Never look back...Tr

While in the Lake District, journalist Emmeline Kirby and jewel thief/insurance investigator Gregory Longdon overhear a man attempting to hire international assassin Hugh Carstairs, a MI5 agent who went rogue. They race back to London to warn Philip Acheson of the Foreign Office and Superintendent Oliver Burnell. But it's a devil of problem to prevent a vicious killing, if the target is a mystery.

More trouble brews as Emmeline pursues a story about shipping magnate Noel Rallis, who is on trial for murder. Rallis is desperate to keep the negative publicity from exposing his illicit schemes, especially something sinister called Poseidon. Lord Desmond Starrett, whose dark past made him easy prey for blackmail, is getting cold feet about their dubious partnership. Hovering in the shadows of this ugly secret world is a Russian mole buried inside MI5. Scorned prima ballerina Anastasia Tarasova makes the fatal mistake of threatening to reveal all she knows. The hunt for the answers takes Emmeline and Gregory up to Scotland, where they learn that the truth has lethal consequences.

Critical Praise for Daniella Bernett

Lead Me into Danger

"Adventure from Venice to London with an engaging cast of characters in this fresh, fast-paced mystery filled with jewel thefts, international intrigue, unexpected twists, and a lovely touch of romance." ~ Tracy Grant, bestselling author of *The Mayfair Affair*

Deadly Legacy

"Stolen diamonds, revenge and murder are served up at a cracking pace as Emmeline unites with Gregory once again in this intriguing second installment of Daniella Bernett's mystery series." ~ Tessa Arlen, author of the Lady Montfort series and Agatha Award finalist

"Emmeline and Gregory's new adventure is a delightful blend of mystery and romance, filled with dazzling twists and turns, unexpected dangers, and old and new tensions in their relationship." ~ Tracy Grant, author of *London Gambit*

From Beyond the Grave

"Escape to Torquay with Emmeline and Gregory for a seaside whirlwind of mystery, romance, and unexpected secrets that will leave you eagerly anticipating the next book in the series!" ~ Tracy Grant, author of *Gilded Deceit*

"Dark secrets, deceit and murder threaten Emmeline and Gregory's future along the scenic Devon coast...A story sure to please fans of romantic suspense." ~ D.E. Ireland, author of the Agatha-nominated Eliza Doolittle and Henry Higgins Mysteries

ACKNOWLEDGMENTS

I would like to thank Editor Susan Humphreys, who gave my book the extra polish it needed and created the beautiful cover.

My continued gratitude to the Mystery Writers of America New York Chapter for its support, particularly Alan Sidransky, and Sheila and Gerald Levine.

I would like to thank bestselling author Tracy Grant, who has been on this journey with me from the beginning. My deepest thanks also go to authors Emma Jameson, Alyssa Maxwell, Meg Mims and Sharon Piscareta, with whom I became friends via Facebook and exchange lively ideas about writing and life.

**Other Books in the
Emmeline Kirby/Gregory Longdon Series**

OLD SINS
NEVER DIE

AN EMMELINE KIRBY & GREGORY LONGDON MYSTERY

By Daniella Bernett

Best wishes,
Daniella Bernett

A Black Opal Books Publication

Black Opal Books

BECAUSE SOME STORIES JUST HAVE TO BE TOLD

GENRE: ROMANCE/MURDER MYSTERY, INTERNATIONAL
THRILLER, AMATEUR DETECTIVES

First Publication: SEPTEMBER 2020

Published by Black Opal Books **http://www.blackopalbooks.com**

DEDICATION

In loving memory of my father,
who is dearly missed every day

PREFACE

Tobermory, Isle of Mull, Scotland November 2010

The few strands of pearly moonlight dangling from the midnight sky shivered in the bracing wind. Soon, they would be swallowed whole by the menacing swath of clouds making its stealthy approach. And never would they be seen again on this miserable, murky night.

Emmeline cast a wary glance at the heavens. They held a teeming, silent threat of rain. Not one of those pleasant showers that freshened the air and coaxed spring blooms from their winter slumber, but rather a pelting assault that sought to punish all humanity for its sins from time *in memoriam.*

Emmeline tore her gaze from the impending doom Mother Nature had in store and squinted at Gregory. He hadn't uttered a word in the last five minutes. What she could discern of his profile was set in taut lines. His body radiated tension as he expertly guided the Zodiac dinghy across the harbor's inky netting of undulating liquid silk. Her fingers clutched for dear life at the rope that ringed the motorized dinghy. Up and down she bounced. Up and down. If, no when—definitely when—it started to rain she probably wouldn't feel a thing. She was already drenched from the spray of splashing water, while the chill had settled deep in her bones—along with fear.

She hunched forward and hugged her arms around her body. A sadistic tentacle of wind managed to find the gap between the collar of her Barbour jacket and her neck. It slithered down her spine with apparent glee. She wanted to shake her fist at the sky. Only the possibility of tumbling backward into the water prevented her from doing so.

It was madness, sheer madness. It wasn't supposed to be like this. They had put the past behind them. *She* had put the past behind her. She was looking forward to the future.

And now this.

Against her will, her gaze was drawn to the huddled lump curled at her feet. The gloom hid the gravity of the situation. But she knew. She knew all too well in fact. It was a man. She could still feel his blood on her hands. She was certain they would be stained forever.

She squeezed her eyes shut. However, she was ambushed by images of the horror she and Gregory had witnessed not more than ten minutes ago. Was it only ten minutes? It felt as if it had been an eternity already. Her mind wouldn't let her forget—would *never* let her forget—seeing the man sprawled, spread-eagled on his back on the floor in the yacht's parlor. From the sinister hole in the center of his chest seeped his blood—thick, crimson, and terrifying.

She shuddered as her eyes popped open. She carefully bent forward, ears straining against the wind. Was he still breathing? She couldn't hear anything. She leaned in closer. Still nothing. Her pulse was racing through her veins.

She shot a look at Gregory. The wind caught the tremor in her voice. "I…I think…"

He cut her off, barely flicking a glance in her direction. "Yes, darling, you're quite right. He's dead."

CHAPTER 1

Dunford House Swaley, England, October 29, 2010

*C**an it be true?* Emmeline wondered. Her gaze snaked across the lawn to where Gregory, at his most dashing in a dove gray morning suit, crisp white vest and tie, had his head bent in earnest conversation with Gran. He must have sensed her eyes upon him because he looked up and gave her a wink.

She smiled, a rush of warmth spreading across her body. Yes, it was true. He was hers. All hers. She held out her left hand in front of her. There, nestled against her pink sapphire engagement ring, was a slim gold band. Its simplicity held a world of meaning and promise. They were bound together now.

Mrs. Gregory Longdon.

She rolled the name around her tongue. It had a lovely, lilting sound.

She had waited for this day for so long. They had been through so much. Had fought so hard to get here. And finally, *finally* they were married.

The first day of their future together. If she smiled any harder, she was certain her face would crack.

Endless days of happiness stretched before them. Nothing would ever pull them apart again. Nothing.

There's always Swanbeck, a niggling voice at the back of her mind whispered.

She gave a violent shake of her head. *No, you're not*

going to ruin today, she snapped back silently. *That man will* not *destroy our lives*.

It had been three months since he disappeared. He wouldn't dare set foot in the U.K. or Europe. again. Every police force from Scotland Yard to Interpol, not to mention MI5 and MI6, were itching to get their hands on him. Besides, if Swanbeck had wanted to exact revenge, surely he would have done it by now?

You're being naive, the voice taunted. *Don't forget the locket he left in your hotel room. It was Swanbeck's sadistic little way of telling you he can get to you at any time he likes.*

She bit her lip, her gaze straying to Gregory again. She knew he worried about Swanbeck too. They never spoke about him. But in unguarded moments, she caught the strained, worried look in Gregory's eyes. She was well acquainted with that look. It was the same one staring back at her every morning she glanced in the mirror.

Emmeline exhaled a long, slow breath. She was determined that Swanbeck would not upset her. Not today. Today belonged to her and Gregory.

Her eyes alighted on Adam Royce, who had just emerged from the marquee that had been set up in the medieval manor house's lush garden. He inclined his head, an amused gleam in his dark eyes. He was about to make his way toward her but was waylaid by another guest. He shrugged his shoulders and lifted his glass in the air in a virtual toast.

She dipped her head, accepting the compliment. She marveled at how close she and Adam had become. Her brother. Well, half-brother. For thirty-one years of her life, she had thought she was an only child. And she was content because she had Gran. Then three months ago, her life was turned upside down when she went to interview Victor Royce, Adam's father. She sighed. It was startling how things could change in the blink of an eye.

She had two other half-siblings as well, Jason and Sabrina. She groaned inwardly. They had *not* been invited to the wedding. Suffice it to say, there was a world of difference between them and Adam. His brother and sister were cut from the same cloth. They both took after their mother Lily Royce. The mere thought of that woman sent a frisson down Emmeline's spine. Never had she met someone so cold and calculating. It was hardly surprising that Jason was preparing to go on trial for murder, among other crimes. And then there was Sabrina, Adam's beautiful, sexy twin, who made no secret of the fact that she wanted Gregory and didn't care what she had to do to get him. Naturally, this did not endear her to Emmeline. Quite the contrary. She wanted claw out her half-sister's eyes. For a start. But she was willing to be magnanimous. After all, it was her wedding day and Gregory had clearly demonstrated that he was immune to Sabrina's siren charms. Granted, this had not deterred Sabrina—if anything it had made her more determined—but soon she would realize it was a lost cause. And if she didn't, Emmeline would devise a painful method to show her big sister the error of her ways.

"May one congratulate the lovely bride?" The well-modulated timber of Superintendent Oliver Burnell's voice broke into her thoughts.

She spun round and beamed up at the burly Scotland Yard detective. "Yes, of course. Thank you for your good wishes. I can't tell you how delighted I am that you were able to come." She nodded at Sergeant Jack Finch, who flanked her on the other side. "And you, too, Sergeant Finch. Today wouldn't have been half as special, if the two of you hadn't been here. I'm certain Gregory agrees with me."

At the mention of her husband's name, Burnell cleared

his throat and Finch tried to bite back a smile.

"We didn't come for Longdon," Burnell mumbled under his breath.

"What he means, Emmeline," Finch interpreted, "is that we wouldn't have missed today for the world. Isn't that right, sir?"

He fixed his deep blue gaze on the sergeant for a fraction of a second and then turned back to Emmeline. "The words were on the tip of my tongue."

She felt her grin widen. "You're both absolutely lovely."

Impulsively, she reached up on tiptoe and kissed each man on the cheek. She couldn't help but notice that Burnell's cheeks flushed a rosy pink beneath his neatly trimmed white beard.

"Yes, well," he stammered.

"What's all this? My back is turned for five minutes and what happens? I find my wife in the arms of another man. Do I need to challenge you to a duel at dawn, Oliver? Your choice, pistols or swords."

They looked around to find Gregory approaching with a masculine grace that cannot be learned. His lips curled into an impish grin, while his cinnamon eyes danced with mischief.

He slipped an arm around Emmeline's waist, as she tilted up her face to accept his kiss. Even the most chaste of kisses were sweeter now. "Hello, darling. We were just talking about you."

"Oh, yes?" His eyes still held a teasing challenge. "From my vantage point, Emmy, it appeared that you and old Oliver here were preparing to run off together to Gretna Green."

Burnell cleared his throat. "Ahem. *Superintendent* Burnell."

Gregory cupped a hand around his ear and leaned in

closer. "I didn't quite catch that, *Oliver*."

"You know perfectly well, Longdon."

Emmeline put a hand on her husband's chest. "Gregory, for once stop needling Superintendent Burnell. I don't want any cross words today." Really, the glee he derived from tormenting poor Burnell was too wicked. It was like he was a five-year-old, rather than a grown man of forty-two.

"It's all right, Emmeline," the detective said. "I should be used to it by now. I hold nothing against you. Your husband"—he allowed his gaze to skim over Gregory, as he shook his head.—"I can't believe I'm actually using that word to describe you, Longdon." Then his attention was back on Emmeline again. "Your husband I'm afraid is a plague on all policemen. He haunts our dreams and waking hours."

"Why, Oliver, you care. I feel a warm glow right here." Gregory rubbed his hand in a circular motion over his heart. "To know I'm always in your thoughts." He paused and lifted a finger to his eye, sniffing melodramatically. "I think I'm going to cry."

Burnell made a dismissive gesture with his hand. "Get off it, Longdon. I said haunt. As in terror."

Gregory winked and lowered his voice. He put his free arm around Burnell's shoulders. "Oh, I understand. You're embarrassed to let the others know your true feelings. Don't worry. Your secret is safe with me."

Finch snorted. "Nothing is safe with you, Longdon. Especially not jewels."

The superintendent shrugged off Gregory's arm. "You're too cocksure of yourself. One of these days you'll use up the last of your nine lives and we'll have you."

Gregory clucked his tongue. "Really, Oliver. I'm quite shocked. I hope Scotland Yard is not is spending taxpayer money to go off on wild goose chases."

"A leopard never changes his spots," Burnell countered.

Emmeline interrupted this volley of words. "Superintendent Burnell, you forget that Gregory has turned over a new leaf. He is Symington's chief investigator. He's well respected."

Burnell and Finch exchanged a stunned glance. "Respected?" they said in unison.

"You *know* he is," she persevered. "He's very good at his job. He's a model citizen."

Burnell gave her a pitying look. "Emmeline, for your sake I hope that's true. I have no doubt that he loves you. Any fool can see that as clear as day. That's Longdon's one redeeming quality. But personally, I have my doubts that he will remain on the right side of the law. The lure of the chase is too strong, the rush of adrenaline too exhilarating. One day soon, it will become too much for him and he'll go back to stealing jewels." He raised an eyebrow. "If he hasn't already."

"You're wrong. He won't." She tilted her head back to look up into Gregory's face. "He promised." These last words were barely a whisper.

Gregory gave her waist a squeeze and pressed a kiss to her forehead. "Don't worry, darling. Oliver, it's ungentlemanly to distress my wife like this on our wedding day."

"Emmeline, I'm sorry," Burnell said, duly chastened. "Truly I am. I didn't mean to hurt you. I would never do so intentionally. But stand warned, if the time comes when I have to arrest Longdon for his crimes, I will do my duty."

"Does the intrepid Assistant Commissioner Cruick-shank know about this obsession of yours, Oliver?"

Burnell sighed. "Let's leave Cruickshank out of this discussion. Actually, Cruickshank is not a fit subject for any discussion."

"There we are in complete agreement. I knew we were of one mind." Gregory extended a hand to the superintendent.

Reluctantly, Burnell shook his hand but they did exchange a conspiratorial grin and the mood lightened.

"I'd say that we're all in agreement that Longdon is a very lucky man to have found Emmeline," Finch observed. "I think we should toast to the gracious and charming Emmeline Longdon." There was only the merest hesitation, before he uttered her new surname.

The superintendent clapped him on the back. "Well done, Finch. I couldn't have said it better myself."

Gregory hailed a waiter and flutes of champagne were handed round.

She felt a blush creeping up her cheeks as Burnell and Finch raised their glasses. "To Emmeline."

"To my darling, Emmy. The woman who captured my heart on a filthy, rainy night two years ago. I'm never going to you let go."

She took a sip of the golden liquid and leaned into his body. She lowered her voice so that only he could hear. "I'm going to hold you that promise."

His lips curled into a smile. "I would expect no less. I'm your slave to command. I can hardly wait to get you alone later." His warm breath tickled her ear. "You look absolutely delectable Mrs. Longdon and the most erotic thoughts are racing through my mind."

His eyebrow arched up suggestively and Emmeline cheeks burned. "Gregory, behave yourself," she hissed, as her elbow nudged him gently in his ribs. "What will the guests think?"

"I don't give a damn what the guests think."

She shot a sideways glance at Burnell and Finch, but they didn't appear to have overheard her exchange with Gregory. Or perhaps they were merely being tactful?

She took another swallow of champagne to hide the secret smile that played around her mouth.

"Ah, there are you," Nigel Sanborn, Gregory's cousin, said as he sidled up to the little group with his older brother Brian in tow.

The brothers shook hands with the two detectives, as Brian's wife, Tessa, approached with her arms outstretched toward Emmeline.

She folded into her embrace. "You look like an angel, Emmeline," Tessa gushed as she drew back. "Isn't that right, Brian?"

Her husband's eyes crinkled into a smile. "An absolute vision." He bent down and brushed a kiss against Emmeline's cheek. "All eyes were on you today."

"You're both very kind. Thank you for coming."

Nigel cleared his throat. "Ahem."

"Yes, Nigel," Emmeline replied expectantly. Of the two brothers, she was closer to Nigel.

He took her hands in both of his own larger ones. "I was wondering when I was going to get my turn. You know how I feel about you. From the bottom of my heart, I wanted to wish you"—he cast a glance at Gregory—"both of you every happiness." He kissed her cheek. "Welcome to the family."

"Hear, hear," Brian chimed in. "Little brother was always more eloquent. I suppose that's why he's the company lawyer and I'm merely the managing director."

They all chuckled as a waiter appeared at their side with a tray of hors d'oeuvres. A brief silence fell as they munched on the tasty morsels.

"Well, Toby," Brian said at last. One of Gregory's eyebrows quirked upward at this. "Sorry. It slipped out."

Brian still often relapsed into calling Gregory by his real name. *Toby*. Toby Crenshaw. But that was another life. A long, sad story. Gregory had shed his past like a snake sheds its skin. At least he had tried to. The only problem is one can never escape the past. It has a funny way of catching up with you when you least expect it, as Emmeline was only too aware.

She looped her arm through her husband's and beamed up at him. But things were different now. They had each other and would face things together. No more secrets.

The awkward moment had past and they were all chatting amiably.

"So where are the two of you going on your honeymoon?" Tessa asked. "Somewhere exciting and exotic, I hope."

"Actually," Emmeline replied, "we've both had more than enough excitement in the past few months to last us a lifetime. All we want is a nice, quiet honeymoon. Just the two of us, no distractions. We've decided to spend a week in Grasmere in the Lake District."

Tessa shook her head. "Only a week?"

An eyebrow arched upward and she shot an outraged look at Brian, who raised his hands in the air. "Don't look at me, love. I'm not a slave-driving ogre."

"But surely now that Emmeline is one of the family, you can give her some more time off. You told me yourself that the *Clarion* is flying off newsstands and subscriptions have doubled since she became editorial director of investigative features."

"Tessa, please. I don't want to cause a family rift. Brian has been very generous since I started working at the paper."

"Ahem." Brian cleared his throat noisily and cast an aggrieved glance at his wife.

"Unfortunately," Emmeline continued, "that's all the time we can take at the moment. I can't leave the paper for an extended honeymoon. I'm working on a profile of the shipping magnate Noel Rallis ahead of his murder trial.

Meanwhile, Symington's has assigned Gregory to a big, new case. Maybe when things settle down, we'll take a fortnight in the spring. We were thinking of Scotland. Edinburgh, of course, and the Highlands. Possibly, the Isle of Mull. We've left the details a bit loose."

"We're going to play it by ear," Gregory echoed. "In the meantime, we're going to enjoy nature in Grasmere. And each other." He winked at her.

Nigel made a disgusted gesture with his hand. "Hmph. How very disappointing. You already sound like a boring, old married couple."

"I heard that, Nigel."

Emmeline's grandmother came barreling toward them, swathed in a flowing creamy beige confection, whose well-cut lines disguised her plump figure. "Boring indeed," she sniffed as she wagged a finger at him, "Don't start putting ideas into their heads. Emmy and this scoundrel"—she latched onto Gregory's free arm—"as much as I adore them both, have spent far too much time the past two years running around in circles being silly." Emmeline rolled her eyes heavenward. "Don't give me that look, Emmy. You know I'm right."

"Yes, Gran," she mumbled under breath. "You're always right. I wouldn't dream of contradicting you. It's more than my life is worth."

Helen gave her a pointed glance. "Hmph. Anyway as I was saying, Nigel," she returned to her lecture, "boring is not a crime. Emmy and Gregory need to spend time *together*. Otherwise, how am I going to get my great-grandchildren? I've been patient for far too long."

They all burst out laughing.

Emmeline felt her cheeks flaming. "Oh, Gran. Really."

For a second, her throat constricted as her mind flew back to the baby she had lost two years ago. Their baby. She swallowed down the tears. The ache in her heart never left her, but she would not cry. Not today.

Gregory pressed a kiss to the top of Helen's head. "You're a treasure. A woman after my own heart." He lowered his voice and whispered in her ear, "I'm willing and ready. It's up to Emmy."

Helen patted his shoulder and beamed up at him. "Good boy. I knew I could count on you."

"Honestly, you two," Emmeline hissed with a disapproving shake of her head. "You're like two peas in a pod. Incorrigible."

Helen leaned across Gregory. "And you, my precious girl, think too much. No more holding back." She straightened up and cupped one of Emmeline's cheeks and touched Gregory's face with her other hand. "Promise me to embrace life and love, and each other. Never let go."

They both hugged Helen. "We won't. We promise." Gregory's voice was a gentle caress in her ear.

"I love you, Gran. More than you will ever know." There was a catch in Emmeline's throat. "Thank you for everything. My life would not have been the same without you."

A sheen of unshed tears sparkled in Helen's soft brown eyes. "Piffle," she said as she disentangled herself from their arms. "You would have been just fine." She touched a finger to the corner of her eyes. "Now, I must go and find out about the cake. Ah, there's Adam. It's a crime that such a nice boy is not married. I will have to do something about that. We can't have him floundering about. Look at the muddle the two of you made of your lives when you were left to your own devices."

Emmeline put out a restraining hand, but it was too late. Her fingers slipped off Helen's arm like raindrops dripping from leaves. "Gran, he's not a boy. You shouldn't meddle…"

Helen was already bustling toward an unsuspecting

Adam.

Emmeline sighed. "Poor Adam. I bet he rues the day I introduced him to Gran."

The others watched with bemused grins as Helen ambushed Adam, looping her arm through his so that there was no means of escape.

"Nonsense," Nigel countered. "Adam is a grown man. He is well aware that Helen is a force of nature. It's easier not to put up any resistance. You simply have to go with the flow. We've all learned that. And we wouldn't have it any other way."

They watched as Adam's face broke into a broad grin as he allowed Helen to lead him off. They saw her throw her head back and laugh at something he had whispered into her ear.

"You see what I mean," Nigel pointed out. "You gave us a gift, Emmeline. Another grandmother who cares about all of us."

She looked up at him. "What a lovely thing to say. I know for a fact that she worries about whether all of you are happy."

"That makes us very lucky," Gregory said.

She reached up on tiptoe and gave her husband a peck on the cheek. "Gran has a big heart, but I still think I'd better go over and pry her away from Adam." She glanced around again. "Oh, they must have gone inside. I won't be a minute. Promise."

"Emmy, leave it."

But she was already walking toward the manor. At the door, she tossed a look over her shoulder and was happy to see that Gregory was once again engrossed in conversation with their friends.

Good, she thought. All she needed was about ten minutes.

"Excuse me," she hailed a passing waiter. "Is there a

telephone I can use? I have to make a rather urgent call to London."

His brown eyes clouded with concern. "I hope nothing is wrong, Mrs. Longdon."

"No, no," she assured him with a smile. "It's just something I neglected to tell the deputy editor. I don't want to worry about the office on my honeymoon. I'm sure you understand."

He grinned back at her. "Of course. There's a telephone in the library at the end of the corridor." He gestured with his chin.

She inclined her head and waited until he had drifted outdoors. Then, she half ran, half walked toward the library.

She pressed the door closed behind her and crossed to the desk. She snatched up the receiver and dialed Jeremy's number. He was a University of London student, who was doing an internship at the *Clarion* this semester. His dream was to become an investigative correspondent and he was eagerly, almost greedily, willing to do anything to further his career. At the moment, Emmeline had him doing research for her.

"Hello *Clarion*. Jeremy Mortimer speaking."

"Hi, Jeremy. It's Emmeline. I only have a minute, if that."

"Emmeline? Isn't today your wedding?"

"It is. Now, hush and listen. I need you to dig into Noel Rallis's business. There have been rumors swirling for years about illegal schemes and possible money laundering. Instinct tells me that he may have murdered his girlfriend because she discovered something."

"Right." His voice was infused with elation. "Leave it to me. I'll check under every rock. If there's anything to find, I'll find it."

"I knew I could rely on you. Ring me on my mobile the

minute you dig up something."

"On your honeymoon?" he asked incredulously.

"Yes. Now, I've got to go." She ended the call before he could say anything else.

She scurried out a French door and across the lawn. She was by Gregory's side again all in the space of five minutes. Her absence had been barely noticed. No one need ever know about the call. She would never hear the end of it, if Gran found out. However, she couldn't stop doing her job simply because she had gotten married. She was a journalist, after all.

"All right. Where are the bride and groom hiding?" a female voice carried over the low buzz of conversation. "Ah, I see you."

Maggie Roth, Emmeline's best friend who was more like a sister, emerged from a knot of guests. She had always been attractive, but today she was stunning with her red-gold hair piled in an elegant chignon atop her head and a sea-green silk dress clinging to her slim figure. As she got closer, a delighted gleam was clearly evident in her mesmerizing emerald eyes. Maggie and Helen were the two people who had been dreaming about this wedding more than Gregory and Emmeline themselves.

"Right, there you are you two. Time to cut the cake. Everyone inside."

Gregory clicked his heels together and gave her a cheeky salute. "Aye, aye, *mon générale*. It is an honor to be commanded by such a beautiful woman. Lead the way."

"Oh, you." Maggie flapped her hand, but she reached up and gave him a kiss. "Save the charm for your wife."

"She knows she has my heart."

"Well, that's as it should be. Now, come on. Chop, chop." She snapped her fingers impatiently as she attempted to herd them toward the tent.

Emmeline fell in step with Maggie. They locked arms

around each other's waists, their heads touching.

"I haven't had a chance to thank you and Gran. No one could have dreamed of a more perfect wedding. The two of you thought of everything."

"We had a long time, a *very long* time, to plan things. I must admit that your and Gregory's silliness—well, your stubbornness really—caused us no end of sleepless nights. He was keen as mustard. We despaired of you. But thank God, in the end you came to your senses. Otherwise, I don't mind admitting, we were going to beat you into submission."

Emmeline merely laughed at her friend's good-natured chiding. "Thanks for everything. It was exactly what we wanted. A small, intimate wedding with only family and close friends." Her eyes darted around the guests who had come out to share their special day. Yes, just right.

"How did you discover Dunford Manor?"

Her gaze roamed over the Tudor manor and the six acres of gardens surrounding it. The house was situated in the High Weald Area of Outstanding Natural Beauty overlooking the border between Kent and Sussex. And on this October day, Mother Nature had outdone herself. Like a chef, she whipped up a cerulean sky. It had exactly the right tinge of blue with a smoky scarf of cloud drifting by to give it texture and make things visually interesting. Meanwhile, a balmy Indian summer breeze whispered sweet-nothings upon the air, making all thoughts turn to love.

They had opted for a civil ceremony since Emmeline was Jewish and Gregory was Church of England. Neither wanted their wedding to be a tussle of religious sensibilities. The ceremony had taken place in what had been the drawing room, which was cozy and snug, and had been perfect for their fifty or so guests.

"Actually, Helen is the one who unearthed this jewel,"

Maggie replied. "She attended a friend's fiftieth anniversary party here several months ago and thought it would be ideal for your wedding. She was bubbling with excitement when she rang to tell me about it. That very weekend I came down to Kent and we visited the manor together. I was instantly smitten. Then, it was merely of question of working on you and Gregory." She cleared her throat and one red-gold eyebrow rose up accusingly. "As I said before, *you* presented no end of trouble. Now, Helen and I can finally stop worrying." She paused. "Of course, you know we are expecting an announcement in the very near future about a little Longdon on the way."

They both giggled.

Emmeline swatted her friend's arm. "Honestly, Mags, you're as bad as Gran. Give us a chance."

"Oh, no. We're not leaving anything to chance anymore. Too much time has been wasted. You need a firm guiding hand—well, two firm guiding hands."

"Don't let my darling wife browbeat you, Emmeline. Stand firm," Philip Acheson said as he joined them as they ducked into the marquis. "Otherwise, you'll turn into a cowering shadow of yourself. Look what happened to me."

"Beast," Maggie snapped without rancor, allowing Philip to press a kiss against her temple. "I married a beast."

There was a mischievous glint in his blue eyes as his blond brows waggled up and down. "But a lovable beast, you must admit."

Maggie tossed her chin in the air and teased, "Hmph. Arrogant too. Emmeline, you're fortunate that Gregory is gallant and charming and knows how to treat a lady properly. Some people around here could learn a thing or two from him."

Philip snorted. "Darling, it's no use trying to make me jealous. The only thing that Longdon could possibly teach me was how to steal jewels."

Even without Maggie stepping on his toes, he regretted it the instant these words tumbled out of his mouth. "Sorry, Emmeline. I didn't mean to…"

Maggie gave him withering look. "Never mind my husband. His tongue can often be a menace to his life. No one believes those ridiculous rumors about Gregory being a jewel thief. It's merely vicious gossip. Isn't that right, Philip?"

His eyes widened and his gaze fixed on Emmeline's face. He shrugged his shoulders. "Oh, definitely nasty gossip. What else could it be?"

"Exactly," his wife concurred as she patted Emmeline's arm. "Anyone can see that someone as sophisticated as Gregory couldn't possibly be a jewel thief. So we're not going to dwell on these rumors ever again, understood?" There was a warning note in her tone that was clearly directed at her husband.

He flashed her a brilliant smile. "I've already forgotten it."

Secrets, Emmeline thought. *Everyone harbored secrets. It's amazing that relationships survived at all.*

She cast a sidelong glance at Philip as Helen and Maggie fussed about arranging them around the cake. Maggie, like most people, thought her husband worked for the Foreign Office's Directorate of Defence and Intelligence. However, a small group, which included Emmeline, Gregory, Burnell and Finch, knew he really worked for MI5, Britain's counterintelligence agency.

She sighed. She understood that Philip only wanted to protect Maggie and the twins, even though he wasn't a field agent. It certainly wasn't Emmeline's place to tell her friend the truth. That was their business. Still, it made her feel a bit dirty having to pretend.

She shook her head trying to physically banish these

thoughts from her mind. The only thing she should be concentrating on today was her marriage to Gregory. For better or worse, their new life stretched out before them.

A boring, old married couple.

A smile spread over her face. She could hardly wait.

CHAPTER 2

Emmeline and Gregory lingered at Dunford House for an hour after the cake was cut. The champagne flowed freely and more toasts were offered to their future happiness. They made a circuit of the marquee. Once they were certain that they had spoken to every guest, or nearly everyone, they quietly snuck upstairs to one of manor's fifteen rooms, which had been made available to the wedding party.

Gregory closed the door behind them and drew her into his embrace. Her arms snaked up around his neck. Her fingers buried themselves in his dark, wavy hair, which was beginning to be threaded with silver strands.

He gave her a roguish smile and tightened his arms around her waist. "Mrs. Longdon." His voice was low and husky.

She leaned into him and lifted her face to his. She thought she would drown in the liquid cinnamon depths of his eyes. "Yes, Mr. Longdon?"

"May I have the honor and the pleasure of kissing the bride?"

She gave him a coquettish grin. "Again you mean?" Then she made a show of thinking the matter over. "I suppose so. If you must."

"Oh, I must." He dipped his head closer, his face only a hair's-breath from hers. "I definitely must."

Their lips met in a long, passionate kiss that was infused with a pent-up ardor that left them both slightly breathless when they finally drew apart.

"Well," Gregory said with a smug smile, as he dabbed at his mouth to wipe away any lingering lipstick, "if that was any indication of what the future has in store. I suggest we change at once and get cracking. It's a good five hours to the Lake District and there isn't a minute to waste. The sooner we start our honeymoon the better."

She had to look away. That gleam in his eye sent a fiery tingle coursing through her blood to every nerve in her body.

Surely it must be a sin to be so deliriously happy? she marveled.

Ten minutes later, they were tiptoeing down the staircase trying to avoid the boards that creaked. It was quite unnecessary because Helen and Maggie, arms folded over their chests, were waiting for them at the bottom of the steps.

"I hope you weren't trying to slink off without anyone noticing?"

Emmeline bit her lip and cast sheepish glance over at Gregory.

"Guilty as charged my dear, Helen," he said, hurrying down the last few steps. "Can you forgive us? And you too, Maggie?"

He bent down and kissed the cheek of each woman in turn, which had the effect of mollifying them slightly. He also flashed one of his dazzling smiles, which makes the recipient forget everything except how devilishly attractive he is.

That did it. Emmeline could tell that he was once again

in their good graces. That was her husband—suave, dashing, and a menace to the female species. Ah well, she could be magnanimous. She had the man. Everyone else would have to be satisfied with the dollop of charm he chose to dole out now and then.

"Sorry, Gran and Maggie," was Emmeline's humble apology. She, too, kissed them. "I know it must seem terribly ungrateful of us after all of this." She waved her hand about, her gesture encompassing the entire front hall. "We're truly touched. No one could have asked for a more beautiful wedding. It's just that we…Well, we…"

Helen's mouth curved into a smile, as she put her arm around Emmeline's shoulders. "Silly girl, there's no need to explain. Maggie and I were only teasing. We simply wanted to see you off. No need to worry about the guests. Everyone is having a smashing time." She jerked her head toward the door. There was a tear trembling on her eyelash now. "Go on."

Emmeline threw her arms around her grandmother, hugging her fiercely. "I love you, Gran." Her words were muffled against Helen's neck, since she was shorter than her grandmother.

Helen sniffled and pushed her away. "Off you go. It doesn't do to keep your new husband waiting."

Emmeline smiled and then gave Maggie a quick hug as well. "Thanks, Mags."

"My pleasure. Now start practicing on that baby."

Gregory gave her cheeky wink as he looped his wife's arm through his. "Darling, you heard Maggie's order. I'm certain all manner of evil things will come down on our heads if we disobey. I, for one, wouldn't want to incur her wrath." He shot a look at her grandmother. "Or Helen's for that matter."

Emmeline shook her head and sighed. "I give up. I'm outnumbered. The only thing to do is to retreat with my dignity still intact." She blew a kiss to Maggie and Helen from the doorway. "We'll be back in the middle of next week, but we'll ring you…"

Helen flapped her hands at the door. "Shoo already. And don't you dare ring. A honeymoon—especially one as abbreviated as yours—is no time for calls home to grandmothers. Unless, of course, it is to inform me that I will become a great-grandmother. That's perfectly all right."

"I'm flattered by your confidence in me," Gregory tossed over his shoulder, "but even I can't work that fast."

"All manner of things are possible, when you think positively," Helen called after their retreating figures.

Gregory's deep-throated chuckle carried on the wind, before the Jaguar's door slammed and they were gone.

ᶜᔆᶜᔆ

Gregory eased the Jaguar off the A591 and into the car park of the MacDonald Swan Hotel in Grasmere around six o'clock. Set against a backdrop of undulating fells, the white-stucco exterior of the former coaching inn, built in the 1650s, gleamed in the early evening light.

"It's absolutely perfect," Emmeline gushed, her face aglow with a mixture of love and elation.

He leaned over and kissed her cheek. "I'm glad that it meets with your approval, Mrs. Longdon. However, I don't intend to spend my entire honeymoon in the car park." He jerked his chin toward the door. "Shall we go in?"

She nodded her head vigorously. "Oh, yes." She was halfway out of the car before he had a chance to unfasten his seatbelt.

"That's what I like. Enthusiasm," he said over the roof as he got out.

"Stop chuntering on and hurry up," she said with impatience. "I'm dying to see inside."

He chuckled as he took their bags out of the boot and came around to join her. *Only a few hours married and Emmy's already giving orders*, he thought. *Ah, well, he wouldn't change her for the world.*

She cocked her head to one side, eyeing him suspiciously as he joined her. "Why are you looking at me like that?"

"Like what, darling?"

"You have a funny expression on your face."

"Oh, that. It must be the look of a man standing in awe of his wife. I had a flash of what twenty years at hard labor would be like."

She swatted his arm. "Ooh. You beast. If you go on like that, I have a good mind to have this marriage annulled." She tossed her chin in the air.

"What? *Before* the honeymoon?" He shook his head with mock gravity. "That would be a crime. Why not take a few days to think the matter over? Who knows? I might grow on you."

Emmeline burst out laughing, no longer able to contain her mirth. She stood on tiptoe and pressed a kiss to his lips. Her voice softened. "I do love you."

He gave a dramatic sigh. "Well, that's a relief to hear. For a minute, I thought it was touch-and-go."

Gregory allowed Emmeline to precede him into the hotel. The interior was warm and inviting. To their left, there was a fireplace surrounded by two sofas, one chocolate leather and the other rust-colored upholstery. A pair of wing-back chairs in the same rust upholstery flanked the fireplace. A gilt-edged mirror hung above it giving the lobby the impression of added depth. Glowing sconces were fixed to the eggshell painted walls, bathing the reception lounge alternately in muted shadows and light.

A man of medium height and slim build, with a head of thick steel-gray hair, a round face and a pair of amused cornflower-blue eyes, beamed at them from behind the reception desk.

He greeted them with a hearty, "Good evening."

They both returned his smile as they crossed the lounge. Gregory set the bags down on the floor. "Good evening. We have a reservation. Mr. and Mrs. Longdon."

He smiled down at Emmeline and slipped his arm around her waist.

"Ah, yes," the man said. "The honeymoon couple. The Swan extends its warmest congratulations."

They nodded, accepting his good wishes.

The man tapped at his keyboard. "We've given you a room toward the back. It has a lovely view of the garden and the fells." He lowered his voice and leaned his elbows on the counter. "It's very quiet. You won't be disturbed. I quite assure you. Here are the keys."

He extended them toward Gregory. "We hope you enjoy your stay with us. We've already starting serving dinner in the restaurant." He waved a hand to his right. "Otherwise, I can a recommend some local restaurants, if you like."

"That's very kind of you. We haven't made any decisions about dinner. At the moment, we'd like to settle into the room. We've been driving for several hours."

The man started to come round the counter. "Of course, I completely understand. I'll just nip your bags upstairs for you."

Gregory held up a hand. "There's absolutely no need. I'll take care of them." He flashed a smile at him as he scooped up their bags. "Just point us in the right direction and we'll take it from there."

Five minutes later, after going up and down, and around

several corners, they stood in front of their room. Emmeline slipped the key into the lock and opened the door.

She was about to walk inside when Gregory halted her with, "Eh, hang on. What do you think you're doing?"

She looked up at him in confusion. "What do you mean?"

"My dear, Mrs. Longdon. You were about to commit a sacrilege."

He clucked his tongue and dropped the bags. Before she knew what was happening, he had scooped her up into his arms.

"Gregory, what are you doing?" she said, squirming.

"I must say I'm utterly shocked, Emmy. Don't you know it's tradition for the groom to carry his bride over the threshold?" He shook his head in mock disapproval.

"Oh," she mumbled as he stepped into the room and kicked the door closed with one foot.

He set her down gently and took a step forward. She tilted her head back and trailed her finger along his jawline. "I can't believe we're finally married," she whispered.

He dipped his head closer and smiled. The next second, their lips met in an ardent kiss.

Without breaking their embrace, Gregory guided her into the room. They stopped when she felt the back of her knees bump against the edge of the bed.

"There's nowhere else to go," she murmured against his neck.

"Who said we were going anywhere?"

He pulled away, his mouth convulsing into a seductive grin. He gave her a gentle shove so that she fell onto the bed. Her gaze never left his face.

He stretched himself out next to her and drew her toward him. She put her palms against his chest. "Darling, we can't do this now. We've just arrived. What will everyone think?"

He merely chuckled and started kissing a sensitive spot behind her left earlobe, sending the most delicious sensations all over her body.

She made one last, half-hearted attempt at decorum. "Our bags are still in the corridor."

His lips found hers. And then all other thoughts flew from her mind.

CHAPTER 3

Emmeline was curled on her side, her hands tucked under the pillow, watching the rhythmic rise and fall of Gregory's chest as he slept on. She had been awake for an hour and was content simply to lie there gazing at him. It had been so long since she had awoken with him by her side. But they had made up for the time they had been apart.

She felt her cheeks suffuse with heat. They never did make it downstairs for dinner last night. At least, Gregory had brought the bags into the room at one point.

He stirred, emitting a groggy "Mmm."

One arm stretched above his head as he arched his back. A hand rubbed the sleep from his eyes. Slowly, they blinked open. His head shifted on the pillow until his cinnamon gaze found her face. He reached out and cupped her cheek.

Her lips curved into a smile. She pressed a kiss to his warm palm. "Good morning," she murmured.

He rolled onto his side, a smile tugging at the corners of his mouth as a hand slid down to her hip.

She needed no further encouragement to snuggle up against his chest. He nuzzled his cheek against her neck.

His lips traced a line to the hollow of her throat, where his kiss left its burning imprint in her skin.

He propped himself onto one elbow. "Good morning," he said, his voice thick with desire. Then his eyes widened. "Wait a minute. My dear lady, I don't recall inviting you into my bed. If my wife catches you, there will be hell to pay. You mark my words. She has a devil of a temper." He nodded his head gravely to emphasize his point.

Emmeline chuckled and swatted his arm playfully. "Oh, you. Why did I marry such an exasperating man?"

He lowered his head to hers and whispered, "I have hidden depths that are well worth exploring."

She smoothed his tousled hair from his forehead. "Is that so?"

"Mmm," he murmured as he nibbled at her ear. "You should make an effort to expand your horizons. You might be pleasantly surprised by what you discover."

A laugh burst forth from her throat. "Oh ho. Did anyone ever tell you that you have an enormous ego?"

He lifted his head and looked down at her. "Really, darling. Must we start our married life with insults? I'm a sensitive soul, you know." He affected a wounded look.

"Rubbish. You're as cunning as they come."

He rolled onto his back and touched his wrist to his forehead theatrically. "It gets worse. In the cold light of day, my eyes have been opened. I have married a cruel and unfeeling woman."

That earned him a thump over the head with her pillow. "I'll show you cruel and unfeeling." She whacked him again. And again.

He quickly snatched the offending weapon from her hands and pinned her to the bed as he tickled her mercilessly.

She tried to wriggle free but could not. "Gregory," she said breathlessly between giggles. "That's not fair."

He stopped for a second, a naughty gleam in his eyes. "Emmy, all's fair in love and war."

She fluttered her eyelashes demurely. "Is this love or war?"

"My dear girl, what a silly question." He shook his head and sighed piteously. "You have left me no choice. I see I must educate you in the ways of the world. We'll start now. Lesson one."

He nestled closer and covered her mouth with his.

℘ℑ℘

It was ten o'clock when they finally emerged from their room and went downstairs to the restaurant. The hostess seated them at a corner table overlooking the garden. It was quiet. The low buzz of conversation mingled with the tinkle of utensils and the clink of cups against saucers. A few of the other tables were occupied.

Gregory snapped his napkin open and dropped it onto his lap. "You needn't have worried, Emmy. The other guests enjoy a lie-in too."

He rubbed his foot playfully against her leg under the table, an innocent smile spreading across his face.

"I say, darling, you're turning the most becoming shade of pink. What's the matter? Was it something I said?"

Her eyes locked on his face. His eyes were alight with mischief. "Behave yourself," she hissed through clenched teeth.

He propped his elbow on the table and rested his chin on one hand. "Now, why would I want to do that when the alternatives are so much more enticing? I have an idea. How about if we forget about breakfast and nip back upstairs?"

He waggled his eyebrows up and down.

She bit back a smile and cast a quick glance around the

restaurant. "No. We are not going to spend our entire honeymoon in our room."

"No?" he said, his features drooping into a crestfallen expression. "How disappointing. You are a hard woman, Mrs. Longdon. A *very* hard woman."

"Yes, well," she sniffed, airily. "We can't give in to temptation all the time."

His eyes widened in surprise. "Temptation? Hmm. That sounds promising," he whispered as he reached out to take her hand, his thumb rubbing the delicate web of skin between her thumb and forefinger. "Perhaps it's not a lost cause after all. It's simply a matter of redoubling my efforts."

He lifted her hand to his lips and grazed her knuckles with a kiss.

Emmeline cleared her throat. "We'll discuss it later. Right now, I'm ravenous."

Gregory straightened and hooked one arm casually over the back of his chair. "Really? I can't understand why."

She avoided looking at him, concentrating on the view of the garden instead. She was certain that a self-satisfied smirk lurked on his face.

"Maybe it has something to do with the fact that we never made it downstairs for dinner last night."

"What could have happened last night to prevent you seeking sustenance?"

Her cheeks were burning again. "You are not making this easy," she mumbled.

"I'm delighted to hear it, darling."

A waitress suddenly materialized at their table.

"Good morning," she said, beaming at both of them. "I trust your room is all right and that you slept well."

Emmeline heard Gregory chortle and she shot a sharp look at him.

"The room is…extremely comfortable," she replied.

Gregory leaned forward again and flashed a smile at the waitress. "I can't speak for my wife, but I slept like a baby."

She should have given him a swift kick in the shin, but her heart melted as she stared at him.

My wife.

The two little words rolled off his tongue effortlessly. As if he had been saying them his entire life.

"Emmy? Have you decided?"

She shook her head to drag herself from her reverie. "What? Sorry, my mind drifted for a moment. What did you say?"

"Darling, this nice lady asked whether you'd like toast. Otherwise, you'll find everything else at the buffet."—he waved a hand toward the bar teeming with an assortment of hot dishes as well as freshly baked rolls, pasties and fruits—"It's a full English breakfast for me." He patted his stomach. "I need to keep up my strength for all that tramping about fields and other activities you have planned for us."

There was only the merest pause before he said *other activities*.

Emmeline cleared her throat. "No toast. Thank you."

The waitress took their menus. "Two coffees or would you prefer tea?"

They both opted for coffee and then the waitress left them.

They took a turn around the buffet. Emmeline selected several slices of pineapple and cut herself a chunk of the freshly baked brown bread, adding a dollop of orange marmalade and raspberry jam on the corner of her plate. Gregory, as he had announced, piled his plate with all the trimmings of a full English breakfast: sausages, bacon, eggs, and grilled tomatoes and mushrooms.

Emmeline stared at his plate. "You don't really intend

to eat all that, do you? You don't normally have so much in the morning."

"Ah," he said, as he popped a forkful of egg into his mouth. "As you pointed out earlier, we did miss dinner last night. However, I could leave all this if you'd like to continue this discussion in the privacy of our room."

Emmeline daintily spread jam on her bread. "We are going to enjoy a lovely walk in the countryside today."

He lifted one eyebrow "So there is nothing I can say to convince you to go back upstairs? To help settle things in your mind, that is. It doesn't do to make a hasty decision. You know, they say you think more clearly lying down."

She snorted. "You made that up."

His features assumed a solemn expression and he crossed two fingers over his heart. "Honestly, darling. It's perfectly true. I'm quite sure there's scientific data to back it up."

"You do talk a lot of rubbish. If *you'd* like to remain in the hotel, you're perfectly welcome to do so. But I am going for a nice ramble."

He let out a reluctant sigh. "I see you leave me no choice. Although I don't know how I am going to keep my promise to Helen."

Her eyes narrowed. "Gran? What promise?" she asked suspiciously.

"Really, Emmy. I am surprised." He clucked his tongue. "Don't you remember? Helen gave us strict instructions about a grandchild." The impish gleam was back in his eye. "I would hate to disappoint her, but I can't see how we can fulfill her wishes if we're out and about communing with the flora and the fauna. Can you?"

She took a sip of her coffee, holding his gaze over the rim of her cup. "The two of you are a bad influence on each other."

"Ah, but it's such a worthy cause," he countered, one

eyebrow arching up suggestively.

She put the cup back down on her saucer. "Walk today and a boat ride on Lake Windermere tomorrow."

He smiled. "Fine. Marriage is about compromise. As a gentleman, I will let you arrange our daytime outings while I take care of the evening entertainment. What do you say?"

"I say that you could charm a snake out of its skin."

"Now, why would I want to do anything so revolting? You, on the other hand, Mrs. Longdon"—he reached out and trailed his finger along the curve of her cheek—"present a much more alluring prospect. I'll begin tonight by trying to persuade you to shed your inhibitions. And we'll see where things take us, shall we?"

CHAPTER 4

The next day was Sunday. A froth of smoky amethyst mist still hovered above the verdant fields or swirled among the still-dozing shadows. The air invigorated the soul with its crisp purity as the sun pierced the clouds, glissading down lemony-gold strands to drizzle warmth with indiscriminate glee.

On such a day, anything was possible.

Emmeline and Gregory enjoyed a leisurely breakfast in the restaurant and then set off on the short drive down to Bowness to catch the boat.

Gregory paid for their tickets and they joined the queue of eager holiday travelers waiting to get on the launch for their journey on Lake Windermere.

Once they were allowed aboard, Emmeline quickly dragged Gregory to the top deck of the two-level boat. She didn't want to miss a single riparian delight. Who wanted to be cooped up inside on the lower deck, when one could feel the delicious caress of the wind in one's hair?

She found a perfect spot toward the front of the launch and rested her elbows on the railing, eager as a child, as they pulled away from the pier.

Gregory placed a hand between her shoulder blades.

"Happy, darling?"

She cocked her head to one side to gaze up at his face. "Deliriously happy." She stood up and slipped her arms around his waist. "We've been through the wars these past couple of years—the secrets, the lies—everything. And here we are, still standing. A bit battered, I'll admit, but the most important thing is that we're together. It can only get better from here."

He pressed a kiss to her forehead and pulled her deeper into his embrace. "Eloquent, as always. I suppose that's why you're the journalist and I'm merely a humble insurance investigator."

He felt her smile against his chest. "There's nothing humble about you." Her words came out muffled.

He held her at arm's-length. "You sounded like dear, old Oliver."

She chuckled. "Why do you insist on needling him? Although he pretends otherwise, Superintendent Burnell is terribly nice. You just have to ignore all the bluster. He respects the law and is serious about his duty. Things would be much easier between the two of you, if you didn't make yourself so...so insufferable when you're around him."

"Me insufferable? Emmy, you must be confused with someone else. I'm charm personified." She snorted, but he persisted, "I bring a sense of fun to Oliver's day. I get the blood flowing through his veins..."

"I doubt he views your verbal tussles in quite the same way."

He went on as if she hadn't interrupted. "Think how much more dour his life would be if he didn't have me around to see to his emotional well-being?"

"He probably wouldn't have an ulcer. The poor man."

"You can't lay blame for his ulcer at my doorstep. It's likely his punishment for some deep, dark indiscretion in his past. Besides, the only reason he's nice, as you put it, is because he's utterly smitten with you, which, my darling, I can't blame him for."

"That's ridiculous. You know as well as I do that Superintendent Burnell is honest and upstanding to a fault. He can't possibly have a 'deep, dark past.'"

One corner of his mouth quirked into a half-smile. "I seem to remember something about still waters running deep."

"This conversation has devolved into the realm of fantasy. You can't really believe that, can you?"

A laugh burst forth from his lips. "No. Old Oliver would trip over his conscience at the merest suggestion of committing a crime. This sceptered isle is in safe hands with Oliver ensconced at Scotland Yard."

She stood on tiptoe and gave him a peck on the cheek. "Good. I'm glad that you agree. From now on, try to behave when you're around him. For me. Please."

He rolled his eyes heavenward and exhaled an exaggerated sigh. "The things I do in the name of love. It rather goes against the grain, darling. I assure you Oliver will not thank you for your intervention. He'll plunge into a downward spiral of withdrawal and then where will we all be? A grumpy detective is much preferable to a depressed one. I don't know about you, but I don't want to find Assistant Commissioner Cruickshank crying on our doorstep one morning because his top detective has gone a bit gaga. Can you imagine?" He gave a shudder at the thought.

"I would rather not. That man is just as bad as Fenton in some ways."

"Precisely. A closed-minded copper who makes snap judgments. That's why Oliver needs an outlet for his stress." His sensuous mouth curved into a broad smile. "I have taken it upon myself to provide that outlet and everyone is happy."

"I give up. I'm never going to win this argument. Let's forget about everyone else and concentrate on the two of us." She shifted her gaze to the water, where tiny white embers of sunlight winked upon the undulating surface.

"Eminently sensible. I knew I married a wise woman."

"And to my regret, I married an unscrupulous rogue." But her tone was soft and teasing.

He nudged her with his elbow. "Ah well, we'll just have to muddle along as best we can." He sidled a little closer to her and lowered his voice. "We'll have to discuss the matter at greater length tonight in the privacy of our room."

"You have a one-track mind."

His eyes widened and he put a hand to his chest, feigning shock. "Whatever can you mean, Mrs. Longdon? My thoughts are so pure the angels bask in their glow."

A chuckle rumbled from her throat. "What piffle. Remember who you're talking to. You can't sway me with your purple prose. I'm completely immune. I know all your tricks."

There was a playful glint in his cinnamon eyes. "Tricks are for conjurers. A gentleman woos a lady with dulcet words and tender kisses. But to get back to what we were saying, what I had in mind for tonight was a deep philosophical debate. I can't imagine what you were thinking."

Emmeline leaned her elbows on the railing and sighed. "I can't wait to hear what the great philosopher has to say."

"You'll be fascinated. I promise you'll hang on my every word."

"Hmph. I'll bet." A cool breeze trickled down her spine, causing her to shiver. "You see. I'm already trembling with anticipation."

He rubbed her back. "Emmy, you're cold. The wind has

picked up a bit out here on the open water. It's heated downstairs. Shall we go down?"

She straightened up and spread one arm in a wide arc to encompass the lake. "And miss this view? Certainly not." She ran her hands up and down her arms. "A little chill never hurt anyone. I'm fine."

"Well if you won't go inside, how about if I nip downstairs and get you a cup of tea?"

She smiled. "Yes, that would be lovely. We'll go down together."

He put a hand up to stop her. "No, stay here and enjoy the view." He gave her a wink. "It'll give you a chance to miss me."

She flapped a hand at him. "Don't flatter yourself."

He jerked his chin to his right. "Why don't you sit over there? It's more sheltered from the wind. I'll be back in a tick."

She nodded. "All right."

Her gaze followed him as he made his way across the deck and then disappeared down the staircase at the back of the boat. She could feel the smile on her lips.

She spied an empty seat next to a man who had his head averted. She couldn't see the expression on his face, but his shoulders and upper body appeared ridge with tension. Oh, dear. Apparently, someone wasn't having a pleasant holiday.

She craned her neck around, but there weren't any other seats out of the wind. She shrugged her shoulders. There was nothing for it. She cleared her throat and asked, "Excuse me, is this seat free?"

The man's head whipped round. An angry scowl had embedded itself in his furrowed brow. "What?"

"This seat." She gestured at the empty chair. "Is it taken?"

He stared at it for a second as if she were speaking

another tongue. Then, he shook his head, as if letting go of whatever disagreeable thought had been lodged in his mind.

He looked up at her again and this time, to Emmeline's surprise, his mouth broke into a broad grin. "Forgive me. No, it isn't occupied. Please sit down, miss."

As she lowered herself onto the seat, she marveled at how his smile changed his entire demeanor. She wouldn't say that he was handsome or even striking, but his features melded together in such a way that they made him attractive. It was a nice face, she decided. Wide chestnut eyes set in a rounded face with an aquiline nose and a strong jaw. Fine lines radiated from the corners of his eyes and bracketed his mouth. Obviously, he wasn't morose all of the time and did know how to laugh on occasion. Thick, sandy-brown hair, closely cropped, fell diagonally across his broad forehead. Though he had a boyish air, she guessed he was somewhere between his late-thirties and early forties.

She returned his smile. "Thank you. Isn't it beautiful here?"

Her gaze strayed to the wooded shorelines drifting past as the boat hugged a curve in the lake. Her mind barely registered the commentary about the area's history and local attractions being broadcast from the public address system. She was content to allow her senses to form their own impressions.

He nodded in agreement. "Mmm. A little glimpse of what heaven must look like, don't you think?"

She turned her attention back to him. "Yes, that's it exactly. Are you on holiday?"

For a fraction of a second, a shadow clouded his eyes and his lips pressed into a thin line. However, the mood was dissipated as quickly as it had manifested itself "Let's say it's a working holiday. And you?"

"Yes, we're—my husband and I, that is—are on holiday. Actually"—she gave him a sheepish grin and felt a blush creeping up her cheeks—"we're on our honeymoon. We were married on Friday."

Her companion sat up straighter and extended a hand, which she accepted. His handshake was firm, cool, and confident. "Well, that's the best news I've heard in a long time. Hearty congratulations. May you both be very happy."

She couldn't help beaming at him. "Thank you very much. We intend to be. Nothing can stand in our way."

"That's the spirit. You have the whole world in front of you, grasp it with both hands before..." His jaw tightened and he swallowed hard. "Just don't let anyone or anything stand in your way. And never look back. Regrets are cold comfort and they'll eat you alive, if you let them."

A brooding silence fell between them.

Emmeline searched his face. How does one respond to such a grave pronouncement? She wondered what could have hurt this man that it had left him cynical and disillusioned. Clearly, he was still nursing a long-ago ache—or was it the bitter taste of betrayal?

She was determined to change the subject and lighten the mood again. "You mentioned that this was a working holiday. What do you do?"

"I was in...the civil service." His lips twisted into an angry line. "But I'm not anymore."

Hmm, interesting, she mused. She leaned in a little closer, her curiosity piqued. *You said what you* used *to do, but not what you* are *doing now. Why are you being evasive?*

"I see. You look far too young to be retired, so how do you fill your days?" she asked. "I love my job and can't imagine not working. I'd go stark raving mad."

He didn't respond straightaway. Instead, he raised one

sandy eyebrow.

She felt herself squirm under the intense scrutiny of his probing gaze. He was sizing her up from the inside out.

"I have a little business," he said at last. "I run boat tours from Tobermory to the Isle of Staffa."

She nodded, digesting this information. "How interesting. Tobermory? That's on the Isle of Mull, isn't it?"

"Yes." He didn't elaborate further. His eyes remained locked on her face.

"It's rather remote up there isn't it? Are you from Tobermory? I don't detect a Scottish lilt."

"I'm not." He gave her a bland smile.

Uh. Huh. A most unsatisfactory answer, a voice inside her head said.

She couldn't stop now. Her journalist's instinct was aroused and she *needed* to know more. She studied him more closely. There was a story here. She could smell it.

"Then I take it you're not from there originally. Where are you from?"

He pursed his lips. "The South. London, originally. But I've lived in different parts of the world."

"I didn't realize that the civil service required a lot of traveling. That sounds more like the diplomatic corps." She offered him a disarming smile intended to loosen his tongue.

His smile matched hers, but now a wary look lurked in the recesses of his eyes. "I told you I'm not in the civil service anymore."

"Yes, yes. I remember. You operate boat tours to the Isle of Staffa. Surely you don't do that year-round? The weather in the winter months must be pretty bleak. I wouldn't think many tourists would venture up there. But I may be wrong."

"I do some consulting work in the off-season," he

replied quietly, but there was an edge of irritation in his tone. "Look, why this third degree? My business is exactly that. Mine. Not yours."

Emmeline tucked her chin to her chest, suitably chastened. Stupid, she chided herself. She had overplayed her hand. Damn. Two days on honeymoon and she was losing her touch.

She turned to him again. "Please forgive me. It's an occupational hazard."

His brows knit together. "What is?"

"Asking questions. I'm a journalist. Questions are my stock in trade. It's just that I'm naturally curious about people."

"Journalist. I see," he murmured. In that instant, he seemed to retreat within himself.

Damn *and* blast. She could almost feel a wall being erected in the small space between their seats.

"Ah, there you are, Emmy," Gregory's voice drifted to her ears. She swiveled her head around and saw him approaching with two cups. "Sorry for the wait. There was a bit of a queue downstairs at the bar."

He handed her a cup. She took a tentative sip, glad of the distraction. "Ooh, it's nice and hot." She curled her fingers around the cup. "Perfect. Thank you, darling."

If Gregory sensed any awkwardness, he didn't show it. He merely smiled and slipped into the empty seat in the row in front of her, hooking one elbow over the back. "Did you miss me?"

She giggled and tossed her head in the air. "I didn't even notice that you were gone."

Gregory directed himself to her taciturn companion in a bid for male solidarity. "I ask you, what do you do with such a heartless woman?"

"I'd tell your wife to mind her own business, before her prying gets her into trouble," the man mumbled.

Gregory's eyes widened and his back stiffened. He shot a quizzical glance at Emmeline and rose. He took her by the elbow and gently drew her to her feet.

"Would you really? My wife has a mind of her own. We don't believe in being in each other's pockets." His tone was clipped. "I don't believe we've met. Emmy, who is your charming new friend?"

"I...I," she stammered. "We never got around to introducing ourselves."

Gregory thrust out his hand. "Then allow me to do so. I'm Gregory Longdon."

The other man looked down at Gregory's outstretched hand for a long moment, before reluctantly shaking it. "Smythe...Just Smythe."

Gregory cocked an eyebrow and inclined his head. "Smythe? Not Smith? How very...original. And no Christian name. Interesting." He tilted his head to one side and stroked his chin. "Hmm. I wouldn't have said you looked like a Mr. Smythe." He smiled genially and shrugged his shoulders. "But then I guess you can't judge the proverbial book by its cover. Mr. Smythe, this is my wife, Emmeline."

For the second time that morning, the man proffered his hand to her. "Mrs. Longdon, forgive me for being churlish just now. I assure you it's not you. Don't let my bad temper mar your honeymoon."

She dipped her head, accepting his apology. "Think nothing of it. We all have days when we're out of sorts." She lowered her voice conspiratorially. "Gregory can attest to the fact that I *sometimes* have a short temper."

Her husband gave her a pointed look. "A classic case of British understatement."

She elbowed him in the ribs. "Yes, sometimes," she replied through gritted teeth.

Smythe chuckled at their playful banter. "Thank you for

being understanding. Now if you'll excuse me, I'll leave you to enjoy the rest of your honeymoon."

They shook hands civilly and he wandered off to the other end of the deck.

Gregory slipped his arm around Emmeline's waist. "Odd chap."

"Yes," she murmured. "He must be hiding something quite awful if he wouldn't give us his real name." She snorted. "Smythe, indeed."

He looked down at her. "Emmy, we're on our honeymoon."

"The world doesn't stop simply because we're on our honeymoon."

"*Emmy.*" There was a warning note in his tone.

"What?" she replied innocently.

"You know what. Don't go looking for trouble."

"What a silly thing to say. I don't go *looking* for trouble."

"No. You just invite it into your parlor like the spider and the fly."

Go ahead and roll your eyes at me, darling, Gregory thought.

But he was not overly enamored of the fact that there was a slight bulge beneath Mr. Smythe's jacket. A suspicious mind would say it was a gun.

And alas, he was cursed with a very suspicious mind.

CHAPTER 5

The rush of adrenaline, inspired by a string of questions about the reticent Mr. Smythe, had chased the chill from Emmeline's body.

"Emmy, where are you going?" Gregory hissed as he snatched her elbow.

"I wanted to see the view from the other side of the deck."

"If you sit here, you'll be able to see it just as well." He pointed at the chair she had been occupying a few moments ago.

She reached up and gave him a peck on the cheek, as she gently prized his fingers from her arm. "It's not quite the same angle. I might miss something."

"Like your newfound friend Mr. Smythe's conversation with that chap over there?"

She tossed a casual glance over her shoulder in the general direction of Smythe. "Is he speaking to someone?" She squinted into the sunshine. "So he is? I hadn't noticed." She gave a dismissive wave of her hand. "I wasn't thinking about him at all."

Gregory pursed his lips and shook his head. Clearly, he saw right through her.

She put her hands on his chest and lowered her voice, "You must admit to being a teeny bit curious."

He smiled down at her, took her hands in his larger ones, and kissed each one in turn. "No."

She made a moue of exasperation at him and tried to break free of his grasp. "Liar."

"Hurling insults about will not help your cause, Emmy. Leave it alone."

Her chin jutted in the air. "Fine," she sniffed. "Have it your way. I've put Mr. Smythe completely out of my mind."

"There was a distinct lack of sincerity in that statement."

She shrugged and plonked herself down onto the chair. "You, my darling husband, can never be satisfied."

He chuckled and sat down next to her. "I'm not a bad sort once you get to know me."

She crossed her arms over her chest. "Hmph. There are two schools of thought on that matter."

He slipped his arm around her shoulders and drew her closer. "I'll grow on you."

"I doubt it," she murmured, but she nestled up against him.

They were lulled into silence by the rhythmic rocking of the boat as it glided through the water. The wind died to down a breathy whisper, allowing them to pursue their own thoughts.

When he glanced down at her a few minutes later, he noticed that two vertical lines had appeared between her brows and she was biting her lip. "If you think any harder about Smythe, you'll do yourself an injury. Forget you ever met him."

She withdrew from his embrace and sat up straight. "What?" she asked in confusion. She flicked a quick look toward the back of the boat where Smythe was sitting next to a rather stout fellow in a flat cap that had been pulled low over his eyes. But she shook her head. "I wasn't thinking about him at all. Well, maybe just a little. It was something else entirely."

"Right. Are you going to tell me what's bothering you or is it like charades and I'm meant to guess?"

"Darling, I'm worried…"

"Yes, that much I can see. All the telltale signs are there. Taut jawline." He ran a finger along her jaw. "Furrowed brow." He smoothed the lines on her forehead with his thumb. "And pursed lips." He gave her a soft kiss and whispered, "So tell me."

She drew a deep breath. "Are you absolutely certain that you want to move into the Holland Park house? Tell me the truth."

Gregory threw his head back and laughed. "Is that what this is all about? I thought we had settled this weeks ago. I've already sold the Primrose Hill flat. Besides, you know I've always loved your house. What's brought this on all of a sudden?"

"Where we live is an important part of our married life. I'm concerned that you sold your flat and agreed to move into the house because you wanted to please me. Out of sentimentality. Because it was the house my parents left me. I was thinking that when we get back to London we should look for somewhere else to live. Somewhere we bought together. I could use some of the money that my fath—" She swallowed hard."—that Victor Royce left me."

He caressed her curls and then took her face in his hands. "Emmy, you worry far too much for your own good." He kissed her forehead. "I'm perfectly content moving into the house."

"Truly? I don't want you to spare my feelings now and end up resenting me later."

He bit back a smile at the concern reflected in her dark eyes. "Truly. And I could never resent you."

"I want you to consider it our house."

"Darling, my slippers are already waiting for me under the bed, as are the rest of my bits and pieces. Unless you throw me out on the streets, I don't intend to live anywhere else."

She released a breath and her body visibly relaxed. "I was hoping you would say that." A smile spread over her face. "I…"

But she would never finish her sentence because her mind suddenly became conscious of Smythe's conversation, low and furtive though it was.

"I want two million for the job." She distinctly heard Smythe demand just above the wind. Then his voice was carried away by an ill-timed gust.

"Emmy, what is it?" Gregory asked, a frown puckering his brow.

She dug her fingers into his thigh and hissed, "Shh."

She burrowed up against him and he casually draped his arm around her shoulders. Outwardly, they appeared to be enjoying the boat ride but Emmeline's neck was leaning back a tad too much to be natural or comfortable. Her ears were straining to separate Smythe's conversation from the desultory chatter around them.

"Half deposited into my account in Geneva upfront and the rest when it's over," Smythe said, his tone inflexible. "Take it or leave it."

"Now listen, you cocky bastard," the other man grumbled.

Smythe cut across him. "No, you listen." His voice was as hard and brittle as shards of broken glass. "You came to me with your little problem, remember? I didn't seek you out. In fact, I could really care less. I'm clean here in the U.K. However after this job, I can never work again. I'll have to disappear. If you want the best—and I'm the best in the business—then you have to pay. My fee is ten million pounds. Period. I don't haggle."

Several minutes passed without either man uttering a word. Emmeline groaned inwardly. It was agony. She shifted her head a fraction and pretended to nuzzle Gregory's neck as she stole a peek at the two men over his shoulder.

They were glaring at one another like two caged lions ready to pounce. They were oblivious to everything else around them.

In the end, Smythe proved to be the stronger-willed of the two. The man in the cap heaved a reluctant sigh and pursed his lips. "You have a deal."

Smythe permitted himself a brief smile before getting down to business. "I knew you would see it my way. As soon the first half is in my account, then I will proceed. This is the last time we will ever see each other. Don't contact me again."

"But how…"

Smythe gave a curt shake of his head. "No questions. Those are the rules."

The other man did not appear happy with this arrangement because he persisted, "That's not good enough."

"If we're going to pay your extortionate fee," the man in the cap muttered, "then we have a right to…"

"Wrong," Smythe snapped. "I work alone. I don't need unsolicited advice."

The other man threw up his hands in exasperation. "Fine. Just tell me when you're going to do it. You can tell me that much at least. Otherwise, how will we know when to pay the other half of your fee?"

"Sorry. When you read his obituary in the paper, you'll know it's time to pay up."

Emmeline sucked in her breath. Her gaze locked on Gregory's face. He grabbed her wrist and gave an imperceptible warning shake of his head. They didn't dare move or get up because Smythe would surely notice them.

"One thing I'd like to stress"—Smythe was saying as he leaned closer so that his head was nearly touching the other man's—"don't even think about double-crossing me. If the money is not in my account within twenty-four hours of the job's execution, I will come after you."

The man in the cap swallowed hard. He appeared to shiver involuntarily. "Don't worry. You'll get your money. Just see that the job is done and that nothing ties it to us."

"Since I don't know—or care—who 'us' are, that won't be a problem."

CHAPTER 6

"Did you hear that?" Emmeline whispered.

"I may be twelve years your senior, but I am not in my dotage yet. I still have all my faculties." She swatted his arm. "Be serious. We have to do something."

"I agree." Gregory took her hand and drew her to her feet just as several passengers were beginning to make their way toward the stairs. "We're going to get off the boat. We've docked at Brockhole."

"Are you mad?" she asked, her nostrils flaring in outrage. "We can't let Smythe get away." On her tiptoes, she craned her neck this way and that to try to keep him in her sights. "Blast I can't see him anymore. We have to alert the police. We have to call Superintendent Burnell."

Gregory pulled her aside and took her by the shoulders. "And tell Oliver what? We know absolutely nothing."

"We know that Smythe is going to assassinate someone. We can't sit back and just let it happen."

"Darling, we don't know Smythe's real name. We don't know who is the target. We don't know when or where the hit is going to take place. We don't know who the other chap is. No one is going to believe us."

She balled her fists at her sides. "Ooh." She hated it when he was right. She also hated feeling helpless.

There had to be *something* they could do.

She smiled. "There's one thing we can do." She grabbed his hand and tugged him to the top of the stairs. "Come on. Let's get off the boat. I'm suddenly dying to see Brockhole."

A few people gave them dirty looks as they unceremoniously nudged their way onto the pier. Gregory flashed an apologetic smile at a few ladies as he squeezed past, which seemed to smooth things over a bit.

Emmeline caught a glimpse of Smythe first. He was several hundred feet ahead of them on the path that led to Brockhole's extensive gardens, which were designed by Thomas Mawson in a series of south- and west-facing terraces that sloped gently down to the shores of Lake Windermere.

"There he is." She couldn't keep the eagerness out of her voice as she fumbled in her handbag for her camera.

Gregory bustled her into the pool of shadows cast by the woodland. "Let's not give the game away, shall we?"

He took the camera from her. They lingered in the woodland for several more minutes to put more distance between themselves and Smythe. He stopped once in the middle of the meadow, making a slow, deliberate circle. He appeared to be looking directly at them.

Emmeline held her breath. Had he seen them?

Gregory snapped a few photos of Smythe's profile. "Come on old chap," he mumbled. "How about a smile for dear old Mum?"

"How about a bullet in the head instead?" a detached male voice said from somewhere behind his left shoulder blade.

The hairs on the nape of Gregory's neck prickled as the cold muzzle of a gun was pressed against the top of his spinal cord. His back stiffened, every nerve in his body alert. The click of the safety catch being eased off echoed with forbidding menace as it rumbled round his ear, while Emmeline's sharp intake of breath struck a jarring note amid the bucolic susurration of the leaves in the trees.

A large hand waggled in front of his face. "Don't turn around. Just give me the camera."

Gregory's fingers gripped the camera harder. "That's bloody cheek for you. Get your own camera."

"I'm not going to ask you a second time, Longdon."

Longdon? Interesting. How do *you know my name, old chap?* Gregory asked himself.

He flicked a sideways glance at Emmeline. She held herself stiffly, fear darkening her gaze. He saw that she, too, had recognized that this was not some random act of theft.

"The camera." the man pressed.

"Sorry, old chap. But I'm afraid not. All our honeymoon photos are on it. You'll have my wife in tears. You know how women are about such things. All gushing sentimentality. For the rest of our lives, she'll be harping about how I allowed a rather pushy fellow to steal our photos."

Emmeline's eyes narrowed, but she held her tongue.

The man exhaled an exasperated sigh. "I'm not playing games, Longdon. I'm not interested in your bloody honeymoon photos."

Gregory took a risk and slowly turned around. His face broke into a broad grin. "Oh, good. That is a relief. Then you can run along and we'll say no more about all this unpleasantness, will we, Emmy?"

She shook her head and clamped her hand on his forearm, her body pressed close to his side.

The purported thief, who had to be at least six-foot-three and in his mid-forties, was all lean muscle mass. His wavy brown hair was threaded with gray and fine lines fanned out from the corners of his gray-green eyes.

His lips pressed together in a tight line. He appeared to be momentarily thrown off balance by Gregory's unexpected defiance.

After a fraction of a second, he grunted and his brows knit together. He snatched the camera out of Gregory's hands. Without a word, he turned it on and flipped through the memory. He hit the erase button when he found the two of Smythe.

He tossed the camera back to Gregory, who caught it with one hand. "There. Honeymoon snaps intact. If the two of you want to remain that way, I suggest that you keep your noses out of things that are none of your concern." He jerked his thumb over his shoulder. "Oh look, the boat's about to leave. If you hurry, you can catch it. Go back to The Swan. Have a drink by the fire. There's nothing for you to see here in Brockhole."

Gregory slipped his arm around Emmeline's waist. "But my wife had her heart set on seeing Brockhole's famous gardens."

The man cocked the gun, a 9mm Beretta Gregory noticed on closer inspection, and brought it level with Gregory's chest. "The gardens are closed today."

Gregory sniffed. "How disappointing." He shrugged and looked down at Emmeline. "Darling, what do you say? Shall we go back to Grasmere?"

She nodded vigorously.

"Wise woman," the man said, as he lowered the gun to his side. "Now off with the pair of you, before I change my mind."

He followed them at a distance and remained on the jetty, arms folded over his chest, until the boat had pulled away from the shore.

Although she was still trembling, Emmeline fumed,

"Don't you dare tell me not to pursue this story. I *am* going to find out who Smythe and his partner are."

"I had no doubt about it. Heaven help those who stand in your path," Gregory murmured as he dropped his arm around her shoulders. "I needn't have to remind you that Smythe is a paid assassin."

She tilted her head back and shielded her eyes from the sun. "No, you don't. I know that this disturbs you just as much as it does me, so there's no use hiding it."

"Mmm" was his noncommittal response.

She lowered her voice. "We can't stand by and let Smythe kill someone in cold blood. That would make us morally culpable. I'd never be able to live with myself."

His mouth curved into a lopsided smile. "You know what this means, don't you?"

She nodded and wrapped her arms around him.

As if of one mind, they said, "We go back to London in the morning."

⌀⌀⌀

Although there was no way that Gregory and Emmeline could have slipped off the boat, the man stood there on the dock until it disappeared around a bend in the lake. Then he made a hasty retreat and retraced his steps until he reached the house that served as the visitor center in Brockhole.

He saw Smythe stalking back and forth along the terrace immediately adjacent to the house. He had to stop for a moment, though, to drink in the beauty of the Langdale Pikes. However, he didn't permit himself the luxury of lingering long to admire the view.

"Carstairs," he called out.

Smythe's restless perambulations halted and his sandy brown head whipped round. He stood still for an instant before giving a curt nod of acknowledgement. They met midway down a path bordered by herbaceous and other scented plants.

The man thrust out his hand. "Carstairs." His voice softened. "Hugh, my dear fellow, it's good to see you."

Carstairs/Smythe hesitated a moment before clasping the other man's hand. "How did you find me, Reynolds?" There was a clipped bite to his words.

Reynolds took his hand between both of his and gave it a vigorous shake. "Reynolds? Why so formal? Have you forgotten your old friend Sam?"

Carstairs lifted his chestnut gaze to meet the other man's eyes. Ghosts chased themselves across his face.

"No, I haven't forgotten. That's the problem. But that was before." His jaw clenched. "Before Laurence bloody Villiers saw fit to destroy my career based on innuendo. And then"—he pounded a fist against his open palm—"when he realized it was a tissue of lies, all he could say was 'Sorry, old chap, but you must see how it looked.' He didn't lift a finger to undo the damage he had inflicted. He just left me hanging in the wind with nothing and nowhere to go. I was tainted goods. So forgive me if I prefer not to have any reminders of the past."

Reynolds hated hearing the bitterness in his friend's voice. He clapped him on the shoulder. "Shall we stroll?"

Carstairs nodded and reluctantly fell in step beside him. They meandered in silence past a variety of ornamental trees and shrubs. Reynolds gestured toward a wooden bench in a secluded corner at the end of a path. It was flanked by two rose bushes with a few stray dusky pink blooms that dandled in the light breeze.

As they lowered themselves into the bench, force of habit made the two men cast a glance about them as a precaution. It was unnecessary. They were quite alone.

"We're well out of earshot here and from this vantage

point we can see anyone stumbling down the path," Reynolds said.

"Yes," Carstairs murmured distractedly as he stared straight ahead. Or was it into the past? Reynolds couldn't be sure.

He allowed Carstairs to mull over his thoughts in silence for several minutes. Without looking at him, Carstairs finally asked, "How did you find me?"

Reynolds rested both elbows on the back of the bench. "It wasn't easy. I can tell you that. It was as if you dropped off the end of the earth."

Carstairs permitted himself a smile and turned to his old friend. "Good. That was the intention."

"I was quite surprised to find that you had gone into business as a tour boat operator. And in the back of beyond of all places."

"That comment just proves what a London snob you are. Tobermory is not the back of beyond. It suits me. I like the quiet. It gives me time to think. The inhabitants are friendly, but they don't pry. They leave me to my own devices."

"Hmph. Quiet? I'd go mad. I can't believe a man like you, a man so used to action, can be content in such a godforsaken hole."

Carstairs's fingers curled until the skin across the back of his knuckles were distended and white. "Well, believe it," he snapped.

Reynolds put his hands up. "All right. All right. No need to get your back up. It was merely an observation on my part."

"Keep your observations to yourself," he muttered.

"Right. You can't run tours to Staffa year-round. How do keep yourself occupied in the off-season?"

Carstairs's mouth quivered into an enigmatic smile. "A

bit of consulting on the side."

"What kind of consulting?"

Carstairs waved a hand in the air. "Oh, a bit of this and a bit of that. Let's just say I've honed the skills Her Majesty's government taught me and put them to good use."

Reynolds frowned. This vague reply unsettled him. Unbidden, the rumors he had heard from time to time over the past couple of years flew to his mind. He studied his companion, whose face was devoid of expression. The rumors couldn't be true, could they?

"What's that supposed to mean?"

Carstairs smiled in lieu of answer and shifted his gaze to some invisible point down the path.

Reynolds decided to try a different tack. "It's funny that you mentioned Villiers…"

"I find nothing remotely amusing when it comes to Laurence Villiers."

"It might interest you to know that he's on gardening leave at his house in Berkshire at the moment."

This caught the other man's attention. His head snapped back and his eyes locked on Reynolds. "What do you mean gardening leave?"

"The old man took a bullet in the back trying to protect someone else. It all happened this past June. It was that mess involving Max Sanborn and a former IRA commander named Doyle, and a looted Nazi painting that tied the bastards together. You must have heard about it. It was in the papers, well not all of it of course." He touched the side of his nose with one finger in a knowing gesture. "Surely even in the isolated environs of Tobermory, you must get the papers?"

"Your snobbery is showing again. Of course, we get the papers. I must have missed this little item, though. So the great deputy director of MI5 is on gardening leave." A broad smile broke out across Carstairs's face. "Temporarily prevented from assuming his favorite role of *éminence grise*. How it must chafe."

"By all accounts, his recovery taking longer than anticipated. There have been whispers that Villiers will get the push. It's more a matter of when, rather than if. He is sixty-eight after all."

"Knowing the old man, he expects to live forever and this very instant is hatching some scheme against God to make sure he gets his way."

"Ye-es. The thing is," Reynolds hedged, rubbing the back of his neck.

"Spit it out, Sam."

"As we're old friends…"

"That depends on what you want."

Reynolds cleared his throat. "I was asked—ordered really—to find you."

A dark shadow passed over Carstairs's face. "Why?"

"Since Villiers is incommunicado, Her Majesty's government needs…your help."

Carstairs blinked twice and then a laugh rumbled forth from deep within his throat. "Pull the other one, Sam."

"It's not a joke," Reynolds replied softly. "Your country needs you."

Carstairs scowled at him. "Where was my country when I needed it? Her Majesty's government and MI5 left me out in the cold," he hissed through gritted teeth. "They can take a flying leap."

"Granted, mistakes were made. No question about it. Be reasonable, Hugh," Reynolds pleaded.

Carstairs shot to his feet. "Mistakes? Reasonable?" His voice thundered with barely suppressed outrage. "Under the circumstances, I think I'm being more than reasonable. I was set up. Granted it was an elaborate scheme, but *no one* would believe me. They all became deaf. I was an embarrassment…*persona non grata*…something that had to be hushed up before—God forbid—it contaminated someone who really mattered, like Villiers."

He shook his head. "You've wasted your time, Sam. Go back to London and tell whoever sent you that he can go to the devil. Then leave me in peace. Nothing personal, but I never want to see you again."

"Hugh, you don't mean that. If you come back, all sins will be forgiven. The slate will be wiped clean."

"I'm to receive special dispensation, am I?" The laugh that escaped Carstairs's lips was more of a snarl. "That's extremely generous. You seem to forget one thing. I didn't commit *any* sins." He thumped his chest with the flat of his palm. "*I* was the one who was sinned against."

"That's not quite fair. There were some of us who tried…to help. Me and certainly Acheson," Reynolds finished lamely.

Carstairs thrust his balled fists into his pockets and leaned down so that their heads were nearly touching. "Well, you didn't try hard enough, did you, old friend?"

Reynolds stood up. "Look here, what happened to you was a disgrace and you have a right to be bitter…"

"Do I? Thank you very much. I'm glad that I have some rights."

Reynolds ignored this acid retort. "Yes, you have every right to be bitter. However rather than wallowing in self-pity, why don't you actually *do* something to clear your name? Come back to London with me."

"The answer is still a categorical no." Carstairs shrugged and started pacing. "Besides, you haven't told me what you want."

A glimmer of hope swelled in Reynolds's chest.

"It has to do with your old nemesis Noel Rallis"

Carstairs froze. He turned slowly on his heel. "Rallis."

A simple name, but when uttered with such venom it

was like a bullet seeking to tear flesh.

He slumped down on the bench again. "I'm all ears. What has Rallis been up to? Nothing legal, that's for certain."

CHAPTER 7

"It's a long, complicated story," Reynolds began.

Carstairs chuckled, but it was devoid of mirth. "Why am I not surprised? Noel Rallis is a study in contradictions. Suave, sophisticated, well-educated, but mercurial as hell."

"Precisely. A rather toxic mix. As you know, MI5, MI6, and Interpol have been trying for years to nail him. He's far too cozy with the Russians and the Chinese for anyone's liking, but he has always managed to stay in that gray area where no one can touch him."

"That's because he has help. The NATO mole. I told the MI5 boffins, but my theories were dismissed out of hand. Villiers dismissed my theories. And then came Rudenko's bungled defection and assassination. It was straight out of the old Soviet Cold War playbook, but fingers started pointing in my direction and suddenly I was out. Funny that."

Reynolds nodded sagely. "Indeed."

"It's all well and good for you, Sam. I was never fully cleared. The best they could do was to come up with a conclusion of 'extenuating circumstances' to shove me out the door. The suspicions will hang over my head for the rest of my life. I'm no longer trusted by a country that I swore to protect. Do you know the boys from London still keep a watch on me?"

Reynolds head snapped around. "What do you mean?"

Carstairs waved a hand airily. "Oh, the usual. My house in Tobermory has been searched. Twice in the last fortnight, as it happens. Nothing has gone missing. Perhaps they're getting a bit bored by the whole exercise. I find it rather amusing that I still merit such attention. After all, it's been three years."

"If nothing's been taken, perhaps you're just being a bit…"

Carstairs tilted his head one side and gave Reynolds a pitying look. "A bit what? Paranoid?" He clucked his tongue. "Really. Remember I used to do this job myself."

Reynolds stared straight ahead and said nothing for a long moment. Then he exhaled a long breath and turned back to his friend. "You were the best so I trust your instincts. I just can't fathom why they're still keeping an eye on you." He shook his head. "It doesn't make sense. Until Rallis reared his ugly head again, I thought when it came to you it was a matter of out of sight was out of mind."

"Mmm. Well, obviously someone misses me. It's curious, though. When I first got the boot, the surveillance was quite intense. I could smell it a mile away. It was quite amusing to lead the chaps on a merry chase. Then interest in me appeared to gradually drop off. In fact, I had the impression that the boys down in London had given up entirely and had decided to leave me alone. Until a fortnight ago."

Reynolds's brow furrowed. "I don't like it, Hugh. Something's amiss. Your name hasn't been mentioned around the corridors of power until I was sent to persuade you to come back to London."

The corners of Carstairs's mouth twitched into a smile. "Perhaps, I have a secret admirer."

"It's not a laughing matter, Hugh. Don't you want to know who these chaps are and what they want?"

Carstairs shrugged nonchalantly. "I'm not worried about it. I can handle whoever it is." But there was tiny flutter deep within his belly. Some would call it a gut feeling. He knew better. It was a survival reflex that had never failed him. It had kept him alive more times than he could count. It was too potent to be ignored and could be lethal if dismissed.

"No one is infallible. Don't let your pride make you a fool."

"I can handle whoever it is," Carstairs growled. "Now what did you want to tell me about dear, old Noel? And why do you want me to come back to London?"

Reynolds rubbed the back of his neck and slid a sideways glance at him. He must have seen by the set of Carstairs's jaw that it was useless to argue any further.

"Right. Rallis's temper has finally been his undoing. He's going on trial next week for the murder of his mistress. Her name was Jessica Markham. An aspiring actress. He beat her senseless. She was virtually unrecognizable when her body was found in her Mayfair flat. I saw photos of her before. She had been an absolute stunner."

"Silly girl for getting involved with Rallis."

"Yes, well, all morals aside, unfortunately Jessica saw the error of her ways too late. She had contacted us a few days before her death and offered to give us everything on Rallis's businesses. She told us that the naughty boy had passed on to the Russians the designs for the new fighter jets on which the British Navy spent three and a half billion pounds to modernize its fleet. How he got his hands on the designs is anyone's guess. My feeling is that it was some sort of tit for tat."

Carstairs let out low whistle. "Someone's been asleep at the helm."

"That's not all. There are whispers that Rallis is aggressively maneuvering behind the scenes to further destabilize the UK's Merchant Navy and our shipping industry."

"How the devil is he doing that? Britain's always been a seafaring nation."

"As you know, there's been a decline in the number of British-registered ships for decades. Nautilus, the maritime union, has been warning that if this trend continues Britain could be backed into a corner because it relies on the shipping industry for virtually all its exports and imports. Foreign powers could control the volume and price of goods entering and leaving our ports by manipulating shipping rates. The matter is quite grave. Currently, Britain ranks nineteenth among countries with the largest merchant fleets.

"Step in our friend Rallis to take advantage of the situation. He's rubbing his hands together, hoping to make a killing. No pun intended. Although he was born in London, he has dual British-Greek citizenship. He still feels an affinity with 'the old country,' despite the fact that his grandfather Dimitrios came here in 1947. Dimitrios and his son, Cyril, built the company into one of the world's largest shipping operators, but young Noel has made it what it is today. However, he's not as scrupulous and is willing to do anything as long it makes him pots of money. He's abandoned the UK flag on his ships and registered them wherever maritime regulations are less stringent. In addition, Noel has forsaken British crews and has found cheaper replacements from around the world. Consequently, the majority of officers working on his ships are not British."

Carstairs slumped back and grunted. "Hmph. Hence an opening for our Russian friends."

Reynolds tapped the side of his nose. "Got it one, old chap. For a long time, MI5 and MI6 have had suspicions about Rallis and the Russians, but we've never been able to get someone on the inside to get the dirt. Jessica Markham told us just enough to know that she was a treasure trove of information. Among these nuggets was the fact that there's a Russian mole in NATO who has been greasing the pole on the sly for Rallis. If that wasn't enough, he had recently become involved in something rather hush-hush. Over the past few months, his yacht has made five trips up to Scotland. She promised to find out what it was. But in the end, she didn't get a chance to give us a damn thing."

"Rallis got wind of it and decided to teach her a lesson." Carstairs spat these words with disgust. "A lesson she took to her grave. Now, she'll have an eternity to lament her poor taste in men."

"Yes. In any case, the Crown Prosecution needs you to testify against Rallis."

Carstairs said nothing. He merely blinked.

Reynolds held his breath as he waited for the other man's reply.

Finally, Carstairs found his voice. "You've taken leave of your senses."

Reynolds squared his shoulders and sat up straighter. "I'm deadly serious." His voice was low and steady. "Rallis's lawyer contends that his client is the victim of a government witch hunt. His client is an honest business-man and a patriot."

Carstairs snorted. "Patriot indeed. He doesn't know the definition of the word honest."

"Precisely. Rallis also claims that he wasn't in London the weekend Jessica was killed. Therefore, she is another sad statistic of what appears to be a wave of violent crime sweeping the city that Scotland Yard is powerless to stop."

"I'm sure the Met didn't take too kindly to that characterization."

"No, in fact Assistant Commissioner Keith Cruickshank has launched an all-out media blitz to reassure the public that the city is safe."

"Good luck to him. I still don't see why the Crown needs me to testify. I didn't know the Markham woman."

"No, but you know Rallis. You can testify about his suspected activities over the last decade. You can sow doubt in the jury's mind and make them believe that Jessica Markham posed a threat to him and had to be eliminated. Of course, murder is not treason. But at least Rallis would be behind bars where he belongs."

"His lawyer would appeal. The case could drag on for years."

"Yes, but your testimony would make the Crown's case stronger. Much stronger. Maybe you could even help to find the evidence on his dealings with the Russians?"

Carstairs pursed his lips. Why should he stick his neck out?

"Come on, Hugh. You know you want to wipe that smug smile off the bastard's face. Why not help the Crown mop the floor with him? I'm certain MI5 would look kindly upon your assistance."

"Are you? I don't owe my loyalty to anyone. I have nothing prove."

"No, but you have everything to gain." Reynolds's voice softened. "Come back into the fold. It's easier to fight the system from the inside. What do you say?"

Carstairs sighed and reluctantly extended a hand to his friend. "I say it's sheer folly."

Reynolds grinned and gripped his hand with both of his. "No one would ever mistake you for a fool. That would be a dangerous miscalculation."

"We'll see. I have two conditions."

Reynolds searched his face warily. "What are they?"

"I testify anonymously." Carstairs crossed one arm over his chest and stroked his chin with his hand. "I think Mr. X will do. Yes, Mr. X. It has a nice ring to it."

"And the second?" Reynolds prompted.

"No press. I don't want my face splashed over papers or on the BBC at ten."

"Your first demand should be no problem. After all, it's in the Crown's best interest to keep your identity mum. As for the second"—Reynolds shook his head and spread his hands wide—"that's going to be rather difficult. When they pick up the scent of blood, the press are ferocious. In any case, it's too late."

Carstairs's back stiffened. "What do you mean?"

"You've already attracted the attention of the most tenacious hack of the bunch. Emmeline Kirby. The editorial director of investigative features at the *Clarion*. She followed you here to Brockhole. She was trying to snap your photo for posterity. I scared her and her husband off for the time being. But be warned, once she sinks her teeth in, she doesn't let go of a story."

"You mean that pretty little brunette on the boat?" Reynolds nodded. "She mentioned that she was a journalist, but she said her name was Longdon."

"That's because she just married Gregory Longdon. A jewel thief with honeyed charm, who *supposedly* has seen the error of his ways and has landed the plum job of chief investigator at Symington's. Talk about cat among the pigeons. An odd coupling if there ever was one. But there you have it. They say love is blind."

Carstairs fixed his gaze on the other man's face. "You must be joking."

"Afraid not, old chap. I would have thought you had

more sense than to chat up a journalist."

"I didn't chat her up." His tone was laced with irritation. "We just sort of fell into conversation on the boat. She seemed harmless enough. Inquisitive, but harmless."

"Looks can be deceiving, especially when they come in such a lovely package. Hugh, you of all people should have been more circumspect. You forgot the rule. *Never let your guard down.* Now not only do you have some shadowy individuals watching you for God knows what reason, but you have the bulldog of Fleet Street hot on your trail."

Carstairs made an impatient gesture with his hand. "What do you take me for? I wasn't reckless enough to give her my real name."

"It's only a matter of time before she finds out."

CHAPTER 8

Eyes widened in disbelief and heads turned on Tuesday morning, when Emmeline swept through the newsroom on the way to her office. She bit back a smile as the murmured comments floated to her ears. "The honeymoon is over already?" "A marital tiff?" Then there were the mean-spirited ones, who gleefully validated their own prognostications. "What did I tell you? I knew it would never last."

With her hand on the door handle, she pivoted on her heel to face the sea of faces. A hush descended. "Before the wild speculation spins out of control, Gregory and I are not on the way to divorce court." She waited for the ripple of conversation to peter out. "We have simply postponed the rest of our honeymoon because a story has dropped into my lap that is too tempting to pass up. Surely all of you can appreciate that. All right? Subject closed."

There was a collective nodding of heads as the newsroom settled back into its vigorous rhythm once more. Reporters started tapping on their keyboards, while others reached for their phones. Her unexpected reappearance was quickly relegated to the old news file.

Ah, yes, Emmeline thought as she stepped into her

office and closed the door. An electric tingle radiated throughout her body. The one she always felt when she was investigating a new story.

The hunt begins.

But how exactly would she and Gregory prevent a hit when they didn't know either the target or the assassin's real name? She rested her chin on her hand as she waited for her computer to fire into life. The elusive Mr. Smythe, she mused. Who are you?

Blood throbbed against her temple. It was a race against time. She just hoped it wasn't already too late.

"Right, none of that negative thinking," she briskly chided herself. "Do your job and find the answers."

❧❧❧

Superintendent Burnell stalked down the corridor to his office on the seventh floor of the steel-and-glass tower that housed the Metropolitan Police, more commonly known as Scotland Yard. Uniformed constables and detective sergeants scattered when they saw the infamous scowl etched on his features. The skin beneath his neatly trimmed beard was turning a shade of pink that looked becoming on a woman, but which made him appear even more ferocious. God help the unsuspecting soul who crossed his path.

He was muttering a string of invectives—each more vitriolic than the last—all directed toward Assistant Commissioner Keith Cruickshank. The Boy Wonder and the bane of his existence.

He flung open his office door. It didn't take kindly to this brusque treatment, rattling on its hinges in protest. Burnell took a half-step into his office and stopped dead in his tracks. His eyes latched on to something most disturbing.

"What the devil are you doing here, Longdon? Did Emmeline finally see you for what you are?"

"Hello, Oliver. I know how much you love surprises, so I toddled along to give you one. Surprise."

Gregory placed his hands behind his head as he leaned back even farther in Burnell's chair. His elegantly tailored legs were propped up on the desk and crossed at the ankles.

The superintendent crossed the room in two strides and made a violent swipe at Gregory's legs. "Get off. And get out of my chair," he growled.

"Certainly. You only had to ask, Oliver. You know your wish is my command."

In one fluid motion, Gregory was on his feet. He shot his cuffs and flicked an imaginary piece of lint from his sleeve. He was immaculate and debonair—as always—in a navy double-breasted suit, which naturally fit him like a glove. A teasing smile played about his lips.

Damn the man, Burnell thought. *No one learns such grace. You're born with it. Longdon certainly knows how to wield his charm and good looks to great effect. He would be a likable chap, if he wasn't so insufferable—and a thief.*

He sighed and plonked down into his chair, which groaned under his weight. "I'm not in the mood for your games. What do you want?"

Gregory lowered himself into the chair opposite without being invited. He clucked his tongue. "Oh, poor old Oliver. Has someone been unkind to you?" Gregory asked, his voice dripping with sweetness.

Burnell propped his elbows on the desk and buried his face in his hands. "Why are you bothering me?" The words came out muffled.

"Bothering? You are having a bad day. How can you say such a thing? We're like two peas in a pod. Strawberries and cream at Ascot. Holmes and Watson.

Mates for life."

"Mates for life," the superintendent whimpered as he ran a hand over his face. He sat up and tipped his head back to stare at the ceiling. "Why, Lord," he asked, "why did you place this curse on me?"

Gregory reached out and gave his arm a reassuring squeeze. "Come now, Oliver. Things can't be as bleak as all that. Chin up and stiff upper lip. You are British after all."

Burnell shook off his hand. His eyes narrowed. "*Superintendent Burnell*," he replied through clenched teeth. "How many times do I have to tell you?"

Gregory put a hand to his mouth. "Oops. I forgot. You know I have terrible memory." He favored Burnell with a smile that only served to irritate the detective even further.

"Longdon, why aren't you on your honeymoon? Was three days alone with you enough to last Emmeline a lifetime?"

"Very droll, *Oliver*." This earned him a withering look from the superintendent. "There's no need to worry yourself over our marriage. We are blissfully happy and more in love than we were on Friday when we exchanged our vows."

"For Emmeline's sake, I'm happy to hear it. Now, make it quick. My patience is wearing thin. The Boy Wonder is driving me mad with his campaign to reassure the citizens of London that they are safe in their beds. He put me in charge of the bloody thing. Can you believe it?" He shuddered in outrage.

Gregory shook his head and *tsk tsked* in sympathy.

"I've got a stack of cases this high." The detective gestured with his hands to emphasize his point. "And he has me holding hands with every Nervous Nelly who jumps at her cat's shadow. If this campaign goes on much longer, I'll throttle him."

"Then I've arrived just in time to save your immortal soul from the devil's clutches. You know crime doesn't pay, Oliver."

"Hmph," Burnell snorted. "That's rich coming from you."

"I won't infer anything from that statement. I know you're not in your right mind at the moment."

Burnell thumped his fist on the desk. "Longdon."

Gregory put up both hands. "All right. There's no need to get tetchy. It's not good for your ulcer. The reason why Emmy and I chose to cut our honeymoon short is that we overheard a man hiring an assassin."

The superintendent stared at him without blinking. After an interlude of silence, he cleared his throat and asked, "I couldn't have heard you properly. Can you repeat that?"

"Perhaps your hearing is another of your faculties that is going. I suggest you visit your GP as soon as possible. I'd hate to see you become a shell of a man."

Burnell murmured something unintelligible.

"You know, Oliver, I can almost see steam coming out of your ears. It might simply be a buildup of wax."

"Longdon, I will have you arrested for wasting police time if you don't get on with it."

"If you insist, as I said, we heard someone taking out a contract."

"Who is the target?"

"We have no idea."

Burnell's eyes widened. "What?"

Gregory shrugged apologetically and spread his hands wide.

The detective swallowed hard. "Can you at least tell me when the hit is supposed to take place?"

"Afraid not, old chap."

Burnell made a choked gurgling sound in the back of his throat. "What *can* you tell me?"

"The assassin's name."

"At last, something tangible to be getting on with. Well, what is it?"

"Mr. Smythe."

CHAPTER 9

Burnell slumped back in his chair and squeezed his eyes shut. "You did it to me again, didn't you, Lord?" he asked *sotto voce*.

"Oliver, everything has its time and place. This is *not* a time to commune with the divine one. It's time for Scotland Yard's finest to get cracking. I don't think the citizens of this great city will feel safe knowing there's an assassin roaming free along its streets. Assistant Commissioner Cruickshank will not appreciate a panic."

The superintendent's eyes flew open and he planted his feet on the floor with a thud. He wagged his forefinger at Gregory. "Listen to me, Longdon, if you…"

Sergeant Finch burst in and interrupted the blistering harangue that he was warming up to give. "Sir, Cruickshank wants to see"—he paused, his gaze flitting between the detective and the "reformed" criminal—"Ah. Longdon. Aren't you supposed to be on your honeymoon?" He cast a glance about the room. "Emmeline's not with you?" He tried to keep the disappointment from his voice.

Gregory's mouth curved into a grin. "Lovely to see you too, Finch. No, Emmy is not with me as you can see. I'll give her your regards, though. Alas, I came to inform your fearless leader here"—with a languid flick of his wrist, he indicated the superintendent—"that Emmy and I decided to curtail our honeymoon for the greater good of society."

Finch digested this information. "Oh, yes?" He shot a quizzical glance at his boss, who was clearly fuming.

Burnell folded his arms over his chest, a malicious gleam in his deep blue eyes. "Go on. Tell him," he snapped.

Finch had to admit, if only to himself, that he was curious to see what mess Longdon was embroiled in at the moment. His gaze drifted back to Gregory who didn't keep him in the dark long.

"There Emmy and I were enjoying a boat ride on Lake Windermere—such a beautiful area, the Lake District. I highly recommend it to you both…"

Burnell drummed his plump fingers on his desk. "Longdon, we are not interested in a personal travelogue."

"Right, Oliver. Sorry. Well, it just so happens that Emmy and I overheard a chap hiring an assassin."

Finch's eyebrow arched upward. "Pull the other one. You don't really expect us to believe that, do you?"

Gregory solemnly crossed two fingers over his heart. "I assure you, Finch, I'm completely serious."

The sergeant's gaze raked his features for signs of duplicity, but apparently he found none.

"But…but that's absurd." He shook his head. "This would only happen to the two of you."

Gregory shrugged. "What can I say?"

"Not much," Burnell complained. "He hasn't finished his little tale of intrigue. Ask him who the target is, Finch."

In the foul mood the superintendent was in, the sergeant knew better than to utter a word. He merely waited for Longdon to continue.

"Oliver, with his razor-sharp mind, has hit the nail on

the head. Things are a bit tricky."

"They always are when it comes to you," Finch mumbled.

Either Gregory didn't hear this comment, or he chose to ignore it.

"We didn't actually catch who the intended target is or when the hit will take place."

Finch exchanged a look with his boss, who gave a lugubrious nod of his head.

"But they were able to provide one important nugget of information, isn't that correct, Longdon?" Burnell prodded.

"Yes. We heard the killer's name."

"That's wonderful. Isn't it, sir?"

"In normal circumstances, I agree it would be. These are not normal circumstances." The sergeant frowned. "Enlighten him, Longdon."

"The assassin's name is Mr. Smythe."

"That's it. Isn't that a tremendous help?" the superintendent observed facetiously. "We'll have him behind bars in no time."

"Now, now, there's no need to take on that tone. Emmy and I thought it was our civic duty to come to you. Emmy was especially insistent. Something about her conscience not allowing her to turn a blind eye. You know how she gets about justice being served."

"As opposed to you," Finch shot back.

Gregory favored him with a broad smile. "Let's just say, I have a more malleable disposition. I can recognize the significance of the gray areas."

"Hmph," Burnell grunted.

"In any case, you'll be delighted to hear that Emmy is also pursuing the mysterious Mr. Smythe. She spoke to him briefly on the boat. She did manage to wheedle out of him the fact that he operates boat tours from Tobermory to the Isle of Staffa. We tried to follow him when he got off at Brockhole. But his cohort, who waved a rather nasty looking gun about I might add, rather put a damper on those efforts. So we were forced to make a tactical retreat and here we are alive to fight another day."

Burnell exhaled an exasperated breath. "Bloody hell. That's all we need. Much as I admire your wife, Longdon, she does manage to place herself in harm's way."

"That's the dedicated journalist. She won't let go of a story until she finds the truth." Gregory's flippant manner had evaporated and he intoned with all seriousness, "None of us can change her, nor would I want to, we simply have to make sure she doesn't get in over her head. I know I can trust you chaps to keep an eye out for her when I'm not around."

"Naturally," Finch replied without hesitation, all trace of antagonism absent from his voice.

"You needn't bother asking, Longdon. But damn it all." Burnell slammed his open palm on his desk. "Why are the two of you such a magnet for trouble?"

Gregory rose and shot his cuffs. His cinnamon eyes danced with mischief. "It's a gift, Oliver. Either one has it, or one doesn't."

"I can think of better talents to take pride in," the superintendent sneered.

Gregory chuckled. "There's no need to be jealous or to feel inadequate. I know I speak for Emmy, when I say we adore you just the same. Besides, you must admit that we add a dash of spice to your otherwise humdrum daily existence."

"My ulcer can do without so much spice."

ᘓᕲᘓ

Gregory had barely departed, when the telephone

began to peal.

"It's probably Cruickshank," Finch said. "He wants to see you. That's what I came to tell you, but we got sidetracked with Longdon and his phantom assassin."

The superintendent shot an accusatory look at Finch, as if he was in league with the Boy Wonder. He silently conceded that this was unfair, but he was not in a particularly generous mood at the moment. If he had to suffer, so would everyone else around him.

His hand hovered over the receiver. He took a deep breath before snatching it up. "Burnell."

"Good morning, Superintendent Burnell." It was Sally Harper, the assistant commissioner's secretary. As always, her tone was clipped and edged with scorn.

The voice of doom, Burnell thought.

"Good morning, Sally." He boomed down the line. He tried—really he had—to inject a note of enthusiasm into the words. However, he had sneaking suspicion that he had failed. After all, it was quite a strain to pretend to be pleasant to someone you despised with every fiber of your being. Of course, he knew the feeling was mutual. Beneath the patina of politeness, there was a raging fire of loathing and disgust.

"What a delightful surprise. I trust you're well this morning?"

Finch, who sat across from him, winced at the false saccharin heartiness. Burnell flapped a hand at him.

"Are you drunk, Superintendent?" was Sally's snippy rejoinder. "Assistant Commissioner Cruickshank does not tolerate alcoholism in his team."

Burnell curled his fist until the skin across the knuckles was white and distended. "No, I am not drunk," he roared into the receiver. "Nor have I *ever* indulged to excess."

Finch clutched his belly and did his best to stifle the laughter struggling to burst forth from his chest.

Burnell covered the receiver and mouthed, "You are not helping matters."

"Sorry, sir," Finch whispered, all contrition. "You shouldn't let her get your back up. You know she does it on purpose. Just let it wash over you."

"Easier said than done."

"Superintendent, are you listening to me?" Sally asked with asperity.

"Every word. How can you doubt it?"

"Hmph," she snorted. "Don't get me started. You exhibit a great many dubious qualities. I'm surprised that you weren't pushed off the force long ago. But then, it's not my place to comment."

You're certainly doing an admirable job of not offering your condescending opinion, you bloody cow, Burnell mused silently.

"Therefore," Sally was nattering in his ear, "Assistant Commissioner Cruickshank expects to see you in his office in twenty minutes. He wants a detailed report on the public outreach campaign."

"It's actually not convenient at the moment. I'm in the middle of a stack of cases. In fact, we've just received word about an imminent assassination attempt and…"

She cut him off. "I needn't have to remind you that your top priority is the public campaign. Make sure you don't keep the assistant commissioner waiting. He's a busy man."

She severed the connection before he had a chance to reply.

As he replaced the receiver, he wondered idly if there might be a vial of Bubonic Plague locked away in some government laboratory. He would only need a tiny amount to add to Sally's coffee. Then he would have to come up with something even more insidious for the Boy Wonder.

"Ah, there are you, Burnell," Assistant Commissioner

Keith Cruickshank said as the superintendent entered his office for the appointed audience. With exaggerated deliberateness, he glanced at his watch. "And only seven minutes late. You're improving, but your time management skills still need polishing. Remember, an efficient office makes the job easier."

He flashed a smile at the superintendent that was intended as encouragement and gestured for him to sit down.

As he lowered himself into the chair across from the assistant commissioner, Burnell bit his cheek and immediately tasted the salty tang of blood in his zeal to rein in his temper.

You do like living dangerously, don't you, Boy Wonder? his mind screamed. *One of these days, you're going to go too far and then I won't be responsible for my actions. It will be an open-and-shut case of self-defense. Any jury would see that I was pushed beyond what a reasonable man could possibly endure. I would be acquitted on the spot.*

Aloud, he replied, "Sorry, sir. I will try harder. I can only plead pressure of work."

Cruickshank, his ginger hair all aglow in the sunlight streaming in through the window and his brown eyes burning with revolting enthusiasm, accepted this at face value. "Then we'll say no more about it, shall we?"

But you will, the little voice inside Burnell's head predicted. *You'll look down that oh, so superior nose of yours and get in a subtle dig every chance you get.*

He plastered a smile on his lips and gripped his knees. "Now, what was it you wanted to discuss with me, sir?"

Cruickshank frowned at him. He leaned forward and folded his hands on his desk.

Burnell supposed he was attempting to appear authoritative. However since the man had barely passed the age of forty, the pose lacked the convincing gravitas of experience and instead merely made him look constipated.

"Surely Sally told you that I expected a report on the public outreach campaign?"

The superintendent smacked his forehead with his open palm. "Oh, that."

"Yes, that," Cruickshank prompted. "I ordered you to make it your top priority." Burnell bit back a smile at the note of irritation in his boss's voice.

"Indeed, it is, sir. My every waking hour, as well as my dreams, is consumed with how to carry out the campaign."

Am I doing it a bit too brown? Burnell wondered. *Is Longdon rubbing off on me? God, I hope not.*

That vacuous smile touched assistant commissioner's lips again. "I will be frank with you. I had reservations about placing you in charge of the campaign. But I always like to give my team a chance to prove themselves and you have certainly exceeded my expectations. Keep up the good work."

A broad grin spread over Burnell's face. "Thank you, sir. It helps to know that you have confidence in my abilities. If there's nothing else," he said as he pushed himself to his feet, "I'll be off."

"Of course, I won't detain you any longer. I'm glad we had this chat. I find it always helps to boost morale, if I take an interest in the team's work."

"Oh, indeed it does, sir." Burnell dipped his head and slowly backed away to the door.

He had opened the door and had one foot over the threshold, when Cruickshank called him back. "Burnell, before you run off, what was that you mentioned to Sally about an assassination attempt?"

Over his shoulder, the superintendent said, "I really couldn't say, sir. Perhaps you should ask her." He lowered his voice. "Between you and me, she does tend to get a bit muddled. Or hadn't you noticed?"

The Boy Wonder's brow furrowed again. "I hadn't actually, but I will make a point of keeping an eye on her now that you've brought it to my attention. Thank you, Burnell. I appreciate it."

"One does one's best for the good of the team, sir," he replied with what he hoped sounded like humility.

"That's the spirit."

Burnell escaped before the Boy Wonder realized he had not provided a progress report on the public outreach campaign.

He ran into Finch by the bank of lifts.

"How did it go with Cruickshank?" the sergeant asked.

Burnell made an impatient gesture with his hand. "Let's not waste time talking about that fool. We have a little breathing room for the time being anyway. I managed to sow some seeds of doubt in his mind about Sally's efficiency."

Finch's features creased into a smile. "You devious devil."

"Watch it. Show some respect. I'm still your superior." The smile on his lips belied the stern tone of his words.

The sergeant became circumspect. "Sorry. You devious devil, sir."

"That's more like it. Besides, what goes around comes around. And Sally deserves every ounce of scrutiny coming her way."

There was a soft *ding* as the lift doors slid open and they stepped inside the car.

Burnell dropped his voice and leaned his head close to Finch so that the others would not hear. "Now, I'd like you to do some digging. See if you can find out anything about Mr. Smythe, the shadowy assassin."

"You're not serious? You actually believe all that rot that Longdon spouted?"

"I know, I know. It sounds too ridiculous. And yet, it has the ring of truth. I don't think Longdon would make it up. You must admit that Emmeline has been a positive influence on him. I wouldn't go as far as to say that he is a reformed character, but there is a glimmer of hope."

The stunned expression on the sergeant's nearly made him chuckle. It was apparent that Finch thought he had gone gaga.

Finch swallowed hard and shrugged. "Right, sir. I defer to you. Who am I to question your vast experience of the criminal classes?"

The doors opened on the seventh floor and they squeezed off the lift. "All right. None of your cheek."

Before they parted ways, Burnell reached out and put a restraining hand on the sergeant's arm. "Work fast, Finch. Check with all your sources. See if there have been any recent whispers in the underworld. I'll make a few calls to some well-paced contacts. Philip Acheson is at the top of my list. My ulcer tells me it's a race against a seasoned professional and he already has the lead."

"What if we can't stop the hit in time?"

"Failure is not an option. You and I both know that Emmeline and Longdon won't give up the hunt. The more questions they ask, the greater the risk the killer will have them in his crosshairs. It's our job to uphold the law. We can't allow them to place themselves in such danger. It would be unconscionable." The slight tremor in his voice betrayed his concern.

Finch attempted to lighten the mood. "I agree about Emmeline. But surely Longdon is expendable?"

Burnell gave him a slightly lopsided smile. "We are charged with protecting all the citizens of this city, even Longdon. That is, until the day he reverts to his old, wicked ways—which I'm certain will be soon because the role of Symington's chief investigator is beginning to chafe. Then it will be my pleasure to personally welcome him into Her Majesty's prison system."

Finch's grin stretched from ear to ear. "You've restored my faith in you, sir. I knew you couldn't have gone completely crackers."

"That only goes to show that you should never second guess those older and wiser. Now, go redeem yourself by finding Mr. Smythe before he kills again."

CHAPTER 10

Gregory leaned against the door frame to the kitchen as Emmeline bustled about humming a merry tune as she prepared dinner. She hadn't heard him come home. He felt warmth swell in his chest as he watched her. This woman who had captured his heart on a rainy night three years ago and had never let go. He had lost her once and nearly a second time because of his secrets and lies. It had taken a long time to repair the damage, but here they were, married at last. He vowed that he would never do anything to hurt her again. He would rather die.

However, one thing he had discovered about himself was that he was not prepared to give up jewels. Diamonds, rubies, emeralds, sapphires, it didn't matter. He liked the electric feel of them between his fingers and the way their fiery facets trapped the light. He also enjoyed the surge of adrenaline after a successful heist and the look on poor Oliver's face when another robbery landed in his lap.

It was love. Of course, it was quite different from his love for Emmy, which was unwavering and eternal, but it was love all the same. Was it a character defect? An addiction? Perhaps a psychiatrist would say it was a bit of both. After all, no one is perfect. His appetite had been whet again at the Sotheby's auction back in July when the Blue Angel, a flawless 12-carat blue diamond, had come up for sale. A Russian mafia boss named Igor Bronowski purchased it, but there appeared to be some question after the auction about its authenticity. Sotheby's and the police had done an admirable job of hushing it up to save face. Gregory's mouth curved into a smile, but his lips would be sealed forever.

He couldn't give up such a deep and abiding love. There was absolutely no need for Emmy to be jealous. Jewels held a completely separate corner of his affections. He reasoned that stealing jewels wasn't such a bad vice. Every man has to have a hobby. He couldn't possibly allow his unique talents to atrophy. That would be a terrible tragedy indeed.

"Oh." Emmeline stopped in the midst of setting the table. "You startled me."

She walked over and twined her arms around his neck. He obliged by giving her a tender kiss. "I approve, Mr. Longdon," she said when they pulled apart. "You're forgiven for creeping about. How long had you been standing there?"

"Only a few minutes. Is it a crime for a man to enjoy looking at his wife?"

She caressed his cheek and gave him another kiss before breaking their embrace. "One of us has to be the strong one, otherwise the dinner will burn and we'll go to bed hungry like we did in Grasmere."

He took a step closer and placed his hands on her waist. His gaze traced every angle and plane of her face, as he whispered, "Was that such a bad thing? I don't recall any complaints at the time, quite the contrary in fact."

He hoped he would always be able to bring that delightful pink flush to her cheeks.

She cleared her throat and gave him a gentle shove.

"I...I have to check on dinner."

He stepped out of the way. "Right. Of course. We can continue the conversation later, when we're upstairs. I could give you a massage. It will help the blood to flow to your brain, allowing you to think more clearly."

He chuckled as he saw her blush deepen.

"Blood flowing, yes. Thinking clearly? No. Not if you're anywhere in the vicinity. Now, if you don't behave I'll send you upstairs for an icy shower."

"You really know how to dampen a chap's ardor. Need I remind you that we are still technically on our honeymoon?"

"Yes, well," she said, evading the question as she placed two bowls of steaming vegetable soup on the table. "We have important things to discuss. I found out who Mr. Smythe is."

Her excitement was palpable. He knew he should praise her industriousness, but it was difficult to feel sanguine when a cold dread clutched at his chest. He would know soon whether her information matched what he had discovered from some old friends who were at home outside the law. Perhaps she was on the wrong track. This thought buoyed his spirit. Then he wouldn't have to worry about his wife chasing after a killer-for-hire.

He slipped into the chair at the blond wood table and draped his napkin across his lap. He picked up his spoon and tried to arrange his features into a neutral expression. "I'm all ears, darling. We can compare notes."

"His name is Hugh Carstairs. He's a former MI5 agent who left the agency under a cloud. I haven't been able to find out what that was all about, yet. At least we have a name."

Gregory's heart sank. No, she wasn't on the wrong track. If he were honest, there was never any doubt on that score.

"It took me a few hours of searching to find Carstairs," Emmeline was saying as they took their coffees through to the living room after dinner. She settled on the sofa and tucked her legs under her, while Gregory eased himself into the adjacent winged-back chair.

"There are about four or five companies that do tours to Staffa and the surrounding islands," she went on, "but the difficult part was trying to find information on their owners and crew." She took a sip of her coffee. "I was beginning to go crossed-eyed, when I found a photo of Carstairs. Things got a bit easier from that point. I think it might be the only photo of him in existence. Once I had a name, I decided to check if there was anything on him in a government database. That's when I hit a dead end. There was a passing reference to his leaving MI5 and that was it. I'll have to ring Philip. He may know more about Carstairs. If he doesn't, he might be able to find out or at least point me in the right direction."

She set her cup and saucer down on the coffee table. "You seem preoccupied. You were very quiet through dinner. Is something the matter?"

"Other than the fact that we've come face-to-face with an assassin?"

"You know what I mean. Did you discover anything else about Carstairs?"

No more lies, he reminded himself. *A marriage demands implicit trust. The only exception being jewels. Then what Emmy doesn't know won't hurt her.*

He sighed. "Nothing good. I put the word out in certain circles that I was looking for information on a killer-for-hire who may go by the name of Smythe. It's a small world and everyone knows one another, as well as the competition. It didn't take long before my mobile started ringing. Carstairs was one of MI5's best agents until he bungled the defection of Ivan Rudenko, a top Russian official, in 2007. Rudenko was assassinated. An internal investigation determined that there was a leak. Carstairs was Rudenko's handler. It was only a matter of time before fingers started pointing in his direction. He protested his innocence, of course. His only defense was that there was a mole. But no one would listen to him. The investigation's findings were inconclusive, but too many questions had arisen about Carstairs so naturally he had to go. Apparently, Laurence Villiers insisted on it for the good of the agency and morale."

Emmeline stared at him. Reflected in those dark eyes was the terrifying image of a June afternoon when they had been trapped in some dank, dark tunnels by a ruthless former IRA commander. Villiers had stepped in front of a bullet to save Gregory's life. The deputy director of MI5 was tough, but at sixty-eight his recovery was taking longer than the doctors had hoped. Although grateful, to this day Gregory wondered why Villiers had done it. Their relationship could be termed fractious at best. Many years before, Gregory had foolishly agreed to carry out "little jobs" for the old man from time to time. Villiers had appealed to his sense of patriotism. It was for Queen and country after all.

Gregory would never forgive Villiers. His path would never have crossed with Walter Swanbeck and his even more sinister son, Alastair, if hadn't been for Villiers. Alastair had vowed revenge for his father's death. And now, Gregory and Emmeline would never be free of him. Alastair had vanished back in July. No one—not Scotland Yard, MI5, MI6, or Interpol—had heard a peep about him. It was as if the man had been swallowed up by the earth. But Gregory knew better. Swanbeck was merely biding his time, until he was sure he could extract his revenge in the most spectacular way possible.

Was it fair—or even wise—to have married Emmy, knowing Swanbeck would never give up? He didn't know the answer. What he did know was that he couldn't live without her.

"I suppose a man could snap and turn rogue." Emmeline's voice drew him back to the problem at hand.

There was no use borrowing trouble. Swanbeck would have to wait for another day.

"Darling, Carstairs was already disgraced. He could never work again in intelligence or in the government. No one would risk the taint by association. A security firm wouldn't touch him because of all the whispers about the Rudenko fiasco. So what did he have to fall back on? His training in the art of murder."

Two vertical lines appeared between Emmeline's brows. "Yes, but to go from protecting the UK to…" She let her sentence trail off.

She shook her head and threw up her hands. "I don't know."

He came and joined her on the sofa, taking one of her small hands in his. "People betray their country for much less. If it's any consolation, thus far Carstairs has only taken jobs outside the UK. As far Her Majesty's government is concerned, he's as pure as the driven snow."

She sighed as she snuggled up against him. "A twinge of conscience?" she posited.

He pressed a kiss among her dark curls. "If he had a conscience, I rather think he would have chosen a different profession, don't you?"

"Yes, you're right. But something doesn't add up. I spoke with Carstairs, granted it was only for a few minutes, but I'm ashamed to say that I liked him. Beneath the bitterness, there was…something else. A sadness. A sense of loss."

He did not like the turn the conversation had taken. He

pulled back and held her by the shoulders. His gaze locked on her face. "Emmy, you're a journalist. Look at the facts. He's an assassin and he's planning another job. You *know* that. You heard it with your own ears."

"Yes, but a good journalist must rely on her instincts and follow new leads to get to the truth. In this case, I think we're missing a huge chunk of the story. What if Carstairs was right about the mole? Shouldn't we try to find out?"

And that's why, my darling, I despair, Gregory lamented inwardly. *Your instincts, while spot on, lead you into danger.*

CHAPTER 11

Philip entered the antechamber where his secretary, Pamela, was typing away at her keyboard. He had been huddled in a meeting all morning at Number Ten with the prime minister and the Foreign and Defense secretaries.

"Anything important while I was out, Pamela?"

She stopped in mid-stream and handed him a stack of messages and a file.

He nodded and flicked through the messages. "Superintendent Burnell? Did he say what he wanted?"

"No, but he stressed it was rather urgent."

Philip sighed. "It always is. I'll give him a ring right away. Thanks."

He started to walk toward his office, when Pamela cleared her throat. "Mr. Acheson, there's just one more thing that needs your attention."

"Oh, yes?" He turned on his heel. His eyes widened in surprise when he saw Emmeline rising from the sofa across from Pamela's desk, where people who had meetings scheduled with him waited until they were called in. He didn't have a meeting with her. This couldn't be good.

"Emmeline, what are you doing here? You're supposed to be in the Lake District on your honeymoon." His eyes narrowed. "Has Longdon done something?" he asked suspiciously.

"Hello, Philip. It's nice to see you too. No, Gregory hasn't done anything. I wish everybody would give him a chance," she replied with a touch of asperity.

"Here, here," he heard Pamela mutter under her breath. "Mr. Longdon is such a lovely man."

She and Emmeline exchanged a look that was infused with that peculiar phenomenon known as instant female camaraderie. A hapless male like himself was powerless against its force.

Terrific, Philip thought, *even my own secretary is in Longdon's camp. Like Maggie and the entire female species. Honestly, what* did *they see in the man?*

"Philip, we had to cut our honeymoon short because Gregory and I overheard something rather disturbing."

"I don't know what it is—and frankly I don't want to—but I'm quite certain that I'm not going to like it. You have that look in your eye."

Emmeline squared her shoulders and drew herself to her full height, which was not saying much since she was five foot two. However, the way her mouth quivered in outrage she could have been a giant.

"What look? I wouldn't have come to you if it wasn't important."

"I'm afraid you've caught me on a bad day. I have a lot on."

"No, you don't, Mr. Acheson," Pamela interjected unhelpfully. "You're completely free for the next two hours before your next meeting. I told Miss Kirby...Sorry, Mrs. Longdon"—she inclined her head in apology to Emmeline—"that you would be more than happy to squeeze her into your schedule. I've penciled her into your diary so there wouldn't be any conflict."

Pamela beamed sweetly at him.

He pinched the bridge of his nose between his thumb and forefinger. He knew he was going to regret it. But there was nothing for it than to surrender with his dignity still intact.

"Pamela, remind me to sack you this afternoon."

"Yes, Mr. Acheson. And the reason?" his secretary asked nonplussed.

"For efficiency. What else?"

He jerked his head at Emmeline. "Come."

He opened his door and stood aside for her to pass. She stopped, put her hands on his shoulders, reached up on tiptoe and brushed a kiss against his cheek. "Thanks, Philip."

"That changes nothing. You will not weaken my resolve," he replied grudgingly. Someone had to maintain a sense of propriety.

Emmeline bit back a smile. "No, of course not. It would be unethical to try to influence you in any way."

To his consternation, she gave Pamela a wink before slipping into his office. *Women*, he scoffed silently.

He wagged his forefinger at his secretary. "Remember. You're sacked."

"Yes, Mr. Acheson. I'll bring in a tray of tea, shall I?"

He nodded and stepped into his office, pressing the door closed behind him. Emmeline had already installed herself on the claret-leather Chesterfield sofa to his right in the area next to the large window overlooking King Charles Street. He chose one of the two wing chairs in the same claret leather opposite her. He propped his elbows on the arms and steepled his hands over his lean stomach.

She opened her mouth to say something, but he forestalled her. "I would like to make it clear from the outset that I've only agreed to listen to you. Nothing more.

I also would like to stress that whatever is said here today is completely off the record. Therefore, no attributions for your story."

"How do you know that I'm working on a story?"

Philip threw his head back and laughed. "Even in your dreams, you're working on a story. If Longdon didn't harm you in any way, then the only other thing that would induce you to sacrifice your honeymoon would be a juicy new story. So no notebook and no tape recorder. By the way, you know Maggie and Helen will not be best pleased when they hear about this."

"Yes, well, perhaps we can delay their finding out as long as possible." He almost chuckled at the sheepish expression on her face.

There was a brief lull in the conversation as Pamela appeared with a tray laden with a Royal Doulton teapot decorated with tiny pink rosebuds and matching cups and saucers, and a plate of chocolate biscuits.

Once the tea was poured, Emmeline settled back on the sofa and took a sip of the perfectly steeped Darjeeling. With a biscuit held aloft between two fingers, she fired off her first question, "What can you tell me about a former MI5 agent named Hugh Carstairs?"

Philip scalded his tongue. He sloshed some tea on his saucer as he set it down with a trembling rattle on the highly polished cherry coffee table.

"*Hugh Carstairs*," he spluttered, as he dabbed at the corners of his mouth with a napkin. "Who…How…"—he swallowed hard in a bid to regain his composure—"how did you find out about Hugh Carstairs?"

Emmeline was watching him closely. "He's an assassin. Gregory and I overheard a man hiring Carstairs to kill someone."

"You what?" He ran a hand distractedly through his hair. "I can't believe my ears. This is going from bad to worse."

"By your reaction," she remarked calmly, "I take it you knew him."

He lifted his gaze to meet hers. "I did. A long time ago. He was…He was a good man. A friend. And then…" His voice trailed off.

"And then he botched the Rudenko defection." She paused. "Or maybe not."

"What are you insinuating? How do you know about that mess?"

"I never divulge my sources, off the record or not. I have my journalistic integrity to uphold."

"At this moment, I don't give a damn about your journalistic integrity, much as I respect you as a professional, and a friend."

"We seem to be at a bit of an impasse."

He slumped back and sighed wearily. Silence stretched between them.

Hugh Carstairs. A ghost from the past. It had been such a long time since he had heard his name. Hugh an assassin? It wasn't possible. There must be some mistake. And yet. Had it been anyone else other than Emmeline coming to him with this, he would have dismissed it out of hand. But it *was* Emmeline and that meant he couldn't ignore it.

"Are you certain it was Carstairs?" he queried, his voice cracking as he said his old friend's name.

"Yes, I spoke to him for a few minutes on the boat when we were taking a tour on Lake Windermere. When Gregory joined us, he told us his name was *Mr. Smythe*. As soon as we returned to London, I started doing some research. I found a photo of him online. He owns a company that does boat tours from Tobermory to Staffa and some of the other Scottish islands."

Philip reached for his cup and took a careful sip of tea this time. It had cooled in the meantime.

"But you said that you and Longdon overheard someone...hiring Carstairs for a hit?"

Her jaw was set in a tight line. "Yes. I'm not lying to you. I never would."

He waved a hand impatiently in the air. "I know that. It's just that it doesn't make sense. None of it makes any sense. Yes, Hugh was treated badly. It never crossed my mind for an instant that he could have been the leak."

"Ah, then you believed his claims about a mole?"

He took another sip of tea as he watched her over the rim of his cup. "I commit myself to nothing."

"We're off the record," she pointed out.

"It doesn't follow that I would suddenly become indiscreet. I have a loyalty to Her Majesty's government. I have signed the Official Secrets Act. I needn't have to remind you that you and Longdon have as well."

"Don't go all official on me, Philip. We are merely two friends having a casual conversation."

"A causal conversation about treason and murder," he scoffed. "Oh, yes. Definitely a fair assessment."

"You're not going to help me?"

"Help you with what precisely? Who is Carstairs going to kill? Is it a high-ranking official?"

"Well, the thing is," she hesitated. Then the words tumbled out in a rush. "We don't actually know who the target is."

His eyes narrowed. He had the satisfaction of seeing her squirm. "You don't...know." He slumped back in his chair and shook his head in incredulously.

"I know it sounds..."

He cut her off. "Mad, insane, crackers? You're the one who is good with words. I'll allow you to choose the perfect *bon mot*. Why did you come to me?"

She took a deep breath. "Because all my instincts are screaming that something is not right. I think Carstairs was set up. What if he was right? What if there was a mole and he was getting too close?"

He stared at her for several seconds. No one's brain worked like Emmeline's. She would have made a formidable MI5 agent, if it hadn't been for her temper and impatience. Hadn't he tried quietly to look into the Rudenko defection at the time? But after several months, he had nothing to show for his efforts and had been forced to give up. Now in hindsight, he reproached himself for not carrying on.

"Let say, for the sake of argument, that your theory is compelling. It would be dangerous—not to mention unwise—to stir up the waters by asking questions. The mole is sure to feel threatened and would lash out in retaliation."

"Then we'll simply have to tread carefully, won't we?" she observed.

We? Did she mean we as in she and Longdon? Or was it a collective we that involved himself, Burnell and Finch?

Either way, he didn't like it one iota.

ℰ⁄ℊℰ⁄ℊ

Hugh Carstairs, Philip murmured to his empty office. Emmeline had left half an hour ago, but their conversation had left him uneasy. He had tried to concentrate on his work but couldn't. His mind kept wandering back to one unsettling subject: *the mole*. Who was it?

He shook his head as he picked up the receiver and punched in Superintendent Burnell's number. Perhaps he could gain some perspective by focusing on something else.

"Burnell," he heard almost instantly.

"Hello, Superintendent. It's Philip Acheson returning your call. My secretary said it was urgent."

"Yes, Philip. Thanks for getting back to me so quickly. We have a problem and time is of the essence."

Philip hunched over his desk and pressed the receiver to his ear. "Of course, I'll provide any assistance I can."

There was a slight pause. "It involves Longdon and Emmeline."

Philip groaned. "Don't tell me. The assassin."

"Yes, how did you know?"

"Emmeline's just left my office. I can tell you his name. It's Hugh Carstairs. He's a former MI5 agent."

"Bloody hell. Are you sure?"

"Yes. It gets more complicated I'm afraid."

Burnell grunted. "Naturally. Why should my life become any easier in my old age?"

Philip couldn't help but chuckle. "You're far from your dotage, Burnell."

"When Longdon is involved, a man can age at the speed of light."

He couldn't argue. Burnell had all his sympathy. At the moment, Philip felt as if he were a hundred. Emmeline was a force of nature that sucked every ounce of one's energy, dear friend that she was.

CHAPTER 12

Edinburgh, Scotland

The lanky fellow with the head of thick coppery curls ducked into Advocate's Close, the narrow alleyway just off the Royal Mile. The bulb from the overhead light must have burnt out. Without the light, the damp chill from the rain earlier in the evening infiltrated the murky gloom, leaving a clammy kiss upon the old stone walls of that confined space. It seeped into the marrow of his bones, sending a frisson up his spine. He thrust his hands deeper into his pockets and hunched his shoulders forward against the breeze whispering upon the air.

Right. He had a job to do. No good dawdling.

His footfalls echoed against the slick flagstones of the steep staircase. If he continued straight on, eventually he would reach Cockburn Street and the Old Town. Ahead of him, over the rooftops of the surrounding buildings, he could see Princes Street and the top of Scott's Monument, which honored the great writer Sir Walter Scott. However tonight, he was not interested in the view. He only cared about one thing. Passing on the information he had meticulously gathered over the last three months. Then he would get out. Had to get out. He had no choice. Every day the risk was greater.

At the bottom of the second set of wide steps, he stopped beneath the gleaming black-and-white sign proudly proclaiming the Devil's Advocate. The pub's two charcoal-gray wooden doors were flung wide open, inviting him to step inside and stay a while. He glimpsed several chaps seated at the bar. The sound of laughter and the low murmur of conversation floated to his ears. He cast a quick glance over his shoulder to his right and left, just to make certain he hadn't been followed. But no, he was quite safe. He allowed his muscles to uncoil slightly as he crossed the threshold of the pub.

He unzipped his jacket. His cornflower-blue eyes adjusted quickly to the half-gloom as he scanned the pub. It was doing a brisk business on this Wednesday night, even the upper floor appeared to be brimming with customers. There was a small crowd of blokes huddled around the bar. They were engaged in a voluble discussion about the latest football match and the disappointing play by the star of the local team.

Most of the tables were occupied, but he spied one tucked in the shadows in a back corner that was unoccupied. He elbowed his way up to the bar, caught the bartender's attention, and ordered a pint. Once he had his drink in hand, he unobtrusively slipped across the room to the empty table. It had a clear view of the door. There was no way he would miss the chap he had come here to meet.

He lowered his weary body into the hard wooden chair and took a long swallow of his beer. The malty taste lingered on his tongue as it slid down his throat. He took another sip and put the pint down on the table. He rubbed his eyes with the heels of his palms. His brain felt heavy and sluggish, weighed down by a mixture of fatigue and…anxiety. Yes, anxiety that was the word. He wasn't prepared to admit that he was frightened. Not just yet.

But he *was*. That was the devil of it.

He took a hasty gulp of beer and was unnerved to see a tremor ripple through his fingers. He sloshed some of it onto the table. Damn and blast. It wouldn't do to come undone. Not now. There was so much at stake.

He glanced at his watch. Where was the fellow? He was already ten minutes late. His eyes slid to the door. There was no sign of him.

Just as this thought crossed his mind, the sturdy bulk of a man filled the doorway. At last. Relief trickled through his body and he slumped back in his chair. The next instant, he realized that the newcomer was not the man he was here to meet.

Rather, it was two burly chaps who should have been in Aberdeen at that very moment. That they were in Edinburgh could only mean one thing. *He was compromised.* He slouched lower in his chair. His pulse started to tingle as the blood coursed through his veins.

He had to get out of the pub. But how? They would see him if he stood up.

He sucked in his breath. Too late. The gaze of one of the men fell on him. His mouth went dry as he saw the fellow nudge his companion in the ribs and jerk his head in his direction.

Well, that was that. His chair scraped against the floor and tipped over backward, landing with a *thud* against the stone floor as he jumped to his feet. He used his elbows, his hands, his shoulders to shove his way across the room. He had to get to the door. His ears rang with a number of "Oy, watch it." and a string of expletives as he fought against the human tide steeped in drunken confusion and outrage. Vaguely, his brain registered that a fight had broken out behind him. He didn't look back, though. He knew the two chaps chasing him were momentarily swept up in the chaos.

He plunged through the open doorway. He drew a greedy gulp of the nippy air into his lungs and bounded up the stairs two at time. He stumbled, regained his balance, and continued on. He couldn't stop until he reached the top of Advocate's Close. Beads of moisture erupted across his forehead. The nape of his neck was drenched in sweat. His toe caught on the edge of a step and he stumbled again.

Almost there, he told himself. *Keep going.*

It will rain again tonight, he remembered thinking. Then his mind was wiped clean.

Only the white-hot, searing pain of the knife being thrust under his rib cage and into his heart consumed his senses. He never saw it coming. He should have known they wouldn't have been alone. He cursed himself for a fool.

He slumped to his knees. He was losing blood and his head was spinning. He felt a foot between his shoulder blades and then a great kick sent him tumbling back down the staircase.

Before oblivion swallowed him into its embrace, he whispered, "Damn you, Carstairs. I trusted you with my life."

CHAPTER 13

The taxi's tires crunched on the gravel sweep as it drew up in front of the Tudor manor in Oxford. A single passenger descended. With a practiced eye, he surveyed his surroundings without seeming to do so. He was certain that he hadn't been followed from the station. The only one watching him was the person inside the house who twitched the curtain in the front room ever so slightly.

He placed his bag on the ground and paid the driver. He waited until the taxi had disappeared from view and allowed his eyes to do another careful circuit of the bucolic landscape. Satisfied that only the birds exhibited any curiosity about him, he scooped up his bag and turned toward the house. The door opened before he had even climbed the three shallow stone steps.

The interior was plunged in gloom. He could make out only the vague outline of a person hovering just beyond the threshold. He didn't say a word until he was inside the oak-paneled great hall and the door was firmly closed behind him.

His host was the first to break the silence. "Good of you to come down, Carstairs," a hoarse voice said.

Carstairs extended a hand. "Not at all, sir."

The hand that gripped his was cool and dry. Had it lost some of its strength?

Villiers stepped out of the shadows. His breathing was a bit labored. "I thought we'd have tea in the library. I've had a fire lit." He pulled his cardigan around his shrunken form. "I seem to feel the cold more these days."

"Of course, sir. Lead the way."

Three arched entryways branched off from the great hall. One led to a spacious dining room, the library, and a rear hall.

They said nothing until they were settled in front of the fire in the library. A low table nestled between two wingback chairs in front of the fireplace. Someone had thoughtfully laid out a pot of tea, cups, saucers, and a plate of what looked like freshly made scones accompanied by strawberry jam and clotted cream.

Villiers lowered himself with great care into one of the chairs. Carstairs pretended not to notice that it took him several seconds to recover his breath.

"Shall I be Mother?" Carstairs asked, reaching for the pot.

Villiers nodded and slumped back in his chair. The hand that accepted the cup trembled slightly. Carstairs ignored that too.

"Would you like a scone, sir?"

Villiers took a sip of tea and waved a hand in the air. "Not just now. But do tuck in. They melt in your mouth. Mrs. Turner, my housekeeper, is a wonderful cook."

Carstairs smiled. "Right. How could I refuse after such praise?"

He felt Villiers's eyes on him as he placed a scone and dollop of jam on his plate. He balanced the plate on one knee as he raised his cup to his lips to take a sip of tea.

He studied the older man over the rim of his cup.

Villiers, although still elegant, seemed to have lost some of his vitality.

"Do you find me much changed?" Villiers appeared to have read his mind.

How should he answer? Carstairs thought.

"Well, sir," he hesitated, "Being shot does take a toll on one's body." He saw Villiers's eyebrows shoot up. "Sam Reynolds told me about it in general terms when he came up to see me."

Villiers leaned forward and placed his saucer on the table with a clatter. Carstairs saw a spark of his former self in the action. "He doesn't suspect, does he? About you I mean?" His tone was edged with anxiety.

Carstairs shook his head. "As far as Sam, or anyone else for that matter, is concerned I've run off to lick my wounds after being treated abominably by the agency. He still thinks that you gave me the boot because you believed that I was the mole."

One by one, Villiers's fingers loosened their grip on the arms of the chair. "Good." He reached for his tea and took a meditative sip. "By the way, we rounded up the chap who tried to hire you in the Lake District. We've shut down his whole network. He doesn't suspect you had a hand in it at all. After all, we wouldn't want our elaborate fiction that you're an international assassin to go up in smoke, would we?"

"No, sir. But may I ask why you didn't tell me about your...about your injury? I thought the reason I hadn't heard from you in all these months was because the trail had gone cold from your end. I had no idea that..."

Villiers made an impatient gesture with one hand. "It was nothing. All in the line of duty."

"Yes, but sir, Sam told me that you took a bullet for Gregory Longdon, a known jewel thief who now is Symington's chief investigator."

Villiers exhaled a weary breath. "It's a long story. We don't have time to go into all of that just at the moment. In our business, we have to deal with all sorts of people to get the job done. You know that. Longdon has…assisted me with certain jobs over the years. In this instance, he and that girlfriend of his got into a spot of bother. It was my fault. I made a miscalculation. Let's leave it at that."

"Of course, sir. I met Longdon and Emmeline Kirby— I assume she was the girlfriend you are referring to. Apparently, they were married last week."

"Yes, I know," Villiers replied quietly as he stared at some invisible spot over his shoulder.

Did he detect a note of sadness in the old man's voice? Carstairs shrugged. He must have imagined it. Why would the old man even care?

"Anyway," he continued, trying to draw Villiers out of his reverie, "They seem to be an odd couple. She asks a lot of questions."

The other man snorted. "That's an understatement. That young woman was put on this earth to plague the devil himself. She won't let go of a story. If I'm honest, we need more journalists like her. However, you didn't hear that from me. As for her and Tob…"—Carstairs frowned when Villiers corrected himself—"As for her and Longdon, they're more alike than anyone realizes."

"But he's a thief. Or doesn't she know?"

A quiver of a smile touched Villiers's mouth. "She didn't at the beginning, but she knows now. She tried to reform him. Then, she issued an ultimatum: Either he found a legitimate job or she wouldn't marry him."

"Mmm. He must love her, if he gave up his wicked ways."

"There's no doubt in anyone's mind that he loves her."

"Yes, but sir, how long can someone like Longdon toe the line? Surely he'll get bored and then what will happen?"

Carstairs thought Villiers said, "I hope he doesn't make the same mistake." But he couldn't be certain. It had been barely more than a whisper. Then in a more forceful voice, Villiers replied, "When she finds out, she'll kill him naturally. If I've learned anything observing that young woman, it's that she has a temper. On several occasions, it has gotten her into trouble."

Carstairs smirked, but there was a touch of admiration in his tone. "That I can well believe. Perhaps I should feel sorry for Longdon. Meanwhile, I wonder how he landed such a plum job at Symington's. Their background check leaves a lot to be desired."

Villiers pursed his lips and developed a keen interest in his fingernails.

"Sir, *you* didn't pull strings at Symington's, did you?" Carstairs asked incredulously. "Why?"

Villiers raised his cinnamon eyes to regard him steadily. "I don't have to explain my actions. I suggest that you concentrate on your mission. Distractions can be lethal."

Carstairs nodded. He knew when it was time to move on. "Speaking of distractions."

Villiers tensed and drew himself to the edge of his chair. "Yes? Has something happened?"

"You could say that," Carstairs said matter-of-factly trying not to worry his boss unduly. "Someone murdered that Treasury chap MacQuillan last night."

Villiers slapped his thigh with an open palm. His jaw was set in a hard line. "Bloody hell."

"We were supposed to meet last night. He said he found out about something called Poseidon," Carstairs went on. "All I have is that one word. I have no idea what it means. If I hadn't been late, perhaps he'd still be alive." He threw his hands up in the air and shrugged. "I don't know. What

I do know, is that MacQuillan was a damn good fellow. The police were already on the scene when I arrived, so I didn't linger."

Villiers shook his head and waved a hand in the air "That was best. You can't blame yourself. MacQuillan knew the risks."

"Yes," Carstairs grumbled bitterly. "There are always risks in this business, aren't there? And yet..." His voice trailed off.

They were silent for a while. Each man lost in his own troubled thoughts.

Villiers was the first to rouse himself. "Right. Anything else happen that I should know about?" he asked briskly.

"Well," Carstairs hedged.

"Spit it out man," Villiers snapped. "I don't like things being kept from me."

"I'm not certain it is connected with any of this, but someone has searched my house in Tobermory. Twice in the last fortnight. Nothing was taken. Nothing was out of place. Looking back on it now, I'm wondering whether my mind merely imagined it. Maybe I'm beginning to see things in the shadows that are not really there."

"Rubbish. You're not given to hysteria." Villiers rubbed his chin pensively. "I don't like it, especially after MacQuillan. I've left you out in the cold too long. Like everything else lately, I've overplayed my hand. It's time to pull you in."

The grating sound of fine china rattling against the table reverberated upon the air as Carstairs jumped to his feet. "Respectfully, sir, that would be a mistake," he observed. "Don't you see? If I've attracted someone's attention, it means I must be close. Obviously, MacQuillan had something too. He was simply careless. I've had more training."

"I don't want to find your body on my doorstep. It's

time for you to disappear. Permanently. I'll make a few discreet calls. You'll have a new identity in a day or two."

"Sir, I've come this far. I must see the mission through. I refuse to give up now."

Villiers shook his head. He was still for so long that Carstairs thought that he might have had some sort of a fit. At last, he gave a sigh that was infused with a lifetime of weariness.

"It goes against my better judgement."

Carstairs smiled and resumed his seat. "Thank you, sir. I'll be careful, especially in view of Rallis's trial. May I ask why you wanted me to testify, albeit anonymously? Surely, you could have done it."

Villiers pounded his fist against his open palm. "Ask the damn bloody doctors," he growled. "They insist the stress of the trial would be a setback for my recovery. A bunch of old biddies, the lot of them. They think they're God."

Carstairs bit back a smile. *Do I hear the pot calling the kettle black?* he asked himself.

"As for Rallis, aside from me you're the only one who's aware of the whole picture. He's been a dangerous thorn in our side for far too long. The murder of his mistress, forgive me if it sounds harsh, came at the ideal time. Once he's behind bars, it will be one less thing for us to worry about."

"You can't guarantee a conviction. From what Sam told me, Rallis supposedly has an alibi and pots of money to buy the best legal defense. His lawyer may have the jury eating out of his hand."

"His lawyer is Clive Stanhope." A low whistle emanated from Carstairs, when he heard the celebrated barrister's name. "Precisely. That's why you have to be even more persuasive. This affair tumbled into our laps. It's the only chance we're going to get. We have to nail him."

"I'll do my best not to let the side down, sir. I can't see my testimony taking more than a day or two. Then I'll nip straight back to Scotland."

"I'll have a quiet word with the Crown prosecutor. He's a member of my club. Without giving the game away, I'll leave him in no doubt about the importance of wrapping up your testimony as quickly as possible."

"At least, it's a closed courtroom. I'll be able to slip in and out without fear of exposure."

"Don't be naïve," Villiers countered. "The press likes nothing better than a juicy, salacious society murder. And this one stars a handsome playboy shipping magnate. It couldn't be better from their point of view. They'll be waiting to pounce on any little morsel that trickles out of the trial."

"I'm an expert at losing myself in a crowd. I've carried on this charade for three years. There's absolutely no way that I'll give the game away now."

"You forget that even before you take an oath on a Bible, you've managed to throw a spanner into the works."

Carstairs stiffened at the criticism, but he swallowed down the defense rising to his lips. He was a big boy, after all. In this business, a pat on the head was rare. The best way to get ahead was to be alive at the end of the day.

Villiers was going on in the same vein. "Three years' worth of work wasted because you crossed paths with Emmeline Kirby."

Is that what you're chuntering on about? Carstairs asked himself. Aloud, he said, "Surely she can't be that much of a threat. She doesn't even know my real name."

A harsh laugh escaped from Villiers. "You mean she didn't. However, your irresistible charm prompted her and Longdon to cut their honeymoon short and rush back to London. There has been an endless flow of questions ever since. Yesterday, they found their answer. For the moment, all they have is the official story about your supposed treasonous acts and subsequent dismissal. But Miss Kirby popped in to see Philip Acheson today."

Carstairs's head snapped up. "Philip? Why would she go to him?"

"Because his wife is her best friend and she's like an aunt to their twin boys, who adore her."

"That doesn't matter. We're in the clear, since Philip is in the dark about the entire scheme. You intentionally kept him out of the loop."

"That's correct. But what you don't know is that Acheson was disturbed by the circumstances surrounding your dismissal from MI5 and tried to do some investigating on his own. He was beginning to make rather a nuisance of himself. I squashed his efforts as soon as I got wind of them. My bet is that Miss Kirby—Damn, I still can't seem to get my tongue to call her Longdon." He shook his head. "My bet is that her conversation with him has rekindled his doubts. Oh, by the way, I heard it through the grapevine that Longdon paid a visit to a certain Superintendent Burnell of the Metropolitan Police. So you see, your fame appears to be growing by the day."

"Bloody hell," Carstairs cursed.

"Yes, well. Recriminations will do us no good at this stage. Aside from not talking to strange women who bat their eyelashes at you"—he shot a stern look at Carstairs—"I have a way for you to redeem yourself."

"Of course, sir."

"That's the spirit. I want you to go back up to London and attend a party."

Carstairs cut him off. "A party? But, sir, I thought you wanted me to keep a low profile."

"Ah, this is a special party. A black-tie affair the *beau monde* will be talking about for years to come. Models, artists, politicians, diplomats will be clamoring to be seen. Who knows? You might run into an old friend or two."

"I rather doubt that, sir. I don't run in those circles. Besides, I've always felt more comfortable observing from the shadows."

"I know old habits die hard, but I've always found that people let their guard down at one of Lady Starrett's parties."

Carstairs sat up bolt upright. "Lady…" He swallowed hard. "*Starrett*. Lady Fiona Starrett?"

"Yes. She's one of a kind." There was the touch of something malicious in Villiers's smile. "Is there a problem?"

"Problem? No. No." Carstairs shook his head vehemently. "No problem at all."

"Good. The party's on Friday at the Starretts' townhouse in Egerton Crescent. I've made a reservation for Mr. Smythe at the Jarvis Hotel in Queen's Gate. Your invitation is waiting in your room, as is a tuxedo. Let me know how you get on."

All Carstairs could do was to nod dumbly. He took a hasty gulp of his tea, which had gone cold. Grimacing, he set his saucer back down on the table. There was nothing more off-putting than cold tea. Or was it his churning thoughts about the upcoming party that colored his perception?

His chest tightened suddenly and he couldn't seem to catch his breath. It was as if water were rising all around him. Gurgling, bubbling. Soon it would cover his head and he'd be dragged under.

CHAPTER 14

Gregory smoothly glided the blue-gray Jaguar into a spot at the northeast end of the crescent across from the half-moon-shaped communal garden. The traffic had been typical for a Friday night in South Kensington, but it was only a short drive from Holland Park and they had plenty of time to spare.

He got out and came around the car to open the door for Emmeline. She smiled up at him as he gave her his hand.

He bent down and pressed a kiss against her cheek. "You look stunning, Emmy. I will be the envy of all the men tonight."

He allowed his gaze to roam appreciatively over his wife. She wore a silk shawl with embroidered roses draped over a simple, knee-length black velvet dress with a V-neck in the front and in the back. The dress emphasized the graceful curves of her petite silhouette to perfection. A diamond pendant in the shape of a flower with a matching bracelet at her wrist, both of which he gave to her on their wedding night, completed the effect. Her only accessory was the silk clutch she carried in her hand.

"Ravishing," he murmured against her ear as he tucked her arm through his elbow. "Perhaps we should get back in the car and go home."

She swatted his arm. "Behave yourself." Although the words were intended to be stern, the contented gleam in her dark eyes softened their sting. "You know very well you have to be here tonight as Symington's representative. You can't shirk your responsibilities."

"Heaven forbid." He dipped his head a little closer to her as their feet led them along the pavement to one of the 30 white-plastered townhouses that ringed the crescent. "But when you're around, I find it rather difficult to concentrate on my work."

She stopped and reached up to caress his cheek. "Darling, as always you're gallant." He inclined his head and flashed a grin at her. "But I doubt Lord and Lady Starrett would find it amusing, if the rare Tudor and Jacobean jewelry they intend to donate it to the Museum of London is stolen right from under the noses of a hundred guests the night before the transfer can be made. I don't think the museum, or the police, would like it much either."

Gregory sighed melodramatically. "I suppose you're right. I will have to steel myself for the long night ahead."

She giggled. "Come on. It will be fun and you know it."

Yes, he thought, *we need a distraction from Carstairs, the assassin, especially Emmy. She's becoming much too enthusiastic about him.*

Besides with the champagne flowing freely and a crush of wealthy guests, it might not be surprising to find a bauble or two ripe for the taking. Yes, the ideal setting to take his expert skills out for a test run, before leaping headlong back into the game.

His smile broadened as this possibility crossed his mind. Life was full of surprises.

A butler of medium height and rather stocky build answered the door. He inclined his balding head decorously when they gave their names and stood aside to usher them into the hall. Emmeline slipped the shawl from her shoulders and handed it over to the butler, who folded it carefully over his arm and melted away.

Everything about the Starrett's townhouse was clean and crisp. All the walls and doors were a creamy alabaster and the parquet floor was polished to a high gleam. For the most part, the Starretts preferred to leave the floors bare. The only thing that enlivened the hall and gave it a bit of warmth was the Persian runner with a swirling pattern of flowers and curlicues in rich shades of crimson, cream, navy, and forest green. It drew one's eye up the stairs to the delicate antique table residing on the half-landing. Gregory made a mental note to go and explore the upper rooms at some point during the evening.

At the moment, Lord Desmond—Dez to his friends and close acquaintances—Starrett strode up to them and thrust out his hand.

"Longdon, good of you to come," he said in his Scottish burr as he pumped Gregory's hand up and down. "I told Symington's I would feel more comfortable having one of you chaps here tonight. Why Fiona felt it necessary to throw a party and attract attention to the jewels I'll never know. I wanted to hand them over to the museum quietly. Of course, there will be a small plaque acknowledging my donation. But really all this fuss." He waved a hand in the air. He shrugged his shoulders. "Well, water under the bridge. When women set their minds on a thing, there is no changing it."

Gregory smiled pleasantly. He slid a sideways glance at Emmeline and saw that Lord Starrett's comments had not endeared him to her.

He cleared his throat. "Speaking of wives, may I introduce mine?" He placed a hand on the small of her back and gave her tiny push forward. "Lord Starrett, this is Emmeline."

She extended a hand. The smile plastered on her lips threatened to crack any second. However, Helen had drilled manners into her and she managed to reply politely, "How do you do, Lord Starrett? Thank you for inviting us to your lovely home."

Starrett took her small hand in both of his beefy ones and shook it vigorously. "Think nothing of it, my dear. Your husband's presence"—he jerked his thumb at Gregory—"eases my anxiety. Please enjoy yourselves. I don't know where Fiona's got to." He craned his neck round. "She's about somewhere, probably in the kitchen checking on the caterer. I'll introduce you both later. I'm afraid I must attend to our other guests. I'm certain that two of you can mingle on your own. Enjoy the party."

With that, Starrett slipped off into what appeared to be a reception room. It was narrow and rectangular, and then opened up into an airy square space. Starrett joined a knot of men at the opposite end of the room, who were sharing a joke. Emmeline and Gregory peeped their heads round the door and caught a glimpse of three members of the prime minister's Cabinet deep in conversation in one corner, a theater critic Emmeline knew from her days at the *Times* chatting with the producer and star of the latest hit in the West End by the window, and two famous models lounging on a sofa looking terribly bored.

Emmeline arched an eyebrow at Gregory. "An eclectic mix of guests."

"From what I hear, you never know who you'll meet at one of Lady Starrett's parties."

"It should make for an interesting evening."

Gregory smiled at a passing waiter and lifted two flutes of champagne off the silver tray he was carrying. He offered one to Emmeline and then took a sip of his own. "We can't linger about in the corridor all evening," he murmured. "Let's join the festivities."

He guided them through a door to the right of the staircase. It turned out to be another reception room. This one was more intimate. It was not as crowded as the one across the hall. Built-in bookcases lined two of the walls. In the middle of one of the cases, there was a closed cabinet. They suspected it neatly hid the television. There was a bow window that looked out onto the garden.

In the center of the room, two beige leather sofas faced one another across a low glass table. A couple of wing-back chairs were arranged together at one end of the table.

"Well, if it isn't the naughty couple who should still be on their honeymoon."

Emmeline and Gregory both spun around at the sound of Maggie's voice.

"Maggie, what are you doing here?" Emmeline asked, as she embraced her friend and gave her a peck on the cheek.

"I might ask you the same question. Actually, I'm rather upset with the two of you." She tossed her head in the air. "I promised myself I wouldn't speak to the two of you."

Gregory took her elbow and bent to kiss her cheek. "Oh, don't say that. It would break my heart not to hear your lovely voice. I always find that someone with such a beautiful voice has other remarkable qualities as well. Like a forgiving nature."

"And don't forget tender," Emmeline chimed in as she looped her arm through Maggie's. "Maggie is a very tender soul."

"No one can possibly forget the quality of her mercy," Gregory concurred.

They had Maggie trapped between them. They both leaned in close.

Gregory's cinnamon gaze locked on Maggie's eyes. He gave her a lopsided smile. A slight flush colored her cheeks. She gave him a gentle shove. "That's quite enough of that. Your charm doesn't work on me," she replied crisply, but the words lacked any anger.

He put a hand to his chest. "Would I try to play on your sympathies?" His voice was infused with innocence.

"Hmph," she snorted. "Does a bird have wings?" She turned to Emmeline. "You must take your husband in hand. You can't allow him to go about flinging his charm at unsuspecting souls the way he did when he was a bachelor. Heaven knows what would happen. Now, to get back to the subject at hand. I'm willing to give you both a second chance, but Helen is quite a different matter." She wagged her forefinger at them. "She's very cross with both of you."

Emmeline sighed. "Yes, I know. She rang me the other day. It was a rather one-sided conversation."

"What can you expect? What possessed the two of you to cut short your honeymoon? Philip was rather evasive. He wouldn't give me a straight answer. He mumbled something about a story. I was planning to tackle him again about it on the way home tonight."

"Poor Acheson," Gregory muttered under his breath.

Maggie sniffed. "I heard that. Naturally, I would expect you boys to stick together." She turned to Emmeline. "But you have no excuse. What story could be more important than your honeymoon? Your *long* overdue honeymoon."

Emmeline exchanged a glance with Gregory. "It's a bit...involved," she settled on at last.

"When it comes to your life and your work, it always is. It also means that it's likely dangerous." Maggie placed her hands on her hips and her green eyes narrowed. "Don't think you can fob me off with some ridiculous tale. I know when you're lying. And I'm not going to leave here tonight until I find out what you're up to."

"Maggie be reasonable..."

"That's what I'm always telling my darling wife, but she never listens to me. Mags, what are you pestering Emmeline about? As if I didn't know," Philip said as he entered the room. "Hello, Emmeline." He kissed her cheek and nodded at Gregory. "Longdon. I apologize for my overly curious wife."

Maggie gave him a withering look, but was prevented from commenting further because her husband was accompanied by two gentlemen.

"Allow me to introduce Maurice Forestier, the French ambassador, and Yoav Zielinski, the Israeli cultural attaché."

The Frenchman, who was lithe of build and several inches taller than either Gregory or Philip, stepped forward. A man of not more than fifty, he exuded confidence with just a tiny hint of arrogance. He gave a slight nod at Maggie, bent over her hand and brushed a kiss across her knuckles. "*Enchanté*, Madame Acheson." His words were infused with centuries of Gallic charm.

When he straightened up, his cool gray eyes lingered appreciatively on Maggie's face. "*Enchanté*," he murmured again.

A pink flush crept up Maggie's cheeks. She cleared her throat. "A pleasure to meet you, Monsieur Forestier. Are you enjoying the party?"

"I never miss one of Fiona's parties. One always meets the most interesting people." His smile lingered on her face, boldly tracing every curve. Then his gaze fell upon Emmeline and Gregory. "But forgive me." He took Emmeline's hand and kissed it as well.

"Maurice, this is Mr. and Mrs. Longdon," Philip said.

"A pleasure," Forestier replied politely as he shook Gregory's hand.

"And by process of elimination, I must be Yoav Zielinski," the Israeli offered, a bemused gleam in his intelligent onyx eyes.

"Oh, Mr. Zielinski, where are my manners? I'm delighted to meet you at last," Maggie gushed. "Philip has told me so much about you over the years. I know he has the utmost respect for you and prizes your friendship."

The corners of Zielinski's eyes crinkled, when he smiled. "I, too, am happy to meet you, Mrs. Acheson."

Maggie bent her head close to the Israeli's. "It's actually Ms. Roth. I decided to keep my maiden name when I married Philip."

"Yes, of course, Roth. A fine Jewish family, highly esteemed in many circles. The Roth investment bank is a well-known institution. I met your father and brothers at charity event a few years ago. I must tell you that they couldn't stop talking about you. They are all very proud of you, despite the fact that you decided not to go into the bank. Now, the only member of the family I have yet to meet is your mother."

"I'll have to arrange a dinner party. Then you'll know the whole *mishpucha*."

The small man threw back his head and laughed at this Yiddish word for the whole family. "I can't think of anything I'd enjoy more. Philip tells me you're a devotee of classical music and Impressionism. We must have a chat…"

Forestier cut across him. "But not tonight, Zielinski. I can't allow you to keep Madame Roth all to yourself. She looks like she needs a glass of champagne, isn't that so?"

"Well, I'd love a glass, but…"

"Then come with me." Forestier took her by the elbow. "I'm sure your husband won't miss you for a little while." He nodded to the rest of the group as he ushered Maggie toward the door.

She gave a little wave. "I guess I'll see all of you later." However before she disappeared into the corridor, she tossed over her shoulder. "Emmeline, don't think this lets you off the hook. We'll continue our conversation later."

"My advice to the two of you," Philip said, "is to make a graceful exit now."

"I'm afraid that's not possible old chap," Gregory replied. "I'm here as Symington's representative tonight at Lord Starrett's behest. No one was too keen on Lady Starrett's decision to throw a lavish party to show off the jewels before they had been safely turned over to the museum. It's been determined that they're part of the infamous Cheapside Hoard, which as you know were nearly five hundred pieces of rare and beautiful Tudor and Jacobean jewelry. Imagine emeralds, rubies, sapphires and diamonds, some dating back 1,500 years to Byzantium." Gregory's eyes glittered as he warmed to his subject. "Lost centuries ago and unexpectedly unearthed in 1912 by workmen demolishing an old jeweler's premises in Cheapside, a stone's throw from where the Museum of London stands today. It boggles the mind. Can you imagine? The workmen stuffed the lot into their pockets, hats, and in knotted handkerchiefs, wherever they could and walked off bold as brass. They took the jewels to a bloke who ran a pawn shop and was known to acquire objects for museums no questions asked."

"But how did the jewels come to be discovered in Cheapside in the first place?" Emmeline asked. She was fascinated by Gregory's tale as were their companions.

"A gem dealer in 1637 booked passage on an East India ship from the Orient back to England, taking with him two huge chests filled with the treasure," he continued. "Unfortunately, the chap was rather careless and lost a small diamond from the purse around his neck when he was bathing. A fortnight into the voyage, the gem dealer was dead, poisoned by the ship's surgeon. His body was thrown overboard. When the chests were opened in

London, they were half-empty, the contents had been stolen by the officers and crew. The loot was offered to jewelers across the city. Historians believe that some of the jewels ended up in the Cheapside Hoard, but it is unclear who buried the treasure. To this day, not all the pieces have been recovered." He lowered his voice. "The Museum of London was delighted when Lord Starrett offered to donate his pieces and Symington's was only too pleased to insure them. However, no one has bothered to ask how they came into his possession. And I rather doubt anyone will."

"A very interesting story, Mr. Longdon," Zielinski said. He extended a hand. "By the way, I'm delighted to meet you in person at last. You've led a fascinating life from what I hear."

Gregory's mouth twitched into a smile beneath his mustache as he shook the Israeli's hand. "Have you? You can't really believe everything you hear. People do tend to exaggerate. I'm just an ordinary chap, trying to scratch out an existence."

Philip made a choked, gurgling sound at the back of his throat at this last comment. Emmeline shot a warning look at him, but Gregory chose to ignore him.

"Come now, Mr. Longdon," Zielinski coaxed. "You are too modest. Your exploits are almost the stuff of legend."

Another smile slid across Gregory's lips. Was he preening just a *teeny* little bit? Or was it merely Emmeline's imagination?

Gregory took a sip of his champagne. "The same can be said about you. I bet you have a story or two tucked up your sleeve about life in the shadows." He took another swallow of the golden liquid and held Zielinski's gaze over the rim of the glass.

Zielinski threw his head back and laughed. "I assure you a diplomat's life is quite dull. Just ask Philip." He touched Philip's forearm lightly. "He will tell you. My life is an open book. I served in the Army, as every citizen must. I was head of the History department at Hebrew University in Jerusalem until the prime minister asked me to become cultural attaché. It has been a great honor for me to represent my country here in London for the last thirteen years."

"Indeed." Gregory lifted his glass in a silent toast. "All quite admirable."

Zielinski inclined his head. "You're too kind."

In that moment, something unspoken passed between the two men. A sort of understanding, tinged with respect. They couldn't have been more different physically. Gregory was six feet tall, lean, his dark wavy hair touched with gray at the temples, whereas Zielinski, a man in his early sixties was no more than five-foot-six or -seven with white hair that was slowly receding from the broad dome of his forehead.

However, it was precisely the older gentleman's nondescript appearance that made him a master at his job. Not that of cultural attaché, although that required finesse, but rather a high-ranking official in Mossad, Israel's spy agency who was under deep cover in the London embassy. This would never be officially confirmed, but Emmeline knew—knew instinctively—that this was the case. Obviously, Gregory suspected it too. Zielinski had provided her with information over the summer when she was pursuing a story about looted Nazi art and an IRA collaborator named Doyle. She drew a deep breath. He also gave her a file about the murder of her parents. She could never have obtained any of this information through the normal channels. She was honored that Zielinski thought so highly of her work—and her discretion—that he trusted her with the sensitive material.

Well, she was not here tonight to cause a ripple across

the diplomatic pond. She would never divulge Zielinski's secret. Never. After all, it was merely speculation on her part. Granted it was based on strong suspicion, but at the end of the day it was suspicion nonetheless.

She broke into the men's conversation. "Mr. Zielinski, I never had the opportunity to thank you properly for all your help over the summer."

He patted her arm in an avuncular fashion and made a dismissive gesture in the air with his other hand. "Think nothing of it. I…"

A sudden flurry of commotion cut off the rest of his sentence.

CHAPTER 15

They all turned as one to see the prima ballerina Anastasia Tarasova entering the room on the arm of a sour-faced man in his mid-fifties, whose gray eyes appeared to be magnified by his steel-rimmed spectacles. Emmeline shivered involuntarily, when his gaze momentarily locked with hers. From his salt-and-pepper hair down to his toes, the man was stiff, cold, and terrifying.

Philip nudged Zielinski with his elbow and jerked his chin in new arrival's direction. "Look, Yoav, your old friend. I was wondering what had happened to Boris. He's been rather too quiet lately."

Zielinski's brows knit together. "Yes," he replied, without taking his eyes off the man. "Much too quiet. Why is he here tonight, I wonder? And on the arm of Anastasia Tarasova, no less."

"Perhaps he's developed a passion for ballet?" Philip ventured facetiously.

Zielinski snorted. "That man was born a philistine. He doesn't know a Monet from a Jackson Pollock. And you expect him to suddenly recognize all the delicate nuances of a performance of *Swan Lake*?" He shook his head dubiously. "Come now, Philip, you know better. Everything is a calculated chess move."

Emmeline cleared her throat noisily. "You know it's frightfully bad manners to keep up a running commentary on the other guests." She lowered her voice conspiratorially. "That is, unless you are prepared to share the gossip with your friends." She batted her eyelashes at Philip and Zielinski.

"Yes, do tell us who the ugly chap is before my wife dies of curiosity," Gregory chimed in as he slipped his arm around her waist and drew her to his side.

She angled her head to look up into his face, sparks of anger kindling in the depths of her eyes. She pushed him away. "That was not helpful. I will speak to you when we get home."

Gregory wrinkled his nose at her, a smile tugging at the corners of his mouth.

"Before we are the cause of your divorce," Philip interjected, so only they could hear, "Anastasia Tarasova's escort happens to be Boris Petrenko, the Russian cultural attaché. It's an open secret in diplomatic circles that Petrenko is an officer in the FSB, the KGB's successor."

Emmeline's gaze slid to the Russians again. "Really? How very interesting." Her mind was already spinning with a host of questions. Perhaps if she played her cards right, she would leave the party with the seeds of another story.

She watched in fascination as the newcomers were quickly swarmed by the other guests, who clamored for a morsel of attention from the great Tarasova. Petrenko stuck close to her, his eyes scouring the semi-circle huddled around them.

Emmeline had never see Tarasova in person, only on television. Everything about the ballerina was lithe. The diaphanous ivory folds of her silk dress clung to the taut, muscled-toned body beneath. She carried herself with the grace and poise ingrained by the years of discipline demanded by her art. Her straight, sandy blond hair was cut in a sleek bob and fell just above her shoulders. A magnificent platinum necklace, dripping with rubies and diamonds, was draped around her throat.

Emmeline sniffed. She was not impressed with the famous ballerina. The woman was striking, she conceded that much. But there too much arrogance mingled with cruelty in those calculating, smoky blue eyes to make her beautiful. She knew that one glance at the bones of the woman's protruding collarbone and Gran would have said that she was far too thin to be healthy. Emmeline chuckled silently as this thought flitted across her mind. Her amusement vanished, though, when she saw Gregory's eyes fixed on the woman. His mouth was slightly parted and the tip of his tongue flicked over his lips. She thought she heard him mumble "Sheer perfection. An absolute stunner." But she couldn't be sure. She wouldn't have believed that Tarasova was the type of woman who could capture his attention, much less fan the flames of his ardor.

She looped her arm through the crook of his elbow, forcing him to bend down slightly toward her. However, his gaze never left the ballerina.

"I needn't have to remind you that you are a married man," she whispered.

"What?" He shifted his head to meet her eye. "Emmy, you are the only woman in the world for me. Other women pale in comparison."

"Hmph." She wanted to stomp on his foot, but that would have been unladylike in such a public gathering. Instead, she hissed through clenched teeth, "Then why do keep staring at her like that?"

His brow furrowed in confusion. "Like what? At whom?"

Emmeline inclined her head in Tarasova's direction.

"*Her*?" He patted her hand and pressed a kiss against her temple. "Darling, credit me with some taste."

She would, if Veronica Cabot didn't still burn in her memory.

She tugged his arm again, drawing him even closer. "If it's not Anastasia Tarasova, *what* has sent you into this catatonic trance?"

He chuckled. "I have no idea what you're on about, Emmy. I'm simply enjoying the party. It's quite festive, don't you think?"

When she didn't answer, he drew her to his side again. "Parties always put me in a nostalgic mood. They make me think of old friends." His gaze strayed again to the ballerina. "And missed opportunities." These words were tinged with regret and punctuated by a wistful sigh. But after a pause, he brightened. "Or they could present second chances."

Missed opportunities? Second chances? She balled her fists at her sides. She liked Anastasia Tarasova less and less as the minutes ticked by.

An odd expression settled over her husband's features. The ghost of a smile played about his mouth and there was a mischievous glint in his eyes.

"What are you up to?"

This had the same effect of icy water being doused over his head, as she had intended. "Up to? I don't know what you mean. You're very suspicious all of a sudden."

"I'm afraid you can't blame Emmeline. It's probably old Boris's fault. He has a way of putting the people about him on edge," Philip murmured.

"Shh," Zielinski hissed. "They're coming this way." He plastered a smile on his lips. "Ah, Boris, this is a surprise."

Petrenko gave a stiff bow from his neck and reluctantly extended a hand. "Zielinski, good evening," he intoned lugubriously. He nodded at Philip and they shook hands perfunctorily. "Acheson. May I introduce Anastasia Tarasova, our greatest ballerina?"

She bestowed a regal smile upon them as she proffered a limp hand, weighed down by a thirty-two carat cabochon diamond-and-ruby ring. "Gentleman," she murmured in her husky Russian inflected voice.

"A great honor," Zielinski said. "I had the pleasure of seeing you last year in *Giselle* at Covent Garden. Your performance was magical."

A glimmer of delight lit up her eyes. "Ah, you are a lover of the ballet, Mr. Zielinski. How charming." She cast a sideways glance at Petrenko. "Boris is not so enthusiastic. He only comes to the ballet because my father wants someone watching over me. It's really rather—what is the English word?—Ah, yes. It's really rather a nuisance."

Zielinski bit back a smile as a scowl darkened Petrenko's features.

Philip sought to fill the awkward breach. "Petrenko, Miss Tarasova, allow me to introduce Mr. and Mrs. Longdon."

They all shook hands. "Longdon," Petrenko murmured. "I know this name. Yes, I know it *very* well." His mouth twitched into a knowing smirk. "You have a certain reputation."

"My, the chap does get around," Philip muttered *sotto voce*. Aloud, he said, "Mr. Longdon is Symington's chief investigator. He's here tonight to ensure that the jewels remain safe until they are transferred to the Museum of London."

"Of course," the Russian replied, his tone laced with skepticism. "We wouldn't want them to disappear, would we?"

Unfazed, Gregory offered him a smile. But he remarked

with grave sincerity, "It would be an absolute tragedy. The public would be deprived of an important piece of English history."

What drivel, Philip thought. *History, indeed. Since when did he develop such a concern about preserving the country's history?*

"But rest assured, Mr. Petrenko," Gregory went on, "Lord Starrett's jewels are in no danger."

Petrenko's face broke into what Emmeline assumed was an uncharacteristic grin. It was more unnerving than his grimace because it held no mirth and was purely predatory. "I suppose we have no choice but to accept your word for that. I would have said quite the opposite. But what do I know of such things?" One shoulder lifted in a blasé shrug. "I'm merely a diplomat. You're the expert."

Gregory inclined his head. "Thank you for the compliment, Mr. Petrenko. But don't sell yourself short, I'm certain that there is more to you than meets the eye. You strike me as a fellow with hidden talents. And many secrets."

They eyed each other for several tense seconds without uttering a word. At one point, Petrenko opened his mouth to say something and then snapped it shut, appearing to change his mind.

He took Tarasova by the elbow and gave a curt nod to the little group. "Good evening, Mrs. Longdon. Gentlemen. We must pay our respects to our hosts. We wouldn't want to be rude."

"Certainly not. We can't have bad manners," Gregory mumbled.

Tarasova's brow furrowed with displeasure, but she nodded and said, "Good evening" before she allowed herself to be led off.

Once out of earshot, she halted near the doorway and shook off Petrenko's grasp. They watched in amusement as Tarasova bent her head close to his and appeared to let loose a tirade in hushed tones.

"Ahem," Zielinski cleared his throat. "One almost feels sorry for Boris, almost."

"I know it's not polite to stare. But I've never seen anyone with a complexion quite that shade of crimson, have you?" Philip asked. "He looks like he's going to explode at any moment. Ah, there's Fiona. Things will settle down now."

Curiosity drew Emmeline's attention to the lovely, svelte woman in the forest green floor-length chiffon dress who was engaged in conversation with the two Russians. Her honey-colored hair was swept up above her head in a chignon and held in place by a mother-of-pearl barrette sprinkled with diamonds. The emerald choker nestled against the peaches-and-cream hollow of her throat and the matching earrings dandling to and forth with every turn of her head mirrored the startling intensity of her eyes. She would have to see Maggie and Lady Fiona Starrett standing side by side, but she would wager their eyes were the same fiery green. Two women with spirit. She would definitely like to get to know Lady Starrett. She guessed that Lady Starrett was only a few years older, no more than her mid-thirties, so they would have a lot in common.

The Russians finally drifted out into the corridor. Lady Starrett folded her hands together and scanned the room. She smiled when Philip waved to catch her eye. She started to weave her way toward them, but her progress was slowed by other guests who stopped to exchange a word with her.

She took Philip's hands in both of hers when she reached his side and angled a cheek to receive his kiss. "Philip, I'm so glad that you and Maggie could come tonight. It's been ages since Dez and I have seen you both. How are Henry and Andrew?"

"They're two healthy little devils. I didn't know that two five-year-olds could get up to such mischief."

Lady Starrett laughed and swatted his arm. "Nonsense. You are awful. The twins are delightful."

"Exactly," Emmeline concurred. "I've never seen two such bright and happy children. Philip is just being an ogre." She made a moue at him.

"You're only saying that because Auntie Emmeline can do no wrong in their eyes. You spoil them rotten."

"I don't." She turned to Lady Starrett, looking for support. "Really, I don't. But children deserve treats from time to time, don't they?"

The other woman's silvery laughter hung upon the air. "Of course, they do." She extended a hand toward Emmeline. "I assume that you are Emmeline Longdon. I already had the pleasure of meeting Mr. Longdon. And dear Yoav, of course, I have known for many years." She nodded at Gregory and touched Zielinski's arm lightly. "I'm sorry I wasn't able to greet you when you arrived. A minor crisis in the kitchen with the caterer. But everything's right as rain. The rest of the evening should go smoothly. However there's no rest for the wicked, so please excuse me. I hope we can chat properly later after the presentation of the jewels."

"We look forward to it," Emmeline said.

The next instant her smile froze on her face.

"Emmy, what's the matter?" Gregory asked.

She swallowed hard. "Look who just walked in on the arm of Noel Rallis, a man on trial for murder."

Gregory followed her gaze. "My God, it's Sabrina. Has she taken leave of her senses?"

"Obviously, you know this woman," Zielinski said.

"You could say that," Emmeline murmured. "She's my sister."

CHAPTER 16

Emmeline started to make her way toward the door,
but Gregory snatched her arm and drew her back.
"Emmy, where are you going?" There was a
warning note in his tone.

She whirled round. "I have to talk to Sabrina."

He increased the pressure of his fingers. "No, you don't,
darling. She's a big girl."

"She's a spoiled, self-involved fool," Emmeline replied
through gritted teeth. "But I can't allow her to get tangled
up with a man like that."

"It's none of your concern."

Her voice dropped to barely a whisper. "But he might
kill her. I can't just stand by and do nothing. Even if I can't
stand her."

Gregory gripped her arms and gave her a gentle shake.
"You can and you will. You owe Sabrina nothing. She
certainly won't appreciate it if you intervened."

"Emmeline, I think Longdon's right," Philip observed
quietly. "My advice is to stay out of it. You might make
things worse."

She pinned him with her gaze and then her eyes strayed
to Zielinski. The latter held up his hands in the air. "I, like

these gentlemen, am not the enemy. I do not know your sister, but I suggest you listen to your husband and Philip."

She managed to wriggle free of Gregory's grasp. Her smile washed over each of them in turn.

Gregory didn't like the set of her chin.

"Thank you. I know you all mean well." She paused. "But I'm going to have a word with my sister."

She turned on her heel and swept off before they could offer any other objections.

Emmeline heard Noel Rallis say, "I'll be back in a tick, darling. I have to take this call. It's business. I'm sure you understand." He had his mobile plastered to his ear and was wandering toward a room at the back of the house. The door was ajar. It appeared to be a study.

Sabrina was left standing alone in the middle of the corridor, scowling at his back.

"Sabrina," Emmeline said, with as much calm as she could muster.

Sabrina's head whipped round. "Yes, what…"

Her eyes widened in surprise and then narrowed. Emmeline saw the flash of annoyance reflected in their sea-green depths. She experienced a little stab of joy that she had upset her sister. Why should she be the only one whose evening was ruined?

Sabrina pursed her lips and stared down her nose at Emmeline. After several seconds, she finally replied, "Don't tell me there's trouble in paradise. Where's that dishy husband of yours? Has he left you already?" She smirked. "I'm not surprised."

Her gaze flickered over Emmeline and she lowered her voice. "You can't give a man like that what he really needs."

Emmeline drew in a sharp breath. The blood was throbbing against her temple. Her nails dug into one palm as her other hand pressed her clutch against her belly.

Don't sink to her level, she told herself. *And above all, don't throttle the viper. It's too public.*

This was a mistake. She cursed herself. She should have listened to Gregory, but it was too late now.

"Gregory is perfectly fine. Thank you for asking."

Sabrina tossed her dark tresses over one shoulder and laughed. "How very British." Her smile evaporated almost instantly. "Why are you here bothering me? Adam told me you were on your honeymoon. Why aren't you?"

Emmeline made an impatient gesture with her hand. "Never mind that. What the devil are you doing with Noel Rallis?"

Sabrina took a half-step closer. Emmeline felt her sister's warm breath brush her cheek when she spoke. "Listen to me, Miss Nosey Parker, you are nothing to me. Do you understand? Absolutely nothing." Her nostrils flared and her tone dripped acid. "Just because Dad's blood runs through both of our veins, it doesn't make us one big happy family. Adam can do whatever he likes, but I could care less what happens to you. So stay out of my business."

They stood there eyeing one another with raw hostility. Emmeline was seething.

She licked her lips. Her voice was a hoarse croak. "He's a murderer. Doesn't that bother you?"

Her sister's mouth curved into a malevolent grin. "*Alleged.* Isn't that what you journalists are supposed to say? Alleged murderer. Noel is innocent until proven guilty. It's rather unfair of you to try the poor man in the press." She wagged a manicured finger at her. "If you're not careful, he'll sue you for slander."

"*Poor man?*" Emmeline spluttered. "Either you're crackers or you're being deliberately naïve. He's dangerous. Or is that the attraction? You enjoy the shock value of walking in on his arm. You always have to be the center of attention, don't you?"

"Leave…me…alone," Sabrina hissed through clenched teeth.

"With pleasure. Come along, Emmy."

They had been so embroiled in their heated conversation that neither of them had heard Gregory approach.

He put his arm, firmly, around Emmeline's shoulders. "Darling, Maggie's been asking for you. Come on." He shifted her body a fraction of an inch and inclined his head toward her sister. "Sabrina, we'll bid you good evening."

Her sensuous lips formed a tiny pout. "Don't run away on my account," she purred. "I don't mind seeing *you*." Her voice was even huskier than usual, if that were possible. "In fact, the evening has definitely perked up. We have an awful lot of catching up to do."

"Do we?" he asked. "I don't recall ever having any heart-to-heart chats in the past?"

Sabrina closed the space between them and put her hand possessively on his arm. Emmeline stared at that hand with undisguised malice. If she wasn't wedged between them, she had no doubt that Sabrina would have shamelessly pressed herself up against Gregory.

"There's always a first time. We can have our own private party at my flat," Sabrina said, a suggestive smile playing around her lips.

I'll kill her, Emmeline screamed silently. Violence was so unbecoming and ultimately did nothing to resolve a problem. But it would feel oh, so good—in a primeval sort of way—when she wiped that sneer off Sabrina's face. With this goal in mind, the hand holding her clutch began to rise. At this distance, she couldn't miss. The trajectory was perfect. The blow would land smack in middle of her sister's mouth.

However, before she could give vent to her fury,

Gregory grabbed her clutch. "Careful, Emmy, you nearly dropped it." He gave her a pointed look.

Hmph, men. They were all cowards at heart. All she wanted to do was to teach Sabrina a lesson.

She sighed inwardly. It was her own fault. Once again, she had allowed Sabrina to get under her skin. "Oh, thank you, darling. What would I do without you?"

She reached up and kissed his cheek and then flashed a triumphant smile at her sister.

Sabrina rolled her eyes. "I've had enough of this saccharin display of domestic bliss. Gregory, one these days you'll get bored and come to your senses. When you do, know that my door is *always* open for you. Anytime of the day or night." She had the gall to wink at him. "In the meantime, I must find Noel."

She gave them a dismissive wave and scooted off down the corridor, her hips swaying provocatively.

Gregory cocked his head to one side and looked down at Emmeline. She put a finger up to his lips. "Before you say anything, you were right. I shouldn't have tried to talk to her. I should have known it would get her back up. There is no reasoning with her. It's hard to believe she and Adam are twins. He's kind and she's so...so..." Her fingers curled more tightly around her clutch.

Gregory smiled and pressed a soft kiss against her temple. "Yes, darling, she is. That's why it's best for everyone concerned if you keep your distance. Promise?" One eyebrow arched upward. It was more of a command than a question.

"You needn't worry. I won't murder her. Not tonight anyway," she mumbled.

"I think Lady Starrett will be relieved to hear it, especially since she's gone to such trouble to make the party a success. Look, Emmy, will you be all right on your own for a bit. I've got to discuss a couple things with the curator from the museum about transfer of the jewels tomorrow."

"Yes, of course. Off you go. Don't worry about me. I won't chase after Sabrina. I'll go find Maggie and Philip and Mr. Zielinski."

"Good girl. I think they mentioned something about the buffet in the dining room. I won't be long."

The dining room table was laden with all sorts of delectable dishes intended to tempt guests' appetites and make them run for the gym tomorrow morning. However, there were several that employed their iron control and were munching, without pleasure, on raw carrots and other vegetables from the plate of crudités. Emmeline tipped her hat to them, but she admitted that they did look miserable. Meanwhile, others were circling the table and happily filling their plates. She would wait for Gregory to join her.

She cast a glance around. Her friends were not among the guests scattered about the room chatting and eating in groups of twos and threes. But her eye narrowed when it fell on Noel Rallis next to the window overlooking the garden. Sabrina was nowhere in sight. Good.

Emmeline threaded her way across the room toward Rallis. She was not going to let him get away.

She was only a few feet away from him, when Anatasia Tarasova sidled up to him. Apparently, she had managed lose Petrenko along the way.

"Noel," Tarasova said, with a wide smile on her face. "What a surprise to see you here tonight." She offered her cheek to him to be kissed.

Rallis's handsome features creased in a dark scowl, when he saw who it was. However, he quickly pasted a smile on his lips and leaned forward to give her a perfunctory kiss. "Ah, Nastya, how lovely to see you again after so long." Although his voice dropped, Emmeline clearly heard him say, "This has stop. I told you it's over."

Emmeline's eyebrows shot up. This was an interesting turn of events. She picked up a plate and pretended to be selecting some morsels. With her back turned away from the couple, but with her ears wide open, she blindly threw a few carrot sticks and broccoli florets onto her plate.

"Noel, I had to see you. I couldn't leave things like that. I knew you couldn't mean it," Tarasova hissed.

"Granted, it was fun while it lasted, darling. But it's over between us. I've moved on. Get that through your pretty little head. No more calls. No more showing up on my doorstep in the middle of the night. You are no longer a part of my life. Do you understand, Nastya?" He made the diminutive of her name sound so ugly.

Emmeline gripped her plate harder. For the interval of a few seconds, they didn't utter a word. She was dying to see what was happening, but she didn't dare turn around.

"Bastard." The single word was laced with all the venom and fury of women scorned through the ages. "You can't just cast me aside, as if I was an old cardigan. I'm Anastasia Tarasova."

A deep-throated chuckle rumbled from Rallis's throat. "Oh, Nastya, don't make more of it than it was. We were merely two consenting adults who enjoyed each other's company for a time. That time is over. Please don't ruin things by throwing a childish tantrum. Playing the diva may get you what you want in the theater. It doesn't work with me."

"I wouldn't be so cavalier," Tarasova lashed back. "I'm the daughter of Col. Aleksei Tarasov. I learned at my father's knee. I know things about you that I don't think you would like MI5 or the police to know." Emmeline's ears perked up at this. "I know about Poseidon. All it takes is a single word in the right ear and I can ruin you, Noel *darling*. And I will do it with tremendous pleasure." These last words were an icy caress.

"I wouldn't hurl threats around. If you haven't noticed, many of your countrymen have nasty habit of dying here in the U.K. Alexander Litivinenko immediately springs to mind. Of course, we can't forget Pavel Melnikov, who was mixed up in that squalid affair with Alistair Swanbeck this summer."

He paused, presumably to let this sink in. Then, as an afterthought, he added, "Poor Pavel. He was a particular friend of yours at one stage, wasn't he?" He clucked his tongue and the next second threw salt on the wound. "It makes me shudder. Imagine being impaled on iron railings outside his Mayfair flat. Horrid. Absolutely horrid. It would pain me greatly to see your lovely face all bruised, and battered, and contorted by death."

He exhaled a heavy sigh. "But I'm afraid that will be your fate. One thing Putin hates is traitors. It would be a terrible shame if a little bird whispered in his ear that you've been passing information to the British."

Tarasova drew in a ragged breath. "But I haven't," she croaked. "I would never…"

"Ah, Nastya, by the time all the muddle was sorted out, it would be too late and you'd already be dead. Pity that. So I'd have care whom you started unburdening your soul to, *especially* about my business. Think long and hard. Is your life really worth a fleeting moment of petty revenge?"

A strangled, primeval grunt of frustration was Tarasova's answer.

"There, I knew you'd see sense, darling," Rallis gloated. "Ah, ah. That was very foolish. You don't want to cause a scene, now do you?"

At this, Emmeline gave up the pretense and craned her neck around to see what was going on. Rallis had Tarasova's wrist gripped between his fingers. He must have caught it in mid-air before she slapped his face. Daggers of pure hatred were flying from her smoky blue eyes.

"You will never get away with this," she said through clenched teeth.

Rallis gave a nonchalant shrug. "We'll see."

"Monster." This single word was fired back at him with all the force of a bullet seeking its target.

"Now you're becoming rather tiresome. Have we sunk to personal insults?" He gave a sad shake of his head. "I thought you were better than that, Nastya."

"Don't call me that. Only my close friends call me that. You are nothing. Behind the good looks and polished veneer, you are no better than a common gangster. A vicious mongrel dog that fights dirty because it's amusing." The lashing bite of her words stung with greater intensity as her voice dipped dangerously low. "You made a mistake crossing me, Noel. I will see you dead."

CHAPTER 17

Without another word, Tarasova pivoted on her heel and turned her back on him. She held her head high as she glided out of the room. Rallis was left slightly open-mouthed for several stunned seconds. But his arrogant smirk soon slipped back on his face. One shoulder twitched in a shrug and he chuckled to himself as he lifted a glass of ruby wine from the tray of a passing waiter.

Emmeline bit her lip, momentarily torn. Should she corner Rallis? Or should she go after Tarasova?

She cast a sidelong glance toward the door and made a snap decision. Tarasova, definitely. The woman knew things. Things that no one else did. She had to strike now, while Tarasova was still smoldering with white-hot anger. Anger was an all-consuming emotion and made one forget to think. That was when a sympathetic ear was all the encouragement that was needed for a careless tongue to unwind.

Emmeline tossed a quick glance at Rallis, but he was staring moodily out the window as he sipped his wine.

She hurried out of the dining room. She had to catch Tarasova on her own. The ballerina would never speak freely if Petrenko was lurking nearby. Emmeline was in luck. The Russian cultural attaché was nowhere to be seen, but he could loom forth any second. She had to work fast.

"Oh, Miss Tarasova," she called, willing the blood thrumming through her veins to slow down.

The ballerina whirled around at the sound of her name. Her face was pinched. Two vertical lines had etched themselves between her brows. Her rage was radiating off her body in waves. "Yes? What do you want?" she snapped peevishly.

Calm, cool sympathy. That was the only way to tease the story out. "I was wondering whether you're quite all right," Emmeline cooed, infusing her tone with concern. "You looked rather upset when you left the dining room just now."

Tarasova's eyes raked over her face. Her gaze narrowed. An internal debate appeared to be raging in her mind. Emmeline held her breath and waited.

The ballerina cleared her throat. "Yes, I know who you are now. You're the one who wrote those stories in the *Clarion* about Pavel, weren't you?"

"Pavel?" Emmeline asked in confusion. "If you mean Pavel Melnikov, then yes it was me. I'm the editorial director of investigative features at the *Clarion*."

"Yes, I thought it was you when we were introduced earlier. I admired your stories. You did a very good job to…to get to the truth. You see, Pavel was"—there was a catch in her voice, but she forced herself to go on—"Pavel was a close friend of mine. No one else cared, but you did."

"I was just doing my job. The public deserves to know the truth."

"You're too modest, Mrs. Longdon." One of Tarasova's eyebrows quirked upward. "Or should I say Kirby?"

"Emmeline is fine."

The ballerina nodded. "Well, Emmeline, I don't think that others would have pursued the story as aggressively as you did. I heard that you nearly got yourself killed by that bastard Alistair Swanbeck."

An icy dread seized Emmeline's chest at the sound of Swanbeck's name on the other woman's lips. She swallowed the lump that had lodged itself in her throat. "Things got a bit out of hand."

To her own ears, her voice sounded rough and hoarse. But Tarasova merely laughed. "How amusing you British are. One never is supposed to show emotion or fear. Isn't that right?"

Her smile didn't touch her eyes as they held Emmeline transfixed. The low murmur of conversation all around them made the silence that suddenly fell between them even more pronounced.

Without warning, Tarasova's long, tapered fingers clamped themselves on Emmeline's forearm. Her voice dropped an octave. "I think we can help each other."

Emmeline leaned in closer. "Is that so?"

"I can tell you everything I know about Noel Rallis and his dirty secrets. And you can do a major exposé with big headlines splashed across your front page."

Emmeline saw the glimmer of malicious glee in the ballerina's eyes. "How do I know that your information is reliable and not merely petty revenge? I can't simply take your word for it. I would need corroborating sources."

At this, one of Tarasova's eyebrows shot up. Then her eyes became narrow slits. "Yes, I was right. You *were* eavesdropping. So let's stop pretending. Yes, I want to hurt Noel. He deserves to be hurt. More than you can possibly imagine. I don't care what you think about me. I don't care what anyone thinks. What I know is pure gold and you *know* it. Otherwise, you would never have come after me like this."

"I never intended to deceive you in any way, Miss Tarasova, and I apologize if you feel as if…"

Tarasova cut her off. "Never apologize and never second guess yourself. My father taught me that. Women have enough trouble in this world. You shouldn't have to apologize for being good at your job. You want a story and I have one for you. It's a simple transaction. Nothing more."

Emmeline inclined her head. "Right, now that we understand the ground rules, what exactly do you want to tell me about Noel Rallis?"

The other woman took a deep breath and nervously fingered her diamond and ruby necklace, which instantly drew Emmeline's eyes to its magnificent artistry. The stones' facets trapped the light and seemed to wink at her, as Tarasova's chest rose and fell. She opened her mouth to say something, but clamped it shut when she saw Lord and Lady Starrett shepherding two couples toward the dining room. In the few minutes that they had been huddled together, more guests seemed to have arrived and were wandering in and out of rooms, encroaching upon them.

"I never forget a face," Tarasova mumbled under her breath. "I've always been that way. I only need to see a person once. My mind never allows me to forget."

Emmeline frowned. She glanced around them in confusion. "Is this about Rallis or someone else? I hope you're not playing games."

"What?" Tarasova stared at her as if she were suddenly a stranger. Her fingers bit into Emmeline's arm. Her voice was low and urgent. "We can't talk here. It's too dangerous. Someone will hear."

"But you said…"

Tarasova flapped a dismissive hand in the air. "I will tell you everything. I promise." She flicked a sideways peek to her right. "But not *here*."

An impatient sigh escaped from Emmeline. "Fine. Where then?"

Tarasova cast another wary look about her and pointed at the ceiling. "The master bedroom. Second door on the right. Nine o'clock. No one will disturb us."

Emmeline nodded reluctantly. She was used to sources desperately seeking to cloak their anonymity about their shoulders. "Nine o'clock."

ℰℐℰℐ

Gregory popped his head into the dining room. He scanned the faces of the guests and Emmy's face was not among them. He could have sworn she was here just a moment ago. Where the devil could she have gotten to? He *hoped* that she hadn't gone after Sabrina again.

"Looking for your pretty little wife, Longdon?" a male voice asked.

Gregory turned to find Noel Rallis standing next to him. "I'm afraid we haven't been introduced," he replied crisply.

A throaty chuckle rumbled forth from Rallis, who raised his wine glass in acknowledgement. "No, you are correct on that point, but don't be tiresome and pretend that you don't know exactly who I am. As I know who you are, Longdon. I made it my business to know."

Gregory inclined his head and flashed a smile. "I'm flattered. I had absolutely no idea that I had a secret admirer. Unfortunately, the feeling is not mutual." He allowed his glance to drift from the top of the other man's head to his shoes. "You appear to lack any admirable qualities."

The dig hit home because a shadow fell across the angles of Rallis's face. "I see you are an arrogant bastard. But I admit I have followed your exploits with keen interest over the years. You fascinate me." He cocked his head to one side. "By my calculations, you must be an extremely wealthy man." He lowered his voice conspiratorially. "All those jewels that have never been recovered. Tell me, which is more of a thrill, actually stealing the jewels, or thumbing your nose at the police? I've always wondered."

Gregory accepted a glass of Bordeaux from a waiter. He allowed the wine to swirl about his tongue, savoring its bold taste, before answering, "I think you have mistaken me for someone else, Rallis. I'm the chief investigator for Symington's."

Rallis took a long swallow of wine and studied Gregory over the rim of his glass. Gregory didn't flinch under the intense scrutiny. He held the other man's gaze without blinking, all the while wondering what he wanted.

"Have it your way, Longdon. However now that I've met you, I must admit that I think Toby Crenshaw suits you much better."

Toby Crenshaw? The hairs on the nape of Gregory's neck prickled. He hadn't been Toby Crenshaw since he was eighteen. How did this man know his real name? Not that it made any difference. People change their names all the time. It didn't worry him. Still, it was disconcerting. What else did he know? And why was he taking such an interest in him?

Gregory didn't have long to wait to find out.

"By the way," Rallis was saying, "Alastair Swanbeck sends his regards. He's sorry he missed your wedding to the delightful Emmeline, but it seems he never received an invitation. An oversight one assumes." His mouth curved into a lupine smile.

Outwardly, Gregory's schooled his features into a bland expression. Inside, ice water was sluicing through his veins.

"What no message for your old friend?" Rallis taunted.

Gregory found his voice at last. "What are you playing at, Rallis?"

Rallis put a hand to his chest. "Me? Nothing. It's a party. I'm simply making idle conversation with a fellow guest. But it appears that I've hit a raw nerve. I wonder why that is."

"I'd remember the proverb about those who live in glass houses not casting the first stone. Once the cracks start to appear in the foundation, the whole thing could come crashing down."

Rallis's grin grew wider. "Is that so? I sincerely hope that wasn't a threat."

Gregory shot his cuffs and matched his smile. "I find it rather common, and certainly in poor taste, to hurl threats about." He reached out to flick an imaginary piece of lint from the other man's immaculate lapel and then patted it back into place. "Of course," he mused, "you spend so much time wallowing in the gutter with thugs like Alistair Swanbeck, it's unsurprising that threats and paranoia immediately spring to mind. It must be *such* a strain on your nerves to always have to look over your shoulder because you have something to hide."

The smile never left Rallis's face, but it seemed to harden in place. His back stiffened. "Stay out of my way, Longdon," he said out of the corner of his mouth. "And keep your nosy wife out of my business. One of these days, she's going to ask one too many questions and I won't be able to answer for the consequences."

He turned to go, but Gregory caught his arm. "Obviously, you've never heard that we have something called a free press in this country. Your murder trial is fair game. Secondly, I couldn't, nor would I want to, stop Emmy from doing her job. Heaven help the person who tries. And finally"—he lowered his voice so that only

Rallis could hear—"if you come anywhere near her, I will take tremendous pleasure in breaking every bone in your body. That is, on the off chance she hasn't done so already. You see, I neglected to mention that she has a ferocious temper."

Rallis shrugged off Gregory's grasp and shot his cuffs. "A man with as many secrets as you shouldn't be so reckless. As for your wife, she shouldn't wear her curiosity as a badge of honor. Remember what happened to the cat."

CHAPTER 18

"Darling, there you are at last." Emmeline had turned her head away from the woman she had been speaking with at precisely the instant Gregory crossed the threshold into the reception room.

She made her excuses and hurried over to him. "Lord Starrett certainly kept you a long time. If he was that nervous about unveiling the jewels, he should have waited until the official ceremony at the museum tomorrow."

He took her small hands in his. "I wasn't with Starrett all this time. I ran into Rallis. He was…"

She waved a hand in the air, cutting him off. "That's what I've been bursting to talk to you about. Come on."

She tucked her arm through his and tugged him, none too gently, toward a tiny oasis of space on the other side of the room before she said any more.

Her dark eyes darted a glance about the room, but no one was paying attention to them. Then the words all tumbled out in a rush. "I'm afraid that I will have to knock the lovely Miss Tarasova off that pedestal on which you placed her. Frankly, I can't understand the fascination. She's rather conceited and insipid if you ask me…"

Gregory groaned. "Emmy, I told you that woman holds

no 'fascination' for me."

"Hmph. Well, let's not argue that point for the moment. Our willowy ballerina has extremely poor taste in men. I was in the dining room and I overheard her with Rallis. Apparently, the two of them had a brief affair and he broke it off abruptly. She wants him back. Why? I don't know. In any case, she's been making a nuisance of herself. Showing up at his flat at all hours. Leaving voicemails begging him to take her back. You'd think a woman like that, who has the whole world at her feet, would have a bit more self-respect." She shook her head in disgust.

This was a surprising twist, Gregory mused. "Rallis and Tarasova? Rather an odd couple."

"Not really. They're both arrogant as hell. She got what she deserved. But that's not all."

Of course, it isn't. The fiery gleam in Emmy's eye told him there had to more. Something he wouldn't like.

"Rallis was in a foul mood. He'd had enough of Tarasova's antics. He told her it had merely been a fling, and it had been fun for a time but it was over now. That sent her over the edge. Her ego couldn't accept being tossed away 'like an old sweater.' So she threatened to ruin him."

Gregory stiffened. "Ruin him how?"

"She said that she knew things about him that he wouldn't want MI5 or the police to know. But don't worry, this didn't faze Rallis. He reminded her that so many of her countrymen seemed to be suffering untimely deaths in recent years here in the U.K. and it would pain him greatly to see the same fate befall her. He made a particular point of bringing up her dear friend Pavel Melnikov. That was when she said would see him dead."

Bloody hell, he cursed silently. Aloud, he said, "Rallis. Melnikov. What a charming circle of friends Tarasova keeps."

Emmeline snorted. "I hate to say I told you so. I didn't like her from the instant I saw her. But to get back to the story, I caught up with her after her row with Rallis and I'm going to meet her upstairs at nine. She's promised to tell me *everything*."

No, he knew he wouldn't like what Emmy had to say. It got worse with every word that came out of her mouth. And just look at her. She can barely contain her excitement.

"I'll come with you when you meet Tarasova."

Emmeline snorted. "You won't. Charming as you are, darling, you might scare her off. Besides, it would be breaking all the rules of journalism for me to bring my husband to meet with a source."

"Damn your journalistic scruples."

One eyebrow shot up at this and then her eyes narrowed. The withering look she cast sliced him to pieces. "Care to rephrase that?"

"Emmy, everyone knows that you are the consummate professional with the highest level of integrity..."

"That's better. You were on a slippery slope there a moment ago."

"But sometimes, you're too stubborn for your own good. Rallis is at the other end of the spectrum from a Boy Scout and Tarasova is not much better. You *heard* her threaten to kill him."

"That was in the heat of anger. You know people say all sorts of things they don't mean when they're angry."

"And sometimes, when one's back is against the wall, murder appears to be the only way out."

"You're being melodramatic. Tarasova is not going to kill me. She *needs* me to tell her story. Otherwise, Rallis will never be punished for his crimes. That's what she wants the most. To see him pay."

Gregory shook his head and exhaled a long breath. Her

argument made eminent sense. It was logical. At the same time, it was bloody infuriating because he knew there was nothing he could do to stop her. Isn't that what he had told Rallis earlier? He sighed again.

"Just don't be…gullible. She's out for revenge."

Emmeline squared her shoulders and tossed her chin in the air. "Don't you think I know that?" she hissed through clenched teeth. "When have I ever been gullible? You know I never take anything at face value. I always double and triple check the facts. It's my job. I'm good at what I do."

"Yes, yes," he replied, his tone edged in irritation.

But there wasn't time for more. Lord Starrett caught his eye. Gregory glanced at his watch. Eight-thirty. The moment had come to unveil the jewels.

"Look, Emmy, Starrett's signaling. It's time for his little bit of theater."

She jerked her chin. "Go on. That's what you're here for. *Your job*. I'll hang about for a bit. Then, I'm going to go upstairs to meet with Tarasova. To do *my* job."

"Longdon, are you coming?" Starrett called.

Gregory smiled and gave a curt nod. "In a minute." He turned back to Emmeline. "I don't like it," he said, as his conversation with Rallis replayed itself in his mind. "But I won't stop you."

"Thank you. I don't understand why you're so nervous. What can happen to me in a house full of people?"

After lovingly showing off each piece, Lord Starrett started blathering on about the jewels' history and his delight at discovering that they were part of the Cheapside Hoard.

The jewels' provenance intrigued her, but Emmeline was only half-listening. She kept peeking at her watch. Really, the hands were moving excruciatingly slowly this evening. Was it only ten minutes that Starrett had been speaking?

"Your husband appears to be drooling over the jewels," a silky voice whispered over her right shoulder. "It's rather unwise for Lord Starrett to have invited a thief into his home. All manner of things could go missing before the night is out."

She knew, even before she shifted her head to look up at him, that it was Noel Rallis.

She cleared her throat. "My husband is the chief investigator for Symington's. He's here tonight to ensure that nothing happens to Lord Starrett's jewels."

Rallis threw his head back and laughed. His voice dipped an octave. "We all know what he is, no matter how much you turn a blind eye to the truth, Emmeline."

Her back stiffened at sound of her name on his lips. "A man in your position shouldn't cast aspersions."

He leaned his head closer, his mouth curving into a lupine smile. "And what position would that be exactly?"

She took a half-step backward, trying to put space between them. She felt her shoulder blades brush against the door frame behind her. She slid a sideways glance to her left. She saw Gregory's gaze fixed on her and Rallis. Her husband gave an imperceptible shake of his head, but there was nothing he could do. He was trapped at Starrett's side.

She returned her attention to Rallis. "A man on trial for murder should be more circumspect. Haven't you already attracted enough negative publicity?"

"And whose fault is that? The *Clarion* is worst of the bunch. Your stories in particular, my dear Emmeline, have caused no end of trouble for me and my businesses."

She smiled. "Have they? You were given an opportunity to tell your side of the story. You didn't respond to any of my voicemails and your office said you had no comment. Since you're here now and don't appear to be in a rush"—she opened her clutch and drew out her notebook, which was with her at all times. She flipped open to a clean page and held her pen aloft—"would you care to make a statement about your murder trial and recent rumors about criminal activity being perpetrated by your company?"

A dark shadow fell across Rallis's face. "Listen to me, you nosy cow." All pretense at charm was abandoned. "The trial is a farce. A waste of taxpayer money. The Crown has no case. The whole thing is driven by jealousy."

Emmeline scribbled in her notebook. "Ah ha. I see, 'The Crown has no case….all driven by jealousy'," she mumbled. "That is your statement, is it? Surely the police and the prosecutor must have had some sort of evidence to bring the case to trial," she replied in dulcet tones.

With one swift gesture, he swatted the notebook out of her hand. "I'm not making a statement. I'm telling it to you like it is. The case will be dropped because there is *no* evidence."

She bent and calmly scooped up her notebook from the floor. She didn't dare look in Gregory's direction. She hoped that he was focusing on Starrett's peroration.

When she straightened up, she continued with her questions as if the incident hadn't occurred. "So confident about the trial being dismissed? I wonder why that is."

"You'd better stop wondering about me and concentrate on your own life. Haven't you heard about the shocking trend these days? Journalists around the world are dying while on assignment. Such dedication to the job is admirable. It's also foolish."

Emmeline drew in a sharp breath. This comment ripped open a barely healed wound. Her parents, journalists like herself, had been killed while on assignment when she was only five. *But that wasn't because of their job*, a voice inside her head whispered. *It was* murder. *A completely different matter altogether.*

Yes, it was different. Over the summer, she and Gregory had found her parents' murderer—and a Pandora's box of other secrets that had turned her world upside down. But it was cold comfort because it still hurt. The ache of their loss never left her.

She shook her head as if she could physically push the past to one side. For the moment, at any rate.

She blinked and Rallis's face came into sharp focus once again. "If you're trying to frighten me off the story, Mr. Rallis, you can forget it. I don't scare easily."

He clapped his hands together. "Such brave words. Do you rehearse them in front of a mirror to get the inflection just right?"

Emmeline closed her notebook and tucked it and her pen back into her clutch. "I see that this is an exercise in futility, since you still refuse to give a statement," she said crisply. "You can't very well have it both ways, Mr. Rallis. You can't complain about the stories being printed, if you choose to remain silent. Or is that what your lawyer advised because he was afraid you might say something that could incriminate you?"

The smile on his lips didn't reach his eyes. "I'm as innocent as a newborn lamb." He leaned in close again, his warm breath brushing her cheek. "Mark my words. The prosecutor is going to regret bringing this case to court. He's going to regret it to his dying day." Then, he drew himself up to his full height of just over six feet. "I can't say it's been a pleasure meeting you, but at least you know where we stand." He paused, his smile widening. "By the way, I hear that Alistair Swanbeck misses the U.K. and you in particular. I believe he's looking forward to a reunion very soon."

His words hung upon the air as she stood there staring at his retreating back. A normal person would have wished her good evening. Rallis left her with memories of Swanbeck and cold dread clawing at her chest.

No, no, no, she chided herself. She would not allow herself to cower in fear. Swanbeck couldn't touch them. He didn't dare set foot in the UK again. He'd be arrested on the spot.

She took a deep breath and squared her shoulders. Right. She had a job to do. She glanced at her watch five to nine.

Time to meet Tarasova to get the dirt on Rallis.

CHAPTER 19

Emmeline backed away slowly, trying not to attract anyone's attention as she attempted to make her escape upstairs. Her gaze roamed over the room. In the few minutes since Rallis had left her side, Gregory had disappeared. Probably he was with Lord Starrett. At least, she hoped he was with Starrett and not waiting for her in the master bedroom to confront Tarasova. She'd kill him if he were.

She slipped into the corridor. It was only a few feet to the staircase. She was about to make a dash up the stairs—well as much of a dash as her heels would allow—when two middle-aged women chose that moment to pop out of the dining room. Emmeline hastily stepped in front of the beveled mirror, pretending to pat a stray curl into place. Of course, this gave them an idea and they decided to check their hair to make certain it wasn't mussed.

Emmeline cast a longing glance at the staircase and groaned inwardly. *Get a move on*, her brain screamed at the women. But no, they lingered there in corridor gossiping about another guest.

"Did you see her frock? Very poor taste if you ask me," one whispered to the other.

Her friend merely clucked her tongue.

Emmeline rolled her eyes at the ceiling and silently cursed them to perdition. She made a show of rooting around in her clutch so they wouldn't think she was eavesdropping. There was no need, though. They were so engrossed in their critique of the woman wearing God knows what shocking frock. They were the only thing standing between her and the staircase.

She couldn't stay here forever. How could she get rid of them? An idea struck her. Somehow the contents of her clutch tumbled to the floor and pooled around their feet.

"Oh, how clumsy of me," she murmured. "I'm terribly sorry." She gave them a sheepish grin.

They returned her smile and stepped out of the way of the detritus. "That's all right, my dear," the more aggressive of the two said. She looped her arm through her friend's and said, "Come along, Alice." And off they went, at last.

With one sweep of her hand, Emmeline stuffed her belongings back into her clutch save for her notebook and pen. They were all she would need. She straightened up, tucking her clutch behind a vase on the console table. She would retrieve it later. In the interim, she would say that she had mislaid it and went searching for it in case anyone caught her wandering somewhere she ought not to be.

It was now or never. Heels or no heels, she took the stairs two at a time.

She hesitated for a fraction of a second when she reached the landing and tossed a furtive glance over her shoulder. But no one had seen her.

However, out of the corner of her eye she caught a flicker of movement. When she turned her head, she saw Sabrina, in a rustle of silk, slipping through the second door on the right. The master bedroom.

Emmeline felt a frown etching itself into her features.

What the devil was Sabrina doing up here?

Question upon question chased through her mind. In a lather of anger, irritation, and bewilderment at the lack of plausible answers, she tiptoed down the corridor.

She flung open the door to the master bedroom and collided with Sabrina, who backed into her.

Sabrina put a hand to her mouth. "Oh, my God."

Emmeline followed her gaze. She stood transfixed, when it came to rest on the still form of Tarasova draped across the bed, her smoky blue eyes frozen open for eternity and her lips parted as if she were about to say something—but only the angels would hear her now. Or was it the devil?

Bile rose to Emmeline's throat, but she couldn't take her eyes off the lifeless body of the Russian ballerina. By her side, Sabrina was trembling. Over and over, she repeated, "Oh, my God" until it took on the timbre of a chant—monotone, numb, and *dead.*

She swallowed down her own revulsion and threw an arm around Sabrina's waist. "Come on. Pull yourself together. We've got to…"

The rest of her sentence died on her lips and her mouth went dry. For the first time, she realized that they were not alone in the room. There, on the opposite side of the bed, hovered Hugh Carstairs in a tuxedo, looking what?— surprised? shocked? *guilty?*

"*Carstairs.*" It was a hoarse croak. Then, a bit stronger, though the tremor didn't leave her voice, "What—What are you doing here?"

He scowled at her, a muscle pulsating along his jaw. "I could ask you the same thing. They warned me that you would be trouble." was his caustic rejoinder.

Emmeline's brows knit together. "*They?* They who?"

During this little interchange, Sabrina seemed to come to her senses again. "Hugh? I can't believe it's you."

Emmeline tore her eyes from Carstairs. "You know him?"

Sabrina sighed. Her complexion was losing its grayish pallor. "I should. He's my ex-husband." After a pause, she said, "One of them anyway." Then to Carstairs, she added, "If it counts, I always liked you best."

The room began to swim before Emmeline's eyes. This couldn't be happening. This was *not* happening. It had to be a nightmare. She squeezed her eyes shut. Any second now she would wake up and everything would return to normal.

When she opened her eyes again, Carstairs and Sabrina were staring at her and Tarasova was still dead.

It was a living nightmare.

"You know her?" Carstairs asked Sabrina as he pointed an accusatory finger at Emmeline.

One of Sabrina's shoulders twitched upward in a nonchalant shrug. "What can I say? It's a night for family reunions. Hugh, meet my sister, Emmeline Kirby. Oh, wait. It's Longdon now, isn't it?"

Sister, Emmeline thought incredulously. This was the first time that Sabrina had ever acknowledged her as her sister.

Carstairs pinched the bridge of his nose. "Your sister? Since when do you have a sister?"

"Half-sister, actually. She dropped into the bosom of the family in July. But it's a long story. A very long story."

Carstairs shook his head as if to rid himself of a headache. "I can't believe this."

"I would say that makes three of us," Emmeline murmured. "But we can sort it all out another time. Right now, there are more important matters." She gestured with her chin at the bed. "We have to ring the police."

Carstairs gave a grim nod. "Yes, you're right." He jerked his head at the door. "The two of you get out of here."

"And let you tamper with the evidence?" Emmeline crossed her arms over her chest. "I don't think so."

Carstairs eyes widened in disbelief. "You can't possibly think I had anything to do with this, can you?"

"How do we know? We found you here looming over the body."

"Hardly looming," he said under his breath.

"Let's not quibble, shall we? You're an assassin by trade."

"A *what*? Don't be ridiculous," Sabrina retorted with more than a touch of asperity. "Hugh didn't kill her"—she waved a hand impatiently at Tarasova—"or anyone else for that matter. You've been reading too many spy novels, Little Miss Nosey Parker."

Emmeline glowered at her. "Sabrina, you don't know anything about this man."

"And you do?" She pressed her palm against her chest. "*I* was married to him for eighteen months. I should think that qualifies as knowing."

"Yes and no," Carstairs mumbled.

Although his voice was low, Emmeline heard his remark and for an instant she felt a stab of sympathy for him as Sabrina babbled on. Sabrina was grating on the nerves in the best of times. But now? Her glance fell on Tarasova again, her creamy neck bent at an awkward angle. A dead body tended to bring out the worst in people.

Emmeline felt hysterical laughter bubbling up in her throat. The whole situation was absurd. It would be comic, if it weren't so shocking. Perhaps that was it. She was in shock and everything was frozen in time.

"Sabrina, for once in your life, shut up," Carstairs ordered. Then his chestnut gaze shifted to Emmeline and his tone softened. "You don't know me and there's absolutely no reason why you should believe me, but I didn't kill her. Now, please get Sabrina out of here. We both know she'll only make things worse."

Emmeline couldn't help it, she gave him a crooked smile and nodded. She started to drag her sister toward the door.

"Wait a minute." Sabrina shook off her arm. "What do you mean I'll only make things worse?" she asked, miffed. "I demand an answer."

Carstairs ran a hand through his hair and groaned. "The world doesn't revolve around you, but you were never able to see that." His voice rose an octave and was tinged with exasperation. "A woman has been murdered, in case you hadn't noticed. If you don't want to be considered a prime suspect, it would be best if you left with Emmeline. Please."

Sabrina sniffed. "You only had to be civil. Come on, Emmeline." She cast one last glance at Tarasova and rubbed vigorously at the goosebumps along her arms. "Let's leave Hugh to commune with the dead. He always was a bit odd."

Emmeline opened her mouth to say something but changed her mind. Instead, she bundled Sabrina out the door and gave her a not-so-gentle nudge toward the staircase.

They both gasped when Philip's blond head popped into view, just as they reached the top step.

"What do we do now?" Sabrina said out of the corner of her mouth. "We have to warn Hugh." She started to turn around to go back to the master bedroom.

Emmeline took a firm hold of her elbow and gave it a squeeze, "Shh," she hissed.

"Emmeline, there you are. Longdon sent me to find you. He's tied up with Starrett." His blue gaze shifted suspiciously between the two of them. "Is something wrong?"

She licked her lips with the tip of her tongue. She could feel Sabrina's eyes on her.

"We have to call the police." She was surprised at how even she had managed to keep her voice.

His eyes narrowed. "Why? What's happened?"

"Anastasia Tarasova has been murdered. We...we found her."

That's not all we found, the voice inside her head said.

"What? In the house with a hundred guests roaming about?"

She nodded dumbly and cleared her throat. "We were on our way downstairs to ring the police."

"Where is she?" Philip demanded.

Emmeline and Sabrina traded a look, but neither one replied.

"I said *where* is she?" His tone was more insistent and thrummed with impatience. "Do I have to check all the rooms or are you going to tell me?"

"Sabrina, can you go downstairs and find Gregory? Please," Emmeline asked.

"Why do I have to go? He's your husband," Sabrina replied peevishly.

Emmeline gritted her teeth. "Just go."

Sabrina's eyes narrowed. "What are the two of you going to do?"

Philip was pulling his mobile out of his tuxedo's inner pocket. "I'm going to ring Burnell."

Sabrina clutched at his sleeve. "Not that old duffer. Please. He hates my family."

It's not surprising, when the family tree features two murderers, Emmeline thought grimly.

"Don't be ridiculous," Philip snapped as he punched in the superintendent's number with more force than was necessary.

"You don't understand. Out of spite, he'll arrest..."

She pressed her lips together and left the sentence dangling upon the air.

Philip's blond brows knit together. "He'll arrest whom?" When Sabrina didn't respond, he turned to Emmeline. "There's someone else up here. Who is it?"

Sabrina shot her a warning look. "Don't you dare."

Emmeline lifted her eyes to meet Philip's. Lying was not an option.

She let out a heavy sigh. "We found Hugh Carstairs in the master bedroom with Tarasova's body."

Philip's features contorted and his mobile nearly slipped from his fingers. "What? Carstairs here?"

She nodded.

"Hugh didn't do it. I tell you he didn't do it," Sabrina insisted. "You've got to believe me. I know he couldn't have done it."

"How do you know?"

"He's my ex-husband. I *know* him."

Philip blinked rapidly. "Your ex-husband? I don't believe this."

"It happens to be the truth. Hugh would never have killed that woman. He wouldn't kill anyone for that matter."

But he has, Philip reflected glumly. *He has for Queen and country.*

Burnell's booming voice in his ear jarred him back to the present. "Look, mate, either you say something or I'm going to ring off. I'm not in the mood for games."

"Sorry, Burnell. It's Philip Acheson. I'm afraid there's a bit of a problem at Lord and Lady Starrett's house."

"Oh?" He could hear the wariness in the detective's voice. "What kind of a problem?"

"It seems that Anastasia Tarasova, the prima ballerina, has been murdered."

A brief silence was followed by a low groan. Then, the

superintendent became officious. "Right. Finch and I are on the way. I'll have a SOCO, scenes of crime officer, and a Forensics team out there right away."

"The address is Thirty-Seven Egerton Crescent."

"Got it. And for God's sake don't let anyone near the scene."

"Too late."

"What do you mean too late?" Burnell snarled.

"Emmeline and…"

The superintendent cut him off. "Emmeline? She's there? That means Longdon is there too."

"Ye-es, but it was actually Emmeline and her sister who discovered the body in the master bedroom."

"Her sister? You mean Sabrina Royce?" Philip thought he heard a whimper escape from Burnell. "Not that family again."

Philip's gaze fell on Sabrina. "I'm afraid so."

"What is she doing there? Why are all of you there?" Before Philip could reply, Burnell said, "Never mind. We'll sort it out when we get there. In the interim, don't let the scene become contaminated any more than it already has. Stand guard outside the door for all I care, just don't let anyone else near the body. And no one, and I mean not a single bloody person, is to leave that house. That includes the servants. Is that clear?"

"Crystal. I'm going to send Emmeline and Sabrina downstairs. Lord and Lady Starrett will have to be told."

"Naturally," Burnell grunted. "Why do I get the feeling that there's more?"

"Because you're a great detective?" Philip ventured, attempting to lighten the tension. Well, as much as one could possibly lighten it when there was a dead woman just down the corridor.

"Leave off the flattery and tell me the rest of it."

"There's a house full of guests. About one hundred to

be exact. And Hugh Carstairs apparently was found, and still is, in *locus in quo*."

He heard a soft *thud* in the background and pictured one of the superintendent's plump palms pounding on his desk. "What?" Burnell thundered. "Get him now. Don't let him out of your sight."

Philip was left staring at his mobile as Burnell rung off. The detective could be forgiven for not making his goodbyes. Murder was not a time to follow the pleasantries of polite society.

Philip tucked his mobile into the inside pocket of his tuxedo and with an arm around the waist of each woman, he gently, but firmly, ushered them toward the stairs. "Ladies, you can surmise what Burnell said. Downstairs the pair of you. Emmeline, quietly pull Lord and Lady Starrett aside explain the situation. Burnell said that no one is to leave the house."

Emmeline nodded. "Come on, Sabrina. There's nothing we can do here. We'll only get in the way."

Sabrina tried to twist around and go back, but Philip was having none of it. "Sabrina, Emmeline's right. Everyone would be better off if you both went down-stairs—and stayed there."

"But, Hugh…"

"He's a big boy. He can take care of himself. Trust me."

"I don't trust any of you." Her voice was harsh and dangerously low. "You're all out to get him. There must be a perfectly logical explanation for why he was in the room."

Philip tipped his head back and looked at the ceiling in a bid to rein in his growing impatience. He kept his tone level as his gaze reluctantly returned to her face. "Of course, there is. It's just that everything is in a bit of muddle, as you can imagine, at the moment. But rest assured, Burnell will get to the bottom of things."

"Hmph," was Sabrina's dissatisfied reaction as she turned her back on him and stomped down the stairs, her head held high and shoulder blades rigid.

"At last," Philip muttered under his breath.

Emmeline gave his arm a reassuring squeeze and followed in her sister's wake without another word.

He exhaled a weary sigh. "Now to deal with Hugh."

He dragged himself down the corridor. His hand hovered over the doorknob for only a second before he flicked his wrist and turned it.

Carstairs was on his knees on the floor searching under the bed. His head popped over the edge of the mattress, when Philip entered the room.

"Acheson," he said, stunned. He quickly got to his feet, brushing off his trousers. "Philip. It's…it's been a long time."

Philip laughed without any inflexion of humor. "It would have been nice if it were under happier circumstances."

He shook his head sadly as his eyes took in the scene. Tarasova dead and Hugh Carstairs—of all people—on the spot. Why?

By this time, Carstairs was by his side. He reached out and tentatively touched Philip's arm. "I didn't do it."

"What this?" Philip waved at hand at Tarasova. "Or the mess three years ago?"

"Both. You have to trust me."

"Hmph," Philip scoffed. "It makes it rather difficult when I find you at the scene of the crime."

"I'm terribly sorry. For everything. It all went wrong. But what I'm most sorry about is this."

Before Philip had time to react, Carstairs pulled his arm back and let loose a punch. The blow caught the side of Philip's jaw. He saw stars for a few seconds. His knees buckled under him and he felt himself sinking toward the floor. Carstairs loomed over him.

Damn you and your iron first, Philip swore. He wasn't sure whether he said it aloud or only to himself.

His vision blurred and his mind clouded. And then there was nothing.

Carstairs stared down at Philip for a few seconds. "Sorry."

CHAPTER 20

Carstairs locked Philip in the room and pocketed the key. His nerves tingled. Adrenaline sent an electric shock through his veins and sheer instinct took over. He tiptoed down the stairs with only the balls of his feet making contact with each step to prevent any telltale creaks from giving him away. On the half-landing, he halted and poked his head over the bannister.

Guests were drifting back forth among the reception rooms. No one had noticed him. And why should they? It was a party. They were here this evening to have fun and be seen, as well as to exchange a bit of gossip.

He straightened up, smoothed his jacket and closed the button. He continued down the remainder of the stairs nonchalantly, but his eye was focused on the front door. Just a couple of more seconds and he would slip out into the night, before the hue and cry went up. He forced himself to draw in air through his nose and to expel it out his mouth.

In, out. In, out. Nice and easy, he told himself. *Don't forget to smile.*

He was only a few feet from the door, when a female arm twined itself through his and arrested his progress.

A husky voice whispered in his ear, "Hugh, you didn't really think you could escape without a word, now did you?"

It was like the Sirens call to old Odysseus. How he wished he could ignore it, but the heart is a treacherous thing.

Against his will—and his better judgement—he turned his head and found himself instantly drowning in the liquid depths of the most beautiful green eyes God ever created.

"Fiona," he managed at last, his voice hoarse. "It's...it's been a long time."

Lady Starrett's mouth curved into a lopsided grin. "You were always a master of understatement. Is that all you can say? No tender word for an old friend."

His back stiffened. "Old friend?" He gave a curt shake of his head. "All tender words between us ended the minute you accepted Starrett's proposal." The words came out more harshly than he had intended.

His eye strayed to the front door. He had to get out of this house. The evening was spiraling out of control in more ways than one.

However, Lady Starrett had other ideas. Her brow furrowed and her grip tightened on his arm as she steered him toward the study. She closed the door and pressed her back against it. "I don't think Villiers would like it if you left without doing the job you were sent here for tonight."

Carstairs's eyes widened in surprise. "Are you still in the game? I thought you retired when you married Starrett."

A bemused smile spread across her face. "I keep my hand in now and then. One likes to be useful, you know. It doesn't do to let one's skills waste away."

"I see." He took a moment to digest this news.

His chest tightened and his breath caught in his throat. Lord, how he wished she wouldn't look at him like that.

The taste of her lips was burned in his memory. He took a half-step forward and stopped short.

She's married, you fool, his brain admonished. *Pull yourself together and get far away from this house and her. Especially her.*

His hands clenched at his sides and he cleared his throat. "Fiona, listen to me. There isn't much time. Anastasia Tarasova is lying dead in your bedroom. Her neck's been broken."

Lady Starrett's eyes bulged. Clearly, this caught her off guard. Well, it was not surprising. Most people don't invite a dead woman to their parties.

"What?" she asked, still trying to absorb this unwell-come news.

"That's not all. That journalist, Emmeline Kirby, and her…"—he was about to say sister, although he couldn't believe Sabrina was related to the woman—"and Sabrina Royce blundered in and found me in the room."

Fiona blinked and then he saw her training take over. She shook off the shock and pushed herself away from the door. She was focusing on his every word. "What were they doing upstairs? What was Tarasova doing in our room for that matter?"

"I have no bloody idea. The Kirby woman is suspicious as hell. They must have run into Philip because he…"

She groaned as she crossed the room to him. "Philip too?"

"He…he left me with no choice. I had to knock him out." He drew the key from his pocket and pressed it into her palm. "I locked him in the room."

"You did *what*? Oh, my God. This gets worse by the second. Desmond is going to hit the roof."

The sound of her husband's name on her lips sent a white-hot flash of jealousy to his ego, but he brushed this aside. This was not a time for emotions. His mind had to remain sharp.

"For what it's worth, I'm sorry. I'm fairly certain that the Kirby woman and Sabrina must have rung the police. Likely they'll be here any minute."

Two vertical lines appeared between her brows. "Mmm." She nodded. "Of course, they will. Charging in. Tramping about everywhere with their heavy feet. And bringing this evening crashing about our ears."

He took both of her hands in his. She was nearly his height and his gaze scoured her face. "We both know that I can't be found here. Help me, Fiona. Please," he implored.

She didn't utter a word. She merely stared back at him. For an agonizing moment, Carstairs thought she would drop him in it. Couldn't she at least help him for old times' sake? Just this once. If he could only escape this house, then everything would be all right. He would ring Villiers and let the old man take care of Scotland Yard—and Philip.

"Right." She took him by the hand drew him across the room. "Hurry, come with me. I'll sneak you out through the kitchen into the garden. No one will see you, if you slip out through the gate. It lets out onto the road. From there, I'm afraid you'll have to make your own way."

She opened the door a crack and peeped out into the corridor with one eye. Carstairs held his breath.

She turned back to him. "It's all right. Keep your head down and follow me. The kitchen is at the back of the house to the right of the staircase. Don't stop. Just keep moving. The caterers will be too busy to notice. They'll think you're stepping outside for a smoke. Everyone knows I can't abide smoking. The door to the garden is unlocked. We part ways at the kitchen. I will return to the party—and the unpleasantness that lies ahead."

He touched her upper arm—her skin was as silky as he

remembered. "Wait."

"Hugh, you have to hurry." Her tone was tinged with a touch of anxiety and exasperation.

"You'll never know how grateful I am."

"Yes, yes." She waved a hand in the air. "I couldn't very well allow you to be caught. Villiers would not be pleased, to say the least."

"Fiona, I didn't kill Tarasova." It was simple statement of fact.

She rolled eyes at the ceiling. "Of course, you didn't. I never thought for a minute that you did."

"My money is on Rallis."

"Yes," she mumbled. "It always comes back to Noel Rallis, doesn't it? That reminds me. The reason you're here tonight—aside from the fact that Rallis is at the party—there's a chap that works for him. All I have is a name. Angus MacQuillan."

His back stiffened. "MacQuillan?" he asked suspiciously.

Something in his tone made her turn her head sharply. "Yes. Do you know him?"

"He was a Treasury agent," he said through clenched teeth.

"Treasury agent?" Her brows knit together. "Hugh, you look odd. What does this MacQuillan fellow have to do with Rallis?"

"Not much. Not anymore at least," he replied phlegmatically. "He's dead. He was murdered a few nights ago in Edinburgh. Stabbed in Advocate's Close and shoved down a flight of steps."

She put a hand to her mouth. "Dear God. And now Anastasia Tarasova." It was barely a whisper. "It can't be a coincidence."

He nodded grimly. "The people who come into contact with our friend Rallis appear to have unusually short life spans."

"Hmm. Scotland. What is Rallis up to in Scotland?" she murmured. She stared off at some invisible spot across the room, seemingly lost in thought for a couple of seconds. Then, she recollected herself and clutched at his sleeve. "You must leave. Now."

She put her eye to the crack in the door again. "Let's go."

They slipped into the hall, skirted the stairs and headed straight to the kitchen. She hovered on the threshold and tapped his sleeve. With her chin, she gestured. "The door to the garden," she whispered. "Be careful. Some of the flagstones are uneven. Cross the lawn. The gate that leads into the road is at the back between some bushes."

"Thanks for everything," he mouthed. But before he left her side, he said, "Philip."

"Don't worry. I'll take care of him." She flapped her hands. "Just go before the police arrive."

He gave a curt nod. Without a backward glance, he made his way across the kitchen in two strides. No one took any notice of him. Then he disappeared into the night.

Fiona exhaled a long, shuddering breath. She leaned back against the wall and hugged her arms around her waist to steady herself. She was never a nervy sort of woman, quite the contrary. But at this moment especially, she needed a clear head. Too many things could go wrong. Too many things had *already* gone wrong.

She mustn't dawdle. There was a lot to do before the police made their grand entrance. Chief and foremost was Philip.

Oh, Hugh, she thought with regret as she lifted her dress so that its folds wouldn't get tangled up in her heels as she scurried up the stairs. *You were always trouble. It was a mistake to come back.*

CHAPTER 21

Gregory spied Emmeline huddled in a corner of the reception room whispering furiously with Sabrina. He saw Emmy shake her head a couple of times. Acheson was nowhere in sight. He frowned.

As he threaded his way to their side, he caught a snippet of their conversation. "No, you will not say anything to him. If you do, Rallis will scarper before the police arrive. He's as much of a witness as any of the other guests." This was his wife.

"You make it sound as if Noel has something to hide. He had nothing to do with this" was Sabrina's outraged, breathy response.

Police? Witness? He knew there would be trouble the minute Rallis turned up this evening.

"Emmy? What's the matter?"

Two pairs of eyes—one dark and tense, and the other full of emerald fire—impaled him.

"Gregory, there you are at last. Where have you been?" Emmeline latched onto his arm, drawing him closer and out of earshot of the other guests. "Never mind. It's not important." She lowered her voice. "Anastasia Tarasova is dead. She's been murdered."

"*What?*" His gaze raked her features. He then shot a questioning look at Sabrina, who nodded.

"We…We found her," Emmeline went on, the words tumbling out in a rush. "Apparently, someone broke her neck. We didn't really want to dwell on that too much. He told us to get out and call the police…"

"He? You mean Acheson?"

His wife cleared her throat. "We did run into Philip. Yes. He rang Superintendent Burnell, who is on the way with Sergeant Finch. But we…we unexpectedly…met someone else as well."

"Someone else? Emmy, please tell me that you didn't confront the murderer." His tone held a severe rebuke mingled with concern.

"Not exactly."

"Don't," Sabrina warned, her lovely face twisting into a scowl.

"Oh for God's sake, Sabrina," Emmeline snapped. "He's my husband. I have to at least tell him. More to the point, we're going to have to tell the police. You *know* that. We can't conceal information that may be pertinent to the case. That would be perverting the course of justice."

"You can stuff your justice." Sabrina's words singed the air with spiteful venom. "We both know how it looks. I *know* he didn't do it. Besides, how come you can tell your Adonis"—she jerked her thumb at Gregory—"but I can't say anything to Noel. *He* didn't do it either."

"Have you forgotten that Rallis already is on trial for murder?" Emmeline shot back.

This dizzying conversation was spiraling out of control. Gregory put his hands up to stifle the bickering. "Enough. What the devil is going on?" he demanded. "And where's Acheson?" He craned his neck, his eyes searching for Philip.

"Philip is still upstairs. Guarding the room…and

Carstairs."

Gregory's head whirled round. "*Carstairs*? He's the 'someone else' who's roaming about the upper floor?"

Emmeline nodded. "We found him in the room with Tarasova."

An assassin and a dead Russian ballerina. Brilliant. And who is at the center of this deadly web of intrigue? His darling wife. Again.

He groaned inwardly as his gaze flickered between the two sisters. Never were there two more different women.

"Hugh didn't kill her," Sabrina insisted mutinously. "He doesn't have a violent bone in his body." If she were still a child, he was certain she would have punctuated this statement by stamping her foot. As it was, he caught a flash of her mother in the frosty look of disdain that was intended to put him in his place. But didn't.

"And how would you know that?" Gregory asked.

Before her sister could answer, Emmeline intervened, "That was the other revelation of the night. Carstairs is one of Sabrina's ex-husbands."

Gregory held his tongue as he tried to formulate a suitable response. He, of all people, would be the first to admit that life could be strange and bewildering at times. Hadn't he extricated himself from dozens of tricky situations over the years? However, this state of affairs set his brain reeling.

"I'm not ashamed of it," Sabrina snapped. She squared her shoulders and glared at them defiantly. "We were young. Hugh and I simply wanted different things."

"That's all well and good, Sabrina, but at this precise moment I don't think a postmortem of your late, lamented marriage is going to help matters. What was Carstairs doing at the party? I didn't see him, did you?" he asked Emmeline, who shook her head. "And what was his connection to Tarasova?"

Sabrina gave a helpless shrug of her shoulders. "Hugh was always a bit of a mystery. That's what made him so exciting."

He rolled his eyes. "Bully for you," he murmured.

"Gregory, we have to break the news to Lord and Lady Starrett, before Superintendent Burnell and Sergeant Finch and the rest of the police get here," Emmeline said urgently.

He took her by the elbow. "Right, come with me, darling. Sabrina, you stay here and try not to get into any more trouble. Whatever you do, don't say anything to Rallis. He'll find out soon enough."

"I resent that. I'm not a child. You can't order me about."

"You're also not thinking clearly at the moment. It's not every day you stumble across a dead body. At least, I hope you don't make a habit of it."

"Do I look like I'm a member of the Mafia?" she spat peevishly.

"You look like you might be in shock…"

"And your precious wife isn't?" Her eyes kindled with anger and resentment.

He was not given to bursts of temper like Emmy, but Sabrina always seemed intent on causing ripples in the pond. Although he could feel his patience with her starting to fray, outwardly he exuded an unruffled calm. "We don't have time to soothe your ego. You're a big girl. Do what you like about Rallis." He leaned in closer and lowered his voice. "But this isn't a playful game of seduction. You're playing with fire. At the first opportunity, he'll try to massage your recollection of what you've seen and heard tonight to further his own purposes. He's told so many lies to keep his secrets from seeing the light of day, he can't keep them straight anymore and that makes him all the more dangerous."

They left Sabrina standing there, her mouth hanging open and daggers shooting from her eyes.

ﻌﻌ

Fiona hesitated, her hand hovering inches from the doorknob. She drew deep draught of air into her lungs and steeled herself for the scene she would find on the other side of the door.

She cast a furtive glance toward the staircase. No one had followed her. Thank God, but she couldn't hang about in the corridor. The police would be here at any moment.

She turned the knob. The door creaked on its hinges as she slowly pushed it open.

"Oh" This was emitted by a groggy male voice.

Her eyes alighted first on Philip, who had regained consciousness and had managed to drag himself up onto all fours. She watched as he rose unsteadily to his feet.

Then her gaze strayed to her bed, where Tarasova's lithe body was draped in death's embrace.

"Fiona," Philip said, as swayed for a second.

He raised a hand to his jaw, gingerly moving it back and forth to make sure it hadn't been broken. Apparently, he came to the conclusion it was still in one piece because he gave a brisk nod of his head and then subsequently seemed to regret it.

He groaned, but drew his shoulders back and met her eyes. "Fiona," he said again, this time with a bit more confidence. He took a step toward her and caught her by the elbow. He felt a tremor travel down her arm. "Come on. Let's go downstairs and get you a brandy. This is all rather unpleasant."

He gently, but firmly, tried to guide her toward the door. She craned neck around for one last look at the room.

"How...I mean what...What happened?" was her stunned, stammering croak.

Philip grasped her by the shoulders and gave her a little shake, forcing her to look at him. He was surprised that she was so calm. Perhaps she was in shock and hadn't absorbed the true horror of situation yet. "Fiona, she's beyond help now. The police are on their way. You must be downstairs when they arrive."

She didn't utter a word. The silence stretched out between them for several seconds, before she straightened her spine and drew herself to her full height. "Yes. Yes, of course you're right. I must find Desmond." She put a hand to her mouth. "What am I going to do about all our guests?"

"At the moment, just make sure no one leaves. The police will need to question everyone who was here tonight."

His lips compressed into a tight line, as the image of Hugh's face the instant before he hit him flashed before his eyes. "Damn, Hugh," he grumbled softly. He was certain that he was long gone from Edgerton Crescent by now.

Fiona's head whipped round as Philip quietly shut the door behind them. "What was that?"

"Nothing important. It's going to be a long night. I suggest you have the caterers prepare pots and pots of strong, black coffee. No one is going to get much sleep."

Except, perhaps, for the murderer, he thought grimly.

CHAPTER 22

Gregory and Emmeline traded glances when they saw Philip and Lady Starrett appear on the half-landing together. They quickly rushed to meet them at the bottom of the stairs. When Philip got closer, Emmeline saw that the corner of his jaw was turning a rather ugly shade of purple.

She touched his sleeve. "Philip, what happened to you?" she asked in concern.

His blue eyes narrowed. "Someone hit me." He gave her a pointed look.

"Oh" was the only thing she could think to say. After a moment, she ventured, "Is…is he still…"

Philip slid a sideways glance at Fiona and then shook his head. He lowered his voice. "No, he got away while I was unconscious."

"I see," Emmeline replied. She didn't know why she felt relieved. Carstairs was an assassin by profession, if you could call killing someone for money a profession. She should want him to be arrested. A civilized society had laws to protect its citizens from murderers. And yet, something didn't ring true. She couldn't explain why, but a niggling voice in the back of her mind couldn't reconcile the fact that the man she met on the boat in the Lake District was a contract killer. If Carstairs was a ruthless, cold-blooded assassin, he would have killed her and Sabrina, as well as Philip, without batting an eye. But he hadn't. The only violent thing he had done was to hit Philip. However, the blow hadn't been serious enough to cause permanent damage.

Hmm. Perhaps my initial instincts were right after all, she mused. *Maybe Carstairs was a pawn during that fiasco three years ago with the Russian defector and maybe someone thought he'd make a perfect scapegoat again now.*

She searched Philip's face to try to gauge what was going on in his orderly brain. It was patently obvious he had not mentioned anything to Lady Starrett about Carstairs. She wondered how he had explained being knocked out.

Could it be that Philip had the same feeling about Carstairs as she did? She would have to tackle him about it, as well as do some more digging into the elusive Carstairs and his road to disgrace.

She shifted her attention to Lady Starrett, who was speaking in hushed tones with Gregory. At least on the outside, the woman was cool and composed. She was the personification of British stiff upper lip at its best. Emmeline supposed it came from always being in the spotlight. First as a successful model and then as the wife of a man who was not only a member of the aristocracy but a politician and former diplomat. Getting hysterical was *not* the done thing, nor would it have helped the situation.

"Yes, I understand," Lady Starrett was saying in her well-modulated, husky voice, "Philip said that he rang the police. I must find my husband. Please excuse me."

"Of course." Gregory stepped aside to allow her to pass.

As soon as she was out of earshot, Emmeline pounced on Philip, "Where's Carstairs?"

"I wish I knew. I barely had a chance to say a word to him before he hit me. Everything went black after that and he did a runner. The next thing I knew, I was struggling to come round and there was Fiona standing in the doorway."

"What was she doing upstairs when she was hosting a party?" Gregory asked.

"How should I bloody know?" Philip retorted irritably. "It is her house. Perhaps she had a migraine and needed a few moments of quiet."

"No need to get your back up, Acheson. It was a simple question." Gregory pursed his lips and his brows drew together. "I'm surprised she didn't walk straight into Carstairs. It couldn't have been that long from the time he hit you to when she found you legless. And how did the bloke get away without anyone seeing him?"

"I was hardly legless, but I do admit to being far from my usual clear-headed self. As for Hugh, I don't know how he slipped into the house. None of us saw him downstairs." Philip shook his head morosely. "I can't for the life of me understand what his connection to Tarasova was."

"Fulfilling his contract?" Gregory suggested. "Emmy and I did overhear his negotiations with that chap on the boat ride on Lake Windermere."

Philip made a dismissive gesture with hands. "It doesn't make sense. It also doesn't look good."

"Besides," Emmeline intervened, "we distinctly heard that chap and Carstairs discussing a man as the target. Remember, Carstairs said, 'You'll read *his* obituary in the paper.'"

"Which makes his rendezvous, if it was a rendezvous, with Tarasova even more peculiar. I wonder," Gregory pondered, "whether he…"

His sentence was left dangling upon the air because at

that precise moment Assistant Commissioner Keith Cruickshank's tall, lean figure filled the doorway. Hovering behind him was what appeared to be a rather large contingent from the Metropolitan Police force.

"Bloody hell," Philip swore. "What is Cruickshank doing here? Why the devil did Burnell bring that fool with him? He's the last person we need in this situation."

"Give Oliver some credit," Gregory replied philosophically. "He would never have brought Cruickshank here by choice. Obviously, the illustrious assistant commissioner pulled rank so that he could be the senior officer and ingratiate himself with the toffs. Haven't you noticed that he's an obsequious snob?"

"All I know is that he's going to make a right cock-up of this mess."

"Philip, I've been looking for you," Maggie said as she sidled up to them. "Where..." She drew in a sharp breath as she fingered his bruised jaw. "What *happened* to you?"

Philip winced at his wife's touch, tender though it was. He folded her hand in his own. "It's a bit complicated and rather unpleasant."

Maggie's eyes widened in concern. "That's why the police are here, isn't it? What's happened?"

He put an arm around her shoulders. "Come into the reception room and I'll explain everything. Is Yoav still here?" His wife nodded. "Good. I'd like to have a word with him. We'll also have to ring Janet and tell her that we'll be back rather late."

"I was going to give her a ring anyway to check on the boys." Then she turned to Emmeline and Gregory and said, "We'll see you later."

Emmeline flapped a hand at them. "Of course, go."

Philip nodded at them both. "Tell Cruickshank and Burnell I'm available whenever they want to question me."

Uniformed police constables spilled into the hall and

started herding the guests into the reception rooms. A plainclothes officer was directing the Forensics team toward the staircase. Dr. Meadows, whose brows rose in surprise when he passed Emmeline and Gregory, paused for a fraction of a second and dipped his head in acknowledgement before following the others to the upper floors.

"Emmy, we would be remiss if we didn't say hello to Assistant Commissioner Cruickshank," Gregory said as he took her elbow.

"Behave," she whispered out of the corner of her mouth. "Don't antagonize him."

He stopped and looked down at her. "Darling, I'm a model of proper etiquette."

She snorted, but there wasn't time to say anything else because Cruickshank was upon them in a few strides. His brown eyes narrowed suspiciously as a frown of displeasure creased his brow. "Longdon. Miss Kirby. I mean Mrs. Longdon. What are you doing here?"

Gregory flashed a smile infused with wry amusement. "Ah, good evening to you too, Assistant Commissioner Cruickshank. I must say it's always a pleasure to bask in the glow of your sunny disposition."

"Put a lid on it, Longdon. You are not going to twist me around your finger like you do with Burnell. Why is it that you're at the scene of yet another murder?"

Gregory gave a casual shrug of his shoulders. "What can I say? I only travel in the best circles. I can't help it if my company is in demand."

Emmeline elbowed him in the ribs, but offered a smile to Cruickshank. "What my husband is trying to say in a rather roundabout way"—she glared at Gregory, but was smiling when she turned back to the assistant commissioner—"is that we are guests of Lord and Lady Starrett this evening. Actually, Gregory is here in an official capacity because Symington's is insuring the jewels that Lord Starrett is donating to the Museum of London. I'm certain you must have read about in the papers. The transfer is scheduled to take place tomorrow, but Lord Starrett had a private unveiling tonight for a group of close friends."

Cruickshank's eyes bulged, as he glanced around incredulously. "A group of 'close friends'? There are over one hundred guests here tonight."

"For someone in Lord Starrett's position, *close* is a relative term," Gregory interjected nonchalantly.

"Hmph," Cruickshank grunted. Gregory merely continued to smile at him, which didn't seem to improve his mood. Quite the contrary, in fact.

Gregory made a show of casting a look at the constables bustling in and out of rooms all around them. "Superintendent Burnell and Sergeant Finch not with you? I believe Mr. Acheson spoke to the superintendent."

Cruickshank waved his hand dismissively in the air, puffed out his chest and swayed on the balls of his feet. "I felt this case deserved the attention of a more senior officer."

Senior in rank, not in years and experience, Gregory observed cynically to himself.

He did enjoy his verbal tussles with Burnell. There was a mutual respect at the heart of them. Well, as much respect as there can be between a detective and someone who bends the law to suit his own purposes—from time to time and only when the need arises. However, he would never view a transparent prat like Cruickshank with anything but contempt.

Cruickshank was nattering on, inflating his importance with every word tumbling out of his mouth. "This is rather a delicate matter. It requires someone with finesse and tact. Burnell is...well, you know...a bit rough around the edges."

Gregory saw Emmeline's nostrils flare. A telltale sign that she was incensed by this rather cavalier portrayal of Burnell's capabilities. "Superintendent Burnell has been on the force over thirty years," she bristled with indignation. "He has a vast wealth of experience and knowledge."

That's my darling girl, Gregory cheered in silence.

"Yes, that's true," Cruickshank admitted grudgingly, "but he is resistant to new policing methods. And he rubs the people the wrong way."

"Unlike you," Gregory chimed in.

"Exactly. You see my point," the assistant commissioner offered, smiling at him for the first time and missing the sarcasm completely.

Not a prat, Gregory corrected himself. *A pretentious weasel. Yes, definitely a weasel.*

"Now then," Cruickshank said, becoming officious, "you'll both have to give statements…"

"We can't tell you how much we're looking forward to doing our civic duty," Gregory replied facetiously.

Cruickshank wagged his forefinger at him. "Murder is not a game, Longdon. I want none of your tricks."

One of Gregory's eyebrows lifted languidly. "Tricks, Assistant Commissioner? I don't know what you mean."

Cruickshank took a step forward and lowered his voice. "I want the truth. What do you know about this crime? That is, if you're even capable of telling truth, which I very much doubt."

The smile that touched Gregory's lips did not reach his eyes. "You might be pleasantly surprised to discover that I have a passing acquaintance with truth. I'm quite certain I'm up to the challenge. Meanwhile if I wasn't the amiable chap that I am, I would rather resent your entrenched prejudice, which assumes that I am automatically guilty of murder, or any other crime."

Emmeline touched his arm lightly and opened her mouth to come to his defense, but he silenced her with a slight shake of his head. So she held her tongue and increased the pressure on his arm.

"Hmph" was the assistant commissioner's skeptical response.

Gregory let it drop. It wasn't worth arguing with him any further.

"Can either of you tell me anything about this ballerina Tarasova? Did you know her?"

Emmeline cleared her throat and decided to answer for the both of them, "No, this was the first time we had met her. Naturally, everyone knows who she is…was. She was greatly admired around the world. However, it can't have escaped your notice"—she made a sweeping gesture with her hand that encompassed the corridor—"there are a number of prominent figures here tonight. The Starretts are well-connected in society."

Cruickshank nodded. "Right. Was she on her own?"

"No," Gregory replied. "She arrived with Boris Petrenko, the Russian cultural attaché." His voice dropped. "There is speculation that he's an officer in the FSB. I'm certain, in view of all your seniority, you know that the FSB is the successor to the KGB."

"Of course, I know that," the assistant commissioner snapped. "I'm not an imbecile."

A broad grin spread across Gregory's mouth as he clapped him on the shoulder. "I'm delighted to hear it. Naturally, Emmy and I can't attest to this rumor. Mr. Acheson and Mr. Zielinski are more familiar with what goes on in the diplomatic world. So you'll have to ask them. But to get back to Tarasova, she gave the distinct impression that she was unhappy to have Petrenko as her escort. Apparently, he's a close friend of her father's and keeps an eye on her. But she seemed to chafe under his watchful eye and soon was mingling on her own."

Emmeline took up the tale at this stage and eagerly related the tense conversation she had overheard between Tarasova and Rallis in the dining room, and about subsequently being waylaid by Tarasova.

"Rallis was livid that she knew about 'Poseidon.' That's why he threatened to expose her as a double agent."

"Do you think that was true?"

She shrugged helplessly. "I have no way of knowing, but Tarasova was obviously rattled. That's why she lashed back at Rallis and told him she would tell MI5 everything she knew about Poseidon, whoever or whatever that is. But the bizarre thing in this whole episode is that *she* vowed to kill Rallis, not the other way around. But Tarasova is the one who's lying dead upstairs."

CHAPTER 23

"Noel, are you all right?" Sabrina whispered, clasping his hand and lacing her fingers through his as she rested her head on his shoulder. They were alone in the corner of the reception room overlooking the garden.

He brusquely disentangled their fingers and took a step away from her. "For God's sake, Sabrina, not now. Show a little decorum."

She smarted at his rebuff, but schooled her features so that he would not see how hurt she was by his callousness. "Sorry. You looked upset," she replied lamely.

He wheeled round from the window, his dark eyes ablaze with anger. "Of course, I'm upset. Aren't you? A woman was found dead in this house tonight."

"Yes, it's horrid," she mumbled.

A wave of nausea roiled her stomach as the image of the ballerina's sightless, staring eyes flashed into her mind. And then in the next second, the image of Hugh danced before her. She put a hand to her mouth. She had to get control of her emotions. She shot a nervous glance at Noel. She couldn't allow him to see how distraught she truly was. She couldn't allow him to find out about Hugh. *No one* could find out about Hugh. However, she was certain that Emmeline and that bloody Philip Acheson had already taken great pains to paint Hugh in the most awful light to that oaf Burnell.

Emmeline's too honest for own good, Sabrina complained to herself. *No matter how it looks, I know Hugh didn't murder the ballerina.* Her fists curled into tight balls. *I* know *it*.

Rallis's voice tore her away from these jarring thoughts and back to the present. "I've been thinking, Sabrina. Perhaps we should take some time off from each other."

She felt the air escape from her lungs. "Time off? What do you mean?"

She tossed a glance over her shoulder, but no one could overhear them. She turned back to Rallis, her nails digging deep into her palms. "I thought things couldn't be better between us, especially in the past fortnight. We had talked about moving in together. Or had you forgotten?"

One of those smiles that used to turn her knees to water slipped onto his lips, but it did nothing to take out the sting of his words. "Naturally, I hadn't forgotten. But sometimes one needs to step back to gain a little perspective. It's not forever. Perhaps a few months."

A few months? She stared as his warm fingers caressed her upper arm. "I'm certain you understand." His smile broadened.

Oh, yes, I understand, she thought with distaste. *You're a bastard. Pure and simple. Everyone was right.*

All at once, she felt soiled and cursed herself bitterly for being a bloody fool.

"It was all a game from the start, wasn't it?" Her voice dipped dangerously low. "Answer me."

Rallis pursed his lips, a flicker of annoyance passing over his face. "This kind of behavior is unseemly. It doesn't become you."

She took a half-step closer to him. "If I scratch your eyes out, as you deserve, that would be unseemly. At the moment, I'm showing tremendous restraint."

Rallis snorted and thrust his hands in his pocket. He leaned his head toward her. "I don't know why you're coming over all outrage. It's not as if you were some innocent whom I seduced. We're both adults and walked into this with our eyes wide open. It was a physical relationship. Nothing more. It was never going to last."

Sabrina pressed a hand to her stomach and drew in a ragged breath. Her head was spinning. "But I thought…"

"I can't help what you think," he replied, his tone clipped and unfeeling.

She teetered on her heels for a second, but quickly regained control. She straightened her spine and gathered her tattered dignity about her. "They say what goes around comes around. The clock is ticking. Everyone has to pay in the end. *Even you.* I can't wait for the day that someone plunges a knife in your chest in that black hole where your heart should be."

He threw his head back and laughed. "Oh, how I'll miss your delightful sense of humor." He gripped her by the shoulders and pressed a hard kiss against her lips. "Goodbye, Sabrina."

Then he walked away. By the set of his shoulders, she could tell that she was already a distant memory in his mind.

She roughly dragged the back of her hand over her lips, smearing her lipstick in her attempt to obliterate any remnant of his kiss. What she really wanted to do was to spit in his cruel, attractive face. It was too late to salvage her wounded pride, but she could do everything in her power to see that Noel got what he had coming to him. Because, much as he tried to mask it with his arrogance, she saw fear in the depths of his dark eyes. She was going to find out what he was hiding.

God, I'm beginning to sound like Emmeline, she observed with disgust. *If I'm not careful, I'm going to start nattering on about justice.* She shuddered. *Heaven help me. Justice is useless. But revenge, yes. It may be cold, but it's oh, so sweet.*

⌘

Cruickshank had allowed a number of the guests to leave, after their statements had been taken because either they hadn't spoken to the ballerina at all or it was quickly determined that they could shed no light on her murder.

Yoav Zielinski was among those who had already departed, but Emmeline, Gregory, Philip, and Maggie glumly remained, awaiting Cruickshank's reappearance with more promised questions. At the moment, the assistant commissioner was upstairs with Dr. Meadows and the forensics team.

"It's nearly eleven o'clock," Maggie said, doing her best to stifle a yawn as she settled her head more comfortably on her husband's shoulder. "How long are the police going to keep us here?"

She was sitting on the sofa in the reception room between Philip and Emmeline, who by contrast was wide awake, ears straining and keenly surveying all the activity around her not wanting to miss a single thing.

Emmeline rose to her feet and started pacing back and forth in front of the fireplace, where Gregory casually stood with one shoulder propped against the mantelpiece.

"My question exactly, Mags," she replied. "Perhaps, I'll just nip into the corridor to find out what's going on, shall I?"

Gregory languidly reached out a hand and caught her arm in mid-perambulation. "No, Emmy."

How could he infuse disapproval into such plummy tones? "No? No what?" she asked innocently.

He smiled down into her face and drew her to his side. "Cruickshank is not going to appreciate it, if you get under his feet."

She returned his smile and placed both hands on his chest. "I don't intend to get in his way. I understand that the police have a job to do, but so do I. Anastasia Tarasova's murder is a legitimate story. I happen to be on the spot. The public has a right to know."

"Do they? Just like they have to know about Rallis?"

"Yes, of course. He is on trial for the murder of another girlfriend. He quarreled violently with Tarasova earlier in the evening and now she's dead. Doesn't it bother you? It certainly troubles me."

"Murder bothers me as it does any sane, rational person. But what you're really interested in is where Rallis went after his little contretemps a few moments ago with Sabrina."

Her eyes widened. "*Did* he have an argument with Sabrina? I hadn't notice."

Philip snorted from the sofa.

"Darling, that statement lacked sincerity. You see, not even Acheson is convinced by your assertions."

She spun her head around slowly and impaled Philip with a single glance. "With friends like you," she muttered her breath, which to her consternation made him chuckle.

She turned back to Gregory. "I can't just stay cooped up in here. I'm not a mushroom. I don't do well being kept in the dark. We have a right to know what's going on." She took a step away from him. "I'll pop my head into the hall for five minutes and see what information I can pick up. Five minutes. I promise."

Her husband folded his arms over his chest and cocked his head to one side. "Is this the same woman who warned *me* not to antagonize Cruickshank?"

She reached up and gave him a peck on the cheek. "You're different, darling. The police don't appreciate your charm and wit like I do. It's an acquired taste."

Philip groaned. "Not even a week married and you're already beginning to sound like him. God save us all." Then a muted "Oof" was heard after Maggie elbowed him the ribs.

Emmeline looked up into Gregory's face. "Five minutes. You won't even miss me."

He shook his head. "You forget that I know you. One question inevitably leads to another, and another."

"That's what journalists do. Ask questions."

"Very amusing. Your questions, though, tend to make people nervous and inevitably you end up the target of the most unsavory characters."

"Except for Rallis," she pointed out matter-of-factly, "there aren't any 'unsavory characters' here tonight."

"That is, if you don't count the murderer, of course. Which could be Rallis. Then there's our friendly neighborhood assassin Carstairs, who popped in for a visit. Shall I go on, Emmy?"

She made a dismissive gesture with her hand. "Oh, you're just being argumentative. The house is teeming with police. I couldn't be any safer." Her voice dipped. "Even if the murderer is hanging about."

"And still my intrepid wife wants to do battle with only her mighty pen for protection."

"This is a major story," she countered, irritation creeping into her tone. "I'm on the spot. *The Clarion* will get a jump on everybody else. Besides, the truth is my protection. I simply need to find the answers to unlock it. You do see that, don't you? Then the law can take its course."

They were both silent for several seconds. Her dark

eyes held a challenge. In the end, Gregory sighed. "Boadicea of the Fourth Estate," he murmured.

Her mouth curved into a smile because she knew she had won the argument. "Right. I'll see you in a few minutes."

He watched in amusement as her smile quickly faded, when he said, "We'll go together, shall we? That way, I can watch as you try to cajole answers from the tight-lipped Cruickshank."

Her brow puckered. "It's out of the question. I don't need you hovering over my shoulder."

He took her elbow. "Think of it as an adoring new husband wanting to be near his wife."

"We've never lived in each other's pockets. I certainly don't intend to start now," she retorted with more than a touch of asperity. A thought suddenly stuck her. "Just a minute, do you *know* something that you're not telling me? Is that why you want me to stay put and not ask any questions?"

Gregory's eyes widened in surprise. "What could I possibly know, darling? I never met Tarasova before tonight, or Rallis for that matter."

Her gaze scoured his face, as if she could find the answer if she stared long enough. But she couldn't discern a single thing because he had arranged his features into a bland expression.

She shrugged her shoulders in resignation. However, he was on the receiving end of several sidelong glances as they crossed the room. But she held her tongue. The desire to know what the police had uncovered was too strong.

CHAPTER 24

Several uniformed constables were huddled together, deep in conversation, as Emmeline and Gregory slipped into hall. One lifted his head and Emmeline flashed a smile at him. He didn't seem to be unduly concerned about their appearance because he inclined his head and quickly returned his attention to his colleagues. Obviously, he realized that it was unreasonable to keep a group of adults confined to one room for hours. A number of other guests had followed their lead and trickled out behind them. Two men headed toward the kitchen, mumbling something about getting a cup of coffee.

What Emmeline really wanted to do was to sneak upstairs to see how the investigation was progressing. However, the practical side of her brain told her that would be pushing the envelope. Alternatively, they could ingratiate themselves with the constables. She opened her mouth to propose this idea to Gregory, when Rallis's voice drifted to their ears. It was coming from the study to the right of the staircase at the back of the house.

One glance at Gregory's face told her that he was as curious as she was to find out who Rallis was talking to in such an angry tone.

Gregory casually took her elbow and guided her toward the study. Fortune was in their corner tonight because the door had been left slightly ajar. Gregory slipped his arm around her shoulder and they drew close to the open crack. As it had earlier, eavesdropping gave Emmeline a fleeting twinge. But she reasoned that her conscience would forgive her, if they were able to discover the nefarious scheme that Rallis was up to. She reasoned that it had to be nefarious because he did not possess an honest or legitimate bone in his body.

"You should have thought about that before, Desmond," Rallis was saying.

Desmond? As in Lord Desmond Starrett? Lord Starrett was somehow mixed up with Rallis?

Emmeline exchanged a stunned look with Gregory. She leaned in closer. She didn't want to miss a single, juicy word.

"Be reasonable, Noel," Starrett countered. "It's become too bloody dangerous. You yourself said that Carstairs chap has been nosing around. An international assassin, for God's sake. I don't like it. We're going to get caught."

"Life is full of risks," Rallis scoffed off-handedly. "That's what makes it exciting."

"I can live without that kind of excitement. I'm not like you. I have a reputation to uphold. Poseidon is not worth the risk. Not anymore. I should never have allowed you to talk me into it in the first place."

They heard Rallis roaming about the room. Suddenly, all movement stopped. A tense silence ensued for several interminable minutes.

Emmeline held her breath. This was the second time tonight that Poseidon had cropped up. She *had* to find out what it is.

"We both know why you agreed to become involved, don't we, *Lord* Starrett?"

It was odd, Emmeline thought, how Rallis had placed the heavy emphasis on the other man's title. Was it significant? Or was she merely grasping at straws?

Starrett grunted. "You didn't leave me much choice in the matter."

A deep-throated chuckle escaped from Rallis. "You give me too much credit, old chap. We always have a choice."

Starrett grumbled something unintelligible.

"However, I see your point," Rallis went on. "If I were in your shoes and I was forever hounded by my one youthful indiscretion—or should I say moral transgression?—I can see how it would color my view of the world. It's a matter between you and your conscience, though. But listen to me chuntering on like I'm a philosopher. I'm just a simple businessman trying to muddle my way as best I can in this dog-eat-dog world."

Starrett snorted with harsh laughter. "Come off it. Let's call a spade a spade, shall we? You're nothing more than a common blackmailer, who will stop at nothing to get what he wants."

Rallis sighed. "That's a rather jaded and cynical observation. But you're entitled to your opinion." His tone took on a sharper edge. "It doesn't change the fact that you're in this up to your neck. There's no backing out of Poseidon or anything else. Funny how your scruples weren't bothered one little bit with our other venture when it came to your collection."

"That was an entirely different matter," Starrett prevaricated.

"Was it? What a convenient justification." Rallis paused for a moment, before he hissed, "If you open your mouth to anyone, I promise you will regret it to your dying day."

"Don't you dare threaten me in my own house," Starrett

blustered. Then his voice dipped so low Emmeline and Gregory had to strain to hear what he was saying. "It's bad enough you murdered your other girlfriend, but you couldn't have found some other place to kill the Russian ballerina? Why involve us in your sordid affairs?"

"Don't be vulgar, Desmond," Rallis spat with distaste. "I didn't lay a finger on Nastya."

"Bollocks," Starrett cursed. "I saw the two of you having a heated argument earlier in the dining room. You probably lured her upstairs, where one of your thugs was waiting and he did the dirty work for you. But you're the one who's guilty, Noel. Stand warned that your wicked ways are going to catch up with you. That meddlesome journalist, Emmeline Kirby, smells blood. She and Anastasia had their heads bent together and were whispering furiously shortly after your little contretemps. It doesn't take a lot to guess *who* they were discussing."

"Yes, well. Emmeline Kirby and her husband, for that matter, will have to be taught a lesson if they continue to pry into my business. It's the only way to deal with the overly inquisitive."

Emmeline swallowed hard and shot a sidelong glance at Gregory, who rubbed her back reassuringly.

"You just stay focused on the job at hand," Rallis went on. "There's too much at stake. The next time you have an attack of conscience, remember that you have so much more to lose than I do. I'm certain your good chum Basil Treadgold would give you the same advice. As you said yourself only moments ago, you have a reputation to uphold, *Lord Starrett*."

There it was again. It was more than a lack of deference the way Rallis addressed the other man. The two words were infused with an inexplicable scorn. And who was Basil Treadgold?

Hmm, I wonder what the story is behind it all, Emmeline mused. *Lord Starrett has suddenly turned into a more intriguing figure than I had ever anticipated at the outset of the evening.*

But she didn't have time to take this thought any further because Rallis was coming straight toward them. Gregory grabbed her wrist and hustled her into the kitchen a fraction of a second before Rallis flung the door open and stalked off toward the reception room.

"Emmeline, Gregory, there's plenty of coffee and sandwiches, if you'd like. Please help yourselves. I've told the caterers to keep the coffee coming."

Lady Starrett's voice startled them. They turned around slowly and found her smiling at them.

As usual, nothing could faze Gregory and he was the first to speak. He favored her with one his most dazzling smiles. "Thank you, Lady Starrett. Coffee is exactly what we came in search of. Isn't it, Emmy?"

Emmeline nodded and smiled as well. "My eyes were starting to droop. I need something to keep me awake. Assistant Commissioner Cruickshank said he would like to question us again once they're finished upstairs."

Lady Starrett poured each of them a cup herself. She tilted her head back and shot a look at the ceiling. "Yes," she murmured, as she lowered her gaze and lifted her own cup to her lips. "I hope the police don't intend to be here all night. It's bad enough that poor woman was murdered. But to have complete strangers poking about and touching one's things is really too intrusive."

"Yes, but the police are only doing their job after all," Emmeline pointed out.

"Of course, I understand that. It's just that the whole situation is so distasteful."

Lady Starrett, her brow furrowing, took a distracted swallow of her coffee.

"Don't worry, Lady Starrett," Gregory offered soothingly. "It can't be much longer."

"Oh, I wish you both would call me, Fiona. After all this"—she waved a hand in the direction of hall, where more policemen were gathering—"let's not stand on ceremony."

"Fiona," Lord Starrett bellowed. "Where have you gotten to?"

She made a face at them and mouthed "Sorry." She cleared her throat and raised her voice. "I'm in the kitchen, Desmond."

The next instant, her husband's bulk was looming in the doorway. His face was flushed. "Ah, there you are." He inclined his head at Gregory and Emmeline. "Longdon, Mrs. Longdon, I'm certain you'll excuse us. I need a word with my wife."

"Of course," Emmeline and Gregory murmured in unison.

They placed their cups down on the counter. "Emmy and I were just leaving in any case," Gregory said. He turned to Lady Starrett. "Thank you for the coffee." Then he took Emmeline by the elbow and squeezed past their host.

They were only a few feet away when they heard Starrett's angry hiss, "Why the devil did you invite Noel Rallis tonight without asking me?"

"I didn't invite him," Fiona replied crisply. "He's Sabrina Royce's escort. I believe they're seeing each other."

Emmeline rolled her eyes at the mention of her sister and this sore subject.

"Well, all I have to say is that Sabrina has very poor judgement when it comes to men."

Emmeline nodded, agreeing in silence wholeheartedly with this sentiment.

"I don't want that man to set foot in this house ever

again. Do I make myself clear?" Starrett snapped.

"Calm down, Desmond. All of this lord-of-the-manor posturing simply will not do. I'm your wife, not a servant," was Fiona's brusque retort.

Gregory and Emmeline loitered near the bottom of the staircase to see if the Starretts said anything else about Rallis. Instead, they were nearly run over by Cruickshank and two plainclothes detectives, who were coming down at a trot.

The assistant commissioner was mumbling to the others, when he looked up and exclaimed, "Burnell, what is the meaning of this?"

CHAPTER 25

Gregory and Emmeline turned to see Superintendent Burnell and Sergeant Finch standing in the open doorway.

A huge grin appeared on Gregory's face as he sketched a crisp salute at Burnell, who scowled in reply.

"I distinctly told you that I would be taking charge of this case," Cruickshank said, closing the space between them in two strides. His nostrils flared. "This is gross insubordination on your part."

"Sir," Burnell said quietly, "something's happened and I felt you needed to be informed personally."

He tried to draw the assistant commissioner to one side, but Cruickshank wouldn't budge. He stood fixed in the middle of the hall, his arms folded across his chest.

"I can't tell you how disappointed I am with you at the moment, Burnell. This disruption had better warrant my immediate attention."

Burnell licked his lips and cast a surreptitious glance around the hall. He cleared his throat before speaking again. "I'm terribly sorry to have to tell you this, sir," he hedged. "Just after you left to come here, we were called out to another murder this evening."

The assistant commissioner's smooth brow puckered in annoyance. "Yes, and?"

Burnell coughed and shot a glance at Finch, who was standing at his elbow. The sergeant gave an imperceptible nod of his head.

Burnell gave a curt nod and drew his shoulders back. "Right, sir. We were called out because...Matthew Copperthwaite, QC was found...strangled in his chambers."

Cruickshank stiffened and his complexion took on an ashen hue. "What? He croaked. "Would you...would you mind repeating that?"

In a stronger, more authoritative tone, the superintendent declared, "Matthew Copperthwaite was found murdered this evening, sir."

"Yes, I see. That's what I thought you said," Cruickshank replied, distractedly. "It just didn't sink in the first time."

He swayed slightly on the balls of his feet. Burnell's hand reached out in a flash to steady him. "Are you all right, sir? Shall I have a PC drive you home?"

"Hmm. Home?" He gave a vigorous shake of his head. "No, certainly not. But I must go."

"Yes, of course, sir. I thought you would want to know as soon as possible."

For the first—and probably the last—time, Cruickshank clapped him on the shoulder. "Quite right. You're a good chap, Burnell. Look, you take over this case. You're the most senior officer." He pinched the bridge of his nose between his thumb and forefinger and fell silent.

"Yes, sir. I'll keep you apprised of developments."

The assistant commissioner fixed his brown gaze on Burnell. "Yes, you do that," he replied, but the superintendent could tell that his boss's mind was elsewhere.

Burnell gestured with his chin to a PC, who was hovering nearby. "Whitfield, see Assistant Commissioner Cruickshank to his car."

The constable nodded and stepped forward. "Sir," he prompted hesitantly when Cruickshank didn't move.

The assistant commissioner shot a glance at him and drew himself up to his full height. "Yes, I'm ready, Constable."

Another constable held the front door open and in a minute Cruickshank was gone.

"Well, all of you, don't stand there gawping," Burnell barked. "Get back to work. I need someone to bring me up to date."

Emmeline bit her lip as she watched several officers swoop down on the superintendent and Finch.

"Matthew Copperthwaite," she mumbled under her breath. "Why is that name familiar?"

"What was that, Emmy?" Gregory asked.

"I know that name. The man whose murder unsettled Assistant Commissioner Cruickshank so much."

Gregory opened his mouth to say something, but was prevented from doing so by Burnell.

"Longdon, Mrs. Longdon," the superintendent called as he headed straight toward them. "What the devil are you two doing here?"

Gregory grinned from ear to ear. "A pleasure to see you too, Oliver." His voice dropped on this last word. "We were just saying how much the evening's festivities were not the same without your delightful presence."

"Stuff it, Longdon. There is nothing remotely amusing about murder."

The jovial expression evaporated in an instant from Gregory's features. "Certainly not. It's a horrible business."

"Before I go upstairs, tell me why you're here? We'll get your formal statements later."

Emmeline answered for him. "We were guests of Lord and Lady Starrett. Lord Starrett is donating some jewels to the Museum of London tomorrow and he had a private unveiling tonight. Gregory is here in an official capacity for Symington's."

Burnell stroked his beard as he eyed Gregory. "Is he now?"

"Of course, you already know that Philip and Maggie are here," she added.

Burnell nodded. "Yes, it seems half of London was here tonight, including our elusive assassin Carstairs. I presume he is locked in some room and being guarded by a constable."

"I do hate to put a damper what has become a rather more stirring evening than any of us anticipated, but alas, our friend Carstairs has disappeared into the night."

The superintendent's cheeks flamed a violent shade of pink beneath his beard and his features contorted into a menacing grimace. "*What*?" he spluttered. He craned his neck around. "Where's Philip? I told him to guard Carstairs like a hawk."

Gregory took a risk and patted Burnell's arm in a bid to calm him. "Oliver, it doesn't do to get so emotional." He waggled his forefinger. "You know it's not good for your blood pressure or your ulcer."

Burnell glared down at the hand on his sleeve and curled fists into tight balls at his sides. "Longdon," he growled in warning.

Gregory put up his hands in a placating gesture and replied in cooing tones, "All right, Superintendent Burnell. It's unfair to lay the blame at Acheson's feet. Carstairs apparently has a vicious right hook. It knocked Acheson out cold. When he came round, the fellow was gone and

Lady Starrett was standing over him."

"Hmph," Burnell grunted, only marginally placated. "I'll have a word with Philip later. Any other unpleasant revelations that I should be made aware of?"

"Sabrina's here too," Emmeline mumbled.

The superintendent's gaze latched onto her. "Sabrina Royce?"

Emmeline gritted her teeth. "Yes, she came with…with Noel Rallis."

"*Rallis?*" The name exploded from his lips. "The same Rallis who is on trial for murdering his girlfriend?"

"Got it in one, Oliver. I always knew you were clever," Gregory offered unhelpfully.

The superintendent's eyes narrowed and his lips pursed. "You are living on the edge of a precipice."

"What is Miss Royce doing with Rallis?" Sergeant Finch asked quickly, seeking to diffuse the tension and keep things from spiraling completely out of control.

Emmeline sighed. "It seems she's been seeing him. I don't think it's been going on for too long. I can't be certain, though. As you know, Sabrina and I are not close. In any event, a little while ago she and Rallis appeared to be having a row. There was a lot of heated whispering back and forth. After a bit, Rallis walked away, the epitome of nonchalance. Sabrina, on the other hand, had a face like thunder as she watched him go."

"Fascinating. Finch I'd like you to have a chat with Miss Royce. But right now, we'd better go take a look at the scene of the crime."

Burnell had his hand on the newel post and one foot on the bottom step, when Emmeline cleared her throat. "Ahem."

Both he and Finch halted, turning their heads in her direction.

The superintendent lifted an eyebrow. "Yes, Emmeline,

was there something else?"

"Sabrina was not the only person with whom Rallis argued tonight."

"No? I *am* surprised," he remarked facetiously. "And here I thought he was such a likable fellow."

"Looks can be deceiving, sir," Finch offered.

"Yes," Burnell murmured, brows knitting together. "Rallis knows quite a bit about deceit, doesn't he?" Then, he leaned his elbow on the newel post. "So don't keep us in suspense, Emmeline. Whose evening did Rallis ruin?"

"Anastasia Tarasova and Lord Starrett."

Burnell straightened up and traded a glance with Finch. "The victim and the host. How jolly interesting. We'll be chatting with you later."

☙☙☙

Sabrina slipped the key into the lock of her Mayfair flat. There was a soft click as the bolt unfastened. She cast one furtive glance over her shoulder and then hurried inside. Once the bolt was securely in place, she exhaled a long, tremulous breath. She closed her eyes and leaned her back against the door, relishing its solidity. Her body was trembling. Any second now her knees were going to buckle under her, she was certain of it.

Her skin prickled with goose pimples as the horrible images of Tarasova's dead body flashed into her mind. Her stomach churned violently. She thought she was going to be sick.

And then in the middle of that nightmare, suddenly there was Hugh. After all these years. The corners of her mouth turned up slightly, but instantly transformed into a grimace. She silently cursed Philip Acheson to the depths of hell. She knew, beyond any doubt, that Hugh couldn't have killed the ballerina. Why would he? It was far more likely that Noel was involved.

"Oh, Hugh," she whispered aloud with regret.

Her worries about her ex-husband didn't have time to fully marinate in the recesses of her brain, though. Her eyes bulged open the instant the hand clamped over her mouth. Terror paralyzed her vocal cords, strangling the scream that was clawing to break free.

CHAPTER 26

Burnell and Finch came downstairs with grim expressions half an hour later. A flurry of activity followed in their wake. Dr. Meadows efficiently oversaw to the removal of the body and the Forensics team had departed soon afterward to begin the dismal process of sifting through the evidence. Burnell and Finch stayed behind with a small group of plainclothes detectives to go over the statements of a handful of the guests and some of the same questions anew to make their own assessments.

At the moment, the superintendent and the sergeant were closeted in Lord Starrett's study with Emmeline, Gregory, and Philip. Maggie already had been allowed to go, much to her chagrin because she was dying to know what had been discovered. But they could all see her curiosity was at war with her maternal instinct. In the end, the pull to go home and check on the twins was too strong. However, she extracted a promise from each of them to tell her what she missed.

"Now then," Burnell said as he thrust his hands into his pockets and stood gazing down at the trio huddled on the sofa. Emmeline had just finished relating the conversation she had overheard between Rallis and Tarasova in the dining room. "Are you certain that she vowed to '*see him dead*?'"

"Positive." Emmeline shuddered. "I could never forget those words."

Burnell nodded as he paced back and forth. He halted in mid-stride to face them again. "And yet, she's the one who is lying cold in the morgue. Did she give you the impression that she feared for her life?"

"The contrary, in fact. When I cornered her in the corridor, she was eager to tell me everything she knew. However, now that I think back, at one point she did say something rather odd. We were talking about Rallis and all of a sudden she stopped and looked about furtively as some guests were passing us, as if she had just realized where she was. Then she said something to the effect that 'I never forget a face.'"

"Rather out of context," Finch suggested from his perch on the sofa opposite.

"It caught me off guard for a second. I had been admiring her exquisite necklace and thought I had missed something that she had said. I asked whether she was still talking about Rallis or something else. Then she seemed to withdraw into herself. She became rather brisk and nervous, and said that we couldn't talk there in the corridor. That's when we arranged to meet in the master bedroom at nine o'clock. She promised to tell me everything I wanted to know about Rallis and his shady business dealings."

"And you agreed to meet her?" Finch prompted.

"I tried to dissuade Emmy," Gregory broke in. "But she refused to listen or at the very least allow me to join her when she met with Tarasova."

"All right." Burnell made an impatient gesture with his hand. "We'll get to you in a minute, Longdon," he retorted with irascibility.

"It was out of the question," Emmeline responded primly as her chin jutted in the air and she shot a sidelong glance her husband. "I have meetings with sources all the time. This instance was no different."

"Except for the fact that Tarasova is now dead and you were one of the last people to speak to her," Gregory pointed out. "That makes you a target, darling."

"Ahem." Burnell cleared his throat to draw their attention. "Emmeline, he's quite right. If the murderer saw you and Tarasova together, he or she could very well assume that she took you into her confidence."

Emmeline lifted her eyes to the detective's face. She saw the concern reflected in the blue depths of his eyes. "The thought had occurred to me."

Gregory took her hand in his. "Brilliant. I'm delighted to see that you haven't completely lost your sense of reason."

She pulled a face at him. "Ha. Ha. Very witty."

Gregory raised her hand to his lips and grazed her knuckles with a kiss. "Thank you. One does one's best."

Finch and Philip rolled their eyes at one another, but this exchange eased the tension in the room slightly.

"I'll have a couple of men keep an eye on you for a few days," "Burnell said quietly, sobering the mood once more.

"That's really not necessary," Emmeline protested.

"Let me be the judge of that. Now then, is there anything else you can tell us about Tarasova?"

"Not really. She never told me whatever it is that she knew. She was already dead when Sabrina and I walked into the bedroom. I didn't see anyone else in the corridor. The only other person there was…" Her sentence trailed off.

The superintendent leaned forward. "Go on."

She sighed. "Carstairs was the only one in the room,"

she replied miserably.

Burnell eyes narrowed and his gaze fell upon Philip. "Yes, our friend Carstairs, an international assassin. Funny that he just happened to pop in to the Starretts' tonight."

Philip opened his mouth, but Emmeline spoke before he had a chance to utter a word. "I know how it looks, Superintendent Burnell, but I really don't think that Carstairs is the murderer."

Burnell groaned and plunked down in a nearby wing chair. "Don't give me the same drivel that your sis...that Miss Royce did. She talked our ears off. I couldn't wait to send her off home.

"Let's look at the evidence we have thus far. Carstairs was in the room, alone with the victim. He knocked out Philip and did a runner. That does *not* sound like an innocent man to me. For God's sake, he kills people for money."

"Yes, I know everything *appears* to point to Carstairs," she persevered. "But if he were truly guilty, he could have murdered Sabrina and me without blinking an eye. But as you can see, we're very much alive and well. On the same token, he could have killed Philip. Again, he didn't."

"Emmeline's right, you know," Philip observed. It was the first time he had spoken since they had entered the room.

The superintendent's gaze hovered between the pair of them. He sighed. "My years on the force tell me that it can only be Carstairs."

"As Finch said earlier, looks can be deceiving. Why not keep an open mind, Oliver?" Gregory suggested with a smile. "We do have other possibilities. Rallis springs to mind, of course."

"I don't need advice from you on how to do my job. At this stage, everyone is a suspect."

Gregory put a hand to his chest in mock surprise.

"Surely, you don't consider me a suspect? I'm innocent as a newborn lamb."

A choking gurgle rumbled around in the back of Burnell's throat. He shot a pointed look at Gregory. "Don't even get me started. You're so far from innocent that the guilt simply oozes from your pores."

Gregory gave a sad shake of his head. "Oliver, Oliver," he lamented. "You really know how to wound a chap."

"Bollocks," the detective snapped and regretted it instantly. "Sorry, Emmeline. An unfortunate slip of the tongue. But your husband"—he pursed his lips and shook his head—"one of these days he's going to be the death of me."

"How can you say that? We're bosom mates for all eternity. Your well-being is of uppermost concern to me."

Burnell tilted his head toward the ceiling. "Why me?" he demanded of the Almighty.

Emmeline elbowed Gregory in the ribs. "I apologize, Superintendent. We're all rather tired."

"Speak for yourself, darling. I'm wide awake," Gregory declared cheerfully.

Emmeline sighed and slumped back against the sofa.

"Sir," Finch interrupted, trying to get control of the interview before it devolved further. "We were discussing Rallis."

After offering up a final silent curse at the Lord's betrayal, Burnell returned his concentration to the here and now.

"Rallis, yes." He stroked his beard as he stared at the little group. "It would please me no end to put that man behind bars. We've been after him for years. But just because I loathe the chap is not sufficient reason to arrest him. I need evidence."

Emmeline sat up bolt upright and scooted to the edge of the sofa, eagerly embracing this shift in the conversation.

"Of course, Matthew Copperthwaite. That's why his name was familiar."

The men turned their heads as one to stare at her.

"Matthew Copperthwaite," she repeated again. "He's the prosecutor in Rallis's murder trial."

"Ye-es," Burnell replied. "He's also Cruickshank's stepfather."

Emmeline's dark eyes widened in surprise. "Is he? I didn't know. So that's why the assistant commissioner dashed out of here and left you in charge." The superintendent gave a curt nod. "Lucky for us. He wasn't keen on listening to us. Anyway, don't you see? Rallis must be behind Copperthwaite's murder too."

"Emmeline, let's focus on one dead body at a time."

She pressed on. "It can't be a coincidence that Tarasova and Copperthwaite were murdered on the same night. They both have links to Rallis. When I spoke to him earlier, he *told* me that the Crown has no evidence and his trial is a waste of taxpayer money. He was extremely confident that the case would be dropped. I thought it was merely bluster and bravado at the time. But what if it wasn't? What if Copperthwaite's murder was a cold-blooded attempt to make certain?"

"Sir, she has a point," Finch observed. "Copperthwaite's murder will disrupt the trial or at the very least delay it. Tarasova knew about the skeletons lurking in Rallis's past and present. What if she contacted Copperthwaite and Rallis found out? I'd say Emmeline's theory is quite plausible."

Burnell drew himself to the edge of his chair and rested his elbows on his knees, his hands clasped together and dangling in the air between them. "Yes, it's plausible," he admitted.

Emmeline beamed triumphantly at him and in the next second her smile faded, when he pointed out reasonably,

"You seem to forget that Carstairs was the only one found in the room with Tarasova." He put up a hand to stem the tide of protest about to spill from her lips. "And another thing. That contract you overheard Carstairs accepting in the Lake District. The target was an important man whose obituary would be in the papers. Remember? Matthew Copperthwaite fits that bill. He's a well-respected QC, who has prosecuted and defended a number of high-profile cases in recent years. So my humble policeman's brain, when presented with this curious preponderance of facts, logically comes to the conclusion that Rallis hired Carstairs to eliminate both Copperthwaite and Tarasova. In one fell swoop, he eliminates two threats and with no apparent connection between them. And Carstairs disappears to kill another day."

"It's quite possible that's the way things unfolded," Philip conceded. "But..."

Emmeline cut across him. "I think you're wrong," she asserted mulishly. To soften her words, she added, "With the greatest of respect, of course, Superintendent."

"Emmeline..."

"No, I'm sorry," she insisted. "It's the convenient, the *logical*, solution, but it's all circumstantial. Something doesn't feel right."

Burnell threw his hands up in air in exasperation. "I can't go by feelings," he spluttered. "I can only go by the evidence and so far everything you've told me is hearsay."

"You weren't there when Sabrina and I stumbled into the room. Carstairs appeared just as surprised as we were to see Tarasova draped across the bed. It was horrible. I'll never forget it. Her blue-gray eyes were glazed and focused on nothing. Her neck was twisted at an odd angle. The pale skin of her throat was as white as her dress." She drew in a sharp breath. "Oh my God. The pale skin of her throat."

"What is it? What have you remembered?" the superintendent prompted.

She swallowed hard and lifted her eyes to meet his gaze. "I just realized that when we discovered Tarasova, her neck was bare. Don't you understand? Her necklace, an exquisite cascade of rubies and diamonds, was missing." She put a hand to her mouth. "It must have been stolen."

A hush descended on the room. All eyes slowly came to rest on Gregory.

CHAPTER 27

Hugh, you're an absolute beast," Sabrina said, putting a hand to her chest. Her heart was still hammering against her rib cage. "You made me jump out of my skin."

She swatted his arm, hard. "I'll never forgive you."

A ghost of a smile quivered upon Carstairs's lips. "Same old Sabrina. Everything revolves around you."

"Don't give me that," she snapped as she gave the light switch an angry flick. She stood in the middle of the corridor with her hands on her hips. "It's not fair for a start. It's not every day that I go to party and end up finding my ex-husband looming over a dead woman."

"I wasn't looming. I was just as surprised to find Tarasova as you were."

Sabrina sniffed. "Yes, well. For what it's worth, I don't think you murdered her."

He inclined his head. "Thank you for that."

She exhaled a weary sigh. "Oh, come on through to the living room. You look as if you could do with a stiffner. I know I could after tonight."

She led him down the corridor into an elegantly furnished room. Whatever else that could be said about

Sabrina, she had good taste when it came to interior design. If she could only focus on the design aspect, her company would be booming. However, she couldn't be bothered about all of the niggling details of the business side and that's why the company was floundering.

Carstairs lowered himself like an old man onto the cream silk-upholstered sofa. Suddenly, all his limbs felt heavy, weighed down by fatigue and stiff with tension. He pressed the heels of his palms to his eyes, listening as Sabrina clinked glasses on the drinks table behind him.

"Here," she said.

He dropped his hands and opened his eyes to accept the crystal tumbler she held out to him. It contained an extremely generous tot of whiskey.

He lifted the glass. "Cheers. To old times."

"Hmph." Sabrina plumped down on the sofa next to him, sitting so close their shoulders brushed. "Our old times didn't involve murder."

She took a swallow of her brandy. "Oh, Hugh." There was a plaintive catch in her voice. "I've never seen anyone murdered before." She rested her head on his shoulder. "I've never been so frightened in my life."

He slipped an arm around her waist and drew her closer. "I didn't kill her. You have to believe me." She felt these words as her cheek pressed against his neck.

She broke their embrace to face him. "Of course, I believe you. I'm the only bloody one who does. What devil have you gotten yourself mixed up in? And don't think you can fob me off because I deserve an answer."

The minutes stretched out as he stared at her with those unblinking chestnut eyes that seemed to shut out the world. The silence was suffocating. "Answer me," she demanded.

He took her face between his hands and softly kissed the tip of her nose. "I can't tell you anything. It's too dangerous. The less you know, the better. It's safer that way."

She snorted. "Men. You always think you're so superior and know best. Well, let me tell you. You know nothing. I don't know anything and I'm already in danger after tonight."

"You mean Rallis."

This caught her off guard. "How do you know about Noel?" she asked nervously.

"Never mind. You've always been stubborn as hell, but my advice to you is to stop seeing him at once."

She laughed. It was a harsh sound that lacked any warmth. "It will please you no end I'm sure to hear that Noel dumped me tonight." She snapped her fingers. "Just like that."

Carstairs's body appeared to relax slightly. "Good."

Her back stiffened. "Thank you for your touching concern and words of sympathy."

He grunted. "Only your pride is hurt. You'll get over it."

"Ever the charmer, I see. You still haven't told me what you were doing at the Starretts' tonight?"

"I can't," he replied through clenched teeth.

"You mean you won't."

"Have it your way. I'm in no mood to argue." He grabbed her roughly by the shoulders, his eyes boring into hers. "This isn't a party game, Sabrina. It has nothing to do with us or our past. Your boyfriend Rallis is involved with a lot of nasty people who won't hesitate to kill you. Just stay clear of it."

Anger and fear vied with one another as they chased themselves across his features.

"Noel is hiding something. I don't know what it is, but I think he's afraid that it will all come out."

"A man with secrets lives on borrowed time."

"Before tonight, I would have denied it" She paused to

take a breath. "I think Noel murdered Tarasova."

He nodded his head grimly. "Very likely."

She clutched at his sleeve. "Hugh, the police think you did it."

"I know. Perhaps that's for the best at the moment."

"How can you say that?" she asked, incensed. "You're innocent."

"By morning, they're probably going to lay the murder of Matthew Copperthwaite at my feet."

Her brows knit together in confusion. "This gets worse. Who is this fellow Copperthwaite?"
He shook his head. "It doesn't matter. You'll find out soon enough. I just wanted to make certain that you were all right. But I see now that it was a mistake. I didn't think."

He stood up abruptly. "I should leave. This will be the first place the police will look."

Sabrina scrambled to her feet as well. "But *where* will you go?"

His mouth broke into gentle smile. He gave her arm a reassuring squeeze. "Don't worry. I'll be fine."

"Do you know how much I hate the male ego? You're in deep trouble."

"You're exaggerating. Now, I must go." He gave her a hurried peck on the cheek and crossed the room.

She caught up with him in the corridor. "Hugh, don't do this alone. I want to help you. You don't know how much. But I wouldn't know where to begin." She paused and took a deep breath. "I never dreamed I would be saying this, but there's one person with an open mind who I think might be able to help you. Someone you can *trust*."

He shot her a quizzical glance. "Who? I have to be careful…"

"Emmeline. My sister. Go to Emmeline."

CSCS

Burnell stood without uttering a word. He yanked open the door, rattling it on its hinges, and bellowed into the corridor. "Maitland, Wallis, in here *now*."

Two uniformed constables appeared on threshold to Lord Starrett's study within seconds. The superintendent ushered them inside with an impatient gesture and slammed the door behind them with a *thud*.

"Right," he commanded. "On your feet, Longdon. Look lively." He turned to the constables. "Search him."

Gregory smoothed down the corners of his mustache and held the detective's gaze.

"I said get up," Burnell growled.

Gregory gave a nonchalant shrug of his shoulders and rose slowly, his every movement infused with innate masculine grace. "Really, Ol…"

Burnell's nostrils flared and his cheeks flushed a violent crimson beneath his beard.

Gregory cleared his throat. "*Superintendent Burnell*, is this quite necessary?"

Before Burnell had a chance to respond, Emmeline leaped to her feet and stood in front of her husband, as if to shield him from the law's embrace. However, as Gregory and the rest of the men gathered in the room stood a head taller than she, her body only blocked him from mid-chest down. It would be comical, if the situation wasn't so grave.

"You can't possibly believe that Gregory stole Tarasova's necklace?"

The superintendent glared down at her. "Can't I? Why not?" he snarled.

Emmeline refused to be cowed by that glacial blue stare. She took a half-step forward and drew herself to her full height of five feet two inches. "Gregory is reformed.

He's legitimate now. He works at Symington's. He doesn't steal anymore."

"Darling, I never stole anything in my life," he murmured over her head.

She whirled her neck around. "Shut up. Don't make this worse."

"That's the first sensible thing you've said in the past five minutes," Burnell remarked.

She turned to face him again. She felt tears sting her eyelids. "Please, Superintendent Burnell, don't do this."

"Emmeline, you know that I respect you." His voice softened and some of the anger dissipated. "But you have a gaping blind spot when it comes to your husband. If he's as innocent as you claim, then you should want him to be searched to prove it. Or are you afraid that we might find the necklace?"

She squared her shoulders. "It's a matter of trust."

"Unfortunately, I have a problem trusting people. I've found that in the end they usually let you down. Now then." He nodded to the two constables and jerked his chin at Gregory. "Longdon."

She dipped her head in defeat.

Gregory took her gently by the arms and eased her back down onto the sofa. "Don't worry, Emmy. Everything will be all right." He gave her a cheeky wink. "Superintendent Burnell hasn't had enough excitement tonight. He's merely bored."

"All right. No more of your lip, Longdon. Arms out, legs apart."

The superintendent nodded, and the constables moved in and started patting down Gregory.

"Don't damage the material, chaps. The tuxedo is custom made," Gregory quipped. Then to Burnell, he said with a sad shake of his head, "This is not worthy of you, Superintendent. I wonder how you can sleep at night when you go around harassing law-abiding citizens."

"Hmph" was Burnell's only reply.

After a few more seconds, the constables turned to him and shook their heads. "Nothing, sir. He's clean."

Emmeline beamed in triumph, her grin stretching from ear to ear. But Burnell's eyes widened in disbelief. "What do you mean?"

Gregory dropped his arms, shot his cuffs, and straightened his bow tie. He cleared his throat. "I believe I did mention that it would be an exercise in futility."

He resumed his seat, draped his arm over Emmeline's shoulders, and crossed one elegantly-tailored leg over the other. He bestowed one of his most engaging smiles upon the embarrassed superintendent. There was a smug glint in his eye.

Burnell's gaze strayed to the two constables. "You're sure?"

"Yes, sir," they responded in unison. Was there a hint of disappointment in their voices?

"Right. Back to your duties."

The superintendent waited until the constables had closed the door behind them.

He stared at his feet for several seconds. Everyone held their collective breath.

At last, he raised his chin and looked Gregory directly in the eye. "It would seem"—his voice cracked. There was a deep rumbling in the back of his throat and he started again, more briskly this time—"It would seem I was mistaken. On behalf of the Metropolitan Police, I apologize for any inconvenience you might have suffered."

Gregory made a languid gesture with his hand, waving off Burnell's act of contrition.

"Think nothing of it, *Oliver*. I realize that you've been under a tremendous strain lately and it might have affected your judgement momentarily. It's nothing a good night's sleep wouldn't put to rights. You'll be a new man."

Burnell curled his fingers, one by one, into tight balls at his sides. "Don't push your luck, Longdon," he replied through gritted teeth.

"I never overstay my welcome. It's frightfully bad manners," he asserted with a breezy insouciance.

The superintendent held himself rigidly. He had been so certain that finally, *finally* they were going to catch Longdon red-handed.

But he turned the tables on us again, he thought ruefully. *Where the devil did the man stash the necklace? He's got it all right. Just look at the smug smile. He's enjoying rubbing our noses in it and we can't touch him.*

"What was that, Oliver?" Gregory asked seemingly without guile. Burnell knew better, though.

The detective folded one arm over his chest and stroked his beard with his other hand. "Nothing."

"Oh, I see. Don't feel bad about tonight. We won't say any more about it. I won't hold it against you. I've quite forgiven you."

Burnell traded a pained look with Finch.

"I don't need forgiveness for doing my job. Especially not from you."

"Don't you? I suppose you know best. To err is human and to forgive divine. Well, I'll leave you to sort it out with the Lord in your prayers." He leaned forward and lowered his voice conspiratorially. "I'm certain He gives special dispensation to policemen."

Burnell felt his cheeks flaming again. He dug his nails into his palms. *I'm going to throttle him.*

"Sir," Finch intervened hastily. "We've finished with the questions for Longdon and Emmeline for tonight, haven't we?"

"Questions?" He stared at the sergeant, his brain racing.

He blinked and sought to pull himself together. He drew in a deep breath through his nostrils. "No. No more questions. For now." Finch nodded encouragingly. "Longdon, you and Emmeline may go. And you too, Philip." He had nearly forgotten about Philip in the excitement of the last few minutes.

Gregory rose and extended a hand to help Emmeline up. "Thank you, gentleman." He gave his jacket a tug to smooth it and closed the button. "Frankly, I've spent more pleasant evenings. However, your presence helped to make it special."

"Go, before I change my mind and take you down to the station, where I assure you the atmosphere will be less genteel, Longdon," Burnell muttered.

"Promises, promises. I know you always miss me terribly, Oliver. But I simply must take Emmy home. The poor girl is dead on her feet."

Emmeline tugged on his arm. "Come on."

"You see, gentleman. It doesn't do to have an anxious wife. Come on, Acheson. We'll give you a lift."

Gregory gave a little salute, as Emmeline dragged him into the hall. She waved and offered a smile, before their faces disappeared from view.

Philip shook hands with both detectives and then he was gone too.

Burnell scowled. "Make yourselves available. We'll have more questions," he called after them.

Gregory's voice drifted to their ears. "Your wish is our command."

"Damn the man," Burnell mumbled and plunked down heavily on the sofa. He was absolutely shattered. Every part of his body was tired. He rested his elbows on his knees and dropped his head between his hands. Why did he allow Longdon to get to him? He knew better. And yet, every time he was sucked into these draining tests of will.

Perhaps, he was getting old. He certainly felt as if he were a hundred.

He slid a sideways glance at Finch. With a stab of spite, he was glad to see that the sergeant looked as shell-shocked as he felt.

In the corridor, Emmeline reached up and gave Gregory a peck on the cheek. "I never doubted you for a moment."

Gregory smiled down at her and rubbed a spot between her shoulder blades. "Thank you, darling. I appreciated your impassioned defense on my behalf. But as you can see, it was quite unnecessary. Poor old Oliver." He shook his head sadly. "I felt rather sorry for him. I suppose it's the pressure of working for that prat Cruickshank that has skewed his perception. He's beginning to see criminals everywhere." Philip choked back a laugh. "What was that, Acheson?"

"Nothing." He glanced at his watch. "It's late. Maggie will be worried."

"Of course, we'll get you home in no time. Traffic will be light at this hour. Come on."

The Starretts' butler materialized from nowhere with Emmeline's shawl.

Gregory frowned. All Emmeline had in her hands were her notebook and a pen. "Darling, where's your clutch?"

"Goodness, I'd forgotten about it. I put it down before I went upstairs."

She tossed a glance over her shoulder. She caught a glimpse of her clutch exactly where she had left it on the console table beneath the mirror. "There it is."

"Allow me, madam," the butler intoned solemnly. He was back within seconds.

"Here, I'll take it," Gregory offered, relieving the butler of his burden. "Thank you."

The servant dipped his head deferentially. "Not at all, Mr. Longdon, Mrs. Longdon." He opened the door and stepped back to allow the trio to finally escape the evening's morbid intrigues.

CHAPTER 28

Emmeline rested her head against Gregory's shoulder as he slipped the key into the lock of their Holland Park townhouse. Her eyelids drooped. She did her best to stifle a rather indelicate yawn. Cracking one eye open, she cast a glance at her watch. Half past one. That couldn't be the time. Her body told her she needed to get to bed at once, but question upon question were chasing themselves across her mind. It would only take her about an hour to write up a more in-depth article than the preliminary one she had called into the *Clarion* on the drive home.

Gregory opened the door and put his hand on the small of her back to give her a gentle nudge into the hall. On the other hand, she thought as her husband shot the bolt into place, he might not view her dedication to finding the truth in quite the same way. At least not at half past one in the morning.

Still preoccupied with this conundrum, she was startled when Gregory drew her into his arms and he pressed a kiss to her forehead. She nestled deeper into his embrace and his warmth. After the horrid scene she had witnessed that evening, she just wanted to be close to him. To appreciate

being alive and loved. When they disentangled themselves, he was grinning down at her in the most scandalous
manner. It sent a delicious frisson down her spine. His
cinnamon gaze left her in no doubt about what was in his
mind. And consequently, no question about doing any
work. Not now.

Ah, well. To own the truth, she wasn't overly upset as
she once would have been when a fascinating new story
was begging for her attention. There would be plenty of
time tomorrow—today, she corrected herself—to get the
answers that were eluding her at the moment.

"How about a brandy before we go upstairs?" Gregory
suggested. "I think we could both do with one."

Emmeline rubbed the back of her neck, trying to ease
away the tension of the last few hours. "Mmm. Sounds
lovely," she said as she followed him into the living room
and fumbled along the wall to her right for the light switch.

They both heard the soft *click* in that suspended second
before the room flooded with light. They froze. Every
nerve taut and alert. Emmeline couldn't take her eyes off
the barrel of the nine-millimeter Beretta pointed directly at
them.

"I assure you it's loaded," Carstairs warned. He rose
from the sofa, his hand steady and his finger curled around
the trigger. "I'm rather hoping I won't have to use it.
That's entirely up to you, though."

"What do you want?" Gregory asked, his manner terse.
There was nothing in his clipped tone that betrayed
concern. However, he stepped in front of Emmeline. She
could feel the tension straining across his shoulder blades.

"You won't believe me, but I simply want to talk to the
two of you."

The smile on Gregory's lips did not reach his eyes.
"People generally don't feel it necessary to bring guns
along to have a chinwag. There's always the telephone, of

course. We're in the directory."

"In view of tonight's events…"

Gregory cut across him. "You mean the murders of Anastasia Tarasova and Matthew Copperthwaite?"

"Ah," Carstairs replied, matter-of-factly. "So you know about Copperthwaite too." He shrugged his shoulders in resignation. "It was inevitable. I didn't kill either of them, by the way."

"We only have your word on that." Gregory was not going to give him an inch.

"I believe you," Emmeline murmured, as she stepped around to stand in front of her husband.

She could feel Gregory's disapproving glare boring into the back of her skull. "Emmy," he hissed.

She didn't flinch from Carstairs's steady gaze. "I believe you," she repeated in a stronger tone. "If you had wanted to kill us, you would have done so already."

A smile tugged at the corners of his mouth. "Sabrina was right. She said that you were the only one I could trust." He shot a wary glance over her head at Gregory. "I still have reservations about you."

"The feeling is mutual."

Emmeline's eyes widened in surprise. "Sabrina? Sabrina sent you here?"

Carstairs nodded. "She did. I was a fool to go to her. Her flat is bound to be the first place the police will visit. She said that if anyone could help me it would be you." He lowered the gun to his side. "I don't think this is necessary anymore, do you? It was merely to get your attention. We understand each other. Besides, I know you've both signed the Official Secrets Act. So unless you want to be charged with treason, you won't open your mouths."

Gregory's back stiffened. "How do you know we've signed the Official Secrets Act?" he asked warily, although a sinking suspicion in the pit of his stomach told him he already knew the answer.

Carstairs gestured toward the sofa. "May I?"

Emmeline nodded and settled herself in the wing chair adjacent. Gregory remained standing.

"How does an international assassin know so much about our lives?" Gregory pressed.

"A mutual friend in high places." He paused for effect. "Laurence Villiers."

Damn Villiers, Gregory cursed silently. *Why can't he leave us out of his bloody intrigues? His lies and half-truths nearly got Emmy killed the last time.*

Carstairs leaned back against the cushions and stretched an arm along the back of the sofa. "I take it that there's a bit of history between the two of you. I'm curious to know how the deputy director of MI5 and a notorious jewel thief crossed paths."

"History. Hmm. That's one way of putting it" was Gregory's curt rejoinder.

His mind hurtled back all those years ago when he had first been drawn into Villiers's snare. He had to admit that he had been more than a bit flattered—and amused—that his particular talents could be of use to Queen and country. But what started out as a lark quickly plunged him into a suffocating nightmare. He cursed the day he met Villiers. If it hadn't been for that man, he and Emmy wouldn't have to look over their shoulders for the rest of their lives, worrying when Alistair Swanbeck would come back to exact his revenge.

"Villiers was rather tightlipped about you."

Gregory smirked as he eased his frame onto the other end of the sofa. "I'm not surprised. Villiers likes to keep his cards close to his chest. He has trust issues."

"Wouldn't you, if you were in his position? But I agree. He's not the most congenial of chaps."

"What I'd like to know," Emmeline broke in, "is what

a disgraced MI5 agent and international assassin is doing still chatting with his former boss. It seems odd, to say the least. Unless…" Her sentence trailed off.

One of Carstairs's eyebrows lifted in askance. "Unless what?"

A smile quivered upon her lips. "Unless this whole thing is a ruse. You were never dismissed from MI5, were you? And consequently, you are not an assassin." She sat back in smug contentment, elbows propped on the armrests and her hands steepled over her stomach. "Don't try denying it. I know I'm right."

Carstairs traded a look with Gregory. "Is she always like this?"

Gregory nodded. His body appeared to have relaxed slightly. "Pretty much. Once she gets an idea in her head, she doesn't let go."

Carstairs shot a glance at Emmeline. "A dog with a bone. Villiers was certainly right about you," he muttered under his breath. In a louder voice, he said, "Yes, you're right. I've heard that you've been poking your nose about and asking questions about me ever since you got back to London. So you know about the bungled Ivan Rudenko defection and his subsequent assassination." Emmeline and Gregory nodded. "That was my operation. I planned every minute detail. It should have been a piece of cake, but obviously things went terribly wrong. The only logical conclusion Villiers and I could come to is that we had a mole."

"You never had any suspicions?" Emmeline prompted.

Carstairs's jaw clenched. He gripped his knees until the skin across the back of his knuckles was stretched taut. "None whatsoever. I vetted every one of the team myself." The bitterness of the betrayal echoed in his voice.

He fell silent for several seconds, staring blankly at the opposite wall, his mind lost somewhere in the past.

The spell was broken when he slapped his thigh and jumped to his feet. He started pacing in front of the fireplace, a restless energy radiating from his body. He continued briskly, "I blamed myself for the debacle. Rudenko trusted me." He pounded his chest with his open palm. "I persuaded him to defect. I told him it would be easy. I told him the Russians wouldn't dare touch him. And all the time, they had someone on the inside.

"I had to know who the mole was. It became an obsession. I think I was getting too close for the mole's comfort because suddenly there were murmurings and concerns being raised about *me*. The Russians had turned the tables and went into attack mode to protect one of their assets. They manipulated things to appear that I was the mole to get rid of me. Villiers, to his credit, dismissed the notion out of hand as a lot of rot. And then we thought, why not let the Russians believe they had succeeded? I was summarily terminated in as public a manner as MI5's protocols allowed. We put the story about that I became so disaffected by the whole episode that I turned rogue. Then I appeared to drop off the face of the earth for six months. When I resurfaced again, Villiers had let it be known anonymously through certain channels that I had become a killer for hire. This has allowed me to move about freely anywhere, as I continued my search for the mole."

"But it's been three years. Surely the trail has gone cold," Emmeline remarked.

"It had up until two months ago. I heard whispers and started to make discreet inquiries. I'm making someone very nervous. A fortnight ago, someone broke into my house in Tobermory. Nothing was taken, but someone had definitely been there."

"That's another thing," Gregory chimed in, "if you're supposedly an international assassin, why the charade with a boat touring company up in the wilds of Scotland?"

Carstairs stopped pacing and allowed himself a slow smile. "A cover for the cover adds an air of authenticity to the intrigue."

Gregory sighed and slumped back. "Typical Villiers. Everything is cloak-and-dagger."

Carstairs shrugged and lowered himself onto the sofa once again. "Yes, well. To each his own. 'The wilds of Scotland' have been a hotbed of activity over the last eight months. The area has certainly attracted Rallis's interest."

Emmeline sat up and perched herself on the edge of her chair. "Rallis? A bit out of his usual sphere of influence. He seems to be popping up everywhere all of a sudden."

"He has something in common with the plague," Gregory mumbled.

"Or a slippery octopus," Carstairs concurred darkly. "In the last eight months, Rallis's sleek new yacht has made five appearances up in Tobermory. Each time, it arrived late at night and stayed for only a few days. It would remain anchored in the harbor during the day. The crew could be seen taking the Zodiac into town to do some shopping for supplies during the day. But like clockwork, at midnight every night it would go out to sea and return at dawn. I haven't been able to discover what the devil he's up to. I tried to following the yacht once, but daren't get too close. I think I may have been seen, hence the unexpected visits to my home when I was out."

Emmeline's brow puckered with concern. "Do you think Rallis has found out your cover is a hoax?"

Carstairs exhaled a slow breath. "Anything's possible. But, I don't think so. Rallis is not the type to sit back and wait for trouble to come to him. He lashes out. He wouldn't have waited this long to come after me. However, he's starting to smell that something is not quite right. I have to find out what he's up to before he finds out the truth. I seemed to be getting somewhere. I was working with a Treasury chap named MacQuillan..."

Gregory cut across him. "Now, why do I hear a but coming. Somehow I get the feeling that something happened to MacQuillan?"

Carstairs stared him directly in the eye and sighed heavily. "You're right," he replied softly. "MacQuillan was murdered a few days ago in Edinburgh."

Emmeline put a hand to her mouth. A stunned "Oh" escaped from her lips. Gregory merely shook his head, a shadow marring his handsome features. Clearly, this was an unwelcome bit of news coming on the heels of the nasty events of that night.

"You think it was Rallis?"

"I can't prove it—not yet anyway—but yes, I think it was Rallis."

"Forgive me, but I'm a little confused. Why is the Treasury interested in Rallis?" Emmeline asked.

"I'm not certain what precisely the Treasury is looking into about Rallis's business—nothing legal, obviously— but Villiers put me in contact with MacQuillan. I met him once. He was working undercover on one of Rallis's ships. He thought Rallis might be involved in drugs or some sort of smuggling. Then last week, he rang me and said he finally had something solid and asked me to come down to Edinburgh. He sounded on edge, anxious. I took the train down the next day. We were supposed to meet at a pub just off the Royal Mile called the Devil's Advocate." Carstairs pounded a fist against his open palm. "I was ten bloody minutes late. Ten minutes. When I got there, MacQuillan was lying in a pool of blood on the steps leading down to the pub. A small crowd was huddled around him. It must have just happened. There was nothing I could do for the poor sod, so I slipped away before the police arrived. I couldn't afford to hang about and allow myself to be seen. For all I knew, the thugs who killed him could still be there, waiting to see who MacQuillan was planning to meet."

"And you have no idea what MacQuillan discovered?" Gregory pressed.

"Frankly, he wasn't very coherent. He was in a rush and rather terse, as if he was afraid someone might be listening. He mumbled something about Poseidon and my mole. It didn't make a lot of sense."

Emmeline sucked in her breath. "Poseidon?" Her glance snaked over to Gregory and then slid back again to meet Carstairs's perplexed gaze.

Carstairs leaned forward, alert. "Yes, Poseidon. Why? What do you know about it?"

Gregory was the one to respond. "Nothing, except that we overheard Rallis and Lord Starrett having a heated argument about Poseidon."

Carstairs slumped back. Lord Starrett and Rallis? Bloody, bloody hell. What the devil were they doing mixed up together? He groaned inwardly when he thought of Fiona. It would come as a tremendous shock.

"Perhaps Poseidon is what Anastasia Tarasova was going to tell me about, but she was murdered before she had the chance," Emmeline ventured.

"Yes," Carstairs mused, "but up until this moment I was dead certain Rallis killed her. What you've just told me puts a completely new complexion on the matter. It may very well have been Lord Starrett."

CHAPTER 29

An oppressive silence pressed in around them as Emmeline, Gregory, and Carstairs contemplated the exceedingly real possibility that Lord Desmond Starrett, peer of the realm, former diplomat and art collector, was a murderer.

"It's hard to imagine Lord Starrett as a killer," Emmeline observed.

"Darling, by now you should know that murderers hide behind all sorts of masks," Gregory countered. "Haven't we seen that in the past few months?"

She shivered involuntarily. Indeed, they had. "I'm up to here"—she raised her hand to just below her chin—"with murderers, and traitors, to last me a lifetime." She turned to Carstairs. "Could any of this be connected to your mole?"

"It's looking increasingly likely, especially in view of the fact that Tarasova's father is a high-ranking officer in the GRU, Russia's military intelligence service." Carstairs ran a hand distractedly though his hair. "But at this stage, I'm at a loss to see the link between Tarasova's murder and Rallis's Poseidon."

"Don't forget that David Copperthwaite, the prosecutor

in Rallis's murder trial, met his untimely end as well. London seems to be littered with dead bodies tonight," Gregory pointed out morosely.

"How could I forget that delightful little fact," the other man snapped. "Your Superintendent Burnell would be quite happy to hang both murders around my neck." Then his tone softened. "Sorry. That was just my nerves talking. I haven't had much sleep in the last week. For the moment, perhaps it's better that Burnell thinks I'm guilty."

"How can you say that?" Emmeline shot back, out-raged. "You're an innocent man."

Carstairs allowed himself a wry smile. "Because if the police are focusing on me, it lulls our quarry into a false sense of security. Besides I do my best work in the shadows." His glance flickered to Gregory. "Just like your husband, from what I understand."

Gregory smoothed down the corners of his mustache and inclined his head slightly, accepting the compliment.

"Yes, well," Emmeline replied sullenly. "That was in the past. Gregory has promised that there will no more secrets between us from now on." She gave her husband a pointed look. "Isn't that right, darling?" Her tone was sweet, but there was an edge to it.

A smile tugged at the corners of Gregory's mouth. "Absolutely. As you can see, marriage changes a man," he told Carstairs.

"It had better change you," Emmeline muttered under her breath.

Carstairs bit back a grin. Then his mood sobered. "To get back to our problem…"

Gregory cut him off. "*Our problem*? You mean *your* sordid mess, don't you?"

Emmeline scowled at him. "Gregory." The single word was infused with reproach.

Carstairs sighed. "I need your help." He appealed to

Emmeline, who was obviously the more sympathetic of the two. "My current status as prime suspect rather limits my ability to pursue Rallis and Poseidon. But you can. It's your job to ask questions. Will you help me?"

"Yes," she replied without hesitation, as any good journalist worth her salt would.

"No," Gregory overruled her in a crushing tone.

She rounded on him, her dark eyes full of fire. "We've had this discussion before. And in any case, I was already working on the article about Rallis's trial. Tarasova's murder and the mysterious Poseidon are merely new leads that will allow me to broaden its scope."

"Emmy, are you stark raving mad? You might as well paint a target on your back."

"Don't be ridiculous."

"Stubborn woman," he grumbled. "Tomorrow we get a divorce."

She crossed her arms over her chest. Her chin jutted in the air. "Fine."

Before the argument escalated further, Carstairs cut in, "Look, Longdon, I understand your misgivings."

"Misgivings? Hmph. That's the height of under-statement. You want to make my wife…"

"Soon to be ex-wife. Remember?" Emmeline murmured truculently.

He chose to ignore this dig and went on, "You want to make my wife a pawn in your little game. Why not go to the *éminence grise* himself? We both know Villiers is a master of deception. He put this whole bloody thing in motion. He should be the one to extricate you from it."

"He can't. If Villiers makes the slightest move to help me, my cover is blown and we've lost our chance to get the mole. All my work over the past three years will have been for naught. I can't—I won't—allow that to happen. I'm on my own for the time being."

"Except that you want to draw my wife in to do your dirty work for you. Not very sporting, old chap."

Carstairs grinned. "If it makes you feel any better, I think the unique—skills, shall we say?—that you acquired in your past life could be of use in this situation as well. Not to mention your current position as Symington's chief investigator. So what do you say? Will you help me get the bastard?"

Although he spoke to Carstairs, his eyes locked on Emmeline's face. "I thought you would never ask."

ഈഈഈ

They all agreed that the safest thing would be for Carstairs to remain at the house for whatever was left of the night. Despite his protests, Emmeline insisted on making up the guest bedroom for him. However when she and Gregory awoke after a fitful few hours of sleep, he was gone. He had left a note saying that he would be in touch.

Emmeline plumped back down on the bed and showed the note to Gregory. She frowned. "Where do you think he's gone?" she asked.

He sat up and dropped his arm around her shoulders. "Don't worry, Emmy. Carstairs is a big boy. He knows how to take care of himself. He probably went to see Acheson."

She searched his face. "I hope Hugh heeded our advice and takes Philip into his confidence. He needs someone he can trust. Aside from us and Sabrina, that is."

In their long conversation in the wee hours of the morning, Carstairs had suddenly become Hugh. No longer a stranger or adversary, but rather a comrade-in-arms.

"Acheson is discretion itself. He'll know what to do." Gregory buried a kiss among her tousled curls. "By the way, the divorce is off. For the moment."

A glimmer of amusement entered her dark eyes, as she nestled against his chest. "Oh, yes? What if I want to move forward with the proceedings?"

His mouth twitched into a roguish grin as he looked down at her. "Ah, then you're out of luck, darling. Divorces are not granted on the first Saturday of the month. It's the law."

He felt her warm breath against his neck as she chuckled. "The law. You do talk a lot of rubbish. The long and the short of it is that I'm stuck with you, Mr. Longdon."

"I'm afraid so," he conceded philosophically. "You'll simply have to learn to make the best of it." He sighed melodramatically. "As will I. As will I."

She swatted his arm. "Watch your step. You don't know how good you have it."

"Good? Imagine my shock when I discovered that I married a modern-day Boadicea, who runs headlong into danger wielding nothing more than her mighty pen. I shudder to think what you consider bad."

"You're treading on thin ice again," she cautioned as she tilted her head back to gaze up into his face.

"How about a truce?" he suggested, as he covered her mouth with his and drew her down against the pillows.

She returned his kiss with enthusiasm, but broke free—reluctantly—from his arms after a few moments and stood up, her movements full of purpose. Slightly breathless, she told him, "I have to do some work on the story. If I succumb to your tender ministrations, we'll never get out of bed today."

A smug smile creased his features making him irresistible. "Would that be so bad?" He patted the sheets, which still held the impression of her body.

If he continued to look at her that way, her resolve would melt. How could one man be so devilishly attract-tive? It really was not fair. She felt herself wavering. No. She shook her head and drew upon every ounce of willpower.

"When we're dealing with murder and treason, it would be exceedingly indulgent. I'm going to do some work. And you should do so as well. You must have at least one old crony that you can contact."

With that she flounced out of the room and scurried to the bathroom before her noble inclinations evaporated.

To her chagrin, his soft laughter trailed after her.

CHAPTER 30

Emmeline and Gregory were not the only ones who found themselves working on that lovely November morning. Burnell had been summoned by Assistant Commissioner Cruickshank at the crack of dawn—not that he had really acknowledged the transition from night to a new day. He'd barely crossed the threshold of his flat in Battersea, when his mobile began vibrating in his pocket. He had let loose a fluent string of curses, when he had seen Cruickshank's number. Foregoing a greeting, the Boy Wonder issued an order that the superintendent present himself at his office at eighty-thirty sharp.

And here he sat two and a half hours later, no sleep, his eyes red and scratchy, and his ulcer rumbling in protest at man's inhumanity to man.

It was petty he knew, but he derived a small stab of pleasure from the fact that the Boy Wonder looked far from his usual neatly pressed best. Then he reproached himself. No matter what he felt about his boss—the list was growing by the day and not in a good way—the man had lost his stepfather the night before. No one should have his life snatched away from him. At the station, the details of David Copperthwaite's death trickled to his ears.

Apparently, the highly respected barrister had been strangled in his office. Not content with this violence, the killer had ransacked the place. They would have to wait until Copperthwaite's secretary sifted through the mess to determine if anything had been removed.

Burnell cleared his throat. "My condolences, sir," he mumbled.

Cruickshank blinked. A hollow, haunted look shadowed his brown eyes. "Yes, thank you," he replied awkwardly. "As you can imagine, it's a rather difficult time. My mother"—a pained sigh escaped his lips—"My mother is taking it quite hard. The doctor gave her a sedative. I hope she can get some sleep. David was a good, kind man. He came into my life when I was twelve, a tricky age. But I had been so happy when my mother had found him. She had been alone for three years."

He fell silent for several minutes. Burnell could see that he was attempting to master his churning emotions. When Cruickshank had found his voice again, his tone had hardened. "We have to get the bastard who killed him. Drop all your other cases and make this your top priority."

The superintendent shifted his bulk in his chair. "Sir…"

Cruickshank slapped his fist on the desk, a departure from his cultivated air of staid solidity. "That is an order, Burnell. For once, I don't want any insubordination. Do I make myself clear? The Copperthwaite murder is your *only* case, until the culprit is apprehended."

Burnell gripped his knees hard and counted to ten. He exhaled a long breath. "Sir, with respect, that is not reasonable nor is it wise. You must see it yourself," he suggested calmly. "The public will perceive it as preferential treatment. Aside from that, certain facts came out in our interviews last night that lead me to believe that Copperthwaite's death is connected to Anastasia Tarasova's murder. It's too much of a coincidence that the two were killed the same night."

Cruickshank leaned back in his chair and steepled his fingers over his stomach. "What facts?" the assistant commissioner said at last.

Good, thought Burnell, *at least the Boy Wonder is listening. I'm in with a chance.*

"The biggest tie between Copperthwaite and Tarasova is Noel Rallis."

The assistant commissioner drew in a ragged breath. "Rallis," he snarled. "I shouldn't be surprised that he's at the bottom of this nasty business. It's his style. Vicious and lethal." He folded his hands on his desk. "I had just started interviewing Miss Kirby." He shook his head. "I mean Mrs. Longdon and her husband, when I was called away last night. She told me about the argument she overheard between Tarasova and Rallis, and her agreement to meet Tarasova later in the master bedroom. What else did you discover?"

Burnell related the tense conversation between Lord Starrett and Rallis about their secret dealings, as well as the latter's threats to prevent Starrett from backing out. "It's obvious that Rallis is blackmailing Starrett."

Cruickshank shook his head in disapproval. "Lord Starrett. I must say that this is all rather distasteful. However, as you are well aware, this is all hearsay evidence. We'd be laughed out of court, if we brought this to the Crown prosecutor. We need something concrete to link the two. We need to find out what this Poseidon matter is."

Burnell nodded. "I have Finch digging into a couple of leads." He paused. "Something solid we *do* have, sir, is this fellow Hugh Carstairs. MI5 terminated him after a botched mission resulted in the assassination of a Russian defector. Rumors were swirling about that Carstairs was the one who betrayed him to the Russians. He went underground for six months and then resurfaced on the international stage as a killer-for-hire. Emmeline Kirby and her sister, Sabrina Royce, caught Carstairs in locus quo with Tarasova's dead body. He knocked out Philip Acheson and escaped before we arrived on the scene. Carstairs is currently at large."

"Hmm. I agree this Carstairs fellow is quite likely our man," the assistant commissioner concurred, "but how can we tie him to both Tarasova *and* my stepfather?"

The superintendent permitted himself a brief smile. "That's thanks to Miss Kirby again. During her conversation with Rallis earlier in the evening, he boasted that the Crown had no evidence and that his case would be ultimately dismissed. What happens virtually the next minute? Copperthwaite is found strangled."

"So you think that Rallis hired Carstairs for the hit on my stepfather and Tarasova?"

Burnell nodded. "In one night, Rallis's two greatest threats disappear. In the case of your stepfather, at the very least, the trial will be delayed for months as a new prosecutor will have to start all over again."

"Rather a risk, though," the Boy Wonder remarked.

"Rallis thrives on risk and flouting the law."

"True." The assistant commissioner pushed his chair back and rose. "Right, Burnell. You've made your point. Go ahead and pursue the two cases in tandem."

The superintendent got to his feet as well. "Thank you, sir."

"I can't involve myself with the investigation for obvious reasons, but I want a report on my desk every morning. I want to be kept fully in the loop. Any new piece of evidence, I want to know about it at once."

"Of course, sir. That goes without saying."

Cruickshank gestured with his chin at the door. "Off you go then. You have a killer to catch."

∽∾∽

Emmeline was restive and irritable when she walked into her office on Monday. She turned on her computer with an angry flick of her wrist. She hadn't been able to uncover any new leads over the weekend. Gregory had spoken to several "old friends," but had met with only a modicum of success. He had slipped from bed early this morning, mumbling something vague.

She bit her lip as she stared at her monitor. Her e-mails became a blur before her eyes. What bothered her most of all was that they hadn't heard from Hugh in the past two days. She reasoned that they would have heard something if he was in trouble. Or would they? Had he tried to contact Sabrina again? He said he wouldn't. Had he spoken to Philip? She hoped he had. Philip was a man of integrity. Someone Hugh could trust with his life. She would ring Philip later.

In the interim, she had a story—well, two stories that were intertwined—to write. That made it difficult to find where one ended and the other began. What she did know was that Rallis was at the center of it all. And Lord Starrett, she reminded herself. She couldn't forget him. *Lord Starrett*. She shook her head. Why was it that those with influence in this world were never satisfied? They always wanted more, whether it was power or money, or both.

What were Rallis and Starrett mixed up in? She had to find out what Poseidon was. She was certain that it was the key that would unlock everything. But where should she begin? She leaned her head back against the chair and closed her eyes. Her mind replayed the argument the two men had in Starrett's study, trying to pick up on even the smallest lead that she could follow up.

There has to be something, she told herself. *They were*

angry. Therefore, their guard was down. They had no idea Gregory and I were listening.

Rallis had mentioned a name when he was taunting Starrett. What was it?

Her eyes flew open. She sat up straight in her chair. *Basil Treadgold.*

Her mouth curved into a smile, as her fingers reached for her keyboard. She started tapping away. Aloud to her empty office, she said, "Well, Mr. Treadgold, who are you and what do you know about Lord Starrett's secrets?"

დოდ

Philip halted, his espresso halfway to his mouth, when Boris Petrenko entered the Caffè Nero directly opposite Trafalgar Square that afternoon. He watched as the Russian cultural attaché's gray eyes roamed around the coffeehouse until they finally settled on Philip's face. Petrenko pushed his steel-rimmed spectacles higher up the bridge of his nose and wended his way toward Philip's table, which was in the back under the window that overlooked the back of Admiralty Arch.

The Russian gave a curt nod. "Philip."

Philip rose and extended a hand out of politeness. "Boris, I'm surprised they let you off your leash. A bit out of your way, isn't it? What's the matter? The coffee at the embassy wasn't up to par today?"

A muscle in the Russian's jaw twitched. "I didn't come for the coffee." He cast a glance to his right and left. "I need to talk to you."

"Make an appointment with my secretary," Philip replied, as he bent down to gather up his attaché case.

Petrenko put a raising hand on his forearm. "Please. What I have to say is unofficial. No one knows I've come to see you. I made certain I was not followed. My car is waiting outside." He waved toward the front of the coffeehouse.

Philip glimpsed a black limousine with tinted windows illegally parked along the curb. "Your driver will get a ticket."

"It's important," Petrenko hissed. "It's about Anastasia."

At the mention of the ballerina's name, Philip's ears pricked up. "Why come to me? The Foreign Office is not involved." He lowered his voice. "This is strictly a police matter. If you have information about her murder, go see Superintendent Burnell."

"That's out of the question and you know it. Philip, please hear me out and then you can make up your mind," Petrenko begged.

Philip's instincts told him to walk away and not look back. However, one tiny corner of his intellect admitted to being intrigued.

He held the other man's gaze. The low buzz of conversation around them filled the air. Finally, Philip threw up his hands in resignation. He glanced at his watch. "Right, I only have half an hour to spare. So whatever it is, you had better talk fast."

Petrenko gave a grateful nod. Neither spoke as they wended their way toward the door and out onto the pavement. As they approached the car, Philip heard a faint click as the driver unlocked the back door.

The Russian entered first and Philip settled himself onto the back seat beside him. The car smoothly merged with traffic as it made a right onto Whitehall.

The imposing triple archway that leads into King Charles Street and the Foreign Office slid passed the window as did Number 10, the prime minister's residence.

"Where are we going?" Philip asked in fluent Russian as the car turned onto Westminster Bridge, leaving the

Parliament behind.

Petrenko, a ghost of a smile on his lips, patted Philip's knee. He responded in his mother tongue. "Don't worry. We're not kidnapping you. We know Laurence Villiers would make a big stink if you suddenly disappeared."

"I don't think he'd notice," Philip muttered under his breath. But at the same time, he was more than a tad irritated by the fact that Petrenko knew about his connection to Villiers, and by extension, to MI5. It was not supposed to be public knowledge.

He eyed the Russian warily as the limousine rumbled over the bridge and toward the streets of Lambeth.

"What do you want, Boris?"

Petrenko, highly trained FSB officer that he was, didn't flinch under the intense scrutiny. He exhaled a long breath and plunged in. "I don't know who killed Anastasia, but I think I know why. It has to do with her father."

"Her father? He's not even in London."

"No," Petrenko conceded, "But he will be soon. Aleksei, my oldest and dearest friend, is"—he swallowed hard—"forgive me. This is extremely difficult for me. Aleksei is going to defect."

"*What*?" Philip exploded. "Is this some sort of a joke?"

The Russian shook his head. "I assure you it is the truth." One eyebrow quirked upward. "Villiers did not tell you? I'm surprised."

Philip's hands curled into tight fists. "Why would Villiers tell me anything? I work for the Foreign Office," he replied with bravado in a vain attempt to maintain the carefully constructed façade.

Petrenko cocked his head to one side. "Really, Philip. The tensions between our two countries make it impossible to completely trust one another, I accept that. But I thought that at the very least we had mutual respect."

He was right about one thing, Philip thought. There was

nothing that he trusted about him.

"Aleksei is supposed to come over in two weeks. The preparations are in the final stages."

Philip ran a hand through his hair. If this was true—and it was a very big *if*—Anastasia could have been murdered as a warning to her father. It was something Putin wouldn't hesitate to do to make those foolish enough to cross him aware that he knew everything and he was coming for them.

"For argument's sake, let's say I believe you. Why are you telling me? Aren't you supposed to be one of the cogs that diligently work in the shadows to keep the Kremlin's dirty business running like a well-oiled machine? Or is this merely a fishing expedition to find out details of your friend Aleksei's defection, so that the boys from Moscow can snatch him before he sets foot on English soil? You must admit that from my vantage point, your motives are more than a little suspicious."

"In this case, friendship means more to me than country. Aleksei saved my life when we were boys, I must ensure that the defection goes as planned—whether I agree with it or not. I'm taking a risk coming to you because I thought you were an honorable man." He clutched Philip's sleeve. "Whatever you think about me doesn't matter. Please do everything you can to make sure Aleksei gets to England. You have the connections. *Use them.* Also, I urge you to help heal a grieving father's heart by seeing that Anastasia's killer is found. You must realize that it was someone at the party."

The car unexpectedly drew to a halt and Philip looked up in surprise to see that they were back already. Petrenko glanced at his watch. "As promised, I only took half an hour of your precious time."

Philip opened the door and stepped out onto the pavement in front of the archway that led into King

Charles Street. Petrenko rolled down the window. He leaned his head out and switched back to English, "When you talk to Villiers, give him my best."

He tapped on the window that divided the front seat from the back. The car engine roared into life again. "Oh, just one more thing." His mouth curved into a mocking smile. "The killer was not the only one at the party."

Philip's raised an eyebrow in askance. "No? I'll never guess who it was, so you might as well tell me, which clearly you are eager to do."

The Russian's grin grew wider. "Our mole in MI5 was there too, of course. I wonder if that was merely a coincidence."

Philip returned his smile. "I don't believe in coincidences. Who's the mole?"

Petrenko clucked his tongue. "Professional courtesy and détente only go so far. I'm afraid you'll have to find out on your own—if you can, which I doubt. It's been nice chatting, Philip. We must do it again soon. I'm certain we'll be seeing each other at the usual embassy parties."

He rolled up the window and the car disappeared into the traffic.

Philip felt soiled somehow. *That's what you get for rolling around in the mud with a smarmy Russian bastard*, Philip cursed silently.

The question was could he trust Petrenko? He didn't know the answer. On the other hand, deception was a spy's tool of the trade. It also could be found at the heart of any murder.

The more his mind tried to puzzle it out, the more troubling the questions became.

CHAPTER 31

Gregory's conscience was salved by the fact that he had dedicated the entire morning to Symington's business. No one had cause to complain about the chief investigator's diligence. Therefore, he reasoned, he was at liberty to disappear for a few hours to delve into darker matters, namely Rallis and Lord Starrett—a most unlikely pair of conspirators. Whatever they were involved in took precedence in his mind. Anastasia Tarasova's murder too, of course, but he was certain that would be resolved once the two men's sordid business was exposed.

That reminded him of something equally important and that had occurred the night of the Starrett's party, but which was overshadowed by the ballerina's untimely demise. It was something that required his attention without further delay. He hadn't had the opportunity to deal with it over the weekend. That was why his Jaguar was turning off Kensington High Street and onto the quiet streets of Holland Park in the middle of the afternoon.

He slid into a spot in front of their townhouse. He cast a casual glance around as he got out and locked the car. The park in the square was empty, save for a pair of birds serenading one another. The street was deserted as well.

He bounded up the steps and let himself into the house. He headed directly into the living room.

Ah, there it was. Emmy's clutch. The one she had the night of the Starrett's party. It was lying innocently precisely where he had tossed it on the console table behind the sofa, when they had come home to find Carstairs lurking in the dark.

Damn the man, Gregory grumbled to himself. He had smelled something fishy about Carstairs the minute he laid eyes on him on the boat in the Lake District. And now, things had become even more complicated because of his connection to Villiers. No matter what he did, he couldn't seem to get away from Villiers. Even when the man was recovering from his injuries, his tentacles still had a long reach. He sighed as he scooped up the clutch. Of course, he was going to have to go and see Villiers. He had no choice. But not just yet.

Now, there was something much more important that he had to take care of. He unzipped the clutch and his fingers froze. They hovered in the air for several seconds. It can't be. Perhaps his vision had momentarily blurred. He blinked twice. When he glanced down into the gaping interior, Emmy's notebook and pen, her lipstick, a compact mirror, and a few tissues, were staring up at him. But what *should* have been there—*was not*. Tarasova's ruby and diamond necklace.

She had still been fuming from her argument with Rallis and he had offered her some soothing words. She hadn't even noticed when he had slipped the necklace from her throat. Like a silk scarf it glissaded with barely a whisper off her skin. The corners of his mouth twitched at how easy it had been. He hadn't lost his touch. Later when the hue and cry had gone up after the discovery of the ballerina's body, he thought it best if the necklace were not found on his person. That's when he spied Emmy's clutch tucked behind the vase on the table in the corridor. How it came to be there he didn't know, but fortunately for him it was. He swiftly placed the necklace in the clutch with tender care. It had amused him no end when Oliver had the constables search him and found *nothing*.

It was no longer a laughing matter, though. The unsettling realization that the necklace had vanished disturbed him beyond words. His fingers rummaged—just for the sake of doing something as his mind reeled— among his wife's possessions one more time.

"Gregory, what are you doing home so early?"

The unexpected sound of Emmeline's voice jarred his senses. But he recovered quickly. He flashed a smile at his wife, holding her gaze as he discreetly dropped the clutch on the table on top of the post and crossed over to her.

He took her by the arms and kissed her cheek. "Darling, you are a vision of loveliness. I thought you were still at the paper. What are you doing home?"

She accepted his kiss, but her eyes raked his features. Oh, the suspicion that lurked in their dark depths.

"I asked you first."

"I came to check the post. A friend said he sent me a package."

Her eyes narrowed. "What friend and what package?"

He slipped his arm around her waist and drew her toward him. "Just a friend. No one you know…"

"What else is new," she mumbled under her breath. Then louder she said, "Am I going to have the pleasure of meeting this mysterious friend of yours?"

He threw his head back and chuckled. "There's no mystery about him. Actually, he's quite ordinary. He's not a very social chap." He made a dismissive gesture with one hand. "It was probably nothing important. Forget it."

She said nothing for a long moment. She simply stood there staring up at him. Then her gaze snaked toward the table and back again.

He tried to distract her. "Let's sit down." He led her to the sofa. Once they were settled side by side, he took one of her hands in his and said, "Now, tell me about your day and if you have any new leads. I haven't had a chance to pop into the station to check with Oliver about how things stand."

Her expression lost some of its sternness. She looped her arm through his elbow and rested her head against his shoulder. "You should stop teasing Superintendent Burnell. It only antagonizes him, particularly when he's in the middle of a murder investigation."

"Nonsense. Oliver loves being kept on his toes and I'm just the fellow to do it."

He heard a soft sigh escape her lips. "Right, I won't beat a dead horse." She sat up again. "I haven't been able to find out anything new and I'm terribly worried about Hugh."

He clenched his jaw. "He's probably closeted somewhere with Villiers plotting their next line of attack."

"You know he can't go anywhere near Villiers. He told you that Villiers can't help him now. I just keep praying that Hugh has gone to see Philip. I was going to ring Philip to have a quiet chat. As for new leads, I thought I might try to track down Basil Treadgold."

Gregory frowned, prompting her to explain further, "Remember Rallis mentioned the name when he was arguing with Lord Starrett. He said, 'I'm certain your good chum Basil Treadgold would give you the same advice.' It sounded more of a threat to me."

"I thought so too at the time," he agreed. "Starrett became quite defensive."

"Uh huh. Perhaps Treadgold can provide a clue to what Rallis and Starrett are up to, as well as Rallis's furtive trips up to Scotland."

He squeezed her hand. "Wait a minute. I seem to remember that Starrett has a rambling old family pile up in Scotland. How much do you want to wager it's on the Isle of Mull?"

She sat bolt upright, her cheeks flaming. "I'll check, but I think your instincts are spot on." She clutched his sleeve. "We have to tell Hugh. This might be the break he needs to nail Rallis." In the next instant, a crestfallen expression snuffed out her excitement. "If only we could get in touch with Hugh."

"Emmy, he's all right. Talk to Acheson. Tell him our theory."

"What are you going to do in the meantime?"

"I have a friend…"

She interrupted, "Another one among a seemingly endless circle."

He grinned and trailed his finger along her jawline. "I can't help it if I'm a popular chap."

She shrugged her shoulders in resignation. "Anyway how can this friend help?"

"My friend"—he paused to search for the right word—"dabbles in a lot of areas. He's quite well-connected. He hears things. If he doesn't know what Rallis is up to these days, he'll do everything in his power to find out."

"How can you be so certain? We have to be exceedingly careful."

"Don't worry, Emmy. My friend is discretion itself. He's Greek. He emigrated to England as a young man. He's a proud man. Proud of his heritage. Proud of his success here in London. But, the one thing that makes his stomach turn is Rallis. He despises Rallis with a passion."

"At least your friend appears to be sane. Why does he hate Rallis so much?"

"Because Rallis had his son killed and he's been waiting for just the right moment to make him pay."

Emmeline shivered involuntarily. "Oh, I see. Your friend sounds rather...*dangerous*."

"The only one who has anything to fear is Rallis."

∽∾∽

When Gregory entered the Aegean Dream, the elegant Greek restaurant on King Street a short walk from Covent Garden, the hushed murmur of conversation and clinking glasses floated to his ears. Waiters wended their way between tables to take orders. The most delicious smells wafted from the kitchen, tantalizing his nose and making his mouth water. It had been some time since he had visited Stavros Constantinides's establishment, which had received that most coveted of honors: three stars from Michelin.

A smile touched his lips when he spotted his old friend. Constantinides, a man of sixty-six with a head of thick white hair and dressed as always in an immaculately cut dinner jacket, had just come out of the kitchen and cast a glance around the restaurant to determine whether his patrons were enjoying themselves. His onyx eyes widened in surprise and a smile spread across his broad face, when they fell upon Gregory.

He hurried across the floor, a smile stretching from ear to ear.

He pressed Gregory's extended hand between both of his and pumped it up and down. "Gregory, it's good to see you. It's been a long time. Come sit down." He waved to a nearby corner table. "We'll have a glass of wine."

"I'm afraid I can't stay long. My wife's waiting for me at home."

Constantinides halted in mid-stride and clapped him on the back. "Wife? When did you get married? I thought you were a confirmed bachelor."

"Actually, Emmy and I were married only last week."

"Newlyweds." Constantinides rubbed his hands together in delight. "Marvelous. She must be an extraordinary woman, if she's managed to melt your heart. I must meet her. I insist you bring her here one night soon. I will have the chef prepare a feast for her."

Gregory chuckled as he lowered himself into the chair his friend indicated. "Emmy would love to meet you."

Constantinides hailed a waiter. "Bring a bottle of Assyrtiko," he ordered.

As the waiter scurried away, Gregory said, "Assyrtiko. The best Greek wine from Santorini. I feel honored."

"What do you expect me to serve to my good friend? We Greeks are known for our hospitality." Constantinides raised his glass in the air. "To your marriage. May it be long and full of love."

Gregory inclined his head, accepting the good wishes. "You haven't changed, Stavros. Still as generous and kind as ever."

His friend modestly shrugged off the compliment. They reminisced as the waiter poured out two glasses of the crisp white wine. He left the bottle and a plate of rich brown and black olives on the table between them. They took a few moments to savor the wine.

Gregory popped an olive into his mouth, followed by a sip of wine, and appreciated how two flavors melded together on his palate. He took another sip of wine and put his glass down. He stared into its golden depths as he twirled the stem between his fingers.

Constantinides broke the silence. "Gregory, I can tell that something is praying on your mind, so tell me why you've come to see me."

Gregory lifted his eyes and searched the features of his friend's broad face. While it was true that Constantinides outwardly hadn't changed too much—perhaps there were a few more lines fanning out from the corners of his eyes and the ones that bracketed his mouth were a bit deeper—but the loss of his son had clearly taken a toll. It pained him to see the haunted sadness that had lurked in Constantinides's eyes, where there had always been joy and laughter.

Gregory smoothed down the corners of his mustache and leaned back in his chair. There was no point beating about the bush. "It's about Rallis."

A heavy silence pressed in on them. He watched as his friend's fingers curl, one by one, until his fists became tight balls with the skin distended across the knuckles. A muscle pulsed along his jaw and his lips were drawn into an ugly sneer.

"I wouldn't come to you, unless it was important."

Constantinides's voice was hoarse when he replied at last, "Yes, I know. You are not a cruel man. Not like that bastard, who drew my Yanis into his dirty businesses and then spit him out. You know what Yanis means in Greek?"

Gregory shook his head. "It means God is merciful." Constantinides's huff of laughter was infused with all of the pain of a still-grieving father. "It's ironic, isn't it? God played a despicable trick when he put Yanis in Rallis's path. It's not like the old days. When we were both still in the game, we never hurt anyone. We only stole from those who wouldn't miss things too much." He shook his head and pursed his lips. "All this violence. It's a different world today." He took a gulp of wine.

"That's why I thought you might like to help me to bring down Rallis."

Constantinides sat up straighter, all his senses alert. "I'd like to kill Rallis, but that would make me no better than the animal that he is and I still wouldn't have Yanis. Therefore, I'm prepared to do anything in my power to destroy him."

Gregory leaned his head across the table and dropped his voice to a conspiratorial whisper, "That's the spirit."

In broad terms, he briefly related to Constantinides everything they had learned about Rallis's trips up to Scotland, his connection to Lord Starrett, the murders of Tarasova and David Copperthwaite, and Poseidon.

Constantinides nodded, when he had finished. "Yes, I saw in the papers about that Russian ballerina and the Crown prosecutor. It definitely sounds like Rallis."

"But do you know what he's up to with Starrett? It sounds like Rallis has something on him."

Constantinides snorted a laugh. "Rallis is not above blackmail. In fact, I believe it is an integral part of his business strategy." He took a contemplative sip of wine. "If a man like Lord Starrett—an aristocrat, an MP, a former diplomat—is mixed up with Rallis, it can only mean that there is something so bad in his past that he's willing to do anything to make sure no one ever finds out." He rubbed his chin. "Unfortunately, he wasn't careful enough since he's been forced to do Rallis's bidding. It's very interesting, though."

"Yes, well, interesting or not, we're still completely in the dark. Any ideas what Poseidon could be?"

Constantinides shook his head. "No clue. But don't worry." He put out a hand and gave Gregory's forearm a squeeze. "I will talk to a few of our old friends. Somebody has to know something. In the world we came from, there are always whispers. We'll get to the bottom of it."

He permitted himself a smile. For the first time since they started this tense conversation, Constantinides appeared to relax. Almost like his old self.

"Thanks, Stavros. I knew I could rely on you. However, I needn't tell you to be careful. If Rallis gets even the merest whiff that…"

Constantinides's face took on an aggrieved expression.

"Stop fussing like a mother hen. I may not be in the game anymore, but I do know how to be discreet. I'll ring you tomorrow." He flapped a hand at him. "Now, go home to your wife."

CHAPTER 32

When Philip entered the antechamber of his office the next morning, two female faces glanced up. One was Pamela, his secretary, who murmured "Good morning" and reminded him of the meetings he had scheduled for the day. The other was Emmeline. She was smiling at him as she rose to her feet. He recognized that smile. It was a smile that sought to soften him up and put him slightly off balance, before she started firing off questions. If he wasn't careful, she'd wheedle out of him in five minutes his illuminating discussion with Boris Petrenko. And he couldn't have that. At least not until he had chance to ascertain whether it was true that Aleksei Tarasov was planning to defect.

"Good morning, Philip. Pamela said you can spare me a few moments."

He threw a pointed look at his secretary. "Oh, did she? You're sacked, effective immediately."

However, this directive lacked any hint of rancor. Therefore, Pamela shrugged one shoulder and calmly treated it in the manner it deserved. "Yes, Mr. Acheson, as you say." She came around the desk. "I'll get a tray with tea, shall I? You and Mrs. Longdon can go on through. I've left the file with your notes for your meeting with the Foreign Secretary on your desk so that you can review them."

"Right, thank you," he said as he ushered Emmeline toward his office ahead of him. Before he followed her in, he tossed over his shoulder, "Don't think your efficiency will change my mind." This was punctuated with a smile.

Pamela returned his smile. "Of course, not, Mr. Acheson. I know how set in your ways you are."

Philip chuckled to himself as pressed the door closed behind him and crossed to his desk. He slid into his chair and stared across at Emmeline's eager face. She was perched on the edge of her chair, her notebook already open.

She opened her mouth to say something, but he raised a hand to forestall her. "Whatever information you want to know…"

"How do you know I want information? I could merely have popped in to say hello," she commented airily.

Philip cocked his head to one side and lifted an eyebrow. "Really, Emmeline. If that were the case, you could have picked up the telephone or dropped by the house. Instead, you ambush me in my office so that I'm your captive audience."

She sniffed. "I resent ambush. You make me sound calculating and manipulative."

He leaned back and propped his elbows on his armrests. "Not in the least. Just dedicated to your job. An admirable quality. I respect that, but I have no answers for you." He gathered up his file and began perusing its contents.

"I haven't asked you any questions yet."

Philip closed the file again and folded his hands on the desk. "I have a fairly good idea why you're here."

There was an excited gleam in her eyes. "Do you? Does that mean that Hugh has come to see you and you'll help?"

His back stiffened. "Hugh? As in Hugh Carstairs?" He pinned her with his gaze. "Why would he come to see me?"

She swallowed hard and offered him a watery smile. "No *specific* reason. I just thought as you were old friends...he might...turn to you."

"Emmeline have you seen Hugh?" he asked her point blank.

"Well, we both saw him at the Starrett's party. Remember? So did Sabrina for that matter," she hedged.

"I mean *since* the party. A party where not just any woman was murdered, but the famous ballerina Anastasia Tarasova," he replied through clenched teeth.

An uncomfortable silence closed in around them.

"Emmeline," he prompted.

She gave an exasperated sigh. "All right. But promise me this goes no farther than this room. You have to promise."

"I promise nothing. This could easily become an international incident. Our relations with the Russians are particularly frosty just now. Tell me what you know and then I'll decide."

A rose stain crept up her cheeks and her dark eyes were kindling. "That's not fair," she snapped. "A man's life is at stake. Things are not what they appear."

He spread his hands wide. "I have no way of knowing that, do I?"

Emmeline slumped back in her chair and glowered at him mutinously.

Pamela chose that precise moment to tap on the door. The next instant, she appeared in the office with the tea tray. One glance at Philip and Emmeline telegraphed all she needed to know. She wordlessly pivoted on her heel, leaving them to their silent test of wills.

After an interval, Emmeline cleared her throat and shot

him a glance from under eyelashes. "This is ridiculous. It's not going to help either one of us find the answers we need to do our jobs. Truce?" she offered tentatively.

Philip's smile smoothed away the lines that had etched themselves upon his brow. "Truce."

The tension eased from Emmeline's body. All was right between them once again. And so, in this spirit of détente, she took a deep breath and plunged into the story Hugh had told them the night of the Starrett's disastrous party. She left nothing out. She had no choice. She needed his cooperation and, hopefully, he could provide some corroboration for her story. Or at least point her in the right direction.

Philip listened to her tale without interruption. With each word, his face darkened. When she had come to the end, he couldn't contain himself any longer. "Damn Villiers and his games."

"That was essentially Gregory's reaction too."

His head snapped up. "Longdon?" He searched her face.

"Yes, Gregory was quite upset, when he heard that Villiers was mixed up in this business. I don't quite understand the tension between them." She gave a resigned shrug. "But there it is."

Philip's body relaxed. He needn't have worried, there was no way Emmeline could know about Villiers and Longdon. But this new information about Hugh's elaborate mission to flush out the mole at MI5 set off alarm bells in the back of his mind.

"I knew at the time Hugh couldn't have been guilty of everything they said. It was just not on." He slammed his open palm on his desk. "I should have kept looking into the matter…"

"It does no good to reproach yourself in hindsight. Besides from what Hugh told us, Villiers did his best to torpedo your efforts when he saw that you were getting too close to the truth."

"But that's just it. We still don't know the truth. And now, Anastasia Tarasova's murder only serves to complicate matters. In more ways than you can imagine."

His thoughts strayed to his conversation the day before with Boris Petrenko about Aleksei Tarasov's impending defection. Who the devil is the mole? They had to find out. Fast. Otherwise, they would have another dead Russian on their hands.

Emmeline sat up straighter and flipped to a fresh page in her notebook, her pen poised. "I was open with you. Now, it's your turn. What do you make of Rallis and Lord Starrett?"

Philip reached a hand across the desk and gently pried the notebook and pen from her fingers. "Off the record from here out."

She opened her mouth to protest, but he raised his hand to forestall her. "Off the record or you leave now. It's entirely up to you."

She gave a reluctant nod and he returned her notebook, which she tucked into her handbag.

"I know MI5 has been trying to find something on Rallis for years. He's always been much too cozy with the Russians for anyone's liking. But he's as cunning as a fox. He knows our every move even before we're a shadow on the horizon."

"Obviously, the mole is tipping him off." Her voice rose an octave and there was an eager gleam in her eye.

"Don't get so excited. Hugh was burned because of the mole. That's why he's in the mess he's in today. We have to tread carefully. Otherwise, the mole is going to go so far underground we'll never find him."

"What if he's in plain sight?" she posited. She propped her elbows on the desk and leaned toward him. "What if

Starrett is the mole?"

Philip shook his head. "Impossible."

"Is it? Why? He has high-level connections and is privy to top secret information. He's a peer of the realm, an MP, which allows him to rub elbows with all sorts of people your average Englishman would never even get near. He was in Brussels for years acting as the NATO liaison. He was ambassador to Germany for two years. Think about it. Who would suspect a man like Starrett? Most men would envy him, especially with a young wife who is a former model hanging on his arm."

"It makes sense, in theory," Philip conceded, "but what could possibly have made the Russians turn him. There's never been even the slightest whisper of his sympathies in that direction."

"What if Starrett was coerced into working for them? What if they discovered something in his past? Gambling debts, an illegal business venture"—she threw up her hands—"I don't know. Or what if they trapped him with the old honeypot? It could be anything." She tapped the desk with her forefinger. "But it has to be something so bad that treason appeared a more palatable alternative to exposure. From what Gregory and I overheard, Rallis clearly is blackmailing Starrett. So why not the Russians?"

Philip nodded and lifted his eyes to hers. "Yes, I think you're right."

She allowed herself to preen for just a fraction of a second. Then, she became pragmatic again. "We have to find out *what* is Starrett's deep, dark secret. That and Poseidon. Any idea what Poseidon is?"

He leaned back and steepled his fingers over his stomach. "It means nothing to me."

"Could it be the code name of a MI5 mission?" she suggested.

"It's possible, but if it is I haven't heard of it."

A sigh of frustration escaped her lips. "We keep coming up with more questions and it's not getting us anywhere."

He glanced at his watch. "And, I regret that I'm going to have to put a halt to our conjectures for the moment or I'll be late for my meeting with the Foreign Secretary."

He stood and walked around the desk. He extended a hand and helped her to her feet. "I promise to do a bit of investigating. I'll also have a word with Villiers. He seems to be at the heart of things, as usual."

Emmeline hitched her handbag over her shoulder. "Right, that's all I can ask. I'll be doing the same on my end. Except speaking with Villiers. At least for the time being. But if I hit a dead end, rest assured I *will* be knocking on his door."

Philip smirked. "He'll be thrilled to see you."

She smiled at him as he escorted her to the door. "Good. Then he'll be more than happy to give me the answers I'm looking for and I'll be off on my merry way."

"Emmeline, I hate to wound your pride, but I don't think Villiers finds you quite as charming as the rest of us do."

She reached up and gave him a peck on the cheek. "I'll grow on him. You'll see."

"I doubt it." He took both of her hands in his and fixed his eyes on her face. "Promise me you'll be careful. Two people are already dead and if Rallis and the Russians are involved, then it is much worse than we initially believed. Besides, the boys would never forgive me if I allowed something to happen to Auntie Emmeline."

She smiled and squeezed his hands. "Don't worry. I'll be fine. Give the twins a great, big kiss from me and tell them Gregory and I will take them on an outing very soon."

"I don't dare tell them that. Maggie and I will never hear the end of it, until you appear on our doorstep. Better let it be a surprise."

She shrugged. "You know best." Then in all earnestness, she urged, "Please help Hugh. Superintendent Burnell and Sergeant Finch have him down as the prime suspect in the murders. We both know he didn't do it."

"I haven't the foggiest idea where he is. Even if I did, I can't interfere on that score. If I go to Burnell, it would blow Hugh's cover."

"Just promise to help him when he comes to you."

"*If* he comes to me."

She patted his arm. "He will. Despite his training, he can't fend for himself forever. We all need help at some point. Perhaps Villiers can do something."

"Perhaps," he murmured to her retreating back. "If Villiers feels so inclined. I wouldn't hold my breath, though."

CHAPTER 33

At about the time Emmeline was leaving Philip's office, Superintendent Burnell was ensconced at his desk at Scotland Yard going over the crime scene reports. He pushed up his glasses higher on the bridge of nose. First, he scoured every inch of the photos of the Tarasova murder, searching for something he might have missed the night of the Starrett's party. He shook his head. Nothing that immediately leaped to the eye.

He snatched up the file on the Copperthwaite murder and read the notes that Inspector Halliday had made. Halliday had been the senior officer on the case before Assistant Commissioner Cruickshank had put Burnell in charge of both murders.

Burnell nodded as he read. As usual, Halliday had been thorough. He put the notes down and turned to the photos of the Copperthwaite murder. Of course he and Finch had already visited the barrister's chambers, but he wanted a sense of the scene when the body was in situ.

He grunted to himself and slammed the file shut. Despite his thirty years on the force, he would never get used the cruelty and viciousness one human being could inflict on another. He leaned back and spun his chair around to stare out the window.

He swiveled back and forth as he stroked his beard. Two murders. One victim's neck was broken. The other was strangled. Both quick and professional, according to Dr. Meadows's postmortem reports.

Tarasova and Copperthwaite both were connected to Rallis, he mused. Rallis was swimming in pots of money. Enough to hire an army of assassins, if he wanted. But he only needed one. A man who had been hovering in the shadows from the outset: Hugh Carstairs, an ex-MI5 agent who had been trained in the art of killing. More importantly, not only was Carstairs at the Starrett home the night of the murder, he was caught in the master bedroom with the dead ballerina, whose body was still warm to the touch although her life had ebbed away. Carstairs then took Philip Acheson by surprise and scarpered. To kill David Copperthwaite?

Burnell nodded. *Yes, I'd say Carstairs was our man*, he thought. *Rallis hired him to get rid of his two biggest threats*.

He frowned and turned back to face his desk. It was all well and good *knowing* someone was guilty, but they needed evidence. They also needed to find Carstairs, who apparently had taken lessons from Houdini and vanished.

The sharp peal of the telephone interrupted these troubling ruminations. "Burnell," he growled.

"Superintendent Burnell, you might try to answer your phone in a more seemly manner. After all, you are a senior officer." Sally's clipped tones echoed in his ear.

Burnell tilted his head back and cursed silently at the ceiling. Sally was the last person he wanted to deal with just now. He took a breath and returned his attention to the call. "Sally, is that you?"

"You know who it is. So stop playing silly games."

He curled his right hand into a fist and replied through

gritted teeth, "Was there a reason you rang? Or did you simply want a chat? Because if you did, your timing is extremely poor. I'm up to my eyes in two murders."

"Oh, for Heaven's sake, you conceited and odious man, I wouldn't speak to you for a moment longer than is necessary. I have better things to do with my time."

"As do I. So what *precisely* do you want with me?"

"*I* want nothing from you. However, Assistant Commissioner Cruickshank would like to see you at once."

He groaned inwardly. No, not the Boy Wonder. Not today. He didn't think he had the strength.

"Did you hear what I said?" Sally asked.

"Loud and clear. Look, can you tell Cruickshank that I have nothing new to report? It would be best if he simply let me get on with things."

He heard her indrawn breath. "I most certainly will not tell the Assistant Commissioner something so...so lacking in professionalism and respect," she replied, her voice thrumming with outrage. "If you're not here in five minutes, I will come down to get you."

He dropped his head between his hands. "No, no. I wouldn't want you to pull a muscle getting up from your desk. Tell Cruickshank I'm on my way."

"See that you are," she snarled as she rang off.

Sally barely looked him in the eye as she ushered him into the assistant commissioner's office, which bothered him not in the least.

Cruickshank waved an impatient hand toward one of the chairs opposite him. "I don't have all day, Burnell."

"And I do?" the superintendent grumbled under his breath, "Chatting with you is a bloody great waste of my time."

Cruickshank's brown eyes narrowed with suspicion. "What was that?"

"I said that you're a great model of police efficiency." He crossed his fingers as he lowered himself into the chair. He hoped he sounded sincere.

The assistant commissioner's mouth curved into a smile. "Why, thank you, Burnell. It's gratifying to be looked up to by one's subordinates."

The superintendent choked back a laugh that threatened to erupt from his throat and merely nodded.

Cruickshank almost instantly returned to his officious manner and didn't appear to notice the Burnell's bemused expression. "Now, I can't rest on my laurels. What example would that set for the team?"

The team. Burnell sighed. How he hated Cruickshank's faux attempts to create an air of chumminess. It was quite silly. He was certain no one, from the most junior PC to those who had achieved his own rank, thought of the assistant commissioner as a "mate."

"Yes, sir. You were about to tell me why you wanted to see me," he prompted gently. "I have nothing new to report on either the Tarasova or Copperthwaite case. Finch and I are working on the Carstairs angle, but we haven't been able to find him."

He half-stood in preparation for making a swift escape.

Cruickshank's brow furrowed. "Sit down." The superintendent glumly obeyed, dropping heavily back into his chair. "Now then, I summoned you because unfortunately I have some bad news. Apparently someone has stolen all the files from my stepfather's chambers pertaining to the Rallis trial. To make matters a thousand times worse"—he pounded his open palm against his desk—"all the evidence that had been collected by the Met and stored here in the evidence room has *disappeared*, while all electronic files have been erased from the computer system."

Burnell sat up straight in his chair, his feet thumping

against the carpeted floor. "*What?*" he exploded. "This is a complete and utter disaster. How could any of this have happened?"

Cruickshank drummed his fingers on the desk. "I'm launching an investigation into the matter. But you haven't heard the best part yet." He took a deep breath and stared the superintendent directly in the eye. "In light of the distressing—and embarrassing—situation, the Crown Prosecution Service has no choice but to drop the case against Rallis."

The superintendent jumped to his feet. "Sir, you can't allow that. You must use your influence."

The assistant commissioner's jaw tightened and his brown eyes burned with fury. "I tried. God, how I tried." His voice dripped with bitterness. "I was told in polite, but forceful, terms that the matter is out of my hands and to move on."

"But that means Rallis gets away with murder and who knows what else." Burnell placed his palms down and leaned across the desk. "Let me bring him in, sir."

Cruickshank gave a curt shake of his head. "Out of the question."

"Sir, we have cause to bring him in. At the Starrett party, Rallis gloated to Emmeline Kirby that the trial would be dismissed. The same night, Copperthwaite is found strangled and his office ransacked. Now, everything connected with the case has mysteriously disappeared. Sir, let me bring him in. At the very least, we can make him squirm for a bit before his solicitor comes to his rescue. It might throw him off-kilter. Make him start to doubt all his elaborate plans. We'll watch him like a hawk and when he makes a mistake—which he inevitably will because of his bloody arrogance—we'll have him. It might even flush Carstairs out of the woodwork and we could kill two birds with one stone. Please, sir. Let me bring Rallis in."

Cruickshank pursed his lips. He held Burnell's gaze. After an interminable interval, he cleared his throat. "I want everything done by the book. If Rallis's solicitor files a lawsuit for police harassment, I will hold you personally accountable."

For the first time since Cruickshank became his boss, Burnell offered him a huge grin. "Thank you, sir. Your orders will be followed to the letter."

"See that they are. We both know Rallis is cunning as hell. I don't want this blowing up in our faces." He paused, his eyes anxiously searching Burnell's face. "You don't think that there's any chance Emmeline Longdon will retract her statement?"

The superintendent snorted. "You've met her. She's not the type to be intimidated."

"No," the assistant commissioner agreed cautiously. "She's the interfering type. I don't like the press under our feet. Especially Emmeline Longdon. She tends to make rather a nuisance of herself."

Burnell watched his boss's face contort into a scowl. He wondered if this display of annoyance was truly directed at the press. Or was it at himself because he had tried to chat up Emmeline the first time he met her and then, to his embarrassment, realized who she was? And that Longdon was her fiancé.

"Speaking of Longdon," Cruickshank suddenly said.

Burnell raised an eyebrow. *You are so transparent, Boy Wonder.*

He kept a straight face as he replied, "Were we discussing Longdon, sir? The years must be catching up with me because I don't recall that we were."

The other man made a dismissive gesture in the air with his hand. "You know how it is. When one thinks of one of them, automatically the other springs to mind. They always seem to be together."

"Well, they are married now, sir. It stands to reason."

"Yes." Cruickshank's jaw clenched.

My, my. Is that jealousy rearing its ugly head? Burnell mused.

"As policemen, we're here to uphold the law. Doesn't it bother you that a thief is the chief investigator at Symington's? The world has gone stark, raving mad."

"I find it deeply troubling, but there's nothing we can do about it. Longdon's never been caught. That's the problem."

"What about Tarasova's necklace? Longdon is the most likely suspect. Who else could it have tbeen?"

The superintendent grimaced. This was still a sore point. "I share your frustration, sir. Believe me. But I had two constables search him in front of a room full of witnesses. If he stole it, he didn't have it on him."

"Of course, he didn't have the necklace on his person. He's probably hidden it."

"The only place he could have hidden it was in the Starretts' house. Forensics and God's knows how many of us tramped through every room that night. We didn't find the necklace."

"Longdon has it. Bring him in for questioning too."

"Um, I don't think that would be wise. Rallis is justifiable. This wouldn't be."

Cruickshank grunted. "Damn the man. He's far too clever."

"That has always been my sentiment. Unfortunately, Longdon is the cross hard-working policemen everywhere have to bear."

CHAPTER 34

What is Starrett so desperate to keep hidden? Emmeline asked herself as she tapped her pen on her desk. *And what is Poseidon?*

These were the two issues that had preoccupied her mind ever since she had left Philip's office that morning. She had asked Anthea in the *Clarion*'s research department dig up everything the paper had on Starrett. Emmeline had told her to leave nothing out, even if it appeared inconsequential.

She glanced down at the file in front of her. Anthea had been extremely thorough. In an hour, she had produced a detailed profile. The file was arranged in reverse chronological order, by year, going back to when Starrett was in his early twenties. Emmeline quickly scanned through the most recent stories because they were fairly common knowledge. His secret had to go back at least three years. That was when Rudenko's defection went awry and Hugh was made the scapegoat to lull the Russians and their mole into a false sense of security.

She stopped flipping pages and halted at an article about Starrett's marriage to model Fiona Kendrick. Emmeline remembered that it had been big news. Everyone predicted that the marriage would never last. He was fifty-two. She was thirty-three. Clearly, she was after his money and he merely wanted a trophy wife.

Those with the sharpest tongues had said that Fiona could never hold a candle to the first Lady Starrett, a truly cultured and intelligent woman who died so young and tragically. These gossips could only conclude that, like all men, Desmond Starrett was weak and had succumbed to his baser, carnal instincts.

Thus far, from what Emmeline had observed at the party, Lord and Lady Starrett were happily married and loved one another. Of course, appearances could be deceiving. Starrett had only become bad-tempered with Fiona after his row with Rallis. But that was probably because he was rattled by Rallis's threat and he was lashing out at the first person who crossed his path.

These articles set Emmeline thinking about the Starrett's relationship and the circumstances surrounding the death of his first wife, Isabelle. How did she die? Natural causes? A long illness? From the murmurs swirling about at the time of Starrett's second marriage, there seemed to be unsettled questions—*suspicions?*—about Isabelle's death.

Emmeline's pulse started racing as she riffled the file for any articles from that sad period. Could Starrett have murdered his first wife? Was *that* what the Russians were holding over his head? A smile danced upon her lips. She was certain that she was on to a lead at last.

Ah, here it was. She propped her elbows on her desk and pored over the details of Lady Isabelle Starrett's untimely death at the age of twenty-seven. It had occurred at Rosemont Castle, the sixteenth-century tower house replete with turrets and gargoyles, and set within its own manicured garden on the Isle of Mull.

Hmm, the Isle of Mull again. Hugh has been buried

undercover there. Rallis has been making forays to the
island over the past several months. And there nestled in
the center is Rosemont, the seat of the Starrett's,
Emmeline mused as she read on. Coincidences always
made her suspicious.

The article revealed that young Isabelle had been a
twitcher, since was a girl. *Twitcher*? Emmeline asked
herself. Her question was quickly answered. A twitcher
was a bird watcher. Apparently, Mull was a haven for all
sorts of birds of prey, sea birds, otters, and other wildlife
such as red deer, hedgehogs, polecats, mink, and rabbit.
Isabelle was in heaven and took every opportunity possible
to dash off to the island. Armed with binoculars and
wellies, she loved nothing more than to tramp through the
woods near the castle and farther afield along the rocky
cliffs to the sea lochs, boggy marshes, sandy beaches,
moorlands, and mountains beyond simply to catch
glimpses of her favored species taking flight or nesting.
Her husband did not share her passion for bird watching,
so Isabelle went off on her own. It was not unusual for her
to leave early in the morning and return to the house well
after dark.

Until the day she did not come back.

The servants became frantic. Lord Starrett had been
delayed in London and would not arrive until the next
morning. A search party was hastily called together. Lady
Starrett was known to everyone on the island because she
always stopped to say hello or exchange a few words with
the islanders. No one could have been kinder or more
liked, and therefore everyone joined in the search.

They would have gone on all night without sleep or
food. The only thing that forced them indoors was the
storm that blew in and raged until the early hours of the
morning. At the first pearlescent glimmer of dawn's gray
approach, the search began again. It did not take long to

make the grim discovery. Isabelle, probably in her zeal to see one of her beloved birds, had slipped on the wet rocks and tumbled over the edge of cliff to her death. Her crumpled body lay in the sea loch below.

Lord Starrett was waiting in the hall at Rosemont Castle when the search party returned with heavy hearts. He had been informed by the housekeeper what had happened and anxiously awaited news from that moment on. He refused coffee and breakfast, instead choosing to pace back and forth in the hall. His lordship nearly collapsed when he was told of his wife's death.

The articles over the next few days were full of news about the brief police investigation, the coroner's finding of accidental death and the fact that Lady Starrett had been two months pregnant. Emmeline drew in a sharp breath when she read the latter. It brought up all the churned emotions about the baby she had lost bubbling to the surface. However, she swallowed hard and buried her personal heartache in the past once more, and forced herself to concentrate on the article in front of her about the preparations for Lady Starrett's funeral in London. There was nothing interesting about the funeral itself, but the day afterward it was reported that someone had spotted Lord Starrett on the Isle of Mull the day Isabelle had gone missing. Starrett dismissed this assertion, reiterating that he had been detained in London by debate on an important bill.

The whispers only grew a week later, when Lady Starrett's will was read and it emerged that she had left her entire, rather sizable, fortune to her husband. Suddenly, Lord Starrett was an extremely wealthy man because Isabelle, the daughter of a major British steel manufacturer, came into the marriage with a great deal of money.

Well, well, well. Who's been a naughty boy?

Emmeline closed the file. She would read the rest later about Lord Starrett's younger years, after his return to England from an extended period in Canada. Perhaps, there would be something about the friend Rallis mentioned, Basil Treadgold.

She pushed herself to her feet and crossed to the window, which overlooked the Thames and Tower Bridge. Normally, the view delighted her. Today, she saw nothing. The wheels of her mind were chasing thoughts.

Starrett had murdered Isabelle and the Russians had *kompromat*, or compromising material, to prove it, she thought. That was the only explanation that made any sense about why he would allow himself to be blackmailed into betraying his country. She bit her lip. But was it the same reason he working with Rallis? She didn't think so. From what she and Gregory had overheard of their row, it sounded as if the Russians knew nothing about Poseidon and the two men wanted to keep it that way. So that meant that Starrett had a *second* secret and somehow it found its way to Rallis's ears.

She shook her head. Didn't the silly man know that the truth always come out, no matter how hard one tries to keep it from seeing the light of day? Apparently not.

She went back to her desk and started jotting down notes. She would make some calls to try to get her hands on the police and coroner reports about Isabelle Starrett's death. Perhaps, Superintendent Burnell could grease the way for her. She had to get in touch with Lord Starrett's friend Basil Treadgold. She knew there was a risk that the man might slam the door in her face, but she was willing to take the chance. She needed answers. Besides, it wouldn't be the first time she encountered a recalcitrant source. And finally, in big block letters she wrote POSEIDON, underlining it three times for emphasis.

Poseidon niggled her brain the most. What could it be?

She turned to her computer and typed Poseidon. Of course, the first thing that popped up was that he was the Greek god of the sea. Terrific. Another Greek. Rallis was already bad enough. She was certain that ancient divine intervention would be of no help in this instance. She started scrolling down the page and then stopped.

What if Poseidon had something to do with the sea? And the Isle of Mull? She knew that the island was surrounded by the Sound of Mull in the north, the Firth of Lorn in the south and east, and the Atlantic Ocean in the west.

Her fingers hovered over her keyboard. The sea, she mused. Something maritime? Nautical? She typed the words *Poseidon* and *ship*, and held her breath.

The first thing her search yielded was HMS *Poseidon*. She clicked on the article link. As she started reading, she knew instinctively that she had found her answer. At last.

HMS *Poseidon* was among the 7,500 merchant ships carrying £125 billion worth of gold and other precious metals that had been sunk by German U-boats during the first and second World Wars. Predators in a marine jungle, the U-boats lurked in the waters off Ireland. The gold was being shipped by the British government to pay for munitions and goods. Most of it was being sent to the United States or other parts of the British Empire, primarily from Glasgow or Liverpool. To this day, the gold lay fathoms below the sea—untouched, abandoned, for all intents and purposes lost.

However, Britannia's Gold, a UK firm which had spent the last twenty-five years analyzing lost cargo at sea, planned to launch a salvage operation a few hundred miles west of Ireland, where three wrecks had been located. Naturally, the company had not disclosed the site fearing an attack by pirates. Meanwhile, the article went on to note that if the company did find anything, the government was technically the rightful owner of the cargoes. The company would be required to hand over any cargo recovered in British waters to a government official known as the Receive of Wreck, unless it negotiates another agreement.

Hmm, interesting. Emmeline slumped back in her chair as the wheels of her mind circled ever closer to the truth.

"Is it possible Rallis and Starrett found the ship?" she asked aloud. She put a hand to her mouth.

Could they be insane enough to believe they could remove the gold without anyone finding out? But how? Could that *be the reason for Rallis's trips up to Mull over the past few months? Is that why Anastasia Tarasova was murdered?*

She scrambled for her phone. She had to talk to Gregory. A little voice told her she should probably ring Philip and Superintendent Burnell first, but she ignored it. In this situation, her husband would know the best way to proceed. If only she could get in touch with Hugh too. *God where was that man?*

She impatiently brushed this last thought aside as she punched in Gregory's mobile number. She drummed her fingers on her desk.

One ring. Two rings. Three rings. Damn. She slammed down the receiver, when his voicemail picked up. What was Gregory up to?

She jumped to her feet. She had to do *something* with this knowledge. Correction hypothesis, albeit an educated hypothesis. She had to corroborate whether her suppositions—she freely admitted that they were wild at the moment—were true. Instinct told her that she was right.

She had to follow the trail to the gold. With any luck, it also would lead her to a killer. This sent a frisson slithering down her spine, but she shrugged off the fear and reminded herself that the truth was the most important thing. She couldn't cower in a corner simply because there was a little danger involved. In life, one had to take risks. But was her life worth the risk?

She made an impatient gesture with her hand. Of course, the truth and justice were worth it. Unless she was dead wrong.

No, she wouldn't allow herself to be. She grabbed her handbag and sailed out of her office, her mind on lost gold and murder.

CHAPTER 35

Rallis Shipping Group had its headquarters in one of those sleek steel-and-glass towers on the South Bank near Southwark City Hall. This reminded Superintendent Burnell, as he and Finch got out of the car, they weren't too far from the *Clarion*. Perhaps, they should pop in and see Emmeline, while they were in the area to find out whether Carstairs had been in touch. Although Burnell had a soft spot for her, he admitted that she might not tell him out of a misguided loyalty to protect the underdog. However in this case, the underdog was an international assassin. How could an intelligent and admired journalist like Emmeline turn a blind eye to the glaring truth?

He shook his head. He supposed it was because all humans had their faults and Emmeline was no exception. After all, look at how she had allowed herself to be dazzled by Longdon's charms. He exhaled a weary sigh. He didn't want to think about Longdon just now. Because if he did, Tarasova's missing necklace flew unbidden into his mind. And it gnawed at him unmercifully. He *would* recover it. Longdon was *not* going to get away with this crime.

"What was that, sir?" Finch asked, jarring him back to

the matter at hand.

He hadn't been aware that he had said anything aloud. That's what came of allowing his mind to linger on Longdon, even if for a fraction of a second. "Nothing," he muttered. "Let's go and make Rallis squirm a bit."

"Somehow I don't think that's possible. He strikes me as a chap who keeps himself well under control at all times. Always cool and calculating."

Burnell snorted. "Everyone makes mistakes, Finch. Never forget that. Men like Rallis are too arrogant for their own good. His overconfidence will be his downfall. I'm going to take a tremendous pleasure in picking up the pieces of his miserable life and throwing them behind bars."

Finch grinned as they crossed the lobby and headed for the bank of lifts. "Yes, sir."

They rode up in silence to the twentieth floor. Rallis Global Shipping's suite of offices occupied the entire floor. A pair of glass doors opened onto a spacious and bright waiting area.

The receptionist smiled at them from behind the desk as they walked in. "Good afternoon, gentlemen. How may I help you?"

Burnell and Finch flashed their warrant cards. "Detective Superintendent Burnell and Detective Sergeant Finch to see Mr. Rallis," Burnell replied curtly.

A crestfallen expression flitted across her pleasant features. "Oh, I see." She became flustered. "Did you have an appointment?"

The superintendent plastered a smile on his face. "We're the police. We don't need an appointment."

"Yes, of course. But you see…the thing is…" Her sentence trailed off.

"Is there a problem?"

"It's just that Mr. Rallis is not here."

"Right. Come on, Finch. We'll catch him at home."

They turned to go, but the receptionist called them back, "Wait, you don't understand. I'm afraid he's not at home either."

Burnell swung around slowly, his eyes narrowing. "What do you mean?"

"Mr. Rallis is out of the country. He left this morning for Athens. I believe he'll be back in a week. A fortnight at the most."

"*What*?" the superintendent exploded. "He's a susp"— he bit off the word *suspect* at the last moment—"How could Mr. Rallis have left town?" He bristled with indignation. "He was present in the house where Anastasia Tarasova was murdered. He may be a material witness."

Two rosy spots appeared upon the receptionist's cheeks. Their shade was deepening by the second under the superintendent's intense scrutiny. Her hand trembled slightly as she reached for her phone. "Perhaps, you'd like to speak with Melinda, Mr. Rallis's personal assistant? I'm certain that she would be able to provide any information you may need."

She offered the detectives a watery smile as she rang Melinda, without waiting for their consent. She covered the mouthpiece with one hand. "If you'd like to have a seat over there, please." She pointed to a cream-colored upholstered sofa, which appeared ultra-modern and none-too-comfortable in Burnell's opinion.

She turned her head to one side and in hushed tones hissed her evident distress to Melinda. She quickly returned the receiver to its cradle and smiled at them again. "Melinda will be with you in a moment."

The superintendent was in no mood to return her smile. He was fuming inwardly. He chose to remain on his feet, looming over the receptionist's desk, although God knew that this was not her fault.

Finch raised his eyebrows and stood stoically at his side, swaying slightly on the balls of his feet.

They didn't have to wait long. A tall woman with thick golden hair that fell in waves to her shoulders, clad in a forest green silk wraparound dress that clung to her trim figure, briskly walked up to them and thrust out her hand.

"Superintendent Burnell, I presume." She nodded at Finch. "Sergeant Finch. I'm Melinda Clement, Mr. Rallis's personal assistant. As Carol has just told you, Mr. Rallis is not here. He left this morning on some urgent business in Athens. Is there something that I can help you with?"

Through clenched teeth, Burnell replied, "I'm afraid not, Ms. Clement. Why did Mr. Rallis leave so suddenly?"

"I'm certain you'll understand I'm not at liberty to divulge company business. All I can say is that it was something urgent that required his immediate attention."

Burnell dropped all pretense at politeness. "I don't give a damn about the company. I want to speak to Rallis. He was not supposed to leave town. He may be a material witness in a murder inquiry."

Melinda's brown eyes narrowed. She sniffed. "Mr. Rallis was not aware that his movements were under any restrictions. I suggest that you take up the matter with his solicitor. I will get you his card."

The superintendent opened his mouth to say something else, but she had already turned on her heel and was hurrying down the corridor, her back ramrod straight. She had returned within minutes. Wordlessly, she slipped the solicitor's business card into his hand, nodded to each in turn, and left them.

Burnell stared down at the small, buff card and slapped it against his other palm. "Come on, Finch," he growled. "There's nothing more to be learned here." He shot a look at the receptionist, who was nervously perched on the edge of her chair. Then, he lowered his voice. "Rallis has done a runner and they've all closed ranks."

All thoughts of visiting Emmeline flew out of his head as they got into the car. Finch drove straight back to the station.

Once in his office, Burnell tossed the solicitor's card on his desk, shrugged out of his suit jacket, and rolled up his shirtsleeves as he flopped down in his chair. He took all his frustrations with the case out on his phone as he viciously punched in the number. Finch sat opposite him, waiting to see how the conversation would devolve.

"Mr. Paul Hislop," Burnell snapped into the mouthpiece. "This is Detective Superintendent Oliver Burnell of the Metropolitan Police. I'm investigating the murders of Anastasia Tarasova and David Copperthwaite."

He nodded and pressed a button to switch on the speaker, so that the sergeant could hear what was being said.

"Yes, Superintendent. How may I help you?" a smooth male voice responded in clipped tones.

"My sergeant and I just dropped by Mr. Rallis's office, and to our dismay we were informed that he is not in London."

"That's correct. He's away on business. He'll be back in a fortnight, perhaps a little sooner. May I be of assistance?"

Burnell's right fist curled into a tight ball. "Under no circumstances was Mr. Rallis to have left London. He was at the scene of a murder and, by a strange coincidence, the prosecutor who had been overseeing his trial was killed on the same night. That makes Mr. Rallis a material witness, at the very least."

"I'm sorry, Superintendent, but I don't see what my client—a law-abiding citizen I'd like to stress—has to do with either crime. Mr. Rallis did not mention to me that he had been *expressly* forbidden from leaving London on a perfectly routine business trip. Have you discovered evidence to tie my client to the murders?"

By now, the skin across the superintendent's knuckles was distended and chalk white. "Not yet, Mr. Hislop," he said through clenched teeth. "We don't have any evidence *yet*. But there are one or two points we'd like to discuss with your client."

"Then, you'll have to wait until he returns."

The solicitor's smugness hovered upon the air.

"If there's nothing else, Superintendent, I am rather busy."

"Of course, Mr. Hislop. Thank you for your time."

"Anything to help the police." They heard a soft *click* as he rang off.

"Damn the man," Burnell railed. "He's as smarmy as Rallis."

"You didn't expect anything else, did you?" Finch asked.

"No," he conceded grudgingly. "Have I ever told you how much I despise lawyers?"

Finch leaned back in his chair and chuckled. "I believe you may have mentioned it once or twice, sir."

The superintendent pounded his fist on the desk. "They're always talking out of the back of their heads. They're nothing more than two-face weasels, always trying to twist your words around."

"Yes, sir," Finch agreed, smiling at the familiar rant.

"Well, almost all of them. I must admit that Nigel Sanborn is scrupulously honest. A gentleman in every sense."

Finch nodded. "Yes, he is. His brother Brian is in the same class. It's amazing, considering who their father was and the fact that they're related to Longdon."

Burnell groaned and dropped his head between his hands. "I don't want to talk about Longdon. He's like the plague. If I never saw him again, it would be too soon."

"We'd all be happy to see the back of him. But then there's Emmeline."

Burnell lifted his head and stared at the sergeant. "Mmm. Yes." His lips were pursed in a tight line as he shuffled some papers on his desk. "She has a way of brightening the day, even when she's being infuriatingly stubborn, doesn't she?"

A broad grin broke out across Finch's face. "She does. So I suppose, for her sake, we have to accept Longdon. Especially since they're married now."

"I will *never* accept Longdon." He wagged an accusatory finger at the sergeant. "I'm telling you now, God help him if he stole Tarasova's necklace—which we both *know* he did. No matter our regard for Emmeline, the law is the law. She will have to visit him in prison."

"I hope it doesn't come to that," Finch remarked softly.

"That's up to Longdon." Burnell slumped back in his chair, weary, irritated and thoroughly frustrated. "Right now, we have two murders on our hands, an international assassin running loose, and nothing but a pile of circumstantial evidence that keeps getting higher. You know what this means, don't you?" He didn't wait for Finch to answer. "I have to go pay another visit to the Boy Wonder."

"Better you than me," the sergeant mumbled under his breath as he got to his feet.

"Where do you think you're going?"

"As you'll be busy updating the assistant commissioner, I thought I'd do some detective work. I'll make some calls to the Greek police to ask them to keep an eye on Rallis and I'll ring Interpol about Carstairs."

"Coward," Burnell snarled. "I should make you come

with me to see the Boy Wonder."

Finch was already at the door. "That would be cruel and unusual punishment. And you're too warm-hearted and generous a boss to do that to your faithful subordinate, sir." A ghost of a smile danced on his lips.

"What rubbish." Burnell jerked his head at the door. "Get out, faithful subordinate, and bring me the killer's head on a platter."

CHAPTER 36

As he sliced his way through the crowd of tourists, civil servants, and other government workers walking along Whitehall, the hairs on the back of Philip's neck prickled. He was certain he was being followed. It was only a short walk up to the Caffè Nero in Trafalgar Square, where he liked to escape from the office for a bit to have a late afternoon espresso.

He tossed a casual glance over his shoulder as he turned the corner, but whoever was trailing him was a professional. No one immediately leaped to his trained eye as suspicious. Perhaps his Boris Petrenko's revelations the other day had him jumping at shadows. Instinct, however, told him that he was not mistaken.

The coffeehouse was quiet. Most of the tables were empty and there was only one woman ahead of him in the queue. His double espresso was soon ready and he carried it over to his favorite table at the back, which overlooked Admiralty Arch. He had barely taken a sip of the strong liquid, when a male voice floated to his ears.

"Glad to see that the jaw isn't giving you too much trouble."

Philip set the demitasse cup and saucer down with a

clatter. He spun round to see Hugh Carstairs poking his head from the worn leather armchair that backed onto his. Carstairs offered him a sheepish grin.

Why did everyone insist on interrupting his afternoon coffee? First Petrenko. Now Hugh.

Philip shot a look around to make sure no one could overhear and then hissed, "I'm lucky that you didn't break it."

Hugh chuckled and got up to join him. "I wouldn't do that to a friend."

"Friend?" Philip asked as he watched the other man sit down opposite him. "If that's the way you treat your friends, I shudder to think what you do to your enemies. Oh, wait." He held up a hand. "I remember. You kill them for money, don't you? Quite the professional, if the rumors are true."

Carstairs slid a sideways glance around the coffeehouse, before meeting Philip's unforgiving gaze. "You can't believe everything you hear."

"No?" Philip's voice was brittle. "You seem to have charmed Emmeline with your daring tales. Not an easy task. She seems to think you're innocent and has become your most outspoken champion. Her loyalty had better not be misplaced."

One corner of Carstairs's mouth twitched into a half-smile. "She's a cracker all right. Longdon's a lucky man."

"Never mind about that. She had better not get hurt in whatever you and Villiers are concocting."

Carstairs raised an eyebrow in askance. "So you know?"

Philip gave a curt shake of his head. "I'm completely in the dark, but being well-acquainted with Villiers, and his penchant for intrigue, I can guess that it's some sort of a ruse. You're no more of a contract killer than my twins. However, I resent being taken for a fool. Therefore if you want my help, you had better tell me everything. And I mean *every* detail. Otherwise, you're on your own."

Carstairs nodded and took a deep breath. "It's only fair." And with that, he launched into the whole sordid business, filling in the blanks that of course Emmeline couldn't. He started with the botched Rudenko defection: the subsequent ploy to draw out the mole at MI5: Rallis's mysterious trips to the Isle of Mull: his unholy alliance with Russians *and* Starrett: and now the two murders.

"So Boris was right?" Philip mumbled when Carstairs had finished.

Hugh's eyes narrowed and he asked suspiciously, "Boris?"

"You must remember Boris Petrenko, ersatz cultural attaché at the Russian embassy, full-fledged FSB agent."

"Of course, I remember old Boris. I'm surprised he's still in the game."

Philip rolled his eyes. "It's in his blood. An old agent never retires. You should know that by now."

Hugh slouched down in chair. "Well, Boris certainly has a lot of blood on his hands. I wonder if it keeps him up at night."

"He's Russian. What do you think?"

"You're right. Either he was born without a conscience or it drowned a long time ago in a sea of vodka. I caught a glimpse of Boris at the Starretts' ill-fated party, but naturally I tried to keep clear. No need to attract attention to my presence."

Philip huffed a mirthless laugh. "I hate to tell you, but you failed miserably on that score. Everyone knows you were there. The police, Emmeline, Longdon, and Sabrina Royce—of all people for God's sake." He stared at Carstairs. "How could you have married that woman? You're like chalk and cheese."

The other man grimaced. "It was a long time ago. We

were too young to know what we wanted. For the record, Sabrina is not as bad as everyone thinks. Yes, she's spoiled and irritating, but she has a heart of gold. She's just a bit insecure and that makes her lash out."

Philip shot him a dubious look. "I'll have to take your word on that. But to get back to your predicament, I had an extremely enlightening chat with Boris yesterday. It's about Anastasia Tarasova and your mole."

Carstairs sat up bolt upright. "I'm all ears."

He listened eagerly as Philip relayed the Russian's theory about Aleksei Tarasov's supposed defection and his daughter's murder.

"And then in passing," Philip concluded, "almost as an afterthought, Boris took great pleasure in telling me that the mole was at the party. Naturally, the wily fox didn't give me a name."

Carstairs nodded. "Of course not."

"Emmeline popped by my office this morning…"

"Did she now? That woman certainly gets around."

"She's a bulldog, if you haven't noticed. Isn't that why you took her into your confidence?"

Carstairs merely inclined his head. "Anyway, she thinks that Lord Starrett could be your mole."

Carstairs's brow puckered. "Oh, yes?"

"Starrett was the NATO liaison in Brussels for several years and ambassador to Germany. Not to mention, the classified documents he has access to as an MP."

"But why would he take the risk?"

"The only thing that makes any sense is that it's a case of *kompromat*."

"What the devil could the Russians possibly have on him?"

Philip took a sip of his espresso and made a sour face. It had gone cold. "No idea. Until the murders, Starrett wasn't even on our radar as a potential target for blackmail. But have no fear, our intrepid journalist friend has made it her mission to discover his secret."

"She'll find out. Or Longdon with his criminal connections will. There's no doubt about that. From what I've observed, no one stands a chance when those two put their heads together. Then what? Will they come to you?"

Philip snorted. "Only when they get in over their heads. That's why I'm worried. Knowing Emmeline and Longdon, they'll attempt to confront Starrett and Rallis on their own."

"They'd be damned fools if they do."

"As the professionals, you and I can see that in a flash. Emmeline and Longdon view things in a different light. That's why they're married to each other. No one else would have the stamina to keep up with them."

"Hmm." Carstairs nodded, but his mind had clearly drifted elsewhere. "So either Starrett, or Rallis, or both of them together, are responsible for the two murders. Three if you count MacQuillan."

Philip's ears perked up. "Who's MacQuillan?"

"A Treasury chap in Edinburgh who had been helping me to get the goods on Rallis. He went undercover in Rallis's organization. He found out about something called Poseidon, but he was killed last week before he had a chance to pass on the information."

"Emmeline mentioned something about Poseidon too. No ideas?"

Carstairs gave an impatient shrug of his shoulders. "None whatsoever."

They lapsed into a brooding silence. Each frustrated by questions they couldn't answer.

After an interval, Philip said, "Starrett must be the mole. He probably killed Tarasova because she threatened to expose him as part of her revenge against Rallis." He sat on the edge of his seat, warming to his subject. "And if

Boris is right about Aleksei Tarasov's imminent defection, then murdering his daughter would be the perfect way to make him see the error of his ways. It has to be his lordship. He has to be the mole."

"The evidence seems to be pointing in his direction. But do you really think he could have turned killer?"

"Starrett has a great deal to lose, if it comes out that he's betrayed his country."

"Yes," Hugh murmured. He felt a flutter in the pit of his stomach, as Fiona flew unbidden into his mind. How could she have married Starrett? "We can certainly tie him to Tarasova, but how do we connect him to the Rudenko affair?"

Philip frowned. "I'll do a bit of digging. There has to be something. Starrett is not a professional spy like our friend Boris, so it's more likely he left a careless clue behind."

"We can only hope. In the interim, I need you to get that Superintendent Burnell off my back. He's kicking up rather a fuss with his investigation."

"Burnell is a damned good detective, Hugh. He's honest and reveres the law. He's just following the evidence"—he held up a hand to forestall a protest from Carstairs—"circumstantial, though it may be. You can't really blame him. Burnell doesn't know you, or the scheme you and Villiers concocted. Besides, I think you'll find that he's under pressure from above to close the case as quickly as possible. David Copperthwaite, QC, the Crown prosecutor overseeing Rallis's trial and who was killed the same night as Tarasova, was Assistant Commissioner Cruickshank's stepfather."

Carstairs slumped back in his chair and groaned. "Terrific. Another complication. That's all we need."

Philip patted his knee. "Don't worry. I'll have a quiet word with Burnell and see what I can do."

"Thanks. I also need you to get word to Villiers. Of

course, he can't be seen helping me. It would blow my cover. Tell him all our theories, maybe he can do something from his end discreetly."

Philip nodded. "Done. What are you going to do?"

"At this stage, the longer I linger here in London the odds increase of Burnell catching up with me and we can't have that." He glanced at his watch. "I'm catching the train to Glasgow in two hours. A hired car will be waiting for me at the station. Then, I'm going to drive to Oban, where a couple of chaps I trust will take me to Tobermory by boat. By the way, I rang Rallis's office and found out that he left the country this morning. They said that he'll be back in London in a fortnight. I have a strong feeling that his little jaunt has nothing to do with business and everything to do with what he and Starrett are up to on the Isle of Mull. This time, I mean to expose whatever game they're playing at."

"Oh, so you were just going to vanish *again* without even a by-your-leave. That's gratitude for you."

Carstairs and Philip glanced up to find Emmeline looming over their table, anger simmering in the dark depths of her eyes.

CHAPTER 37

After determining that a client had faked the robbery of his wife's jewels to collect the insurance money, Gregory was hailed as a hero by Symington's management. There were murmurs of a promotion in the offing. He rather doubted it, but he smiled politely. Having earned the goodwill of his boss and considering his duties fulfilled, he took himself off the rest of the day to make the rounds of some his old haunts. His former "business associates" were all delighted to see him, but when it came time to answer questions about Rallis, he was met with blank stares and nonchalant shrugs of shoulders. No one was able to provide any information about Rallis—or they were too afraid to cross him. Gregory thought the latter was more likely the reason and cursed them all to perdition.

He decided to drop by the Aegean Dream again. If anyone could ferret out the dirt on Rallis, it was Stavros. He slipped his Jaguar into a spot near Covent Garden and walked the few blocks to the restaurant on King Street.

He frowned when he was confronted by the locked door. He cupped his hands over his eyes and pressed his face to the window. The interior was shrouded in darkness, but he could hear distant voices coming from inside.

He stood back and for a good five minutes rapped his knuckles on the glass. "I know someone's in there. I'm perfectly prepared to wait."

Another five minutes ticked by, before he heard the bolt being slipped back from the lock and the door was yanked open.

A man in his early thirties with thick, jet black hair and a night's worth of stubble covering his olive complexion, glared at him from behind onyx eyes. "We're closed. Go away," he snarled.

The man attempted to shut the door, but Gregory was too quick for him and pushed his way inside.

"Your trademark Greek hospitality appears to be lacking. So are your manners, Nicky."

"It's Nicholas to you, Greg. Better yet, it's Mr. Constantinides."

"Come off it, old chap. I've known you since you were a teenager."

He cast a glance around the restaurant now that his eyes had adjusted to the dimness. It was a complete shambles. Tables overturned, smashed plates and crystal glasses everywhere, the carpet stained a mottled red from broken bottles of wine.

Cold dread clutched at his chest. His gaze swung back to Nicky. "What's happened? Where's Stavros?"

The younger man tried to turn his back on him, but Gregory was having none of it. He snatched his arm and spun him around. "I said where's your father?"

Nicky shook off his grasp. "Dad's in hospital because of you."

Gregory drew a ragged breath as the blood thundered in his ears. "Tell me what happened." His voice was hoarse and laced with urgency.

Nicky's body tensed and the gaze that raked Gregory's

features was a mixture of anger and fear. Then, he tore his eyes away. Gregory felt the other man's body slacken. The desire to lash out seemed to abate.

"Tell me what happened," he asked again, his tone softer.

Nicky righted a chair that had not been damaged and dropped heavily onto the elegantly padded upholstery.

"I'm not sure exactly. But when I came to open up today, the restaurant was like this." One arm swung out in an arc that encompassed the entire room. He took a gulping breath, before continuing. "Then, I found Dad in the office in the back."

A sheen of unshed tears glistened in his eyes, as he lifted his ravaged face to look at Gregory. "He was lying on the floor. His face covered in blood. One eye swollen shut. They beat him until he was barely conscious."

Gregory's jaw clenched. "Rallis's men?"

Nicky choked back a sob. "Yes, I'm fairly certain. I heard Dad making some calls yesterday about Rallis. He told me...He told me it was important. He told me it was for you. He said you promised to see that Rallis paid for Yanis. He said friends always help friends." He threw up his hands in despair. A tremor shook his voice. "Now look what's happened. Dad is clinging to his life. All because of you. *His friend*." These last two words dripped with venom from his tongue.

A lump rose to Gregory's throat. Nicky's anger was justified. He knew Rallis was dangerous and he had blithely tossed Stavros in the bastard's path. He would never forgive himself if Stavros died.

"What hospital is your father in?"

At first, he thought Nicky wouldn't tell him. A range of emotions chased themselves over the other's man face. In the end, something made Nicky relent.

"St. Thomas' Hospital. Mum is with him." This came

out as a croak.

Gregory nodded. "Right." He clapped Nicky on the shoulder. "Stavros is strong. He'll pull through. You'll see."

He started to turn on his heel toward the door, but Nicky snatched at his sleeve. "He'd better. After Yanis, it would kill Mum if she lost Dad too."

Gregory patted his arm. "She won't. The only one who is going to lose is Rallis. That's a promise."

"When it comes to Rallis, I don't think anyone can keep such a promise."

Gregory flashed one his most brilliant smiles. "Rallis is going to find out that I'm a man of my word. And then he'll be sorry."

∽∾∽

Why were hospitals always such cold, sterile places? Gregory wondered. He had an aversion to them ever since his mother's battle with cancer. The illness ravaged her frail body and took her away from him when he was a teenager. And the doctors could do nothing for her.

He pushed thoughts of his mother aside. This was not the time to open those memories. He couldn't relive the pain. Not now. He had to focus on the present. On Stavros. And Rallis.

His footsteps echoed against the gleaming white floor as he walked down the corridor to Stavros's room. The random thought that flew to his mind as he continued on was that Villiers had been taken to this same hospital after that nasty business with Doyle. The old man had saved his life. He would always be grateful for that. But he would *never* forgive Villiers for nearly getting Emmy killed with all his machinations. And the bloody schemer was still at it now with Carstairs.

He was still frowning when he reached his friend's room and tapped lightly on the open door.

A small, slim woman with graying hair sat by the bed, where Stavros was huddled under the crisp white sheets. Her head snapped up. Her caramel eyes opened wide when she saw Gregory hovering in the doorway. Then they became narrow slits, as she slowly rose to her feet.

"You are not wanted here, Greg. Go away." Her voice was a mere whisper, but her tone was infused with fury and hatred.

He took a half-step into the room. "I'm so sorry, Theodora." The words were a pathetic offering as he struggled to find a way to right the wrong done to his friend.

She cast a glance down at her husband, whose sleep was far from peaceful. His hands were like the talons of a bird of prey as they clutched the sheets, while his head moved about restlessly on the pillows.

Theodora came around the bed to stand directly in front of Gregory. "I said go away. If you don't, I will summon hospital security." She drew in a deep lungful of air. "Why are you here?" she hissed. "As you can see, you've caused quite enough harm to last a lifetime." She craned her neck to look at Stavros again. "If he has any life left." These words were lost on the sob that sent a shudder through her body.

Gregory drew her into his arms and rocked her gently back and forth as a flood of tears was unleashed. After several minutes, she recollected herself and stepped back.

Her voice was unsteady, but she appeared to a bit calmer. "Please leave and don't come back again." She straightened her back and drew her shoulders back. "You've hurt my family quite enough. Just go."

"No." The tone was unsteady, but unequivocal in its determination nevertheless.

They both turned toward the bed, where Stavros lay, one eye completely shut and other bright with a spark of defiance. He lifted one limp hand and dropped it again.

Theodora rushed to the bed and clasped her husband's hand. She kissed the palm and pressed it against her cheek. "Oh, my darling."

Stavros allowed her to gush for a few more seconds and then he said, "I need to speak to Greg."

"No," Theodora growled. "You are here because of him. I won't allow it."

A flash of irritation passed over her husband's face. "Listen to me." He touched her arm with one finger. "Rallis's men attacked me, not Greg."

"Yes, but you would never have been hurt, if he hadn't come around"—she jerked her thumb over her shoulder in Gregory's general direction—"he pulled you back into the business. You promised me that you were finished with all of that. You promised me…." Her sentence trailed off in a sob.

"I am finished. I'm tired of it. I merely made a few calls to some old friends. That's all."

"And look what happened."

Stavros sighed and winced almost immediately.

"I will get the doctor." She wiped her wet cheeks with the back of her hand and stood up with renewed purpose.

"Good. Get the doctor, if it makes you happy," he replied wearily.

"I expect you gone when I return," she said as she passed Gregory.

They waited until she was gone. Then, Gregory approached the bed and took his friend's hand between both of his. "I'm sorry sounds so feeble, but I don't know what else to say."

"Nothing. This is not your fault." He glanced at the door. "Never mind Theodora. She's upset right now. She'll come back to her senses."

A quiver of smile touched Gregory's lips. "If you say so. You know her best."

Stavros squeezed his hand. "No man can ever know a woman's mind. The one who thinks he does is a fool and in for a rude awakening. You are newly married and your eyes are still full of stars, but this is what you have to look forward to. Worry, worry, worry."

Gregory chuckled. "You don't believe a word of what you're saying."

One corner of Stavros's mouth twitched. "Perhaps not." He clutched Gregory's arm. "Now, quickly before the fury comes back. I was able to find out what Rallis is up to. He's been smuggling Greek antiquities."

"What? How is he getting away with it?"

"Actually, it's not surprising. Greece is a mess right now with the economic crisis. The government is in chaos. Unscrupulous people are willing to trade away their country's heritage for money. Everything always boils down to money."

Gregory sat on the edge of the bed. "It's sheer lunacy."

"No one ever said Rallis was a rational man. He's guided by impulses. Besides it's extremely lucrative for those who manage to evade the law. Private collectors, and museums to a lesser extent, are willing to pay a virtual ransom to possess ancient gold coins, vases, marble statuettes, amphora and so many other precious artifacts."

"That's how Rallis probably ensnared Lord Starrett in his scheme. Starrett's collection features all sorts of art pieces and treasures. He probably jumped at the opportunity Rallis dangled before his eyes. But there's something else afoot between those two. I'm certain of it."

"Your instincts appear to be correct. There are whispers that Rallis is blackmailing Starrett, with what I was unable to discover. My contacts tell me that Rallis has grown so overconfident, he smuggles the pieces out on his yacht, *Athena*. The Greek police and customs officials have received many tips over the last year and have raided the boat on several occasions. But each time they have come up empty-handed. His registration, insurance certificate, radio license, etcetera are always in perfect order."

Gregory frowned and shook his head. "There's got to be a way to get him." He was silent for several moments as he mulled over the possibilities.

"The only other information I can offer is that the yacht always leaves from Piraeus and travels up to Scotland somewhere."

Gregory jumped to his feet. "Scotland? You're sure."

Stavros gave a careful nod as he shot him a quizzical look. "Yes, but I don't know where."

Gregory's face broke out in a broad grin. "But I do. How much do you want to wager the *Athena's* port of call is the Isle of Mull, where it just so happens that Rosemount Castle, Starrett's old family pile, is located?"

Stavros's good eye opened wide and then crinkled at the corner as his bruised and battered face softened into a smile. "Yes, it makes sense. Who would think to search the wilds of Scotland for Greek antiquities? But Starrett is taking an awful risk."

"From his point of view, it's probably worth it. His lordship gets to select the pieces he wants and leaves the rest for Rallis to sell."

"It's brilliant," Stavros marveled. "And deadly."

Theodora's animated voice floated to their ears. She was speaking to someone. The doctor most likely.

"Go now," Stavros urged, "before she gets back. Let me know how things turn out."

Gregory nodded and gave his friend's hand a hearty shake and crossed to the door. "Thanks for everything. If there's anything I can do…"

Stavros gave weak flap of his hand. "Nothing. Just take care of yourself. You don't want your new wife to become a young widow."

A roguish smile danced upon Gregory's lips. "No chance of that. Haven't you heard that I have nine lives?"

CHAPTER 38

A h, our favorite journalist. We were just talking about you. Were your ears burning?" Hugh quipped and added a smile for good measure.

It failed to lighten the mood.

"Stuff it," she said as she drew up a chair and plopped down.

Emmeline's eyes narrowed and her lips pursed. For a full minute, she didn't utter a word. But the two men felt the full force of her dark gaze.

At last, she cleared her throat. Her first volley was directed at Hugh. She leaned toward him and hissed, "I was worried about you. I see that I was a fool to be concerned." She sat up ramrod straight in her chair and placed her hands deliberately on her knees. "And you." She rounded on Philip. "You were just going to allow Hugh to run off without a word."

Philip held up both hands in surrender, but Hugh spoke before he had a chance to say anything.

"Emmeline, it's unfair to blame Philip. He's caught up in the middle of this mess. And, you are far from a fool and anyone who thinks so is crackers. It was best that I kept my distance from you and Longdon. *I* was the fool to get you involved. It's too dangerous."

She flapped a hand impatiently. "I would have pursued the story anyway. You only gave me a hint in the right direction."

"Yes, now that I've gotten to know you I can see that quite clearly. The faint of heart don't stand a chance, when you start firing off questions."

Her mouth curved into a Cheshire cat grin. "That's the only way to get answers. That and good old-fashioned research."

Hugh shot a glance at Philip and then turned his attention back to Emmeline. "Does that mean that you *have* discovered something?"

Her smile only grew wider and there was eager glint in her eyes. "I always find answers." She allowed herself to preen for a few seconds and then decided to put them out of their misery.

"I think Lord Starrett murdered his first wife for her money and the Russians have some sort of proof, which they're using to blackmail him into spying for them." She went on to provide them with details from the articles she had sifted through about Isabelle Starrett's death, and her will leaving everything to her husband.

"Your theory is quite plausible," Philip said when she had finished. "Lord Starrett would do anything keep that dirty secret."

"And if he killed once," Hugh chimed in, "the second time would be much easier. My guess is that Tarasova found out that Starrett was playing footsy with the Russians and she threatened to expose him. It wouldn't have been difficult for her to find out the information. She came from that world. Her father is a highly decorated GRU agent.

"Starrett probably lured her to his house with the invitation to the party and promised they would settle everything. With so many people in the house that night, Starrett wouldn't be missed if he nipped upstairs for a bit. After all, it was his house." Hugh shook his head. "But why blackmail him at all if he was working for Russians? And what did Tarasova want from Starrett in exchange for her silence? That's what I can't figure out. Merely to ruin his scheme with Rallis? I don't think Rallis would be overly put out, in view of the fact that Starrett was starting to get nervous."

"Speaking of their scheme." Emmeline allowed her words to dangle upon the air, enjoying keeping them in suspense for a few more seconds. "I *know* what Poseidon is."

Philip grinned. "Why am I not surprised?"

"Well? Do you intend to tell us? Or do we have to play a game of charades to find out?" Hugh prompted irritably.

Emmeline, being impatient and short-tempered by nature, did not take offense. She took a deep breath and in hushed tones regaled them with the tale of the merchant ships loaded with gold that the Germans had torpedoed during the First and Second World Wars.

"Just think of it," she concluded, "all that gold lying thousands of fathoms below the sea. It would be too tempting a prospect for someone whose inclinations were less than honorable. My guess is that Rallis discovered the *Poseidon*. I checked. His shipping company has a salvage unit. The wreck must be located somewhere near the Isle of Mull. That's why he's roped Starrett into the scheme. Perhaps they're using Rosemount Castle as a staging ground for their recovery operations? I don't know. I'm still trying to fit all the pieces of the puzzle into place. I had no idea about these lost ships. What do you think? Am I completely mad?"

She bit her lip and darted a hesitant glance at both men, who stared at one another in stunned silence.

Philip was the first to speak. "No, Emmeline. You are far from mad. No one's imagination has quite the same breadth as yours. No one else could have made the connections you did." He gave an indifferent twitch of one shoulder. "Well, perhaps, Longdon might have," he conceded grudgingly. "Hugh, what's your opinion about Emmeline's theory?"

She could read admiration in the hazel gaze that settled on her face, which suffused with heat.

"I think you're spot on. That's what MacQuillan probably found out, but he was killed before he had a chance to pass on the information to me. Naturally, the Treasury would be interested. Any cargo found in sovereign waters would be the property of the British government."

"That's what I assumed," she replied. "I rang a source at the Bank of England to try to get some corroboration. He was extremely friendly at first, but as the conversation went on he became more and more sullen. In the end, he gave me a brusque 'No comment' and suggested I was wasting my time. I have a feeling he won't be taking my calls anytime soon."

"Leave the official channels to me," Philip said. "I have a few contacts of my own at the Treasury and the Bank of England, whom I intend to approach discreetly. I'll also have to speak with Villiers, of course. He seems to be the thick of things, as usual."

Emmeline nodded, but a frown creased her brow. "One thing that still bothers me is what Rallis is blackmailing Starrett with. From what Gregory and I overheard of their row at the party, I don't believe it's proof that he murdered his first wife. Starrett clearly wanted out of the Poseidon business. But Rallis was not having it. He sounded far from deferential. In fact, he seemed to be sneering at Starrett. Rallis mumbled something about the mistakes of youth.

That's when he mentioned Starrett's friend Basil Treadgold. I haven't had a chance to track him down yet. Have either of you ever heard of Treadgold?" They both shook their heads.

She shrugged at a loss. "Well, let's leave that for the moment. What have you chaps found out?"

Philip crossed one leg over the other and propped his elbows on the armrests of his chair. "We haven't been quite as busy as you, but a few choice nuggets have dropped into our laps."

"Oh, yes?" Emmeline's eyes sparkled with eagerness. She fished out her notebook from handbag. With pen poised over it, she said, "I'm all ears."

"I'm afraid it's off the record again."

Her brows knit together and her lips twisted into a rueful grimace. She gave an angry flick to close her notebook. "This is becoming a rather tiresome habit on your part. What about the public's right to know the truth?"

He spread his hands wide. "As I told you in my office, the choice is yours. If you want the information, you have to abide my rules."

She inclined her head and primly folded her hands in her lap. "Satisfied."

Philip bit back a laugh. He knew her curiosity would win the battle in the end.

"As I was telling Hugh before you swooped down on us with a face like thunder, the other day Boris Petrenko—you remember, our friendly cultural attaché-cum-FSB agent from the party?—told me something interesting. Apparently, Col. Aleksei Tarasov is planning to defect."

He saw Emmeline's eyes widen in surprise and heard her sharp intake of breath, but she held her tongue. "It seems the plans are in the final preparations. Tarasov is supposed to come over to our side within the next fortnight. Or it could be within days. Sometimes these things have to move more quickly than planned, depending on the circumstances. To no one's surprise, Villiers is at the center of these behind-the-scenes maneuvers. He's in his element when he's plotting."

"What Petrenko believes, and we concur," Hugh picked up the thread, "is that Tarasova was killed as punishment to her father and as a warning to other defectors. Putin despises defectors and considers them traitors. Tarasov is high up in the GRU, Russia's military intelligence. He's privy to an awful lot of the Kremlin's secrets. It would be a coup for us."

Emmeline leaned back in her chair and nodded. "Yes, it makes perfect sense. Putin's opponents have often wound up dead. Just look at what happened to Pavel Melinikov and Yuri Sabatov over the summer here in London. Putin has a long reach. International borders mean nothing to him. Do you think that the mole was ordered to assassinate Tarasova? Would she have been aware of her father's imminent defection?"

"She was probably in the dark about the entire plan. It would have been too dangerous for her to know until her father was safely in London. As for the mole, he must have seen me at the party and thought he'd fit me up again. I was the ideal scapegoat."

"The only thing he didn't realize," Philip pointed out, "was that you never went rogue and are still hunting him."

"*He?*" Emmeline's ears perked up. "So you agree with my conclusion that the mole has to be Starrett?"

"Let's just say it's a working theory at the moment," Philip replied noncommittally.

She made a face at him. "Always the diplomat." Her voice dropped. "Even when you're discussing MI5 business."

Philip shot her a pointed look. "Journalists who have

loose tongues will find that their sources will scatter to the winds."

She smiled sweetly at him and lifted one finger. "Ah, ah. Threats lose some of their sting when the conversation is off the record."

Hugh had remained silent throughout this verbal tussle. He was staring at some invisible spot on the opposite wall. His thoughts were clearly elsewhere.

"Hugh, what's on your mind?"

"What?" Philip's voice jarred him out of his troubled reverie. "Our friend the mole should have remained burrowed. It was a mistake. A *grave* mistake to kill Tarasova." His hands curled into tight fists and a hard glint entered his hazel eyes as he spoke these last words.

"You can't blame yourself. You couldn't have prevented Tarasova's murder," Philip observed reasonably.

"Of course, you couldn't have. You didn't even know that she was going to be at the party," Emmeline remarked.

"No, but I knew the mole would be there." His eyes held a fierce challenge. "I was a fool during the Rudenko affair. I was completely blind, but I should have seen it *now*."

Emmeline cast a worried glance at Philip, who shrugged his shoulders.

"Don't worry. We'll get Starrett this time. Thanks to Emmeline we have a fairly good idea where to look. However, I'll get on to Villiers first to see where things stand with the Tarasov defection. As for you"—he shot his cuff and glanced at his watch—"if you don't hurry, you'll miss your train to Glasgow."

Hugh surged to his feet. "You're right. I can't miss that train. Especially now." He stretched across the table and extended his hand to Philip. "You'll have word with Burnell?"

Philip's firm handshake was infused with all the steadfastness of his friendship. "Yes, I did promise."

Hugh gave him a brief smile. "I can always count on you. Sorry again about the jaw. It was all I could think of that the time."

Philip touched his still tender jaw. "Thanks. That makes it much worse."

"I'll be gentle next time," Hugh teased.

"You're not going to get a next time." Philip jerked his thumb in the direction of the door. "Now, get out of here."

Hugh nodded. "I'll ring you in a few days." When he saw Emmeline's brow pucker, he added, "Both of you."

"You had better," Emmeline said good-naturedly. Then a shadow of concern flickered across her features. "Be careful."

He smiled and squeezed her shoulder without another word. They watched him make his way out of the coffee-house.

"Do you think he'll be all right?" she asked. "He seemed terribly angry."

"We're all angry when it comes to treason. The betrayal becomes personal."

"Yes, of course it does, when you're responsible for the country's safety and security."

She was quiet for a few minutes mulling over what they had just discussed. Then she rose. "I had better go too. This story won't write itself."

One of Philip's eyebrows arched upward. "Don't worry. I won't mention anything about Aleksei Tarasov. I'll concentrate on what I've gathered on his daughter's murder and questions that have been raised about Lord Starrett's past. I'm also going to try to locate Basil Treadgold. I'm hoping that he can provide some insight into his lordship. I still have some clippings to go through on Starrett that the Research Department pulled up for me. Perhaps there's a clue buried in them. But first, I'm going to see Superintendent Burnell. I'm hoping in his official capacity he can get me copies of the police and coroner's reports on the first Lady Starrett's death.

"I'll let you know if I discover anything new." She touched his sleeve lightly. "Promise me that you'll keep me in the loop. Let me know how your chat goes with Villiers."

Philip snorted. "Villiers will likely be his usual cagey self. He only gives up the game, when he has no choice."

CHAPTER 39

Burnell stormed back into his office and slammed the door behind him. His ulcer was doing somersaults and grumbling vociferously. The Boy Wonder had been less than pleased—he'd been downright tetchy, if truth be told—when he had informed him that Rallis had left town. It only inflamed the situation when Burnell added that, thus far, they had had no luck in tracking down Carstairs.

"Oliver, what time do you call this? Since when have you been keeping banker's hours? It's been an age, since you've been gone."

Gregory was ensconced in the superintendent's chair, with his long legs propped on his desk and crossed at the ankles, and that infernal roguish grin dancing on his lips.

The growl rumbled from deep within Burnell's throat, as his hand lashed out and swiped Gregory's legs off the desk in one swift motion. "It's *Superintendent Burnell*. Get—out—of—my—chair," he said through clenched teeth.

Gregory took his time rising. He straightened the superintendent's tie, before stepping aside. "You only had to ask, *Oliver*. I was merely keeping it warm for you."

Burnell plopped down heavily. "Hmph. I'll probably have to get it fumigated."

Gregory clucked his tongue as he settled in the chair opposite him. "Now, now. I take it Cruickshank is responsible for your less than the welcoming reception. Since I'm an easygoing chap, I will overlook it this time. That prat is enough to try anyone's nerves."

The superintendent choked back a laugh. "He's not the only one," he muttered under his breath. Then louder, he said, "What do you *want*, Longdon? Make it fast and get out."

"As a law-abiding citizen, I felt it was my duty to inform you of the crime being committed by Rallis and Lord Starrett under the very nose of Her Majesty's Government."

Burnell fixed him with a hard stare. "What are you on about?"

"I mean that I have discovered what the mysterious Poseidon is. Rallis and Starrett are smuggling Greek antiquities into the U.K. and selling them on the black market."

"No, you're mistaken," Emmeline called from the open doorway.

They looked up as one to find her scowling at them.

Gregory stood up as she crossed the room. He kissed her cheek when she reached the desk. He motioned with one hand for her to take his seat, as he shifted to the one beside it.

"Darling, you are a vision of loveliness in the middle of what had been a rather dismal afternoon," he gushed as they sat down.

She couldn't help but smile, as she laced her fingers through his. Yes, it was a bit much. But that was Gregory and now he was hers—all hers—for better or worse.

She cleared her throat and inclined her head toward

Burnell. "Hello, Superintendent Burnell. I'm sorry. Here we are imposing upon your good nature and patience once again."

"Nonsense, Emmy. Oliver counts the minutes until he can see us again. Isn't that right?" The mischief in Gregory's cinnamon eyes was unmistakable.

Burnell glared at him, but his features smoothed into a smile when he turned his attention back to Emmeline. "I'm always happy to see *you*, Emmeline. Your husband, on the other hand, I only tolerate for your sake."

"That hurts, Oliver. It really does," Gregory sniffed. "I treasure our friendship. I consider us mates for life."

The superintendent guffawed. "God help me. That would be a living nightmare."

Emmeline swatted Gregory's arm. "Be serious" she mouthed.

"Look, we both know you're extremely busy so I'll get straight to the point." She repeated everything she had shared with Philip and Hugh about the sunken gold, Starrett's first wife, and the likelihood that Starrett was the MI5 mole and invited Tarasova to the house to silence her. Since both Gregory and Burnell were bound by the Officials Secrets Act, as she was, she also divulged what Philip had disclosed about Aleksei Tarasov's defection and that his daughter may have been killed as a warning.

"Damn and blast." Burnell pounded his fist on the desk. "When was MI5 going to inform the Metropolitan Police about Tarasov's defection? We're supposed to be on the same side."

"Don't forget, we are talking about Villiers," Gregory pointed out. "Nothing is ever simple when that man is involved."

Burnell grunted in agreement. He was definitely not among Laurence Villiers's admirers. Their paths had crossed on the Doyle case earlier in the year. He still resented Villiers's high-handed intrusion, even though the man had turned into the hero at the end and saved Longdon's life. But not before he had put a number of other lives at risk with his intrigues. The superintendent would never forget that.

"I'll have to ring Philip about this so that Scotland Yard can coordinate with MI5."

"I believe he intends to call you to discuss…a few things."

No need to add fuel to the fire for the time being by bringing up Hugh's name again, she thought. However, she had to admit that Burnell appeared convinced that the Russians were responsible for Tarasova's murder. They just had to find conclusive proof.

"Darling, I don't think anything that you've told us is untrue," Gregory ventured. "Far from it. But Rallis and Starrett are more devious and corrupt than we imagined."

He went on to tell them about seeking out Stavros for information on Rallis's illegal business dealings and the heavy price his friend paid for trying to help him. Emmeline touched his arm when he described his visit to the hospital.

"I'll make sure to send him some flowers tomorrow. If there's anything else you think he'd like, we can send that as well," she said.

"Longdon, I'll station two plainclothes officers at the hospital to watch Constantinides, in case Rallis's men are planning a return engagement."

"Thanks. I appreciate it. But I don't think Stavros is wrong about the smuggling. His sources are like gold. No pun intended, in light of what Emmy found out. Who would ever believe that the upstanding Lord Starrett would be involved in antiquities smuggling? It would be considered in the realm of fantasy." He held up a finger. "But it doesn't look so farfetched when we remember his first wife's probable murder, his spying for the Russians, and the operation to recover the lost gold. When we connect all the dots, Lord Starrett no longer looks like a pillar of society."

Burnell sat back in his chair, stroking his beard as his gaze flickered between husband and wife.

"Come on, Oliver. You know we're both right."

The superintendent exhaled a slow breath. "The frightening thing is that I *do* believe you."

Emmeline beamed at him. "The question now is how to do we bring them down for both of their schemes as well as the murders of Tarasova, Copperthwaite, and MacQuillan. Not to mention, exposing Lord Starrett as a Russian spy."

"*You* are not going to do anything. You and Longdon are civilians. Thank you very much for the information you have provided. *We*, the professionals, will take matters from here. I already have Finch coordinating with the Greek police and Interpol to keep an eye on Rallis's movements."

"But that's quite unfair," Emmeline protested. "You can't just shunt us aside. We have just as much of a vested interest in seeing that Rallis and Starrett are punished for their crimes. You can't prevent me from pursuing the story about Starrett's murky past or following up on the murders. Those are legitimate stories. The public has a right to know how the investigation is proceeding and whether an arrest is imminent. The public also has a right to know whether the country's security has been compromised. No matter how much I respect and admire you, Superintendent Burnell, I would hate to think that you were trying to suppress the press. After all, I'm simply doing my job."

Emmeline thrust her chin in the air. Her back was ramrod straight, her expression intractable.

Burnell stiffened and his blue gaze narrowed. His cheeks flushed crimson beneath his beard, when he caught a glimpse of the ghost of a smile upon Gregory's lips.

The superintendent cleared his throat. "You know very well I would never seek to stifle the press. However, we are dealing with greedy, desperate men who care nothing for human life and who have killed to keep their sordid schemes from being exposed. *My* job is to ensure the public's safety and at the same time see that full force of the law comes down on Rallis and Starrett. I cannot in good conscience allow you to go running about London making yourself"—he threw a sideways glance at Gregory—"and your husband targets."

Emmeline felt her cheeks flame. Her eyes had never left Burnell's face during his entire lecture.

"I apologize, Superintendent Burnell. I spoke in the heat of the moment. Of course, I know you support a free press. I hope my thoughtless remarks will not affect our relationship. Or friendship," she added quietly.

Burnell made a dismissive gesture with one hand. "Never mind. It's forgotten." He leaned forward and folded his hands in front of him on the desk. "But I want to stress that the two of you are not to take any unnecessary risks. Is that clear?"

They each felt the full force of his uncompromising blue stare.

Emmeline nodded. "Yes, we promise. We'll check with you and Philip first. Right, darling?"

Gregory offered one of his most brilliant smiles. "Of course. We'll be on the phone to you the instant something juicy falls into our laps."

"Hmph," Burnell grunted. "Now, why does that make me uneasy?"

Gregory spread his hands wide. "I can't imagine. Perhaps, you're suspicious by nature. Oliver, you really need to trust your fellow man. I'm certain it will improve your ulcer."

This earned him another "Hmph."

⌖⌖⌖

Burnell wasted no time in ringing the Scottish police to request copies of all the reports related to Lady Isabelle Starrett's death. He then summoned Finch to update him on everything Emmeline and Gregory had disclosed.

Finch let out a low whistle when his boss had finished. "Bloody hell, sir."

The superintendent gave a curt nod. "That about sums up the situation. Now that we know what to look for, we can hit the bastards where it hurts. Since Lord Starrett is involved and there's the matter of treason to contend with, we have to mind how we proceed. I'm going to ring Philip and MI5 to see if they can fill us in on the Tarasov defection. We'll have to follow their lead on the antiquities smuggling, and the gold operation. We'll provide any assistance that they require."

"Sir, does that mean we are no longer considering Carstairs as the prime suspect in the Tarasova and Copperthwaite murders?"

"Based on what we've just learned, I think it's fairly obvious he was meant to take the fall. On the other hand, we can't drop that line of inquiry entirely because we don't want to arouse Rallis's or Starrett's suspicions. We have no idea whether they have any informants reporting back to them on our progress. But our efforts don't have to be quite so vigorous. What I would like is to put a surveillance team on Starrett starting this minute. I want to know every move he makes."

Finch rose to his feet. "Right, sir. I'll get onto it straightaway. His life will be an open book. Meanwhile, the Greek police said that Rallis's yacht, *Athenian Princess*, left Piraeus a week ago. They're going to send me the itinerary that was filed. As for Rallis, he flew into Athens this morning, spent a few hours in the city, and was booked on the two-twenty British Airways flight to Glasgow, with an hour-and-ten-minute layover at Heathrow."

The superintendent sat up. "Well, what are you waiting for? Alert airport security to hold him."

"It was too late. By the time I discovered all this, the flight had already taken off. It's scheduled to land in Glasgow at seven this evening. Should I have the local police arrest him on the spot?"

Burnell stroked his beard meditatively. "No. Observe, but hands off. Let him run. If his destination is Glasgow, he's probably on his way to the Isle of Mull, where I presume his yacht is also headed. He has no idea that we're on to him, therefore he has no reason to be suspicious. My guess is that Starrett is preparing to join him up in Scotland. Let me know the minute, his lordship leaves London."

Finch nodded and was out the door, his stride full of purpose.

ϲϳϲϳ

Philip had been surprised to learn that Villiers was back at work—albeit on a limited basis according to doctor's orders—in his office at Thames House, MI5's headquarters on the north bank of the river near Lambeth Bridge.

Since the situation was fluid and time was of the essence, Philip didn't bother making an appointment to see him. Needless to say, Villiers's secretary was not best pleased.

"I'm afraid that the deputy director is quite busy at the moment. It would be better if you came back at more convenient time on *another* day," she admonished in clipped tones.

"Sorry, there's no time like the present," Philip retorted, pushing past her and barging into Villiers's office without knocking.

The old man was on the phone, but looked up at the intrusion. He continued his conversation, but waved Philip to a chair opposite him. The secretary pivoted on her heel in a huff and closed the door behind her.

"Yes," Villiers was saying, "I see. It makes things a bit tricky. Leave it to me. I'll handle it. Things will move forward as planned."

He rang off and leaned back in his chair, propping his elbows on the armrests. He was silent for several minutes.

At last, he observed, "I see that your friend has been making a nuisance of herself again. It's amazing how she gets around. She's been asking a great many awkward questions at the Bank of England, and particularly about Lord Desmond Starrett."

Philip's jaw clenched and he gripped his knees so hard that the skin over his knuckles were white and stretched taut. "Emmeline believes in finding the truth, as should we all."

Villiers's mouth curled into a sneer. "The truth can be a double-edged sword. Try to persuade her to stop pursuing Starrett. It can only lead to trouble."

"Sir, there is overwhelming evidence that Starrett is the Russian mole, who was responsible for the failed Rudenko defection and likely the murder of the ballerina Anastasia Tarasova. For God's sake, he tried to make it appear that Hugh was the mole. Doesn't that bother you?"

Villiers remained silent, his face was a mask of inscrutability.

Philip persevered, undeterred, "We believe that the Russians have proof that Starrett murdered his first wife and have been using it to make him work for them. We have no idea how many secrets he's passed on to the other side."

Villiers cleared his throat. "Not everything is black and white," he suggested cryptically.

"What the devil is that supposed to mean?" Philip exploded.

"It means that Mrs. Longdon…and her husband should keep their noses out of what is none of their concern. The public does *not* need to know about Starrett."

"Why? Because it's an embarrassment to Her Majesty's Government? There, I agree with you. But isn't it better if there's a full inquiry to ensure that this never happens again?"

"No." The single word was like a dagger, slicing across the air to kill any further discussion along these lines.

Philip's back stiffened. "I suppose you are aware that Starrett and Rallis are involved in the smuggling of Greek antiquities." The other man stared at him stone-faced. "And they're trying to steal billions in sunken gold that is the rightful property of the government." Philip was gratified when Villiers arched one eyebrow in surprise at this. Finally, it was something that he hadn't known. "Why are you turning a blind eye to all this?"

"Now, if you've quite finished, be a good chap and advise your friend to drop the story. She doesn't understand what is at stake. A dead journalist helps no one. It only leads to more questions and that's the last thing anyone wants in this case."

CHAPTER 40

Emmeline sat at her desk fuming the next morning, after Burnell had rung to let her know that the Scottish police had refused to release the reports on the first Lady Starrett's death. More than that, Burnell had become incensed—she would have too—when he was told that all the files had been sealed. They could only be accessed by officials with high-security clearance.

Why? she asked herself. Why was someone—she suspected Villiers—going to such lengths to protect Starrett? He was a murderer *and* a spy. Could Villiers be a traitor as well?

She shivered involuntarily as the latter idea crossed her mind. "God help us all, if it turns out that Villiers works for the Russians too," she said aloud.

She shook her head in frustration, as she drummed her fingers on her desk. There was no such thing as the perfect crime. Starrett was human—for the sake of the argument—therefore he was not infallible. He must have made a mistake, left some telltale clue that pointed to his guilt. If she could only find it.

The sources she had spoken to thus far could provide nothing, neither could Starrett's colleagues, nor his enemies in Parliament.

She sighed heavily and snatched up the clippings file on Starrett again. There was a gap of several years before he returned to England from Canada to take up the title after Lord Greville Starrett died. The old gentleman was a widower and didn't have any children, so the title passed on to Starrett, a distant cousin and the only living relative. Starrett is the last of the line.

Emmeline was curious what Starrett was doing in Canada. There was nothing in the file about his time out there. She turned to her computer and began a search of the major Canadian papers on the remote—*extremely* remote at this stage—chance that she might discover an item that mentioned Starrett.

After a fruitless twenty minutes, she heaved a frustrated sigh and was about to give up when the headline of small article in the *Toronto Globe & Mail* caught her eye.

BRITISH MEN INJURED IN A HIKING ACCIDENT IN THE ROCKIES

Emmeline quickly scanned the article, which revealed that the two men were in their mid-twenties. She became excited when the article identified them as Desmond Starrett and Basil Treadgold, old friends who had been on a hiking holiday but had gotten caught in a fast-moving storm. It went on to report that one of them had suffered extensive internal injuries after slipping and falling. He was not expected to live. Obviously, it was Treadgold. She slammed her hand on her desk. That's why all her efforts to locate him had been unsuccessful.

Terrific. Another dead end, she thought as she scrolled through the rest of the piece, although she knew it was unlikely that there would be anything of interest. When she came to the end she froze, only her heart hammered furiously against her rib cage.

It was impossible. Yet, here was the proof before her

eyes. And of all the people to have discovered the truth, it was Lord Starrett's misfortune that it had been Noel Rallis.

ぐんぐん

Emmeline had paced in her office for several minutes, trying to think what she should do with the information. Instinct told her to go and confront Starrett. However, she was fully cognizant of the fact that this might not endear her to Superintendent Burnell or Philip.

But she had to do something with the information she had learned. The reason why Starrett was going along with Poseidon, despite his misgivings. Rallis had given him no choice.

She also was well aware that Starrett was feeling cornered. His nerves were beginning to fray and he might lash out. He had already murdered his first wife and Tarasova. Another death would not bother him one iota.

My God, her brain screamed as she drew in a ragged breath. *His wife*. In their zeal to find out what Starrett and Rallis were hiding, they had all forgotten about Fiona. She had absolutely no idea of the crimes her husband had committed. Emmeline remembered how cross Starrett had been with Fiona, when he thought she had invited Rallis to the party. What if he turned on her?

Emmeline put a hand to her mouth. She had to warn Fiona Starrett. She grabbed her jacket and her handbag. Her sprint across the newsroom earned her curious glances, but no one stopped her. All the correspondents and the other editors knew better than to get in her way when she was following up on a hot lead.

As she rode down in the lift, she placed three calls from her mobile. To Superintendent Burnell, Philip and Gregory. Breathlessly, she explained what she had learned and underscored her grave concern for Fiona Starrett's safety. Each man stressed that under no circumstance was she to go the Starrett house. Each plea fell on deaf ears. If there was anything at all that she could do to prevent another murder, she had to do it.

Of course on a day when she was in rush, the Tube chose to have a problem. Everything had gone smoothly on the Northern Line from London Bridge to Monument, where she switched to the District Line. It was at that point that things soured. It took her forty minutes to get to the South Kensington station.

In un-British fashion, she elbowed her way along the corridor and up the escalator until she was out on the pavement. She ran the few blocks to Egerton Crescent.

She arrived to find Lady Fiona Starrett speaking on the doorstep with Superintendent Burnell and Sergeant Finch. Fiona was shaking her head and pointing to her chauffeur who was waiting at the curb with the back door open.

"Superintendent Burnell, I'm afraid you've come at extremely inopportune moment. I have to catch the train up to Glasgow to meet my husband. Can't this wait until we get back from Scotland?"

"No, Lady Starrett, it can't wait. We have strong reason to believe that your life may be in danger."

"This must be some sort of a joke. I must say that I find it in extremely poor taste," she sniffed.

"It's not a joke, Lady Starrett," Emmeline called as she reached the steps. Two plainclothes detectives suddenly flanked her, but backed away when Burnell waved them off.

"Emmeline?" Fiona peered at her in surprise. "What are you doing here?" She turned back to Burnell and Finch. "What is all this about?"

"May we step inside?" Burnell asked. He cast a sideways glance to his right and left. "I'm certain you would not want this discussed out here in the open."

At this point, Gregory appeared on the scene. "Lady Starrett, Fiona," he urged in soft tones, "It's in your best interest to listen to what the superintendent has to say."

Emmeline threaded her arm through his and watched Fiona's finely chiseled features contort in annoyance.

"No, I will not." She pushed past Burnell and Finch, and walked to the car. "I can't miss my train." She glanced at her watch. "I can spare you five minutes. That's all. So you had better get on with it."

Two vertical lines appeared between Burnell's brows as he scowled. "Right, there is strong evidence to suggest that your husband murdered his first wife and likely Anastasia Tarasova."

Fiona drew in a ragged breath and stumbled back stunned against the car. "*What*? You're lying. Desmond wouldn't harm anyone."

A muscle pulsed along the superintendent's jaw. "I assure you it's no lie. There's more," he added brusquely.

Fiona's green eyes widened in disbelief. "More? What more could there be?"

"Your husband is also suspected of treason."

She laughed hysterically. "Now, I know you're all mad. Desmond is the most patriotic man I know. That was one of the qualities which attracted me to him when my uncle introduced us in Brussels." She made a dismissive gesture in the air with her hand. "If you've all finished with this cruel joke, I must leave. We are entertaining one of Desmond's counterparts up at Rosemount Castle for a few days. He's overseeing some delicate negotiations with the Russians."

"Russians?" Emmeline couldn't believe her ears. She swallowed hard and took a chance. "You and your husband wouldn't be hosting Aleksei Tarasov, would you?"

For the first time, Fiona smiled. "Yes, poor man. It's simply dreadful that he's been burdened with these negotiations at the same time that he has to arrange his daughter's funeral. That's why Desmond and I thought it might be better to take him away from London. Scotland is the perfect place to grieve out of the public eye."

Emmeline shot a pointed look at Gregory and Burnell. "Yes, I'm sure it is ideal, far from the madding crowd of London."

"Precisely." Fiona slipped into the back seat and the chauffeur closed the door for her. He walked around the car and got in behind the wheel.

Fiona rolled down the window. "You're quite wrong about Desmond. And I warn you, if you persist in spreading such horrid lies you will be hearing from our solicitor."

The window went up again, shutting them all out as the car pulled away from the curb.

"How can anyone be so utterly blind?" Finch wondered.

"Never mind that now," Burnell snapped. "We have to get on to MI5 and inform them of the situation."

"MI5 already knows because this is Villiers's doing," Gregory concluded matter-of-factly.

"What are you getting at, darling?"

He took her by the arms. "Emmy, Villiers knows everything we've been able to piece together to this point. He bluntly ordered Philip to persuade you to drop the story about Lord Starrett. Why? Because he has something up his sleeve, as usual. Villiers concocted Carstairs's cover story about being an assassin and has been involved from the outset in the planning for Tarasov's defection. He must have a reason for sending the Russian into the lion's den— not that any of us have much sympathy for Tarasov. He was a Kremlin man and a Putin loyalist, until something made him reassess his priorities. Everything has been carefully choreographed. Villiers is the puppet master.

He's pulling all our strings."

"Then Hugh must be involved," Emmeline concluded. "But there is one thing I'm certain no one knows about Lord Starrett, except Rallis. I stumbled across the information this afternoon."

When she told them, they were just as stunned as she had been.

"That's a reason to kill, if I ever heard one," Finch acknowledged.

"Starrett is a man obsessed with money and the power his name wields," Burnell pointed out, his tone laced with disgust. "He's already killed for both. He saw no harm in the antiquities smuggling because he had first choice for his own collection. But Rallis had his eye on a bigger prize and backed him into a corner. Starrett saw the risk with *Poseidon* and tried to back out. That's when Rallis drew out his ace and issued an ultimatum: Either his lordship played along with Poseidon like a good boy, or his entire world would come crashing down around him."

"Starrett is rattled. Murdering Tarasova in his own home was an act of desperation," Emmeline observed. "He's irrational. He feels as if he has nothing to lose. I think he's going to kill both Rallis and Tarasov. How he plans to explain that I can't even contemplate. What will happen to Fiona? She's walking in there blind. We all saw her just now. She won't hear a word against her husband."

Burnell's brow puckered. "Yes, Lady Starrett is a stubborn, foolish woman. But we can't stand around here all afternoon." He signaled to the plainclothes detectives, who hurried to their car. "Finch, you and I are going back to the station. I'll ring Philip to apprise him of the situation on the way." He was already pulling out his mobile from his inside jacket pocket as they walked toward their car. "Of course, I'll have to report to the Boy Wonder. I must give him credit, though. The one thing he's good at is dealing with officious civil servants. That allows us to concentrate on the job at hand."

Emmeline followed Gregory to his Jaguar and called, "We'll get on the next train to Glasgow and make our way to the Isle of Mull from there."

Her husband nodded, a glint of admiration in his eyes. "We'll send you a postcard from the Scottish wilds."

Burnell stopped dead and slammed the car door closed. He walked over to the husband and wife, who stood side by side. He wagged an admonishing finger at them. "The pair of you are not going anywhere," he hissed through clenched teeth. "If you attempt to leave London, I will have you arrested."

"Not very sporting, I must say," Gregory retorted casually.

"Longdon, this is not some lark." Burnell's solid form trembled from the wisps of his thinning hair to the soles of his feet. "Starrett and Rallis are ruthless killers. There is nothing to choose between them. I will not have two civilians with an unnatural appetite for danger blundering into a situation for which they are completely unprepared to deal with. It is out of the question. What do you think you can do? Except wind up dead, that is."

Gregory sniffed. "Emmy and I take great exception to blundering, don't we, darling?" She nodded her assent and looped her arm through his elbow. "We've never blundered our way through life and we don't intend to start now." A smile tugged at the corners of his mouth. "We have a purpose. We're dedicated to justice."

A primitive growl erupted from somewhere deep within the superintendent's chest.

"You really should have that seen to, Oliver," Gregory recommended unhelpfully. "It may be a sign of a more serious condition."

By this time, Finch had joined them and was peering at

his boss in concern. He stepped in between the superintendent and Gregory. "Longdon, you know you're only making matters worse." He turned to Emmeline in appeal. "Be reasonable."

"I think we're being eminently reasonable. We're going to do our civic duty and prevent two, possibly three, murders, as well as put an end to a traitor's rein of betrayal."

Finch sighed, disappointment etched in the lines of his face.

Emmeline sought to diffuse the highly-charged atmosphere. "How about if we promise to go straight to Hugh the instant we land on Mull? We will place ourselves entirely in his hands and abide by whatever directives he deems necessary."

She offered the two detectives her sweetest smile and kept her fingers crossed behind her back.

"Carstairs is a murder suspect" was Burnell's terse rejoinder.

"Come on, Oliver, you're just being argumentative. You know who the real culprits are Starrett and Rallis. Villiers and Acheson can vouch for Carstairs. Are you saying that you don't trust *them*? Villiers I can well understand. No one can completely trust that man. But Acheson?"

He saw that the superintendent was beginning to waver. "I must be going soft. It's sheer lunacy. I'm willing to wager that Philip and Villiers will not like it either. It will serve you right, if you get yourselves killed."

Gregory grinned. "Oh Oliver, you've always had such a charming turn of phrase. It warms my heart to know that you'll miss us."

"Hmph. I hope I never lay eyes on you again, Longdon. However, as one charged with upholding the law, I must take even *your* safety into account."

Gregory threw an arm around the superintendent's shoulders. "I knew a teddy bear was lurking under that gruff exterior," he teased as he patted Burnell's ample mid-section to emphasize his point.

Burnell shrugged himself free. "Leave off. Now, get out of my sight before I come back to my senses."

Emmeline laid a gentle hand on his arm. "Thank you. We just have to see this thing through. You do see that, don't you? We promise not to take any unnecessary risks. Besides, Philip and Villiers don't have to know until we're actually up in Mull," she whispered. "By that time, we'll already be with Hugh. What harm could come to us?"

They got into the car quickly. Allowing the super-intendent to think about her question was only providing him an opening to stop them.

As they were pulling away from the curb, Gregory took his eyes off the road briefly to ask, "Emmy, do you know how to contact Carstairs?"

She leveled a steady gaze on his face. "No."

He nodded and turned back to the traffic. "Right, I thought not. That's my girl. Never give away your advantage." With his eyes on the road, he lifted her hand to his lips and brushed her knuckles with a kiss. "I knew life wouldn't be dull if I married you."

CHAPTER 41

In the end, they didn't take the train up to Glasgow. Gregory had an idea how they could get up to the Isle of Mull faster. They went home, threw enough warm clothes in an overnight bag to last them a few days, and drove to Hampshire instead. Through one of his vast network of contacts, he managed to cadge them a last-minute lift on a RAF Chinook heavy-lift helicopter that was leaving Odiham air station. Apparently, one of Gregory's old friends owed him a favor.

Emmeline had to admit that she was rather impressed. *It must have been a* very *big favor, indeed*, she mused, as the helicopter, which was designed to transport personnel and provide logistics support, rose off the ground. It went against all her journalistic instincts, but she asked her husband no questions. Now was not the time, especially since there were 10 troops on the flight with them as well. However once this was over, she was going to pin Gregory down and *demand* an explanation.

She tucked her arm through Gregory's and settled back for the flight. She smiled and inclined her head at Group Captain Jeremy Taylor, who had been extremely solicitous. He had told her that he and his men were on their way to RRH Benbecula, the defense radar station on North Uist in the Outer Hebrides. "A mere hop, skip, and a jump to Mull," he had assured her with a boyish grin.

Yes, Mull may be a slight detour for them, but the entire trip was highly unusual to say the least. She tilted her head to one side and contemplated her husband's profile. There were still so many secrets about his past that she still didn't know. She bit her lip. *Would she ever*?

Taylor's voice jarred her from these disconcerting thoughts. "I managed to get word to your friend Carstairs. He'll be waiting for you at the Galleon Grill. He said that it's behind the post office on the Main Street, near the town clock. We'll be dropping you on the hill just above the town. It will be short walk down."

Gregory nodded. "Great. Thanks, Group Captain. You've been a tremendous help. My wife and I can't thank you enough."

The other man smiled. "My pleasure. Anything for good old Badger Crisp. Any mate of his is all right in my book."

Badger Crisp? Emmeline mentally filed away the name. It was one tiny clue she would definitely follow up on at her first opportunity.

They were quiet for the rest of the flight. Emmeline even dozed for a half-hour. Shortly after she awoke, Taylor told them that they would be landing. She sat up, all her nerves tingling, and glanced out the window for her first view of Mull. It was seventy-thirty. The sun had set a good three hours earlier. The wind was carrying a gauzy scarf of cloud across the evening sky, which was dotted with a smattering of winking stars.

A cold gust laden with salty sea mist assaulted her as Taylor offered his hand and helped her to descend from the helicopter ten minutes later. Gregory followed without any assistance and one of the soldiers tossed down their bags to him. After shaking hands with both of them, Taylor scrambled back inside. They huddled together, out of the propellers' draft, and waved as the helicopter lifted off again.

They each grabbed a bag and followed the road down the steep hill straight down to the harbor and Main Street. They found the Galleon Grill easily. It was bright and modern inside. The color scheme was black and red. They saw Carstairs immediately. He was seated at a corner table toward the back of the restaurant. He gave them a brief nod of acknowledgement and they quickly crossed the room to join him.

They had barely shrugged out of their jackets and sat down, when Hugh hissed out of the corner of his mouth, "What the devil are you doing here? You can stay the night, but you leave in the morning."

Emmeline scowled at him. "It's no good lecturing us. We are *not* leaving." Her voice dipped low, but it held fierce determination.

Gregory leaned back and rested his head on his interlaced fingers. "You see before you a woman of strong convictions. And a short temper. I advise you not to forget that. The word *no* is not in her lexicon."

Carstairs rounded on him. "How about the word *dead*? Is that in your lexicon?" He spat these words at them, a muscle in his jaw throbbing. "You're a pair of fools. You're going jeopardize everything and get yourselves killed in the process."

"We are not," Emmeline replied calmly. "We came to help."

Hugh slumped back against the red banquette and huffed a bitter laugh. "How? You're not trained professionals. You're just going to be in the way."

"Well if you stop chuntering on and listen, I'll tell you. There's something I discovered about Lord Starrett since you left London."

Hugh blinked at her and sat there without uttering a word for several minutes, while he digested the information.

"That makes him more unpredictable."

"Yes, that's what I thought. I'm terribly worried about Fiona. She's up there at the castle with her husband, Rallis, and Tarasov, a dangerous triangle."

"Tarasov? He's here?" She nodded. "Why bring him to Mull?"

Emmeline shot a sideways glance at her husband. "Gregory suspects that this is all part of Villiers's grand plan. Fiona told us that Starrett was conducting some delicate negotiations with Tarasov. Obviously, MI5 has tasked him with overseeing the Russian's defection. This places Starrett in the perfect position to kill Tarasov, thus exposing himself as the spy. I think he also plans to murder Rallis."

Hugh shot a look at Gregory and grimaced. "Yes, it sounds very much like Villiers." Some of the tension in his body seemed to ease. "Maybe that's why Philip is on his way up as well. At least, that will be one sane person."

"Philip is coming?" Emmeline frowned. "He didn't tell us."

Hugh fixed his hazel stare on her face. "Yes, he should be here by midnight. And since when does he report to you? Philip told me to put the two of you under lock and key, the instant you set foot on the island. He'll deal with you when he gets here. He said under no circumstances am I to allow you anywhere near Starrett or Rallis."

"If Philip's coming, that means he's arranged for backup," she reasoned. "But midnight is an eternity away. So much can happen in the intervening hours." She held his gaze. "Hugh, it might be too late if we wait. We have to do something."

He smirked. "What? All *three* of us?"

"Don't forget David and Goliath," she pointed out.

"Bible stories are not going to help us."

"Carstairs, we have the element of surprise on our side," Gregory chimed in, "You've been watching Starrett and Rallis for months. Now you know that they're after the sunken gold and are smuggling Greek antiquities…"

Hugh cut him off. "What antiquities?"

"Of course, you had already left London, when that scheme came to light." Gregory quickly explained what had learned from Stavros and went on, "You must have some idea of where they've been concentrating their efforts. We can catch them red-handed and present Acheson with a *fait accompli*. Surely, you have enough official authority to be able to call in the Royal Navy to assist you. Emmy and I can serve as your deputies until Acheson arrives."

Emmeline held her breath as Hugh eyed them skeptically.

"The two of you are experts at wearing people down. You keep hammering away until you weaken a person's defenses and he has no choice but to succumb."

She smiled and laced her fingers through Gregory's because she knew they had won the argument. "A very cynical attitude, I must say."

Hugh threw his head back and laughed. "But true and you know it. Now then, deputies, I think you should get a hot meal into you. It's going to be a long night."

Carstairs disappeared for half an hour. While he was gone, Gregory enjoyed a steak filet and Emmeline had a hearty vegetable soup with freshly baked bread because there was nervous flutter in the pit of her stomach.

Hugh slipped back onto the banquette as they were finishing up. "Right, everything's on schedule. The Royal Navy is in motion. I had already made the arrangements *before* the two of you showed up. I had to use Villiers's name, but they agreed to conduct the raid on the gold." He glanced at his watch. "It's mobilizing now. Let's hope they can get here in time. The raid is going to be rather tricky.

"Since I left London, I've been wracking my brain as to where the gold could be located. Based on my surveillance of Rallis over the past year, his salvage boats have been making forays into the Atlantic Ocean at night and returning in the early morning hours. I snuck onto a boat once when the crew went into Tobermory for supplies. The boat was clean. Therefore, Rallis is hiding the gold somewhere near the site of the shipwreck. I think it's in Fingal's Cave on the Isle of Staffa."

"Why there?" Gregory asked.

"The cave has been closed off to tourists for the past year because a wall collapsed. Very convenient for Rallis. It would be a short trip for his salvage boats. They unload the gold in the cave, where it remains until it is collected by Rallis's yacht on its return trip to Greece."

Emmeline shook her head in amazement. "The sheer audacity of it is mind-boggling. I can't even begin to contemplate the planning it required."

"Well, that's Rallis for you. Cunning and devious as hell," Hugh remarked. "The reason I think the Staffa raid is going to prove difficult is because it's open ocean. They'll see us coming. But we have to trust in the might of the Royal Navy.

"Now for the antiquities problem you just dropped in my lap. Over the last few months, I've observed Rallis's yacht docking in the cove just below Rosemount Castle. A cave leads directly into the castle. My guess is that he unloads the smuggled items there and then the yacht slips back out for part two of its mission at Staffa. In the interim, Starrett takes his time examining the artifacts and selecting the ones he wants for his collection. I suspect the rest are hidden away in the castle until Rallis can find a buyer.

"It will be easier to raid the castle. The local police can help." His gaze flickered between them. "Do you still want to be in for the kill so to speak?"

Emmeline could tell he wanted them to say no. She was going to have to disappoint him. "Rather. This is not simply about getting an exclusive. I wouldn't be able to forgive myself, if I didn't see this thing through to the end. We're not turning back now, are we, darling?"

Gregory patted her hand and beamed at Carstairs. "I wouldn't dream of it."

Hugh shrugged his shoulders in resignation. "Wonderful."

CHAPTER 42

The Navy ship dispatched to the Isle of Staffa had not encountered Rallis's yacht *en route*. Hugh didn't know whether that was a good or a bad sign. He paced the length of the deck, his muscles coiled tightly. He was heedless of the icy wind whipping at his face. His mind was on only one thing: the gold. He watched as two Zodiac motorized dinghies with twenty armed sailors were lowered into the roiling waters. Within five minutes, the sailors were disembarking at the yawning mouth of Fingal's Cave, whose hexagonally jointed basalt columns appeared even more imposing and ominous swathed in darkness.

The waiting was excruciating. Finally, the sailors' voices and their splashing footsteps bounced off the cave's walls and drifted out to the ship. Hugh heard the captain's radio crackle into life. "We've found it, sir. The gold's here."

Hugh tilted his head back and shook his fists at the sky in triumph. There was no time to waste, though. He asked the captain to have his crew send a launch to load the gold onto to the ship and had a call patched through to the Treasury. Next, he called Villiers to report on the mission's success.

"Right, no rest for the wicked. Get back to Mull," Villiers ordered. "The job's not done. A RAF helicopter will be there any minute to pick you up. Acheson will be arriving on the island within the hour. He has a Special Branch unit with him, which will take Tarasov under its protection. Acheson will be escorting him to a safe house, until we can finalize the permanent arrangements. Superintendent Burnell and Sergeant Finch are on the way too. They're coordinating with the local police to arrest the ballerina's murderer."

Hugh's elation was snuffed out in an instant. "Yes, sir." He paused and then asked, "You knew along about the mole, didn't you?"

"Not at the outset. But when the Russians attempted to point the finger of blame at you, it confirmed all my suspicions. If it's worth anything, it was brilliantly executed."

"Oh, yes a masterful job," Hugh concurred bitterly.

෧෨෧

Emmeline stalked the perimeter of the living room in Hugh's snug cottage like a caged animal. For caged, they literally were. Gregory was taking the situation philosophically, but she wanted to throw something or alternately hit someone, preferably Hugh. He had played them for fools. After they had finished their meal at the Galleon Grill, he had taken them back to the cottage. He said it would be safer for them to wait there, until it was time for the raids.

The minute they stepped inside the cottage, three policemen—who must have been bred by giants in Emmeline's opinion—materialized and effectively put them under house arrest.

With a shrug of his shoulders and a sheepish grin tugging at his mouth, Hugh apologized for the ruse. "I can't in good conscience allow the two of you anywhere near the raids tonight. It's far too dangerous for amateurs. I'm sorry if I misled you into believing otherwise. Instead, I'm delighted to have you as my guests. Consider my humble abode"—his hand swept in a wide arc around the living room—"as your home, while you are here."

"Hmph," she grunted as she remembered his parting words. She shot a glance at Gregory, who was quietly savoring a tumbler of single malt Scotch. "What are you smiling at?"

The two policemen stationed inside the cottage discreetly removed themselves to the kitchen, not wanting to be in the line of fire between husband and wife.

Gregory stood up and walked over to her. He drew her into his embrace, which she resisted at first. "Emmy, you know Carstairs was right."

"I know no such thing." Her words came out muffled because her face was pressed against his chest.

He held her away from him and gave her a pointed look. He opened his mouth to say something, but whatever it was it died before the words ever reached his lips.

"Oi," shouted the policeman who had stepped into the garden for a cigarette.

In the suspended second between heartbeats, a sickening crack seared the air. A low, almost primitive moan came in its wake, as the *thud* of a man's body crumpled upon the cold, hard earth. The police officers in the kitchen were already scrambling.

"On the ground. Stay inside," one of them yelled to Emmeline and Gregory, as their pounding footfalls carried them toward the unknown danger lurking outside.

With his arm around her shoulders, Gregory virtually tossed his wife behind the sofa and dove beside her. They lay face-down on their stomachs, their bodies pressed close together. They covered their heads with their hands.

The splintering of glass in the kitchen mingled with the desperate, frenzied cries of men scuffling in a mortal struggle to survive.

Gregory could stand it no more. Emmy would be all right where she was. But he had to go help those policemen, who had the misfortune to be here tonight because they had been assigned to guard them. He lifted his head cautiously and peered over the back of the sofa. The living room was empty. He rose to his haunches, his ears straining to discern who had the upper hand.

Emmeline's hand flashed out and clamped down on his arm, her fingers digging with ferocity through the sleeve of his sweater to the marrow of his bones. "Don't you dare take a step outside." A tremor of sheer terror thrummed in her voice.

"Emmy, I have to do something…"

The night shuddered as two more gunshots exploded in quick succession. And then came the throbbing, suffocating sound of *nothing*.

They're eyes locked. They waited, paralyzed. Was it over? Or were the attackers still out there?

They didn't have to wait long to find out the answer. Something came hurtling through the front window. Orange-red tongues of flames greedily started to lick at the drapes, the plush carpet, the tables and chairs. Noxious, charcoal smoke filled the air, stinging their eyes. They grabbed their jackets, which had been dumped on a corner of the sofa, and covered their noses and mouths. A scorching trail snaked toward the front door, danced around its frame, and set it ablaze.

A scream was ripped from Emmeline's throat. Soon the entire cottage would be engulfed.

Gregory gripped her by the shoulders and gave her a

rough shake. "Emmy, we have to get to the kitchen. *Now*." A violent cough wracked his body and it took him a few seconds to get his breath back. "It's our only chance," he whispered.

She gave a curt nod. An unnatural calm seemed to have settled over her. He could still see the glint of terror in her eyes, but equally as strong was a determination to live.

Half-crouched, they scurried to the kitchen, which was at the back of the cottage. Thousands of shards of glass crunched beneath their feet. The flames hadn't reached this part of the house yet, but the smoke was making its skulking approach.

The door handle rattled as Gregory twisted it, but it wouldn't budge. He surmised that the heat of the fire had caused the door to expand. He took the handle between both hands and gave it vicious shake. They exchanged a look at the sound of the living room ceiling caving in, after a support beam collapsed. Gregory gritted his teeth and savagely wrenched the door handle again. This time, it gave way to his touch and opened.

They burst from the cottage, their feet propelling them toward the far end of the garden, where they were seized by a paroxysm of coughing. Bent over, with their hands on their knees, they ravenously gulped lungfuls of air for several minutes.

Above the crackle of the flames, a male voice drifted to their ears. "This is not your lucky day, Carstairs."

Their heads snapped up. Their burning eyes were squinting and blinking desperately. When their vision came into focus, they wished that it hadn't. The silhouettes of two men, guns in hand, loomed before them.

"That's not Carstairs," one of them said. "The boss is not going to like it, Ron."

"What do you mean it's not Carstairs?" Ron snarled.

"It's Longdon and his nosy reporter wife."

Emmeline could see Ron's teeth gleaming in the flickering light. "Well, well, well. Then, I'd say the boss is going be very pleased indeed."

"We came for Carstairs," his mate pointed out.

"So we get rid of three birds with one stone. It's more efficient that way." Without warning, he snatched up a handful of Gregory's turtleneck and yanked him to a standing position. "Where's your friend Carstairs?"

Gregory cleared his throat. Although his voice was hoarse from the smoke, it held his usual flippant tone. "Carstairs? Never heard of the chap. My wife and I are here on holiday."

Ron smiled and drove his fist into Gregory's stomach. A stunned "oof" escaped from a winded Gregory. Emmeline struggled to break free of Ron's friend's grasp, but couldn't so she stomped on his foot instead.

This elicited a string of colorful curses.

He loosened his hold and she ran over to Gregory. Her gaze was full of daggers for Ron.

Ron brandished his gun just inches from her face. "That's enough," he roared.

Gregory fumbled for her arm and pulled her toward him. He straightened up and drew a deep breath.

"There's a bullet in here for each of you," Ron told them nonchalantly, as if he were reading his grocery list. "If it were up to me, I'd do you now and get it over with. Save everyone a whole lot of trouble." Emmeline drew in a ragged breath. "But I have a feeling the boss would like to have a final chat, so we wouldn't want to spoil his surprise. Isn't that right, Matt?" His cohort nodded. "Just tell us where Carstairs is."

Gregory slipped his arm around Emmeline's waist. He felt her body trembling against his and gave her a reassuring squeeze.

He flashed a mischievous grin. "Carstairs who?"

Clearly, Ron was not a man who liked being thwarted. The force of his blow was injected with even more spite than the first one.

Gregory doubled over, the wind escaping from his lungs, but he had to have the last word. "Was it something I said?" This came out as a croak.

CHAPTER 43

Ron and Matt herded them into the backseat of a dark Vauxhall Corsa that was parked about a hundred feet from Hugh's cottage, which by now was entirely engulfed in flames. The fire brigade would be on the scene any minute. They heard sirens in the distance, but it was too late.

Ron drove like a man possessed down to the harbor, where they had a Zodiac moored.

The waterfront was deserted because it was close to midnight by this time. Emmeline and Gregory were dragged out of the car by their necks. The hard muzzle of a gun was immediately pressed between their shoulders.

Ron gave Gregory a rough shove. "Move," he hissed.

Wordlessly, they descended some stone steps to the Zodiac. Gregory stepped in first and offered his hand to help Emmeline to board. Matt waved his gun impatiently and they sat down on one side, their knees touching one another. Matt sat opposite them, his gun trained on them. Ron started the engine and the Zodiac sputtered into life. Emmeline and Gregory had to cling to the rope ringing the dinghy, otherwise they risked tumbling into the netting of undulating liquid silk.

Emmeline's mind was racing. She wondered how deep the water was. Perhaps they should take a chance and jump overboard? She slid a sideways glance toward Gregory. His face was half in shadow. He caught her eye and winked. "Don't worry" he mouthed.

That was all well and good, but worry seemed the only appropriate thing to do in this situation.

Ron drew alongside a sleek yacht and cut the engine. "End of the line." He chortled as he scrambled to the ladder leading up to the deck. "In more ways than one."

Matt shared in his tasteless joke, while Emmeline stared at him stone-faced. "What no sense of humor?" he asked but didn't wait for a response. He waved the gun at the ladder.

Gregory patted her hand and went up first. Emmeline followed close behind him.

Rallis was on deck to greet them with Ron at his side.

"Longdon, Emmeline," he said, a lupine grin upon his lips, "welcome to the *Athenian Princess*. I know you've been *dying* to see her." He put a hand to his mouth. "Oops, poor choice of words."

"Rallis, we're not the only ones who know about the gold and the smuggling," Emmeline retorted. "You and Starrett are deluded, if you think you're going to get away with it."

Rallis tossed his head back and laughed. "My dear, Emmeline, your problem is that you never know when to stop. First, it was the articles about the trial for the late, lamented Jenna's murder. I did tell you that I would be acquitted."

"You weren't acquitted," Gregory sneered. "David Copperthwaite was conveniently murdered, and your trial was dismissed because all the evidence mysteriously disappeared."

Rallis shrugged one shoulder and lowered himself into

a nearby chair. "A mere detail. These things happen. The result was the same. Next, you and your dear little wife started poking your nose into Poseidon and you"—his brows knit together and a dark shadow fell across his features—"sent Constantinides sniffing around my antiquities business." He clucked his tongue. "Not a wise move. How is old Stavros, by the way? I would have sent flowers, but I had to leave London unexpectedly."

Gregory lunged for Rallis's throat, but Emmeline stepped in front of him before his fingers could sink into his flesh.

Rallis chuckled. "And here I thought your wife was the one with the hot temper." He pushed himself to his feet and glanced at his watch. "Well, I can't linger about here chatting all night. I'm rather pressed for time. I must thank you both for saving me the trouble of coming after you in London. It's less messy this way. We'll simply lighten the load by two, when we stop to retrieve the gold." His brow furrowed and his jaw clenched. "I regret that Carstairs couldn't be here to join you. I'll have to catch up with him another day."

Emmeline marveled at the sanguine manner in which he was discussing how he intended to kill them. She inched closer to Gregory and laced her fingers through his.

"Ron, take our guests down to one of the cabins, until we get to Staffa."

Ron grinned. "It would be my pleasure, Mr. Rallis." With faux politeness, he sketched a bow at Emmeline and Gregory, but the sneer on his lips belied the gesture. "After you."

Emmeline swallowed down the panic that clutched at her chest as Ron locked them in a rather luxurious stateroom.

"What are we going to do?" she whispered.

Then she remembered her mobile. She fumbled in the

pocket of her jacket and pulled it out in triumph. However, her elation was short-lived. She had no reception out here on the water.

She threw up her hands. "Useless."

Gregory spied a telephone on the bedside table. He huffed a bitter laugh, when he picked up the receiver. "The line's dead. Rallis probably had it disconnected before Ron brought us down here."

Tears stung her eyelids. No. She shook her head. She was not going to give up hope. They *would* get out of this nightmare. Somehow.

"Gregory, what if we…" But her sentence trailed off at the sound of an approaching boat.

Their eyes locked. All their nerves tingled and their muscles were wound in knots. They were on the other side of the yacht, so it was pointless to shout for help.

They heard muffled voices coming from the deck. They tiptoed across the room and pressed their ears to the door.

Rallis was arguing with the newcomer. "You can bloody well forget it," he snarled. "Your hands are just as dirty as mine, more so in fact, so let's not pretend otherwise. There is no way in hell you can back out now. If I go down, *Lord Starrett*, I'm going to see to it that you lose everything."

Emmeline grabbed Gregory's arm and held her breath.

"I've had enough of you, Noel. You're *nothing*. A common blackmailer. A street thug," Starrett's booming, irate tone rose an octave with each utterance, until it seemed that it reverberated around the entire ship. "I'm a peer of the realm. You can't touch me. You're not fit to lick my boots. And you're never going to open your bloody mouth again."

They heard Rallis laugh. "Bravo, Desmond. How long did you stand in front of the mirror and practice that amusing little speech?" He paused and the timbre of his voice changed. "Hey, hold on. We can discuss…"

Emmeline jumped as two gunshots exploded on the deck above. She and Gregory hit the floor as two more shots smothered Ron and Matt's startled shouts. She prayed that Starrett wouldn't come down below. Panicked footsteps seemed to be thundering in every direction. Most likely it was the crew scurrying to find cover.

In the midst of all the chaos, a boat engine stammered and rumbled, and then died away.

ɔɕɔ

When silence had leached into every nook and there no longer appeared to be any threat, Gregory and Emmeline got to their feet and started pounding on the door with their fists.

"We're locked in," she called, "Please let us out."

They kept up a constant barrage until a male voice tentatively asked, "Who are you?"

"Gregory and Emmeline Longdon. I'm a journalist with the *Clarion* and my husband is Symington's chief investigator," she said. "Rallis had his men put us in here because we were going to expose his crimes. He was going to kill us. Open the door, please. We can prove who we are."

It was quiet for several seconds.

"All right. Stand back from the door."

They did as the man directed. A key turned in the lock and the door was pushed open. One of the crew was standing in the corridor, a fire extinguisher held aloft, prepared to wield it as a weapon if necessary. He was in his late twenties and obviously shaken by the night's events, as they all were.

Gregory raised his hands in the air. "Easy, old chap. We're not armed."

The young man took a deep a breath and gave a curt nod. He lowered the fire extinguisher. "Sorry, we didn't know anyone else was aboard. We didn't know what to expect."

"We quite understand," Emmeline replied with a smile. "We have to return to shore. We must contact the police and Philip Acheson of Foreign Office. They're on Mull to arrest Lord Starrett. They have no idea Starrett murdered Rallis and the others. Rallis's men also burned down the cottage of a man named Hugh Carstairs. He's...with the authorities." She didn't want to say he was MI5. As the official line went, it was on a need-to-know basis and he most certainly didn't need to know.

There was a tremor in his voice. "I believe everything you are saying. Truly. The thing is Mr. Rallis isn't dead."

Gregory and Emmeline exchanged a startled look.

"He's in a very bad way, but he's still alive. Just."

Gregory pushed past him and bounded up the stairs two at a time. Emmeline was close on his heels, with the reluctant crewman bringing up the rear.

Rallis was sprawled, spread-eagled on his back on the floor in the yacht's parlor. From the sinister hole in the center of his chest seeped his blood—thick, crimson and terrifying. A trickle of blood dribbled from the corner of his mouth. His breathing was labored. He shifted his head slightly, when he heard them enter the room. His lips moved, but no words came out.

"He's needs a doctor at once," a more senior crew member said. "We called ashore and the doctor will be waiting. We were about to take him in the Zodiac. The ride might kill him, but he'll die here if he doesn't get treatment."

Gregory made a snap decision. "We'll take him. Radio ahead let the doctor know. Also radio Philip Acheson of the Foreign Office. He's already on the island. The local police will know how to get ahold of him. Your man there will explain." He jerked his head at the young fellow, who had let them out of the stateroom. "There's no time to waste. Tell Acheson that Starrett is headed back to Rosemount Castle to get Tarasov. We're going to leave Rallis in the doctor's care and then we're on our way to the castle. Emmeline and Longdon. Got it?"

The man nodded. "Consider it done."

Four crewmen gingerly loaded a moaning Rallis, who was bundled in several layers of blankets, into the bottom of the Zodiac. Gregory and Emmeline clambered in and soon they were bouncing back toward the harbor front.

Her fingers clawed at the rope as dinghy went up and down, up and down. She no longer had any sensation in them. They were wet and frozen. No matter how skillful Gregory's steering was, the inky water still splashed over the sides. And now, the malevolent wind was sending ominous clouds scudding across the sky.

She carefully bent forward, ears straining against the wind. Was Rallis still breathing? She couldn't hear anything. She leaned in closer. Still nothing. Her pulse was surging through her veins.

She shot a look at Gregory. The wind caught the tremor in her voice. "I…I think…"

He cut her off, barely flicking a glance in her direction. "Yes, darling, you're quite right. He's dead."

CHAPTER 44

Dr. Fordyce oversaw the transfer of Rallis's body to an awaiting ambulance, which would take him to the morgue. Meanwhile, Burnell and Finch were leaning against a nearby car, arms folded over their chests. Not even the merest hint of a smile could be discerned in either detective's face. Foregoing any greeting, they hustled Gregory and Emmeline into the backseat.

Finch took the curves of the narrow, winding road like a demon.

"Here we are again," Burnell said over his shoulder. "Arson, dead bodies scattered about, a murderer on the loose, and who do we find in the thick of things? The two of you."

"Oliver, are you feeling left out? We can't help it if we're in demand. You know it's not easy being popular."

"You should both be in jail," he grumbled, "particularly you, Longdon, for perverting the course of justice."

"That's rather unfair. If it hadn't been for Emmy's intrepid reporting and the information I discovered from my contacts, you would never have cracked these cases. Admit it. Besides, you can't tell me that you're shedding a tear for Rallis."

"Hmph. Certainly not. But in the course of twenty-four hours, I've aged twenty years on your account. You're a menace to yourselves and my sanity." Finch cleared his throat, although his eyes remained on the road. "And Finch's sanity as well. Carstairs was supposed to have you under house arrest."

The superintendent should not have brought up this sore subject.

"That was completely unwarranted," Emmeline snapped, still chafing at the indignity.

Burnell swiveled his neck around to squint at her through the gloom. "Was it? From my vantage point, it was justified. Despite my precautions, you still managed to wreak havoc. I don't think Tobermory will ever be the same again."

"*We* didn't set fire to Hugh's cottage," she pointed out.

"No, but it wouldn't have happened if you hadn't brought attention to Carstairs and yourselves."

She sniffed and focused her gaze on the dark blur flying past her window. She had no idea where they were. She assumed that they were on the way to Rosemount Castle. At least she hoped so.

"Oliver…" Gregory ventured.

"*Superintendent Burnell*," he replied through gritted teeth without turning around again.

Gregory sighed. "Tsk. Tsk. Someone's in a tetchy mood."

"This is not a game, Longdon. You're lucky that Starrett didn't know that the two of you were on the yacht. No more heroics. Philip and the Special Branch team should be at the castle already. If everything works according to plan, Tarasov will already be in their custody. They're going to take him and Lady Starrett to a safe house. That leaves us to deal with her husband. The two of you will remain in the car, *under supervision*. I will not risk you jeopardizing…"

His mobile started to scream in his pocket.

"Burnell," he barked. He listened for several seconds. "Damn and blast. Right. We're nearly there." He severed the connection.

Finch turned his head slightly to cast a glance at his boss. "Trouble, sir?"

"Trouble? No, not at all," he responded facetiously. "That was Philip, by the way. He said that Starrett arrived just as he was walking out the door with Tarasov and Lady Starrett. He pressed a gun to Philip's head…"

"No." The single, breathless word was dragged from Emmeline's lips and hung upon the air. "Please tell me Philip isn't hurt?"

"For the time being no. The Special Branch team had no choice but to withdraw. That means Starrett has Philip, Tarasov, and Lady Starrett. The local police don't dare rush the castle." Burnell chuckled, but it rang hollow. "But wait, I haven't gotten to the best part yet. Starrett has a special request. He wants Emmeline to join them, in view of the fact that she has shown *such* a keen interest in the story so far. How he even knew you were here, I don't know? He felt you'd like to be there for the denouement. So no, Finch, I wouldn't call it trouble. I'd say that we have a bloody ticking time bomb on our hands."

"I'll go," Emmeline asserted with calm assurance.

"No," a trio of adamant male voices overruled as the car crunched onto the gravel forecourt and drew to a halt before the hulking silhouette of the castle.

They all spoke at once.

"Have you flipped your lid?" Burnell rebuked. "Philip said that under no circumstance were you to even contemplate it."

"Emmeline, it's far too dangerous," said the solicitous Finch.

"Oliver, lock her in the boot until it's all over," was her ever-loving husband's contribution for which he received a sharp elbow in the ribs.

"It's my decision. I want to go in. Perhaps, Starrett will let them go if I do."

Gregory grasped her by the shoulders and shook her. "And what if he doesn't?" he demanded.

"Emmeline, we can't put a wire on you. There's no time. You'll be going in naked, so to speak. Please be sensible," Burnell entreated. "And take some pity on me. How will I live with myself, if I have three dead victims on my conscience the rest of my life? I'll be a broken man. You wouldn't be cruel enough to do that to me, would you?"

She bit back a smile. "Superintendent Burnell, you know I have the utmost respect for you, but my mind is made up," she countered. "There must be a reason he asked for me."

"Of course, there is, you stubborn woman. He wants to silence you forever" was Gregory's caustic rejoinder.

Emmeline leaned over, took his face between her hands, and pressed a soft kiss to his lips. "I love you, darling, but I'm going."

Before any of them could stop her, she was out the door and walking across the gravel with slow, measured steps. Vaguely, she registered the shadowy, sculpted shapes of the walled garden to her right. For some unfathomable reason, she wasn't afraid. She heard the car doors slamming behind her, but she kept her eyes fixed on the elegant outlines of the towers and turrets of the looming castle.

She took a deep breath before rapping on the heavy oak door with her knuckles. Almost immediately, it opened and a triangle of golden light spilled onto the gravel.

"Ah, Emmeline," Starrett greeted her with a smile, a

gun dangling carelessly from his hand. "So good of you to come."

Standing before him now, she lost some of her nerve. Her knees felt like water. She was certain that they would buckle under her.

She swallowed hard and did her best to brazen it out. She tried to channel a bit of Gregory's insouciance. "We journalists are curious creatures. You made the offer sound too tempting to resist."

He gave her an odd look. She could not read the expression in his eyes. "Mmm. Please do come in." He stepped aside to allow her to pass. "The others are waiting for us upstairs in the parlor. They must be getting restless. I'm afraid I had to lock them in." He patted his pocket, presumably where he had the key. "Not very hospitable, I know. But I couldn't have them going on walkabout. Shall we?" He waved the hand holding the gun toward the intricately carved oak staircase to their left.

"Seeing the parlor would be the highlight of what has been a rather dull day," she murmured.

The creaking of the floorboards beneath her feet seemed unnaturally loud in the disconcerting hush. She could hear Starrett's breathing behind her.

At the top of the first landing, he led her to the second door on her left. He unlocked it, inclined his head, and ushered her into an elegant room with a high-vaulted ceiling and custard-yellow walls. There was an arched, painted niche above the stone fireplace. The windows were set in arched, recessed alcoves. The drapes were partially drawn.

Three heads glanced up at their entrance.

"Emmeline," Philip groaned and dropped his head between his hands.

He was seated on one of the two sofas opposite one another before the fireplace. A dainty cherry coffee table looked rather forlorn in the space between them.

Next to Philip was a clean-shaven gentleman in his sixties, with a long, lean countenance, whose translucent skin made his veins stand out. He held himself erect. His icy blue eyes missed nothing. This could only be Tarasov. She saw the faint resemblance to his late daughter.

Lady Starrett, meanwhile, was huddled in a corner of the sofa across from them. Her fretful hands pleated the hem of her skirt. She licked her lips as she eyed her husband warily.

"Emmeline why don't you join Acheson? He looks a bit lonely," Starrett said, giving her a nudge with the gun.

Philip's head snapped up, his blue gaze never leaving Starrett's face.

Once she was settled next to Philip, his lordship nodded. "Good. I don't know about any of you, but I need a stiff drink. Aleksei, be a good fellow and pour me a Scotch."

With slow deliberation, the Russian rose to his feet and crossed the small distance to the console table and did as he was ordered. The only sound in the room was the splashing of the liquor into a crystal tumbler. He handed it to the man who held all their lives in his hands.

They watched mesmerized as Starrett took a deep swig. He downed the rest of it in a single gulp.

Out of the corner of his mouth, Philip hissed, "Why?"

Emmeline didn't need to ask what he meant.

Before she could say anything, Starrett answered for her. "I had to invite Emmeline. This little party wouldn't have been the same without her."

"Why invite her to your sadistic game? Let her go, Starrett." Philip shot a look at Fiona. "Let Emmeline and Fiona go," he implored.

"But Emmeline is so desperate to uncover the truth, I didn't think it would be fair to leave her out of the fun."

"Now, then if you stop interrupting, I can get on with things." He cleared his throat. He clapped the Russian on the shoulder. "Aleksei came to the U.K. to defect. He thought he would be joining his daughter. But the poor fellow finds himself alone in this cruel world."

"Whose fault is that?" Philip retorted. "You invited Anastasia to your party to kill her. Her death solved two problems for you. She knew you were the mole and she served as a warning to her father."

"Invited her to her own murder," Emmeline muttered under her breath.

Philip turned to her. "That's right," he concurred.

But it isn't, a voice inside her head told her. *It's all wrong*.

"But *you* didn't invite her to the party," she said almost to herself. Her gaze snaked to Fiona. "*Your wife* extended the invitations."

Emmeline recollected the snippet of an annoyed husband's reproach.

"Why the devil did you invite Noel Rallis tonight without asking me?"

Starrett's gaze locked on her face and he gave a sad shake of his head. "Now, you understand." His voice was low and husky.

And then it finally dawned on her. "You're not the mole. It's Fiona. She murdered Tarasova."

CHAPTER 45

All eyes in the room shifted to Lady Starrett, who stopped fidgeting and became very still under the scrutiny.

"Emmeline, do you realize what you're saying?" Philip whispered.

She nodded without looking at him. "Yes, I was blind. It all happened under my nose. It just didn't click in my mind until this moment."

Fiona crossed one long, leg over the other and tried to laugh it off. "Really, Emmeline, you're too amusing. Such a dramatic pronouncement." However, there was a nervous undercurrent in her tone.

"No, it's the truth. Tarasova knew you were the mole. Probably from her father?" She cast a glance at the Russian, but he gave a negative shake of his head. "Then Boris Petrenko told her. Either way, she knew. You overheard her talking to me in the corridor. And she saw *you*. At that point, she was still upset after her argument with Rallis and wanted to hurt him. Perhaps she thought he dumped her to take up with you, so she decided to punish both of you. You knew we had arranged to meet later in your bedroom at nine o'clock. All you had to do was nip upstairs beforehand and wait for her. You were going to kill her anyway as a warning to her father. It couldn't have been easier for you."

"Yes, my darling wife is quite a manipulator," Starrett took up the thread. "Laurence Villiers had his suspicions, but he couldn't prove Fiona was the mole."

"*Villiers*? Villiers knew about this?" Philip asked, shock echoing in his tone.

Starrett allowed himself a slow smile. "Oh yes. When the Russians tried to blackmail me with evidence about...about my hand in Isabelle's death, I went straight to Villiers and laid everything out in the open. I had no intention of betraying my country.

"He was delighted to hear it and came up with a proposition. The government would turn a blind eye to my crime, if I tried to help them catch the mole while feeding carefully drafted reports full of false secrets to the Russians. He knew Carstairs was innocent and that the real culprit could be one of only a handful of people. His money was on Fiona because she had been helping MI5 from time to time. As a model, she moved in many circles and could provide a trove of information. And she had been Carstairs's lover."

Emmeline's eyes widened in disbelief at this unexpected piece of news, but she held her tongue. She needed to hear all the details.

"Villiers's plan," Starrett went on, "was for me to marry Fiona. Since the day we exchanged vows, I've been trying to prove that my wife is nothing but a cold-blooded traitor."

Fiona drew in a sharp breath. Her features contorted in a malevolent scowl. The look she threw at him was full of daggers.

"Bastard," she spat the word at him, as she rose to her feet.

"It takes one to know one, my darling," he shot back. "She thinks I didn't know she was trying to discover what Rallis and I were up to. She was desperate to find out, so that she could report back to her handlers and they could dig their claws deeper into my soul." He chortled. "It was highly entertaining to watch her, but I was careful about my dealings with Rallis. That is, until he left me with no choice but to fall into line with Poseidon. I knew it was pushing our luck. No one knew about the smuggling. But it was only a matter of time before someone found out about Poseidon." A weary sigh escaped his lips. "He tied my hands. To my shame, I became his lap dog. Each day, I hated myself even more for it. That's why I had to kill him."

"Because he knew that Lord Desmond Starrett had died over twenty years ago and you were Basil Treadgold," Emmeline concluded for him.

"Yes." The single word was barely above a whisper. After a pause, he went on, "It had been so easy to take over Desmond's identity. We had been friends since we were boys. We knew everything about each other. Even our physical appearance was similar. I wasn't about to allow a common thug like Noel Rallis take away my life."

"Whoever the bloody hell you are, I'm going to finish what I started. Tarasov it's time for you to join your spoiled brat of a daughter."

It had been a mistake to let Starrett's confession distract them.

Fiona had inched her way toward the center of the room, a nine-millimeter Beretta with a silencer in her hand.

Where had she gotten the gun? Emmeline wondered. Was it hidden in the cushions the entire time?

As these questions raced through Emmeline's mind, Fiona raised her arm. It was level without the hint of a tremor as she released the safety catch on the trigger.

Emmeline grasped Philip's hand. "No," she screamed.

Fiona whirled round and aimed the gun at Emmeline's chest. "I was going to save you for last, you interfering bitch, but you're grating on my nerves."

Emmeline swallowed hard. She couldn't drag her eyes away from the muzzle of the gun.

Move, her brain screamed. But her limbs refused to obey its command.

EPILOGUE

The fearsome *crack,* unleashed with such fury, was even more devastating when it shattered the menacing silence trapped in that room, for it released the metallic tang of blood upon the air. The muted footfalls of death hovered close by, waiting to claim its victim.

Emmeline's muscles began to twitch, when she realized that she was still alive. Bruised and sore, but *alive*. She was on the floor, crushed between Philip's body and the sofa. She couldn't remember, but he must have knocked her to the floor a second before Fiona pressed the trigger.

"You're not hurt, are you?" he mumbled anxiously, as they gently disentangled themselves and clambered to their feet. She shook her head and gave him a hug.

It was only when they drew apart that she her heard the groan and saw Fiona lying a few feet away. She had collapsed onto the coffee table, crushing it. A bullet had ripped a hole in her chest. Her blood—and her life—were seeping from her. It would not be long now.

Her eyes had been closed, but they suddenly fluttered open. "*Hugh,*" she croaked.

Emmeline glanced around to see Hugh and Gregory

emerging from behind a panel in the wall at the opposite end of the room. It led into a hidden passage. Burnell, Finch, and a number of police officers were close on their heels and spilling into the parlor.

She sliced a path through these guardians of the law and flung herself into her husband's arms.

He kissed the top of her head and murmured against her curls, "Next time, I *will* lock you in the boot."

She couldn't help but smile as she leaned deeper into his embrace.

Across the room, the three men stood back as Hugh dropped to his knees beside Fiona.

"You—shot—me?" He nodded. "I did—love—you," she said on a rasping breath. "Forgive me?"

"Maybe God will forgive you. I can't." He stood up and walked away.

A single tear trickled from the corner of her eye and then her head slumped to one side.

そやぺ

The next few days came and went in a blur. Before Fiona's body was even cold, Philip and the Special Branch unit hustled Tarasov from Rosemount Castle to a destination unknown, where he would be handed off to another team. Philip returned to London immediately. He was now in the bosom of his family again, and diligently dividing his time between his Foreign Office duties and MI5.

Burnell and Finch had arrested Starrett/Treadgold for Rallis's murder and his part in Poseidon and the antiquities smuggling. However, to Burnell's annoyance and chagrin, the Boy Wonder ordered him to release Starrett into the custody of a pair of anonymous, monosyllabic civil servant-types, who swept into the station. He had no doubt that Villiers had sent them.

"You are to forget everything about the Starrett case," Cruickshank instructed him. "Is that understood? I want all the files on my desk by the morning."

The superintendent's suspicions about Villiers's role were confirmed, when the Boy Wonder took pains to remind him that he and Finch were bound by the Official Secrets Act.

Although it went against the grain, Burnell swallowed his pride and obeyed the assistant commissioner's directive. He had to believe that justice would be served sooner or later. Otherwise, why did they have laws?

Emmeline and Gregory decided to spend a few days in Edinburgh, a city they both adored, before rushing back to London. But they could put the demands of their daily lives on hold for only so long. A major story was unfolding and Emmeline was itching to do a bit of digging to get at the truth. Meanwhile, Symington's had called in Gregory to investigate a theft at a tech executive's Belgravia mansion.

They had intended to take the train, but the Rail Maritime and Transport union decided to stage a 24-hour strike. This left Emmeline and Gregory with no choice but to fly back to London.

As they waited for their bags to arrive on the carousel at Heathrow, Emmeline leaned her head on Gregory's shoulder and said, "When things settled down a bit, perhaps we can go back to The Swan and have a proper honeymoon?"

He glanced down at her and flashed a cheeky grin. "Your wish is my command, Mrs. Longdon."

"Speaking of commands, tomorrow you will turn over Tarasova's necklace to the police."

A startled expression was reflected in his cinnamon eyes, but he remained silent.

"I found it in my clutch the day after the Starretts' ill-fated party. Don't worry. It's quite safe at home. A wife cannot testify against her husband. Therefore, my lips are sealed. But"—she wagged a finger at him—"this will never, *never* happen again."

He pressed a kiss on the tip of her nose, without making any promises he knew he couldn't keep. Instead, he said, "Ah, there are our bags at last."

He grabbed them off the carousel. "Let's go home."

They started heading toward exit, when a security guard stopped them. "Madam, would you mind stepping over there?" he indicated a table about hundred feet away, where two officers were standing. "We are conducting random checks."

"Certainly."

Gregory's mobile started to ring. He pulled it out of his jacket pocket. "I'll join you in a minute, darling."

She nodded and followed the officer.

"Hello," he said as he watched Emmeline put her bag on the table.

"Sorry, I couldn't make your wedding, Longdon, but then I wasn't invited."

Gregory froze. Nerveless fingers pressed the mobile closer to his ear. It was a voice he hoped he would never hear again. "Swanbeck," he hissed.

"I thought I'd send a wedding gift anyway. I hope you enjoy it. Give my love to Emmeline."

The connection was severed.

His gaze slithered over to Emmeline.

"Did you pack your bag yourself?" the officer asked her, as he searched through it.

"Yes," she replied with a smile.

He stiffened and straightened up. "Then how do you explain this?"

Between his thumb and forefinger, he held a stiletto knife with a brown crust of dried blood.

Author's Note

The *Poseidon* was not among the 7,500 merchant ships sunk by the Germans during the First and Second World Wars. It was purely my creation. However, to this day, the others remain in perpetual slumber, fathoms below the sea.

About the Author

Daniella Bernett is a member of the Mystery Writers of America NY Chapter and the International Thriller Writers. She graduated summa cum laude with a B.S. in Journalism from St. John's University. *Lead Me Into Danger, Deadly Legacy, From Beyond The Grave, A Checkered Past* and *When Blood Runs Cold* are the other books in the Emmeline Kirby-Gregory Longdon mystery series. She also is the author of two poetry collections, *Timeless Allure* and *Silken Reflections*. In her professional life, she is the research manager for a nationally prominent engineering, architectural, and construction management firm. Daniella is currently working on Emmeline and Gregory's next adventure. Visit www.daniellabernett.com or follow her on Facebook and Goodreads.

CPSIA information can be obtained
at www.ICGtesting.com
Printed in the USA
LVHW021722270920
667226LV00010B/1912